THE WORLD'S CLASSICS

MEMOIRS FROM THE HOUSE OF THE DEAD

FEDOR DOSTOEVSKY (1821–81) was born in Moscow into an impoverished middle-class family. He went to St. Petersburg to study military engineering and had some success at the age of twenty-four when his first novel, *Poor Folk*, was acclaimed by the great critic Belinsky. But Dostoevsky was never at home in the literary circles of high society, and found more congenial company in a group of radical liberals. In 1849 he and others were condemned to death for conspiring to set up a printing press. The sentence was commuted to exile and hard labour, but, in a calculatedly cold-blooded way, only in the very face of the firing-squad. Despite this evidence of authoritarian harshness and the miseries of prison life, Dostoevsky came to accept his punishment as the atonement of his crime and as purifying his conscience. The belief in the doctrine of salvation through suffering was a central tenet of the Orthodox Christianity which he was to expound in his later work.

After his return from Siberia in 1859, Dostoevsky travelled to western Europe, which he saw as the seat of socialism and spiritual decay, and believed it to be Russia's mission to save. In 1864 his wife and brother died and, left to support their dependants, he wrote *Crime and Punishment* faced with heavy debts. In 1867 he married his young secretary, with whom he was to enjoy a happy family life. He produced three more great novels, and at his death was acclaimed by the nation as a great literary celebrity.

RONALD HINGLEY is University Lecturer in Russian at Oxford. His publications include *The Undiscovered Dostoyevsky* (1962) and *Dostoyevsky: His Life and Work* (1978).

D0746852

THE WORLD'S CLASSICS

FEDOR DOSTOEVSKY
*Memoirs
from the House
of the Dead*

TRANSLATED BY JESSIE COULSON

EDITED BY RONALD HINGLEY

Oxford   New York
OXFORD UNIVERSITY PRESS
1983

Oxford University Press, Walton Street, Oxford OX2 6DP

London Glasgow New York Toronto
Delhi Bombay Calcutta Madras Karachi
Kuala Lumpur Singapore Hong Kong Tokyo
Nairobi Dar es Salaam Cape Town
Melbourne Auckland

and associates in
Beirut Berlin Ibadan Mexico City Nicosia

Memoirs from the House of the Dead *first published 1861–2*

*This translation first published by Oxford University Press 1956;
reprinted 1965*
New material in the translation © *Oxford University Press 1965*
First published as a World's Classics paperback 1983
*Introduction, Select Bibliography, Chronology and
Explanatory Notes* © *Ronald Hingley 1983*

British Library Cataloguing in Publication Data

Dostoevskiĭ, F. M.
Memoirs from the house of the dead.—(The World's classics)
I. Title II. Coulson, Jessie
III. Hingley, Ronald
891.73'3[F] PG3326.Z3
ISBN 0–19–281613–6

Library of Congress Cataloging in Publication Data

Dostoyevsky, Fyodor, 1821–1881.
Memoirs from the house of the dead.
(The World's classics)
Translation of: Zapiski iz mertvogo doma.
Bibliography: p.
I. Hingley, Ronald. II. Title. III. Series.
PG3326.Z3 1983 891.73'3 82–14344
ISBN 0–19–281613–6 (pbk.)

*Printed in Great Britain by
Hazell Watson & Viney Ltd
Aylesbury, Bucks*

CONTENTS

MEMOIRS FROM THE HOUSE OF THE DEAD

PART I

PART II

INTRODUCTION

THE first full version of Fedor Mikhaylovich Dostoevsky's *Memoirs from the House of the Dead* was published in serial form in 1861–2. Its appearance straddled the fortieth birthday of an author who is now commonly regarded as Russia's—or even the world's—finest novelist. But the Dostoevsky of the early 1860s had yet to earn so high a reputation, for the great novels of his maturity (from *Crime and Punishment* to *The Brothers Karamazov*) still remained to be written.

House of the Dead is a worthy forerunner to Dostoevsky's later fiction. It emerged after many years of frenzied literary experiment and personal disaster, and it is the first of his works which can be called unquestionably a masterpiece. This is no novel, however. It consists, in all but name, of Dostoevsky's account of his own life as a convict in the stockaded prison at Omsk in western Siberia between 1850 and 1854.

Russia is rich in penological literature, as befits Russian history, and Dostoevsky has not been the country's only major imaginative author to take prison and exile as his theme. Chekhov was to do so in the 1890s with his *Sakhalin Island*, which was soon followed by Tolstoy with the striking pictures of prison and exile in *Resurrection*. But neither of those remarkable works can vie with the literary power of Dostoevsky's *House of the Dead*. Chekhov's *Sakhalin Island* is an academic study based on a systematic census of the island's convict and exile population conducted by the author; it may be the best-written research thesis on record, but a research thesis it remains. As for Tolstoy's *Resurrection*—accurate and detailed though his account of prison conditions may be, the book does not merely pretend to be a work of fiction. It is one.

House of the Dead falls between these two later chronicles of Russian prison life. Dostoevsky is faithful to the essential facts. But he also draws on his creative imagination.

Dostoevsky the prison annalist enjoyed one supreme advantage denied to Chekhov and Tolstoy: he had 'done time' himself, as the result of certain youthful indiscretions. He had been born in 1821, the son of an impecunious army doctor, and into what soon became a large family. The Dostoevskys were poor, but not so poor that they failed to own peasants as their serfs, and Fedor Mikhaylovich inherited from his father the legal status of *dvoryanin* ('gentleman', sometimes translated 'noble'). Hence the contrast, often drawn in *House of the Dead*, between the majority of the convicts (who sprang from the peasantry) and the narrator himself—so conscious of his status as a gentleman, and thus a member of the social élite. But though Dostoevsky was a gentleman in law, it was to the lower fringes of the gentry that he belonged; and his relatively humble social origins helped to generate the acute inferiority complex which permeates all his earliest literary works.

After seventeen years (1821–38) of schooling and family life in Moscow, the budding young gentleman spent six years in St Petersburg as a cadet and junior officer with the Imperial Russian engineering corps. Anything but one of nature's sappers, he resigned his commission in 1844, and two years later gained ecstatic acclaim with his first published work, the short novel *Poor Folk*. He was still living in his favourite city, St Petersburg, but success only depressed him. It helped to intensify traits already evident in his adolescence by confirming him as a spendthrift, a gambler, a hypochondriac, a paranoiac, a nervous wreck, a potential suicide, a self-pitier. But he was also—he needed to be— physically and mentally rugged.

Inspired perhaps by a latent death-wish, the young Dostoevsky drifted into the Petrashevsky Circle—a network of semi-clandestine political discussion groups attended by young St Petersburgers opposed to the harsh regime of the Emperor Nicholas I. After the Emperor's police had penetrated the circle, Dostoevsky was arrested and held for eight months in the dungeons of the Fortress of St Peter and St Paul. Meanwhile he was being put on trial in his absence and sentenced to death for participation in what, by the standards of societies less grimly regimented, had barely amounted to a conspiracy at all.

On 22 December 1849 the young political criminal was led out, with twenty others, for execution by firing-squad in the Semenovsky Square in St Petersburg. But then the sentences were suddenly commuted at the last moment: by prior arrangement and on the express instructions of the Emperor himself. Dostoevsky learnt that he faced *katorga* (penal servitude in Siberia); it consisted in his case of four years' hard labour, to be followed by military service in Siberian exile. On Christmas Eve 1849 he began the 2,000-mile journey by sledge to Omsk. His ankles hobbled by the regulation ten-pound fetters, his every movement watched by his armed escort, he entered Asia a prey to the gloomiest forebodings. Yet he also felt exhilarated. Could it be that he actually thrived on a diet of disaster?

The sequel to Dostoevsky's journey need not be summarized here, for there is no point in retelling what the master himself has to say about that in *House of the Dead*.

How faithful is *House of the Dead* to the facts of Dostoevsky's life? He barely bothers to keep up the fiction floated in his Introduction: that his Memoirs are those of one Alexander Petrovich Goryanchikov, sentenced to ten years in prison for the murder of his wife. Chapter 2 already indicates that this Goryanchikov, described as having been imprisoned for a civil crime, cannot be equated with the 'I' of the narrative, since the latter openly refers to himself as a political offender (page 35). From that point onwards Dostoevsky speaks for himself, remembering his fictional narrator only occasionally.

If the *Memoirs* depart from the truth, as they do in certain minor details to be discussed below, one reason is that they were not composed immediately after Dostoevsky's release from prison in 1854. Five years' compulsory army service in Siberia followed, and it was not until 1859, when he was demobilized and permitted to return to European Russia, that he started serious work on *House of the Dead*. By the time he completed the work in 1862, more than twelve years had elapsed since his first arrival in Omsk. But he had some earlier notes to help him. While still in prison he had begun to keep brief, cryptic, undated jottings. He drew on them when he came to write the *Memoirs*, and they have been posthumously published as his 'Siberian Notebooks'.

A collation of *House of the Dead* with available supporting evidence confirms that the work offers a comprehensive and essentially accurate record of the author's own prison experiences. This evidence includes Dostoevsky's own letters to his brother Mikhail, some of which antedate the completed *House of the Dead* by eight years. It also includes the original prison archives, which have only recently become available to scholars, and the independent witness of two inmates of Omsk prison—contemporaries of Dostoevsky who have also left memoirs of their prison experiences (Martynov and Tokarzewski).

This material all tends to confirm Dostoevsky's picture of the prisoners' routine, leisure activities, working conditions and personalities as comprehensive and basically faithful. For example, not a few of the numerous individuals mentioned in the work can be shown to be portraits of real-life persons. In many cases Dostoevsky has either retained the true names or reproduced them in partly disguised form. But he has also taken artistic licence to render some of these figures even more exotic than they were in real life. For example, the original 'Gazin' was not quite the grand-guignolesque infanticide portrayed on pages 55–6, but just a drunken, thieving soldier serving a sentence for petty crimes committed when absent without leave. Likewise, the quaintly renamed 'Bumstein' (p. 19) and 'Nurra' (p. 71) have been endowed with piquant traits not possessed by their real-life prototypes: the former, for the sake of picturesqueness, is inaccurately credited with adherence to the Jewish religion, while the latter is presented with a record of armed resistance to the Russian colonial power in the Caucasus.

It is perhaps not surprising that Dostoevsky should have decided to spike some of his minor characters with such seasoning, especially as his fictional framework—however flimsy—absolves him from any charge of misleading the reader. Far more astonishing is his adoption of a diametrically opposite policy in the delineation of what is potentially the most exotic figure in his entire cast: himself. While relating experiences and retailing philosophical reflections which are demonstrably his own, he yet remains in the background as a human being. He makes little attempt to equip himself or his narrator (in so far as his narrator can be distinguished from himself) with any sort of vivid profile, whether fictionalized or in the form of a self-portrait. This accords with the policy which he had explicitly proclaimed when planning the work: 'My own personality will disappear.' Hence a contrast which must strike all who compare the heroes of Dostoevsky's previously published fiction with the narrator of *House of the Dead*. Those early fictional heroes—the dreamy, self-pitying young St Petersburgers of his first short stories, Seryozha in *Stepanchikovo Village*, the two 'Golyadkins' in *The Double*—form a series of caricatured self-portraits of the author. Still more strikingly ego-dominated is the distorted mirror-image contained in the longest and most ambitious of Dostoevsky's immature novels: *Insulted and Injured*, publication of which (in 1861) overlapped that of *House of the Dead*. The novel's hero, 'Ivan Petrovich', is Dostoevsky himself as he was in his pre-arrest period, even being portrayed as a young author who has scored a great success with his first essay in fiction; the plot also draws on Dostoevsky's bizarre courtship of his first wife, as waged in the wilds of Siberia in the late 1850s.

How different is the narrator of the *Memoirs*—so reticent, so innocent of the painful ego-gropings characteristic of Dostoevsky's early fiction. It is here that the work most flagrantly offends against historical accuracy, for the real Dostoevsky of 1850–4 resembled his own early heroes more than he resembled the 'I' of *House of the Dead*. One of the other convict-memoirists, P. K. Martynov, has described the caged novelist as taciturn, unsmiling and pathologically suspicious. Dostoevsky was unpopular with the other prisoners, but they did respect him. So Martynov claims, also comparing him to 'a trapped wolf'. Omsk's other convict-annalist, the Polish revolutionary S. Tokarzewski, accused Dostoevsky of snobbishness, of rabid nationalism and of quarrelling about politics. That can easily be believed. It was also, perhaps, in Omsk that Dostoevsky first imbibed one of the many grand hatreds of his life—his loathing of Poles and most things Polish.

Far from aiming at a self-portrait in *House of the Dead*, Dostoevsky omits one salient autobiographical element. It was during his imprisonment, according to the most convincing evidence, that he first experienced attacks of epilepsy—the complaint from which he was to suffer throughout the rest of his life. As for the suggestion that Dostoevsky's first epileptic seizure was brought on by being flogged while in prison, the epilepsy is better documented than the flogging. Dostoevsky says nothing to indicate that the 'I' of *House of the Dead* was ever subjected to corporal punishment, harrowing though his descriptions of its infliction on others most certainly are. On the other hand, Dostoevsky does go out of his way to incorporate in *House of the*

Dead some of his less atrocious real-life experiences: his meeting with the wives of the Decembrists; the copy of the Gospels which he received as a gift; the one-copeck piece which a little girl gave him by way of charity.

How does *House of the Dead* fit into the general pattern of Dostoevsky's creativity? His earlier work contains some remarkable items. The first published novel (*Poor Folk*) has been generally overrated, but the second (*The Double*) is magnificent; despite certain immature features it contains the seeds of the future Dostoevsky, as he himself was to claim in later life. Among the other early works of fiction *Stepanchikovo Village* is a powerful blend of the comic and the macabre. Had Dostoevsky perished in his fortieth year these items would have survived, to earn him more than a footnote in literary history. But he could never have become known to the world at large on the strength of his early work alone. Still less would he have gained world-wide renown from *Insulted and Injured*, the last and longest of his apprentice novels. It shows the Dostoevsky of the early 1860s at his worst, just as *House of the Dead* shows him at his best. And yet the writing and publication of the two works overlapped.

So spectacular is the failure of the novel *Insulted and Injured*, and so spectacular the success of the documentary study *House of the Dead*, that the forty-year-old Dostoevsky might have seemed best advised to abandon fiction altogether and to concentrate on realistic depictions of the Russian scene. Yet, as it turned out, the superb documentary study *House of the Dead* did far more than the miscued fictional effusion *Insulted and Injured* to turn him into a fiction-writer of the front rank.

To this evolution the above-mentioned 'disappearance of my own personality' was crucial. Not that the Dostoevsky of *Insulted and Injured* had finished ringing the changes on his underdog self-portrait hero. Far from it, for two notable specimens of the type were yet to follow—in the heroes of

Memoirs from Underground (1864) and *The Gambler* (1866).
The publication of the latter coincided with that of Dostoevsky's first fully realized major novel, *Crime and Punishment*, and the underdog-hero was to reappear yet again in
A Raw Youth (1875). But by then this character type had been
put in the shade by a whole parade of figures owing more
to the author's creative imagination than to his creative
narcissism.

Dostoevsky could only become the great novelist that —
from 1866 onwards — he proved himself to be if he
abandoned the posture of intense introspection which is
reflected in his earlier works. He shows his awareness of
this on the first page of *Crime and Punishment*, where he
unavowedly contrasts his new hero, Raskolnikov, with the
numerous underdog-heroes who had gone before. Raskolnikov 'was not cowardly and downtrodden, indeed quite the
opposite. ... He was remarkably good-looking with
handsome dark eyes ... above medium height, slim and
well built.' These sterling attributes the cringing early
heroes had markedly lacked. But it was not with *Crime and
Punishment*, it was with the earlier *House of the Dead* that
Dostoevsky first accomplished the vital step of switching a
large part of his attention from his own perennially
fascinating nature to that of other human beings, all of
whom had one important characteristic in common: that
none of them was a Fedor Mikhaylovich Dostoevsky.

Besides helping to dethrone the underdog-hero, *House of
the Dead* performed an even more signal service to Dostoevsky's fiction by furnishing him with a new and splendid
theme: murder.

Murder, murder, murder ... It was to form the hinge of
the action in *Crime and Punishment*, it was to supply the
supreme crisis-point in *The Idiot*. The slaughter of Shatov in
Devils, the mugging of Fedor Pavlovich in *The Brothers
Karamazov*—these were to crown the glorious series. So
fully was unjustifiable homicide to dominate these great

works that one may wonder how the early Dostoevsky ever managed without it. If his early efforts now seem comparatively lame and ineffectual, the absence of this crucial ingredient must take its place alongside excess of author's narcissism among the contributory factors.

It was inside the stockade of Omsk prison that Dostoevsky first met murderers and other violent criminals in the flesh. He brushed shoulders and clinked fetters with them every day, and he reproduced them on the pages of *House of the Dead*, even going so far (as is noted above) as to credit the occasional real-life non-murderer with the crime of crimes. Dostoevsky also expresses an extravagant admiration for the most appalling criminals, marvelling at the sheer strength of his various 'powerful personalities'—the Petrovs, the Gazins and the like. They had not only proved their ability to commit atrocious misdeeds, but had also shown— which was still more important to Dostoevsky—that they could butcher without feeling any tremor of conscience afterwards. Dostoevsky, whose own emotional seismograph could run amok over the simulacrum of a shadow, greatly admired those so different from himself, and his admiration has turned some pages of *House of the Dead* into a kind of Psychopaths' Charter. The contemplation of psychopaths also helped to aggravate Dostoevsky's passionate concern over the origin and nature of evil in man's soul, that abiding theme of his later fiction. In Rogozhin (*The Idiot*) he created a Petrov or Gazin of his own. But the fullest development of the murder theme is only to be found where Dostoevsky has fed a potent philosophical ingredient into his portrayal of murderers. That ingredient *House of the Dead* does not possess in any comparable degree.

Dostoevsky's truly great assassins are not the relatively mindless Petrovs, Gazins and Rogozhins. They are all intellectuals: Raskolnikov, who kills to prove a theory (*Crime and Punishment*); Petr Verkhovensky, who kills as an experiment in personal relations under the pretext of political conspiracy

(*Devils*); Ivan Karamazov, who does not even stoop to carrying out his murder in person, but confines himself to disseminating the powerful ideological taint which makes it inevitable that his creature Smerdyakov should beat out their common father's brains with a heavy paperweight. All this represents a considerable advance on the stage reached in the *House of the Dead*. But that work was the springboard which made the great leap possible.

House of the Dead played a significant role in the evolution of Dostoevsky's social and political views. It stands half way between the early, confusingly documented socialism of his twenties and the very different system of hard-and-fast dogma which he was to champion from his mid-forties onwards. He then began to emerge as an extreme Russian nationalist; as a fanatical conservative; as a devotee of the Russian Orthodox Church; as an idolator of the Russian common people. All of it was somehow combined with a sort of jolly hatred for most of the categories into which the human race falls—including, not infrequently, even the categories which he himself especially favoured. These dogmas of his maturity Dostoevsky was to advocate in his inimitable and creatively self-defeating manner on the pages of his fiction, while also repeatedly trumpeting them forth, in paroxysms of intellectual *musth*, through his journalistic *Diary of a Writer*. In that grotesque and monumental work Dostoevsky emerges as the prophet of revealed truths. He has come near to suppressing the imp of contradiction who seems constantly present in his later fiction—so much so that Dostoevsky the mature novelist hardly appears capable of affirming anything without being prompted to deny it, if only by implication, in the next breath.

As a vehicle for Dostoevsky's thought, *House of the Dead* stands in stark contrast with all his later work: both with the sequence of great novels and with *Diary of a Writer*. There Dostoevsky is the finder, the possessor, the exegete of the ultimate truths which he can so quickly disavow at the flicker of a mental impulse. But in *House of the Dead* he emerges in a very different role—that of a mere investigator of human nature who has not decided in advance what it is that he intends to discover. Unprimed by a priori notions about human psychology, about the essence of existence, about the destiny of Russia or the attributes of God, he reviews a vast gallery of macabre human figures in an attempt to diagnose their inmost qualities by empirical means. Nothing comparable, at least on this scale, is to be found either in the earlier Dostoevsky or the later. It is as if he sought, for once, to anticipate Chekhov rather than to parade himself as a Jeremiah *redivivus*.

Though the years at Omsk preceded and perhaps helped to cause the radical transformation of Dostoevsky's ideas, converting him from a semi-atheist and a semi-socialist into a whole-hogging loyalist and religious fanatic, this transition by no means took place overnight. Not until nearly a decade after his release in 1854 did the great vat of Dostoevskian dogma show signs of definite crystallization. *House of the Dead* represents an interim stage in this process, as may be monitored from Dostoevsky's pronouncements on the Russian *narod* or common people. It was, incidentally, only during his years of prison and exile that he ever experienced—and much against his will—such intimate contact with this section of society. Dostoevsky might idolize the Russian common man in theory. He might preach the common man's virtues in print. But when he was given the choice he avoided the common man like the plague.

How radically Dostoevsky's views of the mid-1850s differed from his views of the late 1860s onwards may be seen from the hostile comments which he made in a letter to his brother Mikhail written immediately after his release from gaol, eight years before the composition of *House of the Dead* was completed. He tells Mikhail that the common people are coarse, irritable, embittered and imbued with hatred for representatives of the gentry such as himself. He describes them as 'a hundred and fifty enemies' who never wearied of persecuting him. And yet 'they always recognized that we were their superiors'—'we' being the gentry, the educated, the élite. But when Dostoevsky came to write *House of the Dead* this extreme view had been watered down, and he is already saying that members of the élite have much to learn from the *narod*. Here, then, is an interim stage between the anti-*narod* remarks in the letter of 1854 to his brother and the extreme idealization of the peasant expressed in *Diary of a Writer*, in parts of the novel *A Raw Youth*, and elsewhere.

Important though it is to see *House of the Dead* in its creative, biographical, sociological and historical settings, this is emphatically not one of the many Russian literary works which matter less for their inner worth than for their context. Readers of the present volume may safely be left to judge the book's quality for themselves, and it is probable that many will feel enthusiasm comparable to that of the first readers well over a century ago. Their reaction was ecstatic. *House of the Dead* 'literally created a furore' commented Dostoevsky himself, in one of his less happily phrased sentences. Even his enemy Turgenev admiringly compared the convicts' famous communal sauna (pp. 142ff.) with that touchstone of supreme literary quality, Dante's *Inferno*.

From Dostoevsky's contemporary Tolstoy, whom he never met face to face, *House of the Dead* drew praise so superlative that it flouts Russian literary taboo by assigning a relatively minor role to Russia's premier poet, a figure normally treated as sacrosanct:

I know no better book in all modern literature, and that includes Pushkin. Tell Dostoevsky I love him.

RONALD HINGLEY

SELECT BIBLIOGRAPHY

BAKHTIN, M., *Problems of Dostoyevsky's Poetics*, tr. from the Russian (Ann Arbor, Mich., 1973)

CARR, Edward Hallett, *Dostoevsky, 1821–1881: a New Biography* (London, 1931)

COULSON, Jessie, *Dostoevsky: a Self-Portrait* (London, 1962)

CURLE, Richard, *The Characters of Dostoevsky* (London, 1950)

DOSTOEVSKAYA, Anna, *Reminiscences*, tr. and ed. Beatrice Stillman, introduction by Helen Muchnic (London, 1975)

FRANK, Joseph, *Dostoevsky: the Seeds of Revolt, 1821–1849* (Princeton, 1976)

GROSSMAN, Leonid, *Dostoevsky: a Biography*, tr. Mary Mackler (London, 1974)

HINGLEY, Ronald, *The Undiscovered Dostoyevsky* (London, 1962; reprinted 1975)

HINGLEY, Ronald, *Dostoyevsky: His Life and Work* (London 1978)

HOLMQUIST, Michael, *Dostoevsky and the Novel* (Princeton, N.J., 1977)

JACKSON, Robert Louis, *The Art of Dostoevsky: Deliriums and Nocturnes* (Princeton, N.J., 1981)

JONES, Malcolm V., *Dostoyevsky: the Novel of Discord* (London, 1976)

KRAG, Erik, *Dostoevsky: The Literary Artist* (Oslo, 1976)

MOCHULSKY, Konstantin, *Dostoevsky: His Life and Work*, tr. with an introduction by Michael A. Minihan (Princeton, 1967)

PEACE, Richard, *Dostoyevsky: an Examination of the Major Novels* (Cambridge, 1971)

SIMMONS, Ernest J., *Dostoevsky: the Making of a Novelist* (London, 1950)

SLONIM, Marc, *Les Trois Amours de Dostoïevsky* (Paris, 1955)

STEINER, George, *Tolstoy or Dostoevsky* (London, 1959)

TERRAS, Victor, *The Young Dostoevsky, 1846–1849* (The Hague, 1969)

TROYAT, Henri, *Firebrand: the Life of Dostoevsky* (London, 1947)

WASIOLEK, E., *Dostoevsky: the Major Fiction* (Cambridge, Mass., 1964)

WELLEK, R., ed. *Dostoevsky: a Collection of Critical Essays* (Englewood Cliffs, N.J., 1962)

YARMOLINSKY, Avrahm, *Dostoevsky: His Life and Art* (London, 1957)

CHRONOLOGY OF
DOSTOEVSKY

Italicized items are works by Dostoevsky listed by year of first publication. Dates are Old Style, which means that they lag behind those used in nineteenth-century Western Europe by twelve days.

1821   Fedor Mikhaylovich Dostoevsky is born in Moscow, the son of an army doctor (30 October).

1837   His mother dies.

1838   Enters the Chief Engineering Academy in St Petersburg as an army cadet.

1839   His father dies, probably murdered by his serfs.

1842   Is promoted Second Lieutenant.

1843   Translates Balzac's *Eugénie Grandet*.

1844   Resigns his army commission.

1846   *Poor Folk*
        The Double

1849   *Netochka Nezvanova*
        Is led out for execution in the Semenovsky Square in St Petersburg (22 December); his sentence is commuted at the last moment to penal servitude, to be followed by army service and exile, in Siberia; he is deprived of his army commission.

1850–4 Serves four years at the prison at Omsk in western Siberia.

1854   Is released from prison (March), but is immediately posted as a private soldier to an infantry battalion stationed at Semipalatinsk, in western Siberia.

1855   Is promoted Corporal.
        Death of Nicholas I; accession of Alexander II.

1856   Is promoted Ensign.

1857   Marries Mariya Dmitrievna Isaeva (6 February).

1859   Resigns his army commission with the rank of Second
         Lieutenant (March), and receives permission to return to
         European Russia.
         Resides in Tver (August-December).
         Moves to St Petersburg (December).
         Uncle's Dream.
         Stepanchikovo Village

1861   Begins publication of a new literary monthly *Vremya*,
         founded by himself and his brother Mikhail (January).
         The Emancipation of the Serfs.
         Insulted and Injured
         A Series of Essays on Literature

1861–2   *Memoirs from the House of the Dead*

1862   His first visit to Western Europe, including England and
         France.

1863   *Winter Notes on Summer Impressions*
         Vremya is banned for political reasons but through a
         misunderstanding, by the authorities.

1864   Launches a second journal, *Epokha* (March).
         His first wife dies (15 April).
         His brother Mikhail dies (10 July).
         Memoirs from Underground

1865   *Epokha* collapses for financial reasons (June).

1866   Attempted assassination of Alexander II by Dmitry
         Karakozov (April).
         Crime and Punishment
         The Gambler

1867   Marries Anna Grigoryevna Snitkina, his stenographer,
         as his second wife (15 February).
         Dostoevsky and his bride leave for western Europe
         (April).

1867–71 The Dostoevskys reside abroad, chiefly in Dresden, but
         also in Geneva, Vevey, Florence and elsewhere.

1868   *The Idiot*

1870   *The Eternal Husband*

1871   The Dostoevskys return to St Petersburg.

PART I

INTRODUCTION

In the remoter parts of Siberia, in the midst of the steppes, the mountains, or the pathless forests, lie scattered a few small towns of one, or at most two, thousand inhabitants, plain little towns built of wood, with two churches—one in the town, the other in the cemetery,—which are more like the prosperous villages of the Moscow region than real towns. They are usually abundantly furnished with district police inspectors, assessors, and other minor officials. Generally speaking, Siberia, though its climate may be cold, provides an uncommonly warm, snug berth for servants of the state. The people there are simple, untouched by liberal ideas; their ways are old and fixed, hallowed by the centuries. The officials, who play the part of a virtual Siberian aristocracy, are either natives, dyed-in-the-wool Siberians, or migrants from Russia, chiefly from the capital, attracted by the supplementary salaries, the double allowances for expenses, and alluring hopes of the future. Those among them who are capable of solving the riddle of life almost all remain in Siberia and gladly take root there. The fruits they subsequently bear are sweet and abundant. The others, the frivolous ones, who cannot guess the answer to life's riddle, soon grow weary of Siberia, and, disheartened, ask themselves why they ever came there. Impatiently they serve out their statutory term of three years and as soon as it has expired begin to petition for transfer, and go back home reviling and ridiculing Siberia. They are wrong: Siberia can be a place of blissful contentment from many other points of view besides that of the civil servant. It has an excellent climate; there are many remarkably rich and hospitable merchants and many extremely prosperous non-Russian inhabitants. The young ladies bloom like roses and are in the highest degree virtuous. Wild game flies about the streets and throws itself in the hunter's path. Champagne is drunk in incredible quantities. The caviare is marvellous. In some places the harvest yields fifteen hundred per cent. . . . The land in general is richly blest; all that is required is the capacity to make the best use of it. In Siberia they have that capacity.

It was in one of these cheerful and contented little towns, full of the nicest and kindest people, the memory of whom will never be erased from my heart, that I met Alexander Petrovich Goryanchikov, a convict settler.* He had been born in Russia, of a noble landed family, and sent to Siberia as a convict of the second class for the murder of his wife, and, after the expiry of the ten years' penal servitude to which the law had sentenced him, had settled down to live out the rest of his days humbly and obscurely in the little town of K—.* He had been assigned to a district which adjoined the town, but he lived in the town itself, where he had the opportunity of making some sort of living by teaching children. In Siberian towns teachers who are convict settlers are often met with; there is no prejudice against them. They teach, for preference, French, which is so indispensable in polite society, and of which these remote regions of Siberia would otherwise have no understanding. I first met Alexander Petrovich at the house of Ivan Ivanovich Gvozdikov, a worthy and hospitable old government official with five daughters of various ages, who furnished the occasion for many sanguine dreams. Alexander Petrovich gave them lessons four times a week, at thirty silver copecks a lesson. His appearance interested me. He was a puny little man, extraordinarily pale and thin, and still quite young, about thirty-five years old. He was always very neatly dressed, in the western European fashion. If you talked to him, he looked at you with extraordinary fixity and attention and listened to your every word with strict politeness, as if pondering each one, or as if you were setting him riddles with your questions, or trying to wring some secret from him; finally, he answered you briefly and clearly, but he weighed every word of his answer so carefully that you began to feel awkward and were glad when at last the conversation ended. I asked Ivan Ivanovich about him on that occasion, and learned that his life was morally irreproachable, or he would not have been invited into his daughters' company, but that he was a terrible misanthrope and shunned everybody; he was very scholarly and read a great deal, but said very little indeed, and was always rather difficult to talk to. There were some who asserted that he was undoubtedly crazed, although they did not, in practice, consider this too important a defect; many people holding honourable positions in the town were prepared to show him every kindness; and he could even be useful in drawing up petitions and in other ways. It was supposed that his family in Russia must be respectable, and not perhaps of the lowest rank, but it was known that he had resolutely broken off all connexion with them as soon as he was sent to Siberia —in short, he was his own worst enemy. Moreover, everybody in our town knew his history, and knew that he had killed his wife in the very first year of his marriage, killed her out of jealousy and then given himself up (which considerably lightened his punishment). Such crimes are always looked on as misfortunes and as deserving of pity. In spite of all this, the crazy fellow obstinately avoided everybody and never put in an appearance except to give his lessons.

At first I did not pay him any particular attention; but, I hardly know why, little by little he began to interest me. There was something enigmatic about him. There was not the smallest possibility of holding any conversation with him. Of course he always answered my questions, answered them, in fact, as though it were a most important duty, but when he had answered me I somehow felt reluctant to ask him any more; and after such conversations, suffering and weariness were visible in his face also. I remember walking away from Ivan Ivanovich's with him one lovely summer evening. Suddenly it occurred to me to ask him to come in for a minute, to smoke a cigarette. I cannot describe how terrified he looked; he quite lost his head, muttered some disjointed words and then suddenly, with a furious glance at me, ran off headlong in the opposite direction. I was quite taken aback. From that time on, whenever he met me, he looked at me with a certain alarm. But I was not to be put off; something drew me to him, and a month later, without any excuse, I called on him. Needless to say, this was a stupid and tactless thing to do. He lodged on the outskirts of the town with an elderly woman who had a consumptive daughter, who in her turn had an illegitimate child, a pretty, merry little girl of ten. Alexander Petrovich was sitting with her and teaching her to read when I went in. Seeing me, he was as disconcerted as though I had caught him committing a crime. In utter confusion he jumped up from his chair and stared at me wildly. We sat down at last; his eyes attentively followed every glance of mine, as though he suspected each had some peculiarly mysterious significance. I realized that he was mistrustful to an insane degree. He looked at me with hatred and all but asked aloud how soon I would go away. I began to talk to him about our little town and about current events; he smiled bitterly and remained silent; it became clear that he had not heard our most ordinary news, known to everybody else, and moreover was not interested in hearing it. I went on to talk of our country and its needs; he listened in silence, gazing so strangely into my eyes that at last I began to repent of having started the conversation. However, I almost tempted him by offering him, still uncut, the new books and magazines, fresh from the post, which I had with me. He looked hungrily at them, but instantly changed his mind and refused the offer on the ground of having no spare time. I took my leave at last, feeling an intolerable weight fall from my heart as I went out. I was ashamed, and it now seemed to me extraordinarily stupid to have pestered a man who made it his chief concern to hide himself as securely as possible from the whole world. But the thing was done. I remember that I saw hardly any books in his room, which meant that people were wrong when they said he read a great deal. But once or twice, going past his windows very late at night, I noticed a light in them. What could he be doing, sitting up till dawn? Was he writing, and if so, what?

Circumstances took me away from our town for about three months. Returning home after the beginning of winter, I heard that Alexander Petrovich had died in the autumn, died alone and without calling in a doctor. He was already almost forgotten in the town. His room was empty. I lost no time in making myself known to his landlady, with the intention of finding out from her what her lodger had done with his time and whether he had not been writing something. For twenty copecks in silver she brought me a basketful of papers left behind by the dead man. The old woman confessed that she had already used two of the notebooks. She was a sullen, silent peasant and it was difficult to get any sense out of her. She could tell me nothing really new about her lodger. According to her, he hardly ever did anything, and for months together did not open a book or take a pen in his hand, but then he would walk up and down his room all night, thinking, and sometimes talking to himself. He took a great fancy to her little granddaughter Katya, and made a lot of fuss of her, especially after he learned that she was called Katya; every time St. Catherine's day came round he had a requiem said for somebody. He could not bear visitors; he left the house only to give lessons to children; he looked suspiciously even at her, the old woman, when she went into his room once a week to tidy up a bit, and in the whole three years he had hardly ever said a single word to her. I asked Katya whether she remembered her teacher. She looked at me without a word, turned her face to the wall and burst into tears. So even he had been able to make someone love him.

I took his papers away with me and spent a whole day going through them. Three-quarters of them were blank sheets, meaningless fragments, or pupils' copy-books. But there was one fairly bulky notebook filled with small hand-writing, but unfinished, abandoned and perhaps forgotten by the author himself. It was a description, although a rather disconnected one, of the ten years' penal servitude under-gone by Alexander Petrovich. In places it was broken by another narrative, some kind of strange and terrible remi-niscences, written in cramped irregular characters, as though under some compulsion. I read through these frag-ments a few times and almost convinced myself that they had been written in madness. But the prison memoirs—'Scenes from the House of the Dead', as he himself called them somewhere in the manuscript—appeared to me to be not without interest. The completely strange world, un-known until that time, the strangeness of some of the facts, some particular notes on those lost souls, attracted me, and I read with curiosity. I may, of course, be mistaken. As a test, I have picked out two or three chapters to begin with; let the public judge . . .

1. The House of the Dead

OUR prison*stood close to the ramparts, on the very rim of the fortress. You would look through a chink in the stockade at God's blessed daylight; surely there was something or other to be seen? But you saw only a glimpse of sky and the earthen rampart, overgrown with weeds, with the sentries pacing back and forth, day and night, and you would think that years would go by and you would come again in just the same way to peer through a chink in the stockade and see the same rampart, the same sentries, and the same tiny strip of sky, not the sky above the prison, but another, remote and free. Imagine a large courtyard, two hundred yards long and a hundred and fifty yards wide, irregularly hexagonal in shape, surrounded by a high fencing or stockade consisting of a ribbing of tall wooden uprights (stakes) driven close together deep into the ground, strengthened with cross-bars and sharpened at the top; this was the outer wall of the prison. In one of its sides were set massive gates, always kept locked, and always guarded, day and night, by sentries; they were opened on demand, to let out those going to work. Beyond those gates lay the bright, free world, where people lived like everybody else. But from this side that world seemed like an impossible fairy-tale. Here was our own peculiar world, unlike anything else at all; here were our own peculiar laws, our own dress, our own morals and customs, a house of the living dead, a life such as is lived nowhere else, and people set apart. It is this special corner that I purpose to depict.

As you enter the enclosure you see inside it several buildings. Along both sides of the wide inner courtyard stretch two long single-storied log buildings. These are the barracks. The convicts live here, distributed according to their categories. Then, at the far end of the same yard, there is another building of the same sort: this is the kitchen, divided between two *artels*;[1] further still is another building where cellars and store-houses of various kinds are all under one roof. The middle of the yard is empty, a fairly large level stretch of ground. Here the convicts are drawn up, and roll-calls and checks take place, in the mornings and evenings and at midday, and sometimes several times a day besides—depending on the degree of mistrustfulness of the sentries

---

[1] A group, properly of workers jointly responsible for the work undertaken and sharing the proceeds on an agreed basis. [*Tr.*]

and their capacity for quick calculation. All round, between the buildings and the stockade, there remains a fairly large space. Here, behind the buildings, some of the prisoners, the most unsociable and moody, liked to walk when they were not working, hidden from other eyes and thinking their own thoughts. When I met them at these times, I liked to look at their sullen, branded faces and guess at their thoughts. There was one convict whose favourite occupation, in his spare time, was to count the pales of the stockade. There were about fifteen hundred of them, and he knew them all by their position and characteristics. For him, each one of them meant a day; each day he counted off one pale, and in this way, from the number remaining still uncounted-off, he could see at a glance how many days he must still spend in the prison before the end of his term of servitude. He was genuinely happy when he came to the end of any of the sides of the hexagon. He had still many years to wait; but in the prison one had plenty of time to learn patience. Once I saw a convict saying good-bye to his friends when, after twenty years in prison, he had at last achieved his free-dom. There were people who could remember him as he was when he entered the prison for the first time, young, careless, unconcerned about either his crime or its punish-ment. He emerged a grey-haired old man, with a sad and sullen face. Silently he went the round of all our six barracks. Entering each, he prayed to the icons and then, bowing low from the waist, took leave of his comrades, asking them to remember him kindly. I remember also a convict, formerly a wealthy Siberian peasant, who was summoned to the gate late one afternoon. Six months before this he had received the news, which profoundly grieved him, that his former wife had married again. Now she herself had come to the prison, asked for him to be sent for, and given him alms. They talked for a minute or two, both wept, and they said good-bye for ever. I saw his face when he came back to the barrack . . . Yes, one could learn patience in that place.

When it grew dusk, they led us all into the barracks, where we were locked in for the night. I always found it painful to return to the barrack from the yard. It was a long, low airless room, dimly lighted by tallow candles, with a heavy, stifling smell. I cannot understand now how I could live ten years in it. My bed was a shelf three planks wide; that was all the space I had. In our room alone about thirty men were accommodated on such shelves. In winter they locked up early; there were some four hours to wait before all were asleep. Until then—a racket of noise, guffaws, curses, the rattle of chains, smoke and soot, shaven heads, branded faces, ragged clothes, everything accursed and ignoble . . . Yes, mankind is tough! Man is a creature who can get used to anything, and I believe that is the very best way of defining him.

There were in our prison about two hundred and fifty men;*the figure was almost constant. Some arrived, others finished their term and left, others again died. And how many different sorts of people there were! I think every Province and every District of Russia had its representative. There were non-Russians as well, and some of the convicts even came from the mountains of the Caucasus. All of these were divided according to the classification of their crime, and, consequently, the number of years of punishment they had been assigned. It is to be supposed that there was no kind of crime without its representative here. The principal element of the prison population was formed by the civilian convict-exiles. These were offenders who had been deprived of all their civil rights and status, fragments broken off from society, with faces branded in perpetual witness of their outcast state. They were sent to hard labour for terms of from eight to twelve years and afterwards distributed about the administrative districts of Siberia as settlers. There were also military criminals, not deprived of their rights, as is usual in Russian penal companies. They had been sent to us for short terms; at the end of them they were returned to where they had come from, as soldiers in the Siberian regiments of the line. Many of them came back to prison almost at once, for second, serious offences, and no longer for short terms, but for twenty years. This category were called 'lifers'. But the 'lifers' were still not completely deprived of all rights. Finally, there was a special, fairly numerous class of the most terrible, predominantly military, criminals. They were called the 'Special Class'. These criminals were sent here from all over Russia. They themselves did not know the term of their sentences and thought of themselves as condemned in perpetuity. They were obliged by law to do twice or thrice the normal tasks. They were kept in the prison pending the opening of the heaviest penal labour undertakings in Siberia. 'You're here for a stretch, but us for the duration', they would say to the other prisoners. I have since heard that this category has been abolished. In our fortress, the Civilian division has been abolished also, and one general penal battalion for military offenders set up. It is hardly necessary to say that the governing authority has also changed. All this means that what I am describing belongs to the past, a state of affairs long gone by and now out of date . . .

This was all long ago; I see it all now as if it were a dream. I remember entering the prison. It was a December evening.* It was growing dark; prisoners were returning from work; preparations were being made for the roll-call. At last a moustached non-commissioned officer opened the door for me into the strange place in which I must spend so many years, undergo so many experiences that I could never have formed even an approximate conception of, if I had not actually endured them. I could not, for example, have realized at all what terrible torment it would be never once to be alone for as much as a single minute, throughout the whole ten years of my sentence. At work always under guard, in the prison with two hundred fellow-convicts, and never once, never once, alone! To this as well, however, I had to get used.

In the prison there were murderers on impulse and murderers by profession, brigands and brigand chiefs, thieves and petty pilferers, and some about whom it was difficult to decide what could have brought them there. But each had his own story, as hazy and disturbing as the fumes of yesterday's drunkenness. In general, they spoke very little of bygones; they did not like to talk, and evidently tried not to think, of the past. I knew even murderers among them so cheerful, so permanently free from all preoccupations, that one would have been prepared to swear that their consciences could find nothing to reproach them with. But there were also those who were sombre and almost always silent. Generally speaking, it was rare for anyone to tell his story and curiosity was not in fashion, was indeed neither customary nor acceptable. Thus if, by some rare chance, somebody did begin to talk, for want of something to do, his hearer would listen with gloomy indifference. Nothing could astonish anyone here. 'We are educated folks', they often said, with a certain strange smugness. I remember that a brigand, who was drunk (it was sometimes possible to get drunk in the prison), once began to tell how he had killed a five-year-old boy, how he first lured him away with a toy and then took him into an empty shed somewhere and killed him. The whole barrack-room, who had until then been laughing at his jokes, cried out like one man, and the brigand was forced to stop talking; they did not cry out in indignation, but simply because *one must not* talk *about that*, because it was not done to talk *about that*. I may remark in passing that these people were indeed literate, and that not in a figurative but in a literal sense. Probably more than half of them could read and write. In what other place, where the common Russian people are collected in large numbers, could you isolate a group of two hundred and fifty, half of whom were literate? I have since heard the deduction from facts of this kind that literacy ruins the common people. This is a mistake; the causes are quite other, although it is impossible not to agree that literacy does develop their self-sufficiency. But this is certainly not a fault.

The different categories of prisoners*were distinguished by their dress; some had one half of the jacket dark brown and the other half grey, and the same with the trousers—one leg grey and the other dark brown. Once, at work, a peasant girl who had come to sell rolls to the convicts stood looking at me for a long time and then suddenly guffawed. 'Well, how disgusting!' she cried. 'They hadn't enough grey cloth and not enough black either!' There were others whose jackets were all of grey cloth except for the sleeves, which were dark brown. Our heads were also shaved in different ways; some had half the head shaven lengthwise, others across.

From the first glance, a vivid family likeness could be observed in all the members of this strange clan; even the most strident and original personalities, dominating the others, even they involuntarily strove to fall in with the tone common to the whole prison. Generally speaking, the whole tribe, with the exception of a few unquenchably cheerful souls, who for that reason enjoyed universal contempt, was sullen, envious, terribly conceited, boastful, touchy, and preoccupied in the highest degree with forms. The capacity not to be surprised by anything was the greatest possible virtue. They were all vitally concerned about one thing: what sort of figure they cut. But not seldom the most arrogant bearing changed with the speed of lightning to the most pitiful. There were a few genuinely strong characters, but they were simple and did not pose. But, strangely enough, some of these really strong people were superlatively, almost morbidly, conceited. Generally speaking, vanity and outward appearance were only the foreground of the picture. The chief part was corruption and terrible perversity. Backbiting and scandal-mongering went on ceaselessly; this was Hell, the nethermost pit and the outer darkness. But against the home-made laws and accepted

customs of the prison none dared to stand; everybody submitted. There were some rugged and unyielding characters
who found it difficult and had to force themselves, but they
did submit. Some who came to the prison had burst all
bounds, broken through every restraint, when they were
free, so that in the end their very crimes were committed,
as it were, not of their own volition but as though they did
not know why they acted so, as though they were delirious
or possessed; the cause was often vanity, raised to the highest
pitch. But with us they were immediately put in their places,
in spite of the fact that some of them, before they came to us,
had been the terror of whole villages and towns. Looking
round, the new-comer soon saw that he had come to the
wrong place and no longer had anybody to astonish, and
imperceptibly he grew tame and conformed with the general
tone. This general tone consisted outwardly of a certain
peculiar personal dignity, with which practically every inhabitant of the prison was imbued. It was just as if the
status of convict, of condemned man, constituted some kind
of rank, and that an honourable one. Not a sign of shame or
remorse! However, there was here some sober reasoning:
'We are a lost people', they said; 'we did not know how to
live in freedom; now it is: "Break the green street¹ and line
up in the courtyard!"' 'You wouldn't heed your father
and mother, now be ruled by the drum.' 'You would not do
fine needlework, now break stones.' All these things were
often repeated, both as moral precepts and as ordinary
proverbs and sayings, but never seriously. They were only
words. There was hardly one of the prisoners who in his
heart acknowledged his own lawlessness. If anyone who
was not one of themselves had reproached a prisoner with
his crime or reviled him for it (although it is not in the
Russian spirit to upbraid the sinner), there would have been
no end to the cursing and swearing. And what masters of
swearing they were! Their oaths were subtle, artistic. They

¹ The reference is to the punishment of running the gauntlet. [*Tr.*]

had raised the use of bad language to a science; they did not strive so much for the offensive word as for the offensive idea, tone, implication—and the maximum of refinement and venom. The ceaseless quarrelling still further developed this science among them. All of them worked under the lash, consequently they were idle, and consequently they were debauched; if they had not been debauched before, they became so in prison. None of them had come here of his own free will; they were all alien to one another.

'The devil wore out three pairs of shoes getting us all rounded up into one herd', they would say of themselves; and therefore gossip, intrigue, cattiness, envy, squabbles, malice, were always to the fore in this life outside life. No woman in the world could have been as womanish as some of these murderers. I repeat that there were strong characters even among them, men who all their lives had been used to rule and domineer, tough and fearless men. They were treated with involuntary respect; for their part, although they were jealous of their reputations, they generally tried not to be a burden to others, did not engage in empty cursing, bore themselves with extraordinary dignity, were reasonable and almost always submissive with the authorities—not on principle, or from any sense of obligation, but rather as though they had entered into a contract for the mutual profit of both parties. Such men, however, were always handled with great care. I remember how one of these prisoners, a bold and resolute man, known to the authorities for his brutal ferocity, was once taken out to be punished for some misdeed. It was a summer day, after work was over. The staff-officer in immediate command of the prison came himself to the guardroom, which was at our gates, to be present at the punishment. This major had a deadly effect on the prisoners, reducing them to a state in which they trembled before him. He was extravagantly strict and was 'always jumping on people', as the convicts expressed it. What most terrified them in him was his eye, as sharp as a lynx's, from which nothing could be hidden. He seemed to see without looking. As soon as he entered the prison, he knew what was happening at the other end of it. The prisoners called him 'Eight-eyes'. His rule was bad. His violent and malicious deeds merely increased the bitterness of already embittered men, and if he had not had as his superior a commandant*who was an honourable and intelligent man and who sometimes tempered his more extravagant and erratic actions, his administration would have been disastrous. I cannot understand how it was that he did not come to grief but was allowed to resign, even though he was court-martialled.

The prisoner turned pale when he was summoned. Usually he lay down resolutely and silently under the rods, silently bore his punishment and got up after it as fresh as paint, regarding the unfortunate occurrence with philosophical detachment. He was always, however, treated with caution. But this time, for some reason, he considered that he was in the right. He turned pale and, unseen by the guards, stealthily contrived to thrust into his sleeve a sharp English shoemaker's knife. Knives and all sharp tools were strictly forbidden in the prison. There were frequent, unexpected, and thorough searches and severe punishments; but since it is difficult to find anything on a thief when he is specially determined to hide it, and since knives and other tools were everyday necessities in the prison, they were never lacking, in spite of the searches. If they were taken away, others were soon procured. The whole prison rushed to the stockade and gazed anxiously through the chinks. Everybody knew that this time Petrov would refuse to lie down under the rods and that the major's end had come. But at the decisive moment the major got into his droshky and drove away, having entrusted the execution of the sentence to another officer. 'It was God Himself who saved him!' the prisoners said afterwards. As for Petrov, he underwent his punishment with the utmost calm. His rage had vanished with the major's departure. A prisoner is obedient and submissive up to a certain point, but there is a limit which must not be transgressed. In passing I may say that nothing could be more curious than these strange outbursts of impatience and rebellion. Often a man endures for several years, submits, suffers the cruellest punishments, and then suddenly breaks out over some minute trifle, almost nothing at all. One school of thought regards such men as definitely insane, and the mad do indeed behave thus.

I have already said that throughout several years I never once saw among these men the slightest sign of remorse, the least gnawing of conscience, and that the majority of them believed themselves to have done nothing wrong. This is a fact. Of course vanity, bad examples, the desire to show off, false shame, were the causes of much of this. On the other hand, who could say that he had penetrated into the depths of those lost souls and read in them what was hidden from all the world? But it should surely have been possible, in so many years, to discern something, at any rate, in those souls, seize some hint, however fleeting, which bore witness to inward anguish or suffering. But there was nothing, nothing at all. Yes, it seems that crime cannot be comprehended from a fixed and settled point of view, its philosophy is rather more difficult than is supposed. Prison and penal servitude do not, of course, reform the criminal; they only punish him and secure society against his further attempts on its peace. In the criminal himself, prison and the most strenuous forms of hard labour develop only hatred, a thirst for forbidden pleasures, and terrible irresponsibility. But I am firmly convinced that the results achieved even by the much-vaunted cell-system* are superficial, deceptive, and illusory. It sucks the living sap out of a man, wears down his spirit, weakens and browbeats him, and then presents the shrivelled, half-demented mummy as a pattern of repentance and reform. Of course the criminal, rebelling against society, hates it and thinks himself innocent and it guilty. Besides, he has already been punished by it and is inclined to feel that this has cleansed him and squared the account. Finally, we may, from some points of view, consider it almost incumbent on us to exculpate the criminal. But whatever point of view one adopts, it is universally agreed that there are certain crimes which, from the beginning of the world, under every code of law, have always and everywhere been regarded as indisputably crimes and will continue to be so regarded while men are men. Only in prison have I heard tales of the most terrible, the most unnatural actions, the most monstrous murders, told with absolutely irrepressible, childishly merry laughter. I cannot forget one parricide in particular. He was a gentleman by birth, had done his government service, and was something in the nature of a prodigal son to his sixty-year-old father. His conduct was thoroughly dissipated and he had run heavily into debt. His father remonstrated with him and tried to restrain him; but his father had a farm and a house, and was suspected of having money, and the son, greedy for his inheritance, killed him. The crime was not discovered for a month. The murderer himself informed the police that his father had disappeared. He spent all that month in the most riotous fashion. Finally the police found the body in his absence. Along the whole length of the farmyard ran a ditch for carrying off sewage, covered in with boards. The body lay in this ditch. It was fully dressed and neatly laid out; the grey head had been cut off and then replaced on the trunk, and under it the murderer had put a pillow. He did not confess. He was deprived of his nobility and his rank in the service and sent to hard labour for twenty years. The whole time that I lived in his company he was always in the most cheerful and excellent spirits. He was a giddy and thoughtless creature and in the highest degree irresponsible, although no fool. I never saw any cruelty in him. The other prisoners despised him, not for his crime, which was never mentioned, but for his folly, for the fact that he did not know how to behave. He sometimes mentioned his father in conversation. Once, talking to me of the healthy constitution hereditary in his family, he added: 'Well, take my father; he never complained of any illness till the day of his death.' Such brutal insensibility, of course, seems impossible. It is exceptional; it shows some defect in the organism, some physical and moral abnormality, as yet unknown to science, and not simply criminality. I need not say that I did not believe in this crime. But people from his own town, who must have known every detail of his history, told me all about the case. The facts were so clear that it was impossible not to believe them.

Once the prisoners heard him crying out in his sleep: 'Hold him, hold him; smash his head for him, his head, his head! . . .'

The prisoners nearly all talked and wandered in their sleep. Curses, thieves' jargon, knives, axes, were what came most frequently to their tongues in these wanderings. 'We are beaten folks', they said; 'the insides have been beaten out of us; that is why we call out of nights.'

The forced labour of penal servitude was compulsory toil, not a calling; the prisoners finished their allotted task or worked the appointed hours and returned to the prison. The work was regarded with hatred. Without his own particular occupation, to which he devotes all his mind and all his calculations, a man in prison could not live. What other means could make these people, all with some degree of development, who have lived intensely and intensely desire to live, and who have been forcibly swept into one swarming mass, forcibly torn from society and normal life, settle down together into a normal and regular existence, of their own free will? The lack of occupation alone would develop among them criminal qualities they could not have dreamed of before. Without labour and normal lawful possessions men cannot live, they grow depraved and turn into beasts. Therefore every man in the prison, driven by natural necessity and some instinct of self-preservation, had his own craft and occupation. The long summer days were almost filled with penal work; in the short nights there was hardly enough time for sleep. But in winter the prisoner, by the regulations, must be locked in as it grew dusk. What was he to do in the long dull hours of the winter evening? And so, in spite of prohibitions, almost every barrack turned itself into a huge workshop. Work itself was not forbidden, but it was strictly forbidden to possess any tools, and work without tools was impossible. The work, however, was done with discretion and in some cases the authorities seemed willing to turn a blind eye to it. Many convicts knew no trade when they arrived in the prison, but they learnt from others and afterwards returned to freedom good workmen. We had cobblers, shoemakers, tailors, carpenters, locksmiths, engravers, gilders. There was one Jew, Isaiah Bumstein, who was a jeweller and also a pawnbroker. These all worked at their trades and earned a few copecks. Orders for work were obtained in the town. Money is coined freedom, and thus is ten times as dear to a man deprived of all other freedom. If it only jingled in his pocket, he would already be half consoled, even though he could not spend it. But money can always be spent, anywhere, and it will, all the more since forbidden fruits are twice as sweet. In the prison it was possible to get even vodka. Pipes were strictly forbidden, but everybody smoked them. Money and tobacco saved men from scurvy and other diseases. Work, moreover, saved them from crime; without work the prisoners would have eaten one another like spiders in a flask. In spite of this, both work and money were forbidden. Not seldom there were unexpected searches in the night, all forbidden objects were taken away, and however carefully money was concealed, it sometimes fell into the searchers' hands. That was part of the reason why it was not taken care of but quickly went in drink; that was why there was trading even in vodka in the prison. After every search the culprits, besides being deprived of all their wealth, were usually severely punished. But after every search, shortages were immediately made up, new industries soon got under way, and the prisoners never murmured against the punishments, although their life was like that of settlers on the slopes of Vesuvius.

Those who had no craft found other ways of making money. Some methods were quite original. Some lived entirely by dealing in second-hand goods, and things were sometimes sold that it would never enter the head of anybody outside the walls of the prison even to think of as things at all, let alone buy or sell. But the convict population was poor and extremely resourceful. The least rag had its value and could enter into some transaction. Because of the poverty, even money had a quite different value in the prison from what it had in the free world. A long and complicated piece of work was paid for in farthings. There were several successful pawnbrokers. The prisoner who had been spendthrift or had no money took his best possessions to the pawnbroker and received a few coppers from him at an exorbitant interest. If he did not redeem his things at the end of the term they were sold ruthlessly and without delay; pawnbroking flourished to such a degree that even government property was accepted as pledges, things like shirts, shoe-leather, and so on, things indispensable to every prisoner at every moment. But when such pledges were made, affairs would take another, not altogether unexpected, turn; the prisoner who had made the pledges and received the money went at once, without more ado, to the senior sergeant, who was immediately responsible for the prison, and informed about the pawning of government property, and it was instantly taken away from the pawnbroker again, even when it was not reported to the higher authorities. It is curious that sometimes this did not even cause an argument; the pawnbroker silently and sullenly returned what he must, and even seemed to have been expecting this to happen. Perhaps he could not help admitting to himself that in his client's place he would have done the same. And therefore, if there was a little cursing afterwards, it was done without malice and only to relieve the feelings.

In general, all the prisoners robbed one another shamelessly. Almost everyone had a box with a lock, for keeping the things issued to him. This was allowed; but the boxes were not sufficient protection. I think it may be imagined what expert thieves we had among us. One prisoner, who was sincerely devoted to me (I say this without any exaggeration), stole from me my bible, the only book one was allowed to possess in prison; he confessed it to me the very same day, not out of remorse, but out of pity for me because I had spent a long time looking for it. We had a number of traffickers in vodka, who quickly grew rich. I shall deal specifically with this trade at some other time; it was somewhat remarkable. There were in the prison many who had been sentenced for smuggling, and there is therefore nothing surprising in the way vodka was brought in in spite of all the guards and inspections. Smuggling, by the way, is by its very nature a rather special crime. Can one imagine, for instance, that with some smugglers money and profit do not stand in the foreground, but play a secondary part? It really is so, however. The smuggler works for love of it, because he has a vocation. He is in some sense a poet. He risks everything, runs into terrible danger, twists and turns, uses his invention, extricates himself; sometimes he seems to act almost by inspiration. It is a passion as strong as that for cards. I knew one prisoner, a man of colossal size, but so meek and submissive that one could not imagine how he came to be in prison. He was so mild and peaceable that he never quarrelled with anybody during the whole time he was there. But he came from the western frontier, had been convicted of running contraband, and, one need hardly say, could not resist trying to smuggle in vodka. How many times he was caught and punished, and how he feared the rods! And the actual smuggling brought him only a trifling reward. It was only the dealer who got rich out of vodka. This queer fellow loved his art for its own sake. He was tearful, like a woman, and how often, after a punishment, he used to vow and swear to renounce the carrying of contraband! He would manfully restrain himself sometimes for as long as a month, but at length he would succumb . . . Thanks to such personalities there was no scarcity of vodka in the prison . . .

Finally, there was one further source of income which, while not enriching the prisoners, was constant and grateful. This was charity. The upper classes of our society have no notion of the solicitude shown for the 'unfortunate' by the upper and lower middle class and all our common people. Gifts come almost uninterruptedly, almost always in the form of various kinds of bread, much less often in money. Without these alms, in many places, life would be too hard for prisoners, especially for those awaiting trial, who are kept in much severer conditions than the condemned. With religious care the gifts are equally divided by the prisoners. If there is not enough to go round, the little round loaves are cut up, sometimes into as many as six equal portions, and each without fail receives his share. I remember the first time I was given money in charity. I was returning from the day's work alone except for a guard. Coming towards me were a mother and her daughter, a little girl about ten years old, as pretty as an angel. I had seen them once before. The mother was a widow. Her husband, a young soldier, had died under arrest in the prison ward of the military hospital at a time when I was ill there. His wife and daughter came to say good-bye to him; they both wept very bitterly. When they saw me, the little girl blushed and whispered to her mother, who immediately stopped, found a quarter copeck in her purse and gave it to her daughter. The little girl ran after me . . . 'Here, poor man, take this copeck in Christ's name', she cried, running round in front of me and thrusting the copper into my hand. I took it and the little girl returned well contented to her mother. I kept that piece of money carefully for a long time.

2. First Impressions (1)

THE first month and the beginning of my prison life in general are vividly present now to my mind. The later years glimmer much more faintly in my memory. Some seem to have faded completely away, merging with others and leaving behind only a general impression, an impression of oppressive, stifling monotony.

But everything that I went through in the first days of my penal servitude rises before me now as though it had happened yesterday. This, indeed, was to be expected.

I remember that what impressed me at the first step into this new life was that I did not find in it anything striking, anything out of the ordinary, or rather, anything unexpected. My imagination seemed to have caught glimpses of all of it earlier when, trudging to Siberia, I had striven to guess what my lot would be like. But soon an inexhaustible stream of the strangest surprises, the greatest enormities, began to arrest my attention at almost every step. And it was only later still, when I had lived for a long time in the prison, that I comprehended to the full the exceptional nature of that existence, at which I wondered more and more. I confess that this wonder accompanied me all through my long term of penal servitude; I could never grow reconciled to that life.

My first impression on entering the prison was of general and extreme disgust; but in spite of this, strangely enough, it seemed to me that it was much easier to live in prison than I had imagined on my way there. The prisoners, although they were confined, and although they wore fetters, were free to move about all over the prison; they cursed and swore, sang songs, worked for themselves, smoked pipes, even (a very few of them) drank vodka, and at night some of them played cards. The very labour, for instance, did not seem to me so very heavy or *penal*, and it was only after a fairly long time that I realized that the oppression and *penal quality* of the work lay not so much in its being hard and unremitting as in its being *forced*, obligatory, done under the threat of the rod. The peasant in freedom works, perhaps, incomparably harder and sometimes even far into the night, especially in summer; but he works for himself and for reasonable ends, and it is infinitely easier for him than for the convict doing forced labour without any advantage at all to himself. The idea occurred to me once that if it were desired to crush and destroy a man completely and punish him with the most frightful possible penalty, which would make even the most terrible criminal quail and fill him with dread, it would suffice to give the penal work the most completely and utterly useless and nonsensical character. Even though work is now dull and uninteresting for the convict, it is itself, as work, reasonable enough; the prisoner makes bricks, digs the soil, plasters walls, builds; there is purpose and an idea in such work. The convict sometimes even grows enthusiastic about it and tries to perform it more neatly, more efficiently, more skilfully. But if he were compelled, for example, to pour water from one bucket into another and back into the first again, grind sand, or laboriously transfer a heap of soil from one place to another and back again, the prisoner, I think, would hang himself after a few days, or commit a thousand new crimes, choosing any way of escape, even death, from such degradation, shame, and suffering. Such punishment, needless to say, would be a reversion to vengeance and torture, and it would be senseless because it would serve no rational purpose. But since some part of that torture, senselessness, degradation, and shame is inevitably present in every kind of compulsory work, penal labour is incomparably more cruelly painful than any free work, simply because it is compulsory.

I, however, arrived in the prison in winter, in December,

and did not yet possess any understanding of the summer work, five times as laborious. In winter there was generally little official work to be done in our fortress. The prisoners went to the River Irtysh to break up old government barges, worked in the various workshops, dug away the snow piled up by the storms round the government buildings, calcined and pounded gypsum, and so on. The winter day was short, work ended early, and all our people returned to the prison, where there would have been almost nothing for them to do if it had not been for their own work. But perhaps only about a third of the convicts had their own occupations; the rest lounged about, wandered aimlessly through all the prison barracks, abused one another, gossiped and intrigued among themselves, got drunk if they could get hold of a little money, at night gambled away the shirts off their backs at cards, and all out of boredom and idleness and having nothing to do. Later I came to know that, besides the deprivation of liberty, besides the compulsory labour, there is another torment in prison life, almost more unbearable than all the rest. This is being forced to live herded together. Community life, of course, exists elsewhere; but people come to prison with whom not everybody would care to associate, and I am certain that every prisoner, the majority of them of course unconsciously, felt this ordeal.

Our food, also, was fairly adequate. The prisoners asserted that there was no such food in the penal battalions in European Russia. I do not undertake to judge of this: I have not been there. Many of us, besides, were able to have our own food. Beef cost half a copeck a pound in winter, three copecks in summer. But only those could procure their own food who had a constant supply of money; the majority of convicts ate the rations issued. However, when the prisoners boasted of the food they were speaking only of the bread; and rejoicing in the fact that it was distributed to the *artels* and not weighed out to us. This last horrified them; when bread is weighed out a third of the recipients go hungry, but in the *artel* there was enough for all. Our bread was especially good and was famous all over the town. This was attributed to the happy construction of the prison ovens. The cabbage soup, though, was of very indifferent quality. It was cooked in a common cauldron and slightly thickened with groats, and, especially on week-days, was thin and watery. I was horrified by the enormous number of cockroaches in it. The other prisoners, however, paid no attention.

For the first three days I was not sent out to work; all new-comers were treated so; they were allowed to rest after the journey. But on the second day I had to leave the prison to have my irons changed. My fetters were not regulation ones, but ring-shaped 'chinkers', as the prisoners called them. They were worn outside the clothes. The regulation prison fetters, adapted for working in, consisted not of rings but of four iron bars, almost as thick as one's finger, joined together by a chain of three links. They had to be worn under the trousers. The middle ring was fastened to a strap which in turn was attached to the leather belt worn immediately over the shirt.

I remember my first morning in the prison. In the guardhouse by the gates a drum beat tattoo, and ten minutes later the non-commissioned officer of the watch began to unlock the barracks. People were waking up. By the dim light of tallow candles, six to the pound, the prisoners were getting up off their planks, shaking with cold. Most of them were silent and morosely heavy with sleep. They yawned, stretched, and wrinkled up their branded foreheads. Some crossed themselves, others had already begun quarrelling. It was terribly stuffy. The chilly winter air rushed in as soon as the door was opened, and steam drifted in puffs through the room. The prisoners crowded round buckets of water; each in turn took the dipper, filled his mouth with water and proceeded to wash his face and hands with it.

The water had been brought in the evening before by the latrine orderly. In each of the barracks regulations required one prisoner to be selected by the *artel* for menial tasks. He was called the latrine orderly and did not go out to work. His duties consisted in attending to the cleanliness of the barrack, washing and scouring the plank-beds and floors, carrying in and out a tub for use in the night, and procuring two buckets of fresh water, for washing in the morning and drinking during the day. Disputes soon arose over the dipper, of which there was only one.

'Where are you shoving to, blockhead?' grumbled a tall, surly prisoner, a lean and swarthy fellow with certain curious protuberances on his shorn skull, elbowing another who was fat and squat and had a ruddy, good-humoured face. 'Keep your place!'

'What are you yelling about? Where I come from it costs money to stay anywhere; you clear off yourself! Standing up there like a monument! I mean to say, lads, nobody's ever chopped no bits off him; no amputifications . . .'

'Amputifications' produced some effect; many of the men laughed. This was just what the jolly little fat man wanted; he was evidently the self-appointed clown of the barrack. The tall prisoner looked at him with the deepest scorn.

'Fat little cow!' he said as if to himself. 'Look at him, getting fat on prison grub; he's going to give birth to twelve little sucking-pigs, come the end of the fast.'

The stout man grew angry at last.

'And what sort of a bird do you think you are?' he burst out suddenly, going red in the face.

'That's just what I am, a bird!'

'What bird?'

'Oh, a bird.'

'What sort of a bird?'

'Just a bird.'

'What bird?'

They were glaring into each other's eyes. The fat man waited for the answer with his fists clenched, as if he meant to fling himself into a fight on the spot. I, indeed, thought there was going to be a fight. This was all new to me and I watched curiously. Later I learnt that all such scenes were extraordinarily harmless and were played like a comedy for the general enjoyment, but almost never resulted in blows. All this was a quite characteristic display of the customs of the prison.

The tall prisoner stood there quietly and majestically. He felt that people were looking at him and waiting to see whether he would disgrace himself by his answer, and that he must keep his end up, show that he really was a bird and indicate exactly what bird. With indescribable contempt he squinted at his adversary, trying to be more offensive by looking at him down his nose and with averted head, as if he regarded him as some sort of small insect, and pronounced slowly and distinctly:

'A great crested grebe . . .'

A loud volley of laughter saluted his resourcefulness.

'You're not, you're a dirty scoundrel!' yelled the fat prisoner, conscious that he had been defeated at all points and growing frenziedly angry.

But as soon as the dispute grew serious the valiant contestants were quickly put in their place.

'What's all the row about?' the whole barrack shouted at them.

'You ought to be going for one another's throats instead of straining your own,' cried somebody from the corner.

'Yes, they'll fight, I don't think!' came the answer. 'We're a lot of dare-devils, we are, full of spunk; we're not afraid of anybody so long as we're seven to one . . .'

'And they're a fine pair! One of them was sent here on account of a pound of bread and the other's a tup'ny whore and got the lash for sneaking some woman's junket . . .'

'Now then, now then! That's enough,' called out the

disabled old soldier who lived in the barrack to keep order and slept on a camp-bed in a corner of the room.

'Water, lads! Here's Daddy Petrovich waked up! Daddy Petrovich, dear old pal, good morning!'

'Pal . . . Since when have I been your pal? We've never so much as had a drink together and he calls me pal . . .,' grumbled the old soldier, struggling into the sleeves of his great-coat . . .

People were getting ready for the 'control'; it was beginning to grow light; an impenetrably thick crowd had collected in the kitchen. The prisoners in their sheepskin coats and parti-coloured caps crowded round one of the cooks, who was cutting up bread for them. The cooks were chosen by the *artels*, two to each kitchen. They had the custody of the kitchen knife for cutting up bread and meat, only one to serve the whole kitchen.

In every corner and round the tables were prisoners in caps and sheepskins, with girdles fastened, ready to go out to work at once. In front of some of them stood wooden bowls of kvass into which, before sipping it, they crumbled their bread. The noise and uproar were intolerable but a few men were talking quietly and sensibly in the corners.

'Good morning, old Antonovich, a very good morning to you,' said a young prisoner as he sat down beside a toothless, scowling old man.

'Well, good morning, if you mean it seriously,' said he, mumbling his bread in his toothless gums without looking up.

'You know, Antonovich, I thought you were dead, I really did . . .'

'No. You die first, and I'll follow you . . .'

I sat down beside them. On my right two sedate and sober prisoners were talking, each evidently trying to preserve his consequence in the other's eyes.

'Nobody's going to pinch anything off me, I can tell you,'

said one. 'I'm half afraid I might steal something myself, though.'

'Well, keep your hands off my stuff or you'll get them burnt.'

'Oh, and how are you going to manage that? You're only an old lag, no different from me . . . She'll fleece you without so much as saying thank you. That's the way my last copeck went, brother. And she didn't wait to be asked. But where could we go? I asked Fedka the executioner; he used to have a house in the suburbs. He bought it from that Jew, Scurvy Solomon, the one who hanged himself . . .'

'I know. He was a moonshiner, and his nickname was Grishka the Dirty Pub . . . I know.'

'You don't know anything. Dirty Pub was another man.'

'What do you mean, another? You don't know what you're talking about! I could bring any number of witnesses to prove it.'

'You could, could you? What do you take me for?'

'You? Why, I used to thrash you, and I'm not boasting. What should I take you for?'

'You used to thrash me? The person who can thrash me hasn't been born yet, and anybody who ever tried it is under the ground now.'

'You be damned!'

'May you catch the Siberian plague!'

'I'd like to see you talk to a Turkish scimitar!'

There was more cursing in the same strain.

'Now then, now then! Kicking up a row!' people began to shout round about. 'You couldn't live outside; be thankful you've got a bit of grub in here! . . .'

This subdued them at once. Cursing, abuse, 'tongue-lashings', were permissible. In some measure they served to entertain everybody. But things were not often allowed to go as far as fighting; only rarely, in exceptional cases, did the adversaries come to blows. Actual fighting would be reported to the major; there would be investigations, the major himself would come—in a word, it would be bad for everybody, and therefore fights were not tolerated. Indeed, the contestants abused one another more as a form of amusement and as an exercise in style than anything else. Not infrequently they got carried away and began to dispute with passionate heat and frenzy . . . and you would think they were on the point of flinging themselves on one another; nothing of the sort happened; they progressed to a certain point and then immediately parted company. All this seemed to me at first extremely strange. I have deliberately brought in here examples of the most usual kind of prison conversation; I could not at first imagine how it was possible to wrangle for pleasure and find it an amusement, an agreeable and pleasing exercise. Vanity, however, must not be forgotten. The man who could argue down or shout down his opponent was highly esteemed and all but applauded like an actor.

On the previous evening I had already noticed that I was looked at askance. I had caught several resentful glances. Some prisoners, on the other hand, hung round me, suspecting that I had brought money with me. They began at once to curry favour with me, showing me how to wear my new fetters and procuring for me (for money, of course) a small chest with a lock in which I could keep the things that had been issued to me and some of my own linen which I had brought with me. On the very next day they stole it from me and drank the proceeds. In course of time one of them became quite devoted to me, although he never ceased to rob me at every opportunity. He did it without any compunction, almost automatically, as if he were obliged to, and it was impossible to be angry with him.

Among other things, they told me I ought to have my own tea and that it would not be a bad thing if I were to acquire a teapot; meanwhile they procured somebody else's for me for the time being and recommended a cook who, they said, for thirty copecks a month would cook me what

I liked if I wanted to eat separately and buy my own pro-
visions . . . It goes without saying that they borrowed money
from me and on that first day each of them came to me three
times for a loan . . .

The prison in general regarded former members of the
nobility with resentment and ill will. In spite of the fact that
they had been deprived of all the rights of their position and
reduced to complete equality with the others, the prisoners
never recognized them as their fellows. This was not the
result of conscious prejudice but happened quite simply,
genuinely, and unaware. They sincerely acknowledged that
we were gentlemen, even though they liked to taunt us with
our fall:

'No more of that, now! Peter used to go strutting round
Moscow but now Peter's picking oakum,' and many more
such civilities.

They watched our sufferings, which we tried not to show
them, with delight. We were particularly severely cursed at
work at first, because we were not as strong as they were and
could not pull our weight. There is nothing harder than to
gain the confidence of the people (especially these people)
and even their liking.

There were a number of gentlefolk in the prison. To begin
with, there were five Poles.* I will speak more particularly of
them at some other time. The convicts fiercely disliked
them, even more than they did the Russian gentleman exiles.
The Poles (I am speaking only of political offenders) bore
themselves towards the other prisoners with a kind of subtly
offensive courtesy, were extremely uncommunicative and
quite unable to conceal their loathing for the others, who
understood this very clearly and repaid them in their own
coin.

I had to live in the prison for almost two years before I
could gain the favour of some of the convicts. But in the
end the majority of them liked me and recognized me as
a 'decent' fellow.

Besides myself, four of the prisoners came from Russian noble families. One, a mean, despicable creature, horribly corrupt, was a spy and informer by profession. I had heard of him even before I came to the prison and I broke off all relations with him in my first days there. Another was the parricide of whom I have already spoken in these memoirs. The third was Akim Akimovich.* I have rarely seen so extravagantly strange a person as this Akim Akimovich. His portrait is sharply etched in my memory. He was tall and spare, naïve, terribly illiterate, extraordinarily moralistic, and as punctilious as a German. The convicts laughed at him, but some were almost afraid to have anything to do with him because of his captious, exacting, and quarrelsome character. He was at home among them from the first moment, wrangling and even fighting with them. He was phenomenally honest. If he saw any injustice he would instantly intervene, although it might be no concern of his. He was simple to the last degree; for example, he sometimes, when he was arguing with them, reproached other prisoners with being thieves, and seriously tried to persuade them not to steal. He had served in the Caucasus as an ensign. He and I were friendly from my first day in the prison and he told me his story at once. He had begun his service, straight from the military academy, with an infantry regiment in the Caucasus, had slaved away for a long time and then been given his commission and sent to a fortress as senior officer commanding. A little neighbouring princeling, who had accepted Russian domination, made a raid by night on the fortress and set fire to it, but was driven off. Akim Akimovich concealed the fact that he knew who was responsible. The affair was ascribed to unreconciled tribes and a month later Akim Akimovich invited the princeling to pay him a friendly visit. He came, suspecting nothing. Akim Akimovich drew up his troops and publicly accused and reproached the princeling; he pointed out that firing the fortress had been an act of treachery. Then he read him a most detailed lecture on how a friendly prince ought to conduct himself in future and, in conclusion, shot him. He lost no time in reporting all this to the authorities. He was tried for it and sentenced to death, but the sentence was commuted and he was sent to Siberia as a convict of the second class, to spend twelve years in fortresses. He was fully aware of the irregularity of his action; he told me that he had known it before he shot the princeling, and known, too, that friendly peoples must be tried in proper legal form, but in spite of knowing this he seemed incapable of a genuine understanding of his guilt:

'But, for heaven's sake! He had set fire to my fortress! What was I supposed to do, thank him for it?' he would say in answer to my objections.

But although the prisoners made fun of Akim Akimovich's craziness, they respected him for his preciseness and skill.

There was no trade that Akim Akimovich did not know. He was carpenter, cobbler, shoemaker, painter, gilder, locksmith, and he had learnt all these crafts in prison. He was entirely self-instructed; he would look at a thing once and then make it. He also made various boxes, baskets, lanterns, and children's toys and sold them in the town. Thus he was never without money, which he quickly spent, on extra linen, a softer pillow, or acquiring a folding mattress. He lived in the same barrack as I, and did me many services in my first days in the prison.

When they were leaving the prison for work, the convicts were drawn up in two ranks before the guard-house; guards with loaded rifles were posted in front of and behind them. The Engineer officer in charge appeared, with several Engineers of lower rank who acted as overseers. The officer told off the prisoners and sent them in parties to where they were wanted.

Together with others I was sent to the engineering work-shops. These occupied a low stone building standing in a large yard, which was encumbered with various materials.

Here were a blacksmith's, a locksmith's, a carpenter's, a paint-shop, and so on. Akim Akimovich came here and worked in the painter's shop, boiling linseed oil, mixing colours, and staining and graining furniture to look like walnut.

While I waited for my irons to be changed, I began to talk to Akim Akimovich about my first impressions of prison.

'No, they don't like gentleman convicts,' he remarked, 'especially political ones; they wouldn't mind murdering them, and no wonder. To begin with, you're a different sort of people, not like them, and in the second place they've all been some landowner's serfs or else soldiers. You can see for yourself whether they can be expected to love you. Life is hard here, I can tell you. It's even harder in the Russian penal battalions. There are some men here who have come from them and they can't praise our prison too highly; it's as if they had crossed over from hell into paradise. It's not the work that's the trouble. They say that there, in the First division, the authorities are not entirely military, at least they behave differently from ours. I haven't been there, but that's what they say. Their heads aren't shaved, they don't wear uniforms; it's a good thing, though, that ours are shaved and we do wear uniform; it's more decent, after all, and it's nicer to look at. Only we don't like it. And then look what a crew! One comes from the army schools, the next is a Circassian, the third an Old Believer,* the fourth an Ortho-dox peasant who's left his dear children and family behind, then the fifth's a Jew, the sixth a gipsy, the seventh God knows what—and they've all got to live together, come what may, and get on with one another somehow, they've all got to eat from the same bowl and sleep on the same planks. And what sort of liberty has anyone?; you can't eat a bit of extra food except by stealth, you have to hide every farthing in your boots, and life is nothing but prison, prison . . . All sorts of queer ideas are bound to get into your head . . .'

But I knew this already. I particularly wanted to ask

questions about our major. Akim Akimovich spoke quite openly, and I was left, I remember, with a not very pleasant impression.

I was destined to spend two years under his rule. Everything that Akim Akimovich told me about him proved to be quite true; the only difference was that the reality always makes a much stronger impression than a mere description. It was just because a man like him had almost unlimited power over two hundred souls that this man was terrible. In himself he was no more than a bad and undisciplined man. He looked on the prisoners as his natural enemies, and this was his first and most important mistake. He had some genuine abilities, but all of them, even the good ones, seemed distorted by his personality. Violent and malevolent, he would sometimes burst into the prison even at night and if he noticed a prisoner sleeping on his back or on his left side, he would punish him in the morning: 'Obey my orders,' he would say, 'and sleep on your right side.' In the prison he was hated and feared like the plague. He had a red, ill-tempered face. Everybody knew he was completely in the hands of Fedka, his batman. The thing he held dearest was his poodle, Trezorka, and he almost went out of his mind with grief when Trezorka fell ill. They said he groaned over the dog as though he were his own son; he drove out the veterinary surgeon and, in his usual way, almost came to blows with him; and then, learning from Fedka that one of the prisoners was a self-taught veterinarian, whose treatments were extraordinarily successful, he sent for him at once.

'Save him! I'll pay you anything, if you cure Trezorka!' he cried.

The prisoner was a Siberian peasant, cunning and shrewd, a very good vet, certainly, but an out-and-out moujik.

'I looks at Trezorka,' he told the other peasants later, long after his visit to the major's, when the whole matter had been forgotten; 'I looks and sees the dog is lying on a sofa, on a white pillow; and I can see he's probably got an inflammation, and ought to be bled, and then he would get better for sure. But I thinks to myself, "What if I don't cure him, what if he dies?" "No," says I, "your excellency, you called me in too late; if it had been yesterday or the day before, now, I could have saved the dog; but now I can't, he won't get better" . . .'

So Trezorka died.

I was told the details of an attempt on the life of our major. There was a certain convict in the prison, who had already been there for several years and was distinguished by the mildness of his bearing. It was also noticeable that he hardly ever talked to anyone. He was put down as a pious simpleton. He had learned to read and write and spent all his last year reading his bible, reading by day and night. In the middle of the night, when everybody else was asleep, he would get up, light a wax church-candle, climb up on to the stove, open his book and read till morning. One day he went to the sergeant and declared that he would not go to work. This was reported to the major, who flew into a rage and came dashing along himself at the gallop. The prisoner flung himself on him brandishing a brick he had secreted for the purpose, but the blow went wide. He was seized, tried, and punished. The whole affair passed off very quickly. Three days later he died in the hospital. As he lay dying, he said that he had borne nobody any ill will, but had simply wished for suffering. Nevertheless, he did not belong to any dissenting sect. His memory was honoured in the prison.

At length my fetters were changed. Meanwhile, one after another, several women and girls selling white loaves had appeared in the workshops. Some were quite little girls. Usually they would continue to bring their loaves until they were grown up; their mothers baked them and they sold them. When they grew up, they still came, but without loaves; this was the almost invariable course of things. There were also some who were not young girls. The loaves cost half a copeck each, and almost all the prisoners bought them.

I noticed one prisoner, a carpenter, already grey-haired, but ruddy-faced, smiling flirtatiously at the girls with their loaves. Just before they began to arrive he had twisted a red fustian handkerchief round his neck. One fat pock-marked peasant put her basket down on his bench. They fell into conversation.

'Why didn't you come yesterday?' began the convict with a smug smile.

'I did, but you weren't there,' answered the woman pertly.

'We were wanted somewhere else, or we'd have been found in the same old spot . . . All your pals came to see me the day before yesterday.'

'Who do you mean?'

'Maryashka came, and Khavroshka, and Chekunda, and Two Farthings, they all came . . .'

'What is all this?' I asked Akim Akimovich. 'Is it really possible . . .?'

'It does happen,' he replied, modestly lowering his eyes, for he himself was unusually chaste.

It did indeed happen, of course, but very rarely, and in circumstances of the greatest difficulty. Generally speaking, more of us wanted, say, a drink, than this sort of thing, in spite of all the naturally burdensome restrictions imposed by our way of life. Women were very hard to come by. The time and place must be chosen, an agreement reached, an assignation made; privacy must be sought, which was very difficult, and the guards must be won over, which was more difficult still, and altogether vast sums, comparatively speaking, must be laid out. All the same, later I did sometimes witness love scenes. I remember one occasion, in summer, when there were three of us in a shed on the banks of the River Irtysh, where we were heating up a furnace; the guards were in a good mood. At last there appeared two 'blowers', as the prisoners called them.

'Well! Why have you been so long? You were at the Zverkovs', I suppose?' was the greeting of one of the prisoners whom they had come to see, and who had been expecting them for a long time.

'I was a long time? Why, just now a magpie sat on the fence post longer than I stayed with them,' answered the woman cheerfully.

She must have been the dirtiest wench in the world. This was Chekunda. Two Farthings had come with her. She was utterly beyond description.

'It's a long time since I saw you,' went on the ladies' man, turning to Two Farthings. 'How is it you seem to have got so thin?'

'Perhaps I have. Before, I used to be terribly fat, but now I'm as thin as a rake.'

'Still hanging round with the soldiers?'

'No! Spiteful people have been stuffing you up about us, and anyhow, why not? All the nice girls love a soldier.'

'You give them the go-by and love us. We've got money.'

To complete the picture you must imagine the appearance of this ladies' man, with shaven head and fetters, wearing parti-coloured clothes and under guard.

I said good-bye to Akim Akimovich and, learning that I might go back to the prison, I returned there with a guard. People were already gathering there. The first to return from work were those who had been set a definite task. The only way of making a prisoner work zealously is to give him a task. Sometimes the tasks assigned are enormous, but nevertheless they are completed twice as quickly as work that must be continued right up to the time when the drum beats for dinner. When he had finished his task the convict was at liberty to go back home and nobody tried to stop him.

We did not all dine together, but in any order, just as we happened to arrive; indeed, the kitchen would not have held all of us at once. I tried the cabbage soup but, not having grown used to it, could not eat it and made myself some tea. We sat down at the end of a table. I had a companion who, like me, was a gentleman.

Prisoners came and went. There was room, however, since they were not yet all there. A group of five had sat down together at a big table. The cooks poured their soup into two bowls and set on the table a whole panful of fried fish. They were having some celebration and eating their own food. They looked at us askance. A Pole came in and sat down beside us.

'I've not been here, but I know everything!' shouted a tall prisoner as he came into the kitchen, embracing with his glance everybody there.

He was a lean and muscular man of about fifty. His expression was at once cheerful and cunning. His thick pendant lower lip was particularly noticeable; it gave his face an extraordinarily comical look.

'Well, how did you sleep? Why can't you say hullo? Here's to all of us from Kursk!' he added, sitting down next to the men who had their own food. 'Good appetite! Welcome your guest!'

'We're not from Kursk, mate.'

'Tambov,* then?'

'Not from Tambov, neither. You'll get nothing from us. You go to the rich moujik and ask him.'

'All I've got in my belly today, mates, is sorrow and hiccups. Where does he live, this rich moujik?'

'That Gazin is a rich moujik; go to him.'

'Gazin's on a binge today, mates; he's drinking. He's drinking away everything he's got.'

'That's twenty silver roubles,' remarked another. 'It pays to sell vodka, mates.'

'What, mates, won't you welcome a guest? Well then, I must eat prison grub.'

'You be off! Why don't you ask for some tea? The gentlemen over there have some.'

'What gentlemen? There are no gentlemen here; they are just the same as us now,' sullenly put in another prisoner sitting in the corner. Up till then he had not said a word.

'I could do with some tea, but I don't like to ask; I have my pride,' said the prisoner with the thick lip, looking at us pleasantly enough.

'If you would like some, I will give it to you,' said I, with a gesture of invitation. 'All right?'

'All right? Why not?' He came over to the table.

'Look! at home he used to eat cabbage soup out of his shoe, but here he's learnt to drink tea. Now he wants the masters' drink,' said the morose prisoner.

'Doesn't anyone here drink tea?' I asked him, but he did not deign to answer.

'Look, they're bringing white loaves. What about a bit of bread as well?'

White bread had been brought in by a young convict who was carrying a whole armful of loaves and selling them round the prison. The woman for whom he sold them allowed him every tenth loaf for himself and on that one he counted for his profit.

'White loaves, white loaves!' he called, as he entered the kitchen. 'All hot, real Moscow bread! I'd eat them myself, but I need the money. Well, lads, there's one left; who had a mother?'

This appeal to mother-love amused everybody and several took loaves from him.

'Well, mates,' he went on, 'I'll tell you what, that Gazin will get himself into serious trouble in one of those wild fits of his. "Eight-eyes" will catch him on one of his surprise visits, mark my words.'

'They'll hide him. Why, is he very drunk?'

'Not half! He's turning nasty and button-holing people.'

'Well, then he'll be getting fighting drunk next . . .'

'Who are they talking about?' I asked the Pole sitting beside me.

'Oh, that's Gazin, one of the prisoners. He sells vodka. When he's taken in some money he drinks it away at once. He is an ill-natured brute but tame enough, sober; when he gets drunk it all comes out; he goes for people with a knife. But they soon shut him up here.'

'How?'

'About ten of the other prisoners rush him and knock him about terribly, until he's quite unconscious, that's to say they beat him half to death. Then they put him on his planks and cover him up with a sheepskin coat.'

'But surely they might kill him?'

'Anybody else would be killed, but not him. He is terribly strong and healthy. The next morning he gets up quite well again.'

'Please tell me one thing,' I went on with my questioning. 'Look, they are eating their own food, too, and I am drinking tea. But all the same, they look as if they resented my having the tea. What does that mean?'

'It's not because of the tea,' answered the Pole. 'You irritate them because you are a gentleman and not like them. Many of them would like to pick a quarrel with you. They are itching to insult and humiliate you. You will see a great deal more unpleasantness here. Things are very difficult for all of us. It is harder for us in every way. We need all the unconcern we can muster to get used to it. You will come up against unpleasantness again more than once, and harsh words about having tea and your own food, although many of them very frequently eat their own food and some always have tea to drink. They can do it, but you must not.'

When he had finished talking he got up and left the table. In a few minutes his words came true . . .

3. First Impressions (II)

No sooner had Miretsky*(the Pole who had been talking to me) left, than Gazin staggered into the kitchen, quite drunk.

The sight of a drunken prisoner in broad daylight, on a weekday when everybody was obliged to go out to work, with a martinet of a commanding officer liable to visit the prison at any moment, with the sergeant in charge of the prisoners constantly about, in face of all the sentries and old soldiers, in face, in a word, of all this watchfulness—completely upset all my newly conceived notions of convict existence. I had, indeed, to live in the prison for quite a long time before I succeeded in explaining to myself all the facts I found so puzzling in the early days.

I have already said that the prisoners always had their own occupations and that this work filled a natural need of prison life; that, besides feeling this need, the prisoner delights in money and esteems it more than anything else, almost equally with freedom, and that he finds solace in the sound of it jingling in his pocket. He is, on the other hand, dejected, melancholy, restless, and downcast when he has none, and is ready to steal or do anything else to acquire it. But, although money was so precious in the prison, it never remained long in the hands of those who were lucky enough to get it. In the first place, it was difficult to keep it from being stolen or confiscated. If the major came upon it in one of his surprise searches, it was immediately taken away. It might perhaps be used to improve the prisoners' food; in any case it fell into the major's hands. But most often it was stolen; it was impossible to trust anybody. Later we evolved a means of keeping it in complete safety. It was confided to the care of an Old Believer, an old man who came from one of the dissenters' settlements . . . I cannot refrain from saying something about him, although it is a digression.

He was a little grey old man, of about sixty years of age. He began his term of penal servitude a year after me, and he made a sharply striking impression on me from the first glance. He was so unlike the other prisoners, there was something so still and tranquil in his look, that I remember looking with peculiar satisfaction at his clear bright eyes, with fine wrinkles radiating from them. I often talked to him and I have rarely met so good and kind a being in my whole life. He had been sent to us for an extremely serious crime. Converts to the Orthodox Church had begun to appear among the extreme Old Believers. The government was strongly encouraging them and had begun to direct its efforts to procuring further conversions of dissentients. The old man, with other fanatics, resolved to 'make a stand for the faith', as he expressed it. The building of a new 're-united' church had been begun and they burnt it down. As one of the ringleaders the old man was sent to penal servitude. He was a well-to-do tradesman; he left a wife and children behind; but he went into exile with fortitude, because he thought of it as 'martyrdom for his faith'. After living with him for some time you would involuntarily have asked yourself how this mild and childishly submissive man could be a rebel. I talked to him several times about 'the faith'. He would abate not one jot of his convictions, but he never expressed any bitterness or hatred. Nevertheless, he had destroyed a church and he did not disavow his action. His convictions apparently obliged him to regard it and the 'martyrdom' resulting from it as glorious. But however deep I probed, however closely I studied him, I never observed any trace of pride or vanity in him. We had others in the prison who clung to the old rites, the majority of them Siberians. They were highly developed people, shrewd peasants, believing pedantically and uncritically in the literal truth of their old books, and very powerful dialecticians in their own way; a haughty, arrogant, crafty, and highly intolerant people. The old man was quite different. With an even more uncritical trust in the printed word than theirs, perhaps, he avoided disputes. He was of an extremely sociable nature. He was cheerful and much given to laughter —not the boorish, cynical laughter of the convict but a serene gentle laughter which contained much childlike innocence and seemed peculiarly appropriate to his grey hairs. I may be mistaken but it seems to me that a man may be judged by his laugh, and that if at the first encounter you like the laugh of a person completely unknown to you, you may say with assurance that he is good. All through the prison the old man won general respect, which he accepted without any touch of vanity. The prisoners called him Grandad and were never offensive to him. I could half understand the influence he must have had over his fellow believers. But in spite of the fortitude with which he bore his sentence there was in him a hidden grief which he strove to keep concealed from all the world. I lived in the same barrack-hut with him. Once, at about two o'clock in the morning, I woke up to the sound of quiet, stifled weeping. The old man was sitting on the stove (the same where, before him, the crazy prisoner who had tried to kill the major used to sit at night, reading and praying), reading prayers from a manuscript book. He was crying and I heard him say from time to time: 'Lord, do not desert me! Lord, strengthen me! My little children, my dear children, we shall never see each other again!' It filled me with indescribable sorrow. It was to this old man that almost all the prisoners began to confide their money for safe keeping. Almost everybody in the place was a thief, but for some reason all of them were convinced that the old man was quite incapable of stealing. It was known that he hid the money entrusted to him somewhere, but the hiding-place was so secret that nobody could discover it. Later he revealed it to me and some of the Poles. In one of the posts of the stockade there was a knot that was apparently firmly embedded in the wood. But it lifted out and revealed a large hole. There

Grandad hid the money and afterwards replaced the knot so that nobody could ever find anything.

But I have wandered from my subject. I had come to the question of why money did not remain long in the prisoner's pocket. Apart from the difficulty of keeping it safe, there is so much misery in the prison, and the prisoner in the nature of things has such a thirst for freedom and is rendered by his position in respect to society so irresponsible and undisciplined, that he is naturally open to the temptation to have his fling, to 'blue in' all his wealth in one wild noisy revel and so to forget his anguish if only for a fleeting moment. It was quite strange to see one of them keep his nose to the grindstone, sometimes for several months on end, simply in order to squander all his earnings, down to the last copeck, in one day and then once more plod away at work for months, until the next outbreak. Many of them liked to get themselves new clothes—'civilian' black trousers, coats, full-skirted tunics—which it was most essential should not resemble any kind of uniform. Print shirts were also fashionable, and belts with brass plates on them. People dressed themselves up in these things on holidays, and then they used to parade through all the barracks to display themselves to all the world. The pleasure of those who were well dressed was positively childish, and indeed many of the prisoners were nothing but children. It is true that all these fine things were apt to disappear suddenly, their owner sometimes pawning them for a mere trifle before the day was out. A 'binge', however, developed gradually. It would usually take place on a holiday or a man's name-day. The prisoner whose saint's day it was, on getting up in the morning, lit a candle before the ikon and said his prayers; then he dressed himself up and ordered dinner for himself. Beef and fish would be bought and Siberian meat dumplings made; he would eat steadily through it all like an ox, almost always alone, but very occasionally inviting his friends to share his table. Then vodka would make its appearance: the man would get as drunk as a lord; then he absolutely must go reeling and staggering all through the barracks in an effort to show everybody that he was drunk and 'having a good time' and thus earn general respect. All over Russia the common people feel sympathy with a drunken man; in the prison he was even treated almost with respect. A drinking bout in the prison had its own code of stylish behaviour. Once he had become a little merry the prisoner never failed to hire a musician. There was a Polish deserter in the prison, a nasty little creature, but he played the fiddle and possessed an instrument—his only property. He had no trade and earned money only by hiring himself out to play cheerful dance-tunes for prisoners on a binge. His duties consisted in following his drunken master from barrack to barrack and sawing away at his fiddle for all he was worth. Often his face expressed boredom and dejection but the cry, 'Play, you've been paid for it!' would force him to begin scraping away again. Any prisoner who set out to get drunk could confidently rely on being looked after if he went too far, put to bed at the right time and hidden somewhere if ever anybody in authority put in an appearance, and all quite disinterestedly. For their part the sergeant and the old soldiers living in the prison to keep order might also be quite easy in their minds: the drunken man would not create any disturbance. The whole barrack would take care of him and if he began to be noisy or disorderly he would be violently suppressed, even bound if necessary. Therefore the lower authorities turned a blind eye on drunkenness and refused to notice anything. They knew very well that if they did not allow vodka, worse things would happen. But where did the vodka come from?

It was bought inside the very prison from so-called 'tapsters'. There were several of them and they did a constant and profitable trade, although there were few drinkers and 'revellers', because drinking required money and prisoners' money was hard-earned. The traffic in drink starts, is carried on, and is tolerated in a rather odd fashion. A prisoner, let us suppose, has no trade and is not willing to work (there are such), but wants to have money and, being impatient, to get rich quickly. He has a little money to make a start with and he decides to deal in vodka; it is a daring enterprise, entailing great risks. One may have to pay with one's back and be deprived of one's goods and capital at one blow. But the 'tapster' makes up his mind. To begin with he has not much money and so, the first time, he brings in the vodka himself, and, of course, disposes of it at a profit. He repeats the attempt a second and then a third time and, if the authorities have not caught him, quickly sells out. Only then can he establish a real trade on a large scale; he becomes a dealer, a capitalist, with agents and assistants; he risks much less and grows richer and richer. His assistants run the risks for him.

There are always many people in prison who have squandered and wasted everything they had, down to the last copeck, on drinking, gambling, and riotous living, men without a trade, destitute wretches, but endowed with a certain degree of audacity and resolution. All they have left by way of capital is their backs; these may still serve some purpose, and it is this last capital that the destitute rake resolves to put into circulation. He goes to the dealer and hires himself out to him for carrying in vodka; a rich 'tapster' will have several men working for him in this way. Somewhere outside the prison there is a person—a soldier, a small tradesman, sometimes even a prostitute—who will buy vodka in a tavern with the dealer's money for a certain commission, comparatively very large, and put it in a secret hiding-place in the place where the prisoners work. Almost always the agent first samples the quality of the vodka and ruthlessly makes up the quantity with water; it is a case of 'take it or leave it' and a prisoner cannot afford to be too particular; it is something that his money has not been completely lost and some vodka has been obtained, watered

down, perhaps, but still vodka. The smugglers, pointed out
to him beforehand by the dealer, then come to the agent,
bringing with them ox-guts. These have first been rinsed
out and then filled with water to keep them in their original
moist and elastic state, so that in due course they can be used
to hold vodka. Having filled the gut with vodka the smuggler
fastens it round his body as inconspicuously as possible.
Needless to say, this is an opportunity for displaying all the
smuggler's skill and thievish cunning. His honour is involved; he must cheat both guards and sentries. He does
cheat them; the guard, sometimes a raw recruit, is never any
match for a good thief. The prisoner has, of course, studied
the guard beforehand and taken into consideration the time
and place of work. The prisoner is a stove-setter, for
example, and he climbs up on top of a stove; who is to see
what he does there? The guard cannot be expected to climb
up after him. When he comes to the prison, the prisoner
takes a little money—fifteen or twenty silver copecks—in
his hand, just in case, and waits at the gates for the corporal.
The corporal of the watch inspects every prisoner returning
from work and runs his hand over him before he unlocks
the prison door for him. The smuggler usually hopes that
delicacy will prevent a too detailed investigation of certain
parts of his body. But sometimes a wily corporal probes as
far even as these parts and feels the vodka. Then there
remains one last expedient: the smuggler silently and without the notice of the guard thrusts the money he has been
holding into the corporal's hand. Sometimes in consequence
of this manœuvre he gets safely into prison carrying his
vodka. But sometimes the manœuvre is unsuccessful and
then he must settle his debts with his sole capital, his back.
The matter is reported to the major, his capital is flogged,
and that severely, the vodka is forfeited, and the smuggler
takes the whole on his own shoulders, without betraying his
employer. Note, however, that this is not because of any
abhorrence of informing but solely because it would do him

no good to inform: he would be flogged just the same and his only consolation would be that both of them would receive the same punishment. But he still needs the dealer, although by prison custom and prior arrangement a smuggler gets not a copeck by way of salve for his lacerated back. As for informing in general, it commonly flourishes in prison. The informer is not subjected to any infamy; nobody so much as thinks of being indignant with him. He is not shunned, his friendship is acceptable, and anybody who tried to demonstrate the full vileness of informing would be quite incomprehensible to the inmates of a prison. That base and vicious gentleman-convict with whom I broke off all relations was intimate with Fedka, the major's batman, and acted as a spy for him; and Fedka repeated to the major everything he learnt about the prisoners. All of us knew this and nobody at any time so much as thought of punishing or even reproaching the wretch.

But I have digressed. It does happen, of course, that vodka is smuggled in successfully; then the dealer receives the ox-guts, pays for them, and begins his calculations. From these it appears that the goods have already cost him very dear and therefore, for the sake of bigger profits, he decants them, once more adding water, up to nearly half the amount, and having thus finished his preparations, sits down to wait for custom. On the first holiday, or sometimes even on a week-day, a customer appears, a prisoner who has worked for several months like a black and saved up his few copecks simply in order to squander them all in drink on a certain day fixed beforehand. The poor toiler has been dreaming of this day long before it comes, both in sleep and in happy reveries over his work, and his spirits have been sustained through the dreary course of prison days by the thought of its enchantments. At last the first glow of that bright day appears in the east; his money has been saved, it has not been confiscated or stolen, and he takes it to the 'tapster'. At first the 'tapster' gives him vodka as pure as possible, that is not more than twice diluted; but as fast as the contents of the bottle are diminished the deficiencies are made good with water. A glass of vodka costs five or six times as much as it would in the tavern. It may be imagined how many glasses of such vodka must be absorbed and how much money must be spent on them in order to get drunk. But because he has lost the habit of drinking and because of his previous abstinence, the prisoner gets intoxicated fairly quickly, and he usually goes on drinking until he has spent all his money. Then his new clothes come into the picture; the 'tapster' is a pawnbroker as well. First the newly acquired 'civilian' things fall into his hands, then it comes to the old rubbish as well, and finally to government property. When everything has been drunk to the very last rag, the drunkard goes to bed; next morning, waking with the inevitable thick head, he pleads in vain for even a mouthful of vodka to clear it. Sadly he bears his troubles, and the very same day sets to work once more and again labours for several months without straightening his back, dreaming of his day of happy indulgence, now receding irrecoverably into the past, and then little by little he begins to cheer up and look forward to another day like it, still far off, which nevertheless will come in due course.

As for the 'tapster', he, when he has at length amassed a vast sum, some tens of roubles, prepares a last batch of vodka, no longer adding any water, because he intends this for himself; enough of trading, now it is his turn for a little celebration! The 'binge' begins, with eating, drinking, and music. He has ample funds; some even of the lower, more immediately interested, ranks of prison officers can be placated. The binge sometimes lasts for several days. The previously prepared vodka is of course quickly drunk; then the reveller goes to another 'tapster', who is expecting him, and drinks until he has spent his last copeck. However much care the other prisoners take of a reveller, he sometimes comes under the eye of the higher authorities, the major or the commander of the guard. He is taken to the guardroom, his capital is confiscated if any is found on him, and in conclusion he is flogged. He pulls himself together and returns to the prison, where after a few days he resumes his trade of 'tapster'. Some of these revellers, of course, the richer ones, dream of the fair sex. In return for a great deal of money they are sometimes allowed to make their way secretly out of the fortress to some place in the suburbs, instead of to work, in the company of a guard who has been bought. There, in some secluded little house on the outskirts of the town, there is a lavish feast and really large sums are squandered. Money removes all fastidiousness about associating with convicts, and somehow a guard who 'knows what's what' has been picked out beforehand. Usually such guards are themselves future candidates for prison. Money, however, can do anything and these excursions are nearly always kept secret. It must be added that they occur very rarely; they require a great deal of money and lovers of the fair sex usually have recourse to other means, quite without danger . . .

In the very first days of my life in prison, one young convict, an extraordinarily handsome youth, especially aroused my curiosity. He was called Sirotkin. He was a rather mysterious personage in many respects. Most of all I was struck by the beauty of his face. He was not more than twenty-three years old. He was in the Special Class, that is among the 'lifers', and consequently thought himself one of the most important of military criminals. He was quiet and modest, spoke little and laughed rarely. He had blue eyes, regular features, a neat, delicate little face and fair hair. Even his half-shaven head did not greatly disfigure him, he was such a pretty boy. He had no trade but he picked up some money, only a very little, but fairly often. He was obviously lazy and always went about looking slovenly. Sometimes somebody else would dress him decently, perhaps even in a red shirt, and Sirotkin was apparently glad of the new clothes; he would walk through the barracks to show himself off. He did not drink or play cards, and quarrelled with hardly anybody. He used to walk behind the barracks with his hands in his pockets, meek and thoughtful. What he could be thinking about it was difficult even to imagine. If you called to him and asked him something, out of curiosity, he would answer at once, almost courteously, not like a prisoner, but always shortly and without wasting words, and he would look at you like a ten-year-old child. If he acquired any money, he did not buy himself any necessities, or have his jacket mended or get new boots, but bought white rolls and gingerbread and enjoyed them as though he were seven years old. 'What a fellow you are, Sirotkin!' the other prisoners would say. 'You're just a refugee!' During leisure hours he would wander about the other barracks where almost everybody was occupied with his own work; he alone had nothing to do. Somebody would say something to him, almost always banteringly (he and his kind were often the butt of sly jokes) and he would turn round without a word and go off to another barrack; sometimes, when the teasing grew too much for him, he would turn very red. I often wondered what had brought this meek and artless creature to prison. Once I was in the prison ward of the hospital. Sirotkin was also ill and his bed was next to mine; during the afternoon we fell into conversation; he became unexpectedly animated and, among other things, told me how he was sent for a soldier, how his mother wept as she walked beside him, and how hard he had found life as a recruit. He added that he could not endure being a recruit because everybody was so stern and angry and the officers were almost always displeased with him . . .

'What was the end of it?' I asked, 'and what brought you here, and in the Special Class, too? . . . Ah, Sirotkin, Sirotkin!'

'I was in the battalion a year altogether, Alexander Petrovich, and I came here because I killed Gregory Petrovich, my captain.'

'I have heard so, Sirotkin, but I don't believe it. Why, how could you kill anybody?'

'I did, though, Alexander Petrovich. It all got too much for me.'

'But how do other recruits get on? Of course, it's hard to begin with, but afterwards one gets used to it, and in the end you have a fine soldier. Your mother must have spoilt you: she fed you on milk and gingerbread until you were eighteen.'

'My mother was very fond of me, that's true enough. When I went into the army she took to her bed, so I've heard, and never got up again . . . In the end, being a recruit got too rough for me. My captain had his knife into me and he used to punish me for everything—but what had I done? I never got uppish; I did everything I ought to; I never took a drink; I never got mixed up in anything, and it's a bad thing, Alexander Petrovich, for a man to get mixed up in things . . . Everybody there was so hard-hearted, and there wasn't anywhere where you could have a good cry. Sometimes you would go into a corner somewhere and cry. Well, once I was on guard-duty; it was night; I had been put on watch at the guard-house, near where the arms were piled. It was windy; it was autumn and the darkness was so thick you felt as if your eyes had fallen out. And I felt so sick, so sick! I grounded my rifle and unfixed the bayonet and put it down by me and then I kicked off my boot and put the muzzle of the gun against my chest and leaned on it and pulled the trigger with my big toe. It misfired! I looked at the gun, cleaned out the touch-hole, put in some fresh powder, knapped the flint and put the gun against my chest. What happened? The powder flashed in the pan, but the gun didn't fire! Well, what can it be? I thought. So then I put my boot back on and fixed the bayonet and went on with my sentry-go without another word. I made up my mind what I was going to do; they could do what they liked with me so long as I got out! Half an hour afterwards along came the captain; he was doing the rounds. He came straight up to me: "Is that the way to stand on sentry duty?" I levelled the gun like in the drill and ran the bayonet right into him up to the muzzle. I had to march all these four thousand versts and here I am in the Special Class . . .'

He must have been speaking the truth. Otherwise, why should they have put him into the Special Class? Ordinary crimes are punished much less severely . . . But Sirotkin was the only one of all his kind in the prison who was so good-looking. As for the others in his category, of whom we had fifteen or so, they were strange even to look at—only two or three were even endurable, and the rest were hideous, lop-eared slovens, some of them grey-haired. Sirotkin, though, was often friendly with Gazin, of whom I spoke at the beginning of this chapter as staggering into the kitchen, drunk, and upsetting my first notions of prison life.

This Gazin was a frightful creature. He produced a hideous and terrifying impression upon everybody. It always seemed to me that there could be nothing more savage and monstrous than he. In Tobolsk I had seen the brigand Kamenev, celebrated for his cruel deeds; afterwards I had seen Sokolov, a deserter and a terrible murderer, when he was awaiting trial. Neither of them produced such an abominable impression on me as Gazin. It sometimes seemed to me that I was looking at a huge, monstrous spider, the size of a man. He was a Tartar, of enormous strength, stronger than anybody else in the prison; he was taller than average and of Herculean build, with an ugly, disproportionately large head; he walked with a stoop and had a frowning expression. Strange rumours about him were current in the prison; he was known to have been a soldier and the other prisoners said among themselves, I do not know with what truth, that he had got away from Nerchinsk, that he had been sent to Siberia more than once, had escaped more than once, and more than once changed his name, before he finally landed in our prison in the Special Class. It was also said that he had had the habit of slitting the throats of little children solely for pleasure; he would take the child to some convenient place and frighten and torment him; then, when he had sufficiently enjoyed the terror and anguish of his wretched little victim, he would slowly, quietly, voluptuously, cut his throat. All of this may have been invented as a consequence of the universal feeling of oppression produced by Gazin's personality, but all these inventions somehow fitted and suited him. In the prison, meanwhile, he bore himself at ordinary times, when he was not drunk, very prudently. He was always quiet, never quarrelled with anybody, and avoided disputes, but out of contempt for others, as it were, and as if he considered himself better than all the rest; he spoke very little and seemed deliberately uncommunicative. All his movements were slow, measured, and assured. His eyes showed that he was far from stupid, indeed extremely shrewd, but there was always something of supercilious mockery and brutality in his look and his smile. He was a dealer in vodka and one of the wealthiest 'tapsters' in the prison. But about twice a year he had to get drunk himself, and then all the bestiality of his nature showed itself. As he grew steadily drunker, he began to annoy people with the most ill-natured, calculated pleasantries, apparently long-thought-out; at length, when he was quite drunk, he flew into a violent rage, seized a knife, and flung himself on people. The other prisoners, knowing his appalling strength, fled before him and hid; he would attack anybody who came in his way. But a means of managing him had quickly been found. Some ten men from his barrack would attack him together and begin to belabour him. It is impossible to imagine anything crueller than the beatings they gave him; he was struck on the breast, under the heart, in the pit of the stomach, in the belly; the beating was heavy and prolonged, and ceased only when he had lost consciousness and lay like one dead. Nobody else would have been beaten like that; to beat anybody else in that way would most likely have meant killing him—but not Gazin.

After the thrashing he was wrapped, still quite unconscious, in a sheepskin coat and carried to his plank-bed. 'He'll sleep it off, all right!' And indeed, the next morning he would get up almost well and go off, silent and morose, to work. Every time that Gazin got drunk, the whole prison knew that for him the day would inevitably end in a thrashing. He himself knew it, as well, but all the same he got drunk. This went on for several years. Finally it was noticed that Gazin was beginning to succumb. He began to complain of various aches and pains and grew obviously sickly; he went more and more often into hospital . . . 'He's broken up, though!' said the convicts.

He came into the kitchen in the company of the nasty little Pole whom the convicts used to hire with his fiddle to give the finishing touch to their merry-making, and stopped in the middle of the floor, carefully and silently scrutinizing everybody there. All talking ceased. Finally, catching sight of me and my companion, he looked at us with an angry sneer, smiled in a gratified way, seemed to be pondering something, and then, staggering wildly, came up to our table.

'Allow me to inquire,' he began (he spoke in Russian), 'how you made the money to regale yourselves with tea.'

I silently exchanged glances with my companion, realizing that it would be better not to answer him. At the first hint of contradiction he would fly into a passion.

'So you've got some money, eh?' the questioning continued. 'You must have heaps of money, eh? And did you come to drink cups of tea? Did you come here to drink tea? Answer me, blast you! . . .'

But, seeing that we had made up our minds to be silent and pay no attention to him, he turned crimson and began to shake with anger. Beside him, in a corner, stood a large wooden tray in which all the bread cut up for the prisoners' dinner or supper was placed. It was big enough to hold the bread for half the prison, but now it stood empty. He snatched it up in both hands and brandished it over us. Another minute and he would have smashed our skulls with it. In spite of the fact that a murder or an attempted murder threatened the whole prison with the most extreme un-pleasantness: there would be interrogations, searches, redoubled severity, and therefore the prisoners made every effort not to bring down such extreme measures on all alike—in spite of this, everybody now was quiet and ex-pectant. Not a word in our defence! Not a single outcry against Gazin, so strong was their detestation of us! Apparently our plight gave them satisfaction . . . But all was well in the end; as he was about to bring down the tray, somebody shouted from the passage:

'Gazin! The vodka's been stolen . . .'

He threw the tray to the floor with a crash and rushed out of the kitchen like one possessed.

'Well, God Himself came to the rescue!' said the prisoners to one another. And so they said for a long time afterwards.

I never could learn whether this news about the theft of the vodka was true or was simply a quick-witted device to save us.

In the evening, when it was already dark, but before the barracks were locked up, I walked round the stockade, and a heavy sadness fell on my heart. Never afterwards in all my prison life did I experience such sadness. The first day of imprisonment is hard to bear, wherever it may be spent, whether in a cell, in a fortress, or in a convict prison . . . But, I remember, what most exercised my thoughts was the problem, which haunted me throughout my life in prison—an almost insoluble problem, one which I cannot to this day resolve—that of the inequality of the punishment for one and the same crime. It is true that crimes cannot be equated with one another, even approximately. This man and that, for instance, have both killed a man; all the circumstances of both cases are weighed and almost the same punishment is meted out to one and to the other. But see what difference there is between the crimes, nevertheless. One man, for example, has committed murder casually, for nothing at all, for an onion. (He went out on the highway and cut down a passing peasant, who had nothing on him but one onion. 'Look, gaffer! You sent me out for plunder; I killed the peasant yonder and all I found was an onion.' 'Fool! An onion is as good as a copeck! A hundred deaths is a hundred onions, and there you have a whole rouble!' So runs the prison legend.) The other killed protecting the honour of his beloved or his sister or his daughter from a lustful tyrant. One man kills because he is a vagrant, beset by a whole regiment of pursuers, trying to protect his liberty, even his life, dying perhaps (it is not rare) of starvation; another cuts little children's throats for the pleasure of killing, of feeling their warm blood on his hands, for the enjoyment of their terror and their last bird-like flutterings under the knife. What happens? Both the one and the other get the same penal servitude. There are, it is true, variations in the terms of sentences. But there are comparatively few of these variations possible, while the variations in the nature of crime are infinite in number. Every different personality means a different crime. Let us concede that it is impossible to reconcile or smooth over these differences, that it is by its very nature an insoluble problem, like squaring the circle— let us suppose it! But look at the other inequality which would occur even if those differences did not exist at all, the inequality consequent on punishment . . . Here is a man who in captivity pines and wastes away like a candle; here is another who before he was imprisoned did not even know that such a gay life, such a happy collection of bold spirits, existed on the face of the earth; yes, there are even such men among those who come to prison. Here, for example, is an educated man, who has an active conscience, a mature mind, and a feeling heart. The pain in his own heart is alone enough to kill him with its agonies before any punishment begins. He condemns his own crime more harshly, more pitilessly, than the cruellest of laws. Here beside him is another who has not once so much as thought of the murder he committed during the whole of his sentence; he does not even think he has done wrong. There are even men who deliberately commit a crime simply in order to be sent to penal servitude and thus escape the incomparably harsher servitude of freedom. 'Outside' this man existed in the last stages of destitution, he never ate his fill, he toiled for his employer from morning till night; in prison, work is easier, he can eat to his heart's content; the food is better than he has ever known; there is beef on holidays, there are charitable doles, there is the chance of earning a copeck or two. And the society? Clever, cunning people who know everything; he regards his companions with astonished respect, for he has never seen anybody like them; he considers them the highest society possible on earth. Is punishment really equally painful to these two? . . . Why, however, concern myself with insoluble problems? The drum is beating, it is time to go in.

4. First Impressions (III)

THE last check was beginning. After this the barracks were locked each with its own key, and the convicts remained shut up till daybreak.

The check was carried out by a non-commissioned officer and two soldiers. Sometimes the prisoners were lined up in the yard and the officer of the watch came along. But more often the ceremony had a domestic character and the checking was done in the barracks. So it was this time. The checkers made mistakes, miscounted, went away and came back again. At last the poor sentries managed to arrive at the desired figure and locked the barrack. There were something like thirty prisoners in it, crowded rather closely on the plank-shelves. It was early yet for sleep. Obviously, everybody must find something to do.

Of the prison authorities there remained in the barrack only the old soldier, whom I have mentioned before. In each barrack there was also a senior prisoner, chosen by the duty-officer himself, for good conduct, of course. It very often happened that even these senior prisoners fell in course of time into serious misdemeanours; then they were flogged, immediately reduced to the junior grade, and replaced by others.

The senior in our barrack proved to be Akim Akimovich, who, to my surprise, frequently shouted at the other convicts. They usually responded with jeers. The old soldier was more sensible and did not interfere in anything, and if he ever had to wag his tongue, it was only for form's sake, to keep his conscience clear. He sat silently on his bed and stitched at his boots. The prisoners paid almost no attention to him.

On this first day of my prison life I made one observation which I later convinced myself was accurate. It was this: all non-prisoners, whoever they may be, from those who come into immediate contact with prisoners, like sentries or guards, to the generality of those who have any connexion at all with prison life, have a somewhat exaggerated view of convicts, as though they were uneasily expecting to be attacked by any one of them with a knife at any moment, without warning. And—what was most noticeable—the prisoners were themselves aware that they were feared and this plainly gave them a certain swagger. The commanding officer who is best for prisoners, however, is one who does not fear them. Generally speaking, all swagger aside, it is indeed much more agreeable to the prisoners themselves if there is confidence in them. This attitude may even arouse their liking. It happened during my time in prison, though extremely rarely, that one of the men in authority visited the prison without an escort. It was worth seeing how much the prisoners were impressed, and favourably impressed, by this. A fearless visitor of this kind always aroused respect, and if there was always the possibility that something unpleasant might happen, it would not be in his presence. The fear inspired by convicts is always present wherever they are, and I honestly do not know what it proceeds from. It has of course some foundation, firstly in the outward appearance of the convict, the acknowledged killer; besides, everybody who approaches a convict prison feels that this mass of people have been brought there not of their own will and that by no means whatever can a living man be turned into a corpse: he will retain his feelings, his thirst for vengeance and for life, his passions and the desire to satisfy them. But in spite of this I am firmly convinced that there is no reason to be afraid of convicts. A man does not so lightly and so hastily attack another with a knife. In short, if danger is possible, if it sometimes becomes actual, yet one may conclude from the rarity of such unhappy occurrences that it is insignificant. Needless to say, I am speaking of convicted prisoners, many of whom are even glad to have reached the prison at last (a new life is sometimes so great an attraction!) and are consequently disposed to settle down in peace and quiet; in addition, they do not allow the genuinely restless and dissatisfied spirits among them to do much blustering and swaggering. Every convict, however bold and hardy he may have been, is afraid of everything in the prison. The prisoner awaiting the execution of his sentence is a different matter. He really is capable of flinging himself on the chance bystander for no reason at all, simply because, for example, he must face a flogging on the morrow, and if a new accusation is brought against him, it means the postponement of his punishment. This is the cause and aim of the attack, to 'change his lot' at any cost and as soon as possible. I know a strange instance of this type of psychological effect. We had, in the military section of the prison, a private soldier who had not lost all his rights, but had been sentenced to two years penal servitude, a terrible braggart and a notable coward. Generally speaking, boastfulness and cowardice are extremely rarely met with among Russian soldiers. Our soldier seems always to be kept so busy that, even if he wanted to, he would have no time to boast and swagger. But if he is a boaster, he is almost always a loafer and coward as well. Dutov (that was our prisoner's name) served out his short sentence and went back to a battalion of the line. But since all the men sent to prison, like him, to reform them, complete their deterioration there, it usually happens that, after no more than two or three weeks of freedom, they find themselves once more in the hands of the law and reappear in the prison, this time, however, not for two or three years but in the long-term class, for fifteen or twenty years. So it was in this instance. Dutov carried out a burglary; on top of this he was insubordinate and mutinous. He was tried and sentenced to a very severe punishment. Being a most pitiable coward, he was frightened out of his wits, and on the eve of the day when he was to run the gauntlet, he attacked the officer of the watch with a knife when he entered the guardroom. Needless to say, he understood very well that such an action would immeasurably increase his sentence and the term of his penal servitude. But his calculations were directed simply to the postponement, if only for a few days, or even a few hours, of the terrible moment of punishment. He was so great a coward that when he attacked the officer he did not even wound him; the whole was done *pro forma*, solely in order to create a new crime, for which he must again be put on trial.

The moment before his punishment is, of course, terrible for the condemned man, and in the course of several years I had to see a fair number of prisoners on the eve of that day so fateful to them. It was a usual thing for me to meet prisoners under sentence in the prison ward of the hospital when I was ill, which was fairly often. All prisoners throughout Russia know that the people most compassionate towards them are the doctors. They never make any distinction between prisoners, as almost all outsiders involuntarily do, except perhaps the common people. They, indeed, never reproach a convict with his crimes, however terrible, and forgive him everything because of the punishment he has borne and because of his misfortunes in general. It is not for nothing that the people all over Russia call crime misfortune and convicts unfortunates. It is a deeply significant designation, and even more important because it is conferred instinctively, unconsciously . . . The doctors, then, are a veritable refuge for prisoners, and especially for those whose sentences are not yet carried out, for whom conditions are harder than for the others . . . Thus a man, having calculated the probable date of the evil day, frequently goes into hospital, wanting to put off the dreadful minute if only for a little. When he is discharged again and knows almost certainly that the morrow will be the fateful day, he is almost always in a state of violent agitation. Some, out of pride, try to hide their feelings, but their clumsy assumption of bravado does not deceive their companions. Everybody knows what the matter is and keeps his thoughts to himself, out of humanity. I knew one prisoner, a young soldier, a murderer, who had been condemned to the maximum number of strokes of the rods. He became so faint-hearted that on the day before the execution of the sentence he brought himself to the point of drinking a jug of vodka, in which he had steeped a quantity of snuff. Vodka, by the way, always makes its appearance before punishment is inflicted on a prisoner. It is smuggled in a long time before the day and acquired in return for a great deal of money, and the man awaiting punishment would rather deny himself absolute necessities for half a year than fail to accumulate the amount needed for half a pint of vodka, which he will drink a quarter of an hour before it begins. The conviction is general among prisoners that a drunken man feels less pain from the lash or the rods . . . But I have digressed. The poor youth, having drunk his jug of vodka, fell sick at once; he began to vomit blood and was taken almost unconscious to the hospital. This vomiting did so much damage that in a few days he began to show symptoms of tuberculosis, from which he died six months later. The doctors who treated his consumption did not know what had caused it.

Since, however, I have spoken of the frequent pusillanimity of criminals facing physical punishment, I ought to add that some of them, on the contrary, astound the onlookers by their extraordinary lack of apprehension. I recall some examples of fortitude amounting almost to impassivity, and such examples were not very infrequent. I particularly remember my meeting with one hardened criminal. One summer day a rumour spread through the prison wards of the hospital that the notorious brigand and deserter Orlov was to undergo punishment that evening and that he would be brought to the hospital after the flogging. The sick prisoners affirmed, while they waited for Orlov, that his punishment would be cruel. They were all in a state of tension and I confess that I also awaited the appearance of the celebrated miscreant with extreme curiosity. I had long heard extraordinary stories about him. He was an evil-doer such as rarely occurs, a cold-blooded murderer of old men and children, a man of terrifying strength of will and proudly conscious of that strength. He had confessed to many murders and was condemned to run the gauntlet. It was late when they brought him in. It was already dark in the ward and candles had been lighted. Orlov was almost unconscious and terribly pale and his thick dark hair was matted. His back was swollen and of a livid and bloody colour. All night long the other prisoners nursed him, bringing him fresh water, turning him over from one side to the other, giving him medicine, as though it were a near relative they were tending, or somebody who had done them many kindnesses. On the next day he had quite come round, and walked the length of the ward two or three times! This amazed me; he had been very weak and exhausted when he came into the hospital. He had undergone at one time a full half of the strokes to which he had been condemned; the doctor stopped the flogging only when he saw that continuation of the punishment would inevitably mean his death. Orlov was a small and puny man and very much weakened besides by having been kept for a long time awaiting trial. Whoever has come into contact with prisoners awaiting trial or sentence has probably long remembered their pale, thin, haggard faces and feverish eyes. In spite of all this, Orlov quickly recovered. His inner, mental energy evidently powerfully assisted nature. He was in fact a somewhat unusual man. Out of curiosity I cultivated his closer acquaintance and for a week I studied him attentively. I can say with conviction that in all my life I have never met a man of stronger, more rock-like character than his. Before this I had on one occasion seen in Tobolsk another celebrity in the same line, a former bandit chief. He was a pure wild beast and if you were near him, not knowing his name, you instinctively felt that a terrible being stood beside you. But what horrified me was his spiritual torpor. The flesh had so much gained the upper hand over all his mental attributes that you might see from the first glance at his face that there was nothing left in him but a fierce thirst for bodily pleasure, sensuality, carnal satisfaction. I am certain that Korenev (that was his name) would have trembled with fear and his spirit would have quailed before physical punishment, although he was capable of murdering unresisting victims. Orlov was utterly contrasted with him. He had achieved a complete conquest of the flesh. It was plain that this man had limitless mastery over himself, despised all punishments and sufferings and feared nothing on earth. In him you saw only boundless energy, thirst for action, thirst for vengeance, thirst for the attainment of his predetermined goal. One of the things that struck me about him was his strange arrogance. He seemed to look down on everything from a fabulous height, not as though he had tried to hoist himself on stilts, but quite simply and naturally. I do not think there was any creature on earth to whose authority he would have submitted.

He took everything with unexpected calm, as though there was nothing in the world that could arouse his astonishment. And although he fully realized that the other prisoners regarded him with respect, he gave himself absolutely no airs. Yet vanity and presumption are characteristic of prisoners almost without exception. He was very shrewd and had a strange kind of frankness, although he was far from talkative. When I asked him he told me directly that he was waiting to recover in order to undergo the rest of his punishment as soon as possible, and that at first he had been very much afraid that he would not be able to endure it. 'But now,' he added, 'it is all over. I can take the rest of the strokes, and then I shall be sent straight off with a party to Nerchinsk, and I'll escape on the way. There's no doubt I can get away! If only my back heals quickly!' And all those five days he waited impatiently for the time when he could ask to be discharged. Meanwhile he was sometimes very cheerful and amusing. I tried to talk to him about the things he had done. He frowned a little at these interrogations but always answered frankly. When he realized, though, that I was working towards his conscience and trying to discover some slight tinge of remorse in him, he looked at me with as much arrogant contempt as though I had suddenly become in his eyes a stupid little boy with whom it was impossible to talk reasonably, as with a grown-up. His face even reflected something like pity for me. After a minute he began to laugh at me with the most simple-hearted amusement, without a trace of irony, and I am sure that when he was left alone and remembered my words he laughed again to himself, perhaps many times more. At last he was discharged with his back not yet completely healed; I was also discharged at the same time and we chanced to leave the hospital together, I to go back to the prison and he to the guard-house beside our gates, where he had been held before. As we said good-bye he shook my hand, a sign of great trust on his part. I think he did it because he was very pleased with himself and with the moment. In reality, he could not help despising me and must have looked on me as a poor, submissive creature, weak, pitiful, and in every respect beneath him. On the next day he was taken out for his second dose of punishment . . .

When our barrack had been locked it suddenly took on a special aspect—the look of a real dwelling, of a home. Only now did I see the prisoners, my fellows, completely at home. By day the non-commissioned officers, sentries, and officials in general might come into the prison at any moment, and therefore all the inmates seemed to bear themselves differently, as though they could not be quite at ease, as though they were constantly, and with a certain anxiety, expecting something. As soon as the barrack was locked up, everybody went quietly to his own place and nearly everybody set to work at some handicraft. The room became suddenly light. Each man had his own candle and his own candlestick, most of them made of wood. One sat down to stitch his boots, another to sew some piece of clothing. The noisome air of the barrack grew thicker from hour to hour. A group of idlers squatted on their heels in a corner, where a piece of carpet had been spread, playing cards. In almost every barrack there was one prisoner who possessed an *arshin*[1] of thin carpet, a candle, and some unbelievably dirty, greasy cards. All this together was called a *maidan* The owner received payment from the players, fifteen copecks a night: this was his source of income. The gamblers usually played very simple games. They were all games of chance. Each player put down a pile of copper coins in front of him, all he had in his pockets, and left the game only when he had lost everything or beaten all his companions. The game finished late at night or sometimes went on until dawn, until

---

[1] Twenty-eight inches. [*Tr.*]

the very minute the barracks were unlocked. In our room, as in all the other barracks, there were some paupers, called by us *baygushi*, those who had gambled or drunk away all their money or were simply paupers by nature. I say 'by nature' and I lay stress on the term. There really are, and always will be, everywhere in our nation, in every possible environment and under all conditions, odd creatures, peaceable and often far from lazy, who are destined by fate to remain beggars for ever. They are always solitary and neglected, they always look downtrodden and downcast, and they are always at the beck and call of somebody, usually some rake or parvenu. Every new departure, every initiative, is distressing and irksome to them. They seem to have been born to originate nothing themselves, but only to serve others, to live at the behest of others, to dance to others' piping; their destiny to fulfil that of others. To crown all, no circumstances, no vicissitudes of fortune, can enrich them. They are always beggars. I have noticed that such personalities do not occur only among the common people, but in all societies, classes, parties, political groups, and associations. The same thing happened in every barrack in every prison, and as soon as the *maidan* was set up one of them appeared to act as attendant. No *maidan*, indeed, could dispense with such an attendant. He was hired jointly by all the players for the whole night, for five silver copecks or so, and his chief duty was to keep guard all night. For the most part he froze for six or seven hours in the darkness of the entrance, in thirty degrees of frost, listening for every sound and every step in the yard. The officer on duty or the sentries sometimes put in an appearance in the prison very late at night, came in quietly and discovered the gamblers, and the workers, and the extra candles, which could be seen from the yard. In any case, when the lock on the door giving into the yard from the entrance began to rattle suddenly, it was already too late to hide, put out the candles, and lie down on the plank-beds. But since the watchers suffered painfully at the hands of the *maidan* after them, such blunders were extremely rare. Five copecks, of course, was a ludicrously paltry payment, even for the prison; but I was always struck by the pitiless harshness of prison employers, both in this and in all other cases. 'You took the money, now earn it!' This was an argument which allowed of no retort. In return for his half-copeck the employer took everything he was entitled to, and more if he could, and still considered that he had laid the recipient under an obligation. The gambler or the drunkard, throwing money recklessly right and left, always cheated his hired follower, as I observed in more than one prison and at more than one *maidan*.

I have already said that almost everybody in the barrack had settled down to some occupation; besides the gamblers, there were not more than five men who were not doing some work; they lay down to sleep at once. My place on the plank-shelf was next to the door. On the other side, head to head with me, was Akim Akimovich's place. Until about ten or eleven o'clock he worked, pasting together some kind of multi-coloured Chinese lantern, which somebody in the town had ordered for a fairly good price. He was very skilful at making these lanterns, and he worked methodically and steadily; when he had finished he put everything tidily away, unrolled his mattress, said his prayers, and lay down on his bed like a well-behaved child. Evidently he carried nice behaviour and seemliness to the most pedantic lengths; plainly, like all dull-witted and limited people, he must consider himself an extremely sensible man. But I disliked him from the very first day, although I remember that on that first day I was very undecided about him, and it seemed to me astonishing that such a person, instead of making a success of life, should find himself in prison. I shall have a good deal more to say of Akim Akimovich later.

But now I must briefly describe the inmates of our barrack. I should have to live many years in it and all these were my future companions. Naturally, I watched them with eager curiosity. To my left were installed a group of Caucasian mountaineers, most of them condemned to various terms for robbery. There were two Lezgians, a Chechen, and three Daghestanian Tartars. The Chechen was a morose and gloomy creature; he hardly spoke to anybody and was perpetually looking around him with an expression of lowering hatred and an ill-natured venomous sneer. One of the Lezgians was quite an old man, with a long, thin, hooked nose, a regular brigand to look at. The second, Nurra, on the other hand, produced a most comforting, a most pleasing impression on me from the very first. He was still quite young, not tall, built like a Hercules, very fair, with light blue eyes and a face like a Finnish woman's, snub-nosed, and bow-legged from being constantly in the saddle. His whole body was scarred with bayonet and bullet wounds. In the Caucasus he had been one of those who submitted to the Russian conquest, but he was always stealing away to the rebellious mountaineers and joining in their raids on the Russians. The other prisoners all liked him. He was always cheerful and friendly towards everybody, did his work without repining and was good-natured and placid, although he often showed his dislike of the filth and squalor of prison life and was roused to fury by every instance of theft, drunkenness, swindling and general knavery, and vice; he never made a row about them but merely turned away in disgust. He himself never stole anything or did one wrong thing all the time he was in prison. He was extremely pious. He religiously observed all times of prayer, kept all the fasts before the Mohammedan feast-days like a fanatic, and sometimes spent all night praying. Everybody liked and trusted him. 'Nurra is a lion', the prisoners would say, and the nickname clung to him. He was firmly convinced that at the end of his term of penal servitude he would return home to the Caucasus, and he lived for that hope. I think he would have died if he had been deprived of it. He made a vivid impression on me from my very first day in the prison.

It was impossible to miss his kind, sympathetic face among all the sullen, spiteful, jeering faces of the other prisoners. In the first half-hour after my arrival he patted my shoulder with a good-natured laugh as he went past me. I did not at first understand what this could mean. He spoke Russian, moreover, very badly. Soon afterwards he approached me again, and again, smiling, gave me a friendly slap on the shoulder. Then again, and again, and this went on for three days. It meant, as I guessed then and was later to know, that he was sorry for me, felt how hard it was for me to get acquainted with prison life and wanted to show me that he was friendly, and to cheer me up and assure me of his help. Good, simple Nurra!

There were three of the Daghestanian Tartars, and they were brothers. Two of them were middle-aged but the other, Aley, was no more than twenty-two years old and looked even younger. His place on the plank-shelves was next to mine. His handsome, candid, intelligent and at the same time naïvely good-natured face attracted my heart to him at first sight, and I was very glad that Fate had sent me him, and not somebody else, as a neighbour. His whole soul was reflected in his handsome—one might almost say beautiful—face. His smile was so trustful, so childishly artless, his big black eyes were so melting and tender, that I always felt particular satisfaction, even a lightening of my grief and longing, when I looked at him. I speak without exaggeration. In his own country his eldest brother (he had five: the other two were in some factory) once told him to take his sword and mount his horse to ride out with him on a raid. Reverence for one's elders is so great among the mountaineers that the boy not only would not have dared to ask, but did not even think of asking, where they were going. Nor did they consider it necessary to tell him. They were all bent on brigandage, the waylaying and robbery of a rich Armenian merchant. This they achieved: they killed the escort, slit the Armenian's throat, and carried off his goods. But the affair was discovered; all six of those involved were caught, tried, convicted, flogged, and sent to penal servitude in Siberia. The only grace shown by the court to Aley was that his term was shorter: he was sentenced to four years. His brothers loved him dearly, with a love that was more paternal than brotherly. He was a comfort to them in their exile, and although they were habitually morose and gloomy they always smiled when they looked at him, and when they talked to him (but they had very little to say to him, as though they still thought of him as a boy, with whom nothing serious could be discussed) their grim faces relaxed and I supposed they were speaking of something amusing, almost childish; at any rate they always used to exchange glances and laugh good-humouredly while they listened to his reply. His attitude to them was so deferential that he hardly dared to address them first. It is hard to understand how this boy could have preserved so gentle a nature throughout his prison term, kept himself so strictly honest, so sincere, and so attractive, and never become hardened or corrupted. His personality, moreover, was strong and direct in spite of all his seeming gentleness. I came to know him well later. He was as chaste as a pure young girl, and any evil, cynical, filthy, or unjust instance of violent con-duct lit the fires of indignation in his fine eyes, making them even more beautiful. But he avoided disputes and strife, although he was not one of those who allow them-selves to be insulted with impunity and was able to stand up for himself. But he had no quarrel with anybody; everybody liked him and was kind to him. To begin with he was merely polite to me. Little by little I began to talk to him; in a few months he learned to speak excellent Russian, a thing which his brothers did not accomplish in all their time in prison. I found him an extremely intelligent youth, extraordinarily modest and delicate and already capable of sound judgement. Before I go further, I will say that I think of Aley as no ordinary being and I remember my meeting with him as one of the most valuable in my life. There are natures so innately beautiful, so richly dowered by God, that the very idea that they could ever alter for the worse seems unthinkable. You can always be tranquil on their account. I am not even now uneasy for Aley. But where is he now? . . .

Once, a considerable time after my arrival in the prison, I was lying on my planks, full of very heavy thoughts. Aley, always busy and industrious, for once was doing nothing, although it was too early for bed. But this was one of their Mussulman holidays and they were not working. He was lying with his hands clasped behind his head and he too was thinking. Suddenly he asked me:

'Are you finding things hard just now, eh?'

I looked at him curiously, finding this abrupt direct question strange, coming from Aley, who was always delicate, always discriminating, always wise of heart; but, looking more closely, I saw such anguish, such an ache of remembrance in his face, that I realized that things were very hard for him also, at this moment. I told him what I had guessed. He sighed and smiled sadly. I liked his smile, which was always tender and warm-hearted. Besides, when he smiled, he showed two rows of pearly teeth, which the foremost beauty in the world might have envied.

'I suppose, Aley, you were thinking of how they are celebrating this holiday at home in Daghestan. It must be nice there.'

'Yes,' he answered with delight, and his eyes sparkled. 'But how did you know I was thinking of that?'

'How could I help knowing? Is it better there than here?'

'Oh! Why do you say that? . . .'

'You must have marvellous flowers there now, a perfect Paradise? . . .'

'O-oh, don't say any more.' He was deeply moved.

'Listen, Aley, had you a sister?'

'Yes, I had. Why?'

'She must be a beauty, if she is like you.'

'Like me? There is not her equal for beauty in all Daghestan! Ah, what a beauty my sister is! You have never seen one like her! My mother was beautiful too.'

'And did your mother love you?'

'Oh, what are you saying? She has probably died of grief for me. I was her favourite son. She loved me more than my sister, more than anybody else . . . She came to me in a dream today, and cried over me.'

He fell silent, and all that evening he did not say another word. But from that time he sought every opportunity of talking to me, although, because of the respect he felt for me, Heaven knows why, he never addressed me first. On the other hand, he was very pleased when I spoke to him. I used to ask him about the Caucasus and his former life. His brothers did not prevent him from talking to me; they seemed, indeed, to like it. They themselves, seeing that I grew fonder and fonder of Aley, became much pleasanter to me.

Aley helped me with my work and did me what services he could in the barrack, and it was plain that it gave him great pleasure to make things even a little easier and pleasanter for me; in this endeavour there was not the slightest abasement or search for personal advantage, but only the warmth of his friendship for me, which he made no attempt to hide. Among other things, he had great manual dexterity; he had taught himself to sew well, was excellent at stitching shoes, and later learnt carpentry as well as he could. His brothers praised him and were proud of him.

'Listen, Aley,' I said to him once, 'why have you not learnt to read and write Russian? Don't you know how useful it will be to you later here in Siberia?'

'I should like to, very much. But who could I learn from?'

'There are plenty of literate people here! Would you like me to teach you?'

'Oh, please do!'—and he raised himself on his planks and joined his hands in entreaty, with his eyes on me.

We set to work the very next evening. I had a Russian translation of the New Testament,* a book which was not forbidden in the prison. In a few weeks, without an alphabet, with nothing but this book, Aley learned to read excellently. In about three months he thoroughly understood the literary language. He learned with zeal and enthusiasm.

Once we read through together the Sermon on the Mount. I noticed that he seemed to pronounce some parts of it with special feeling. I asked him whether he had liked what he read. He looked up quickly and his cheeks were flushed.

'Oh, yes!' he answered. 'Yes, Jesus is a holy prophet. Jesus spoke the word of God. How wonderful!'

'What do you like best of all?'

'Where He says: "Forgive, love, do not offend, love your enemies." Ah, how beautifully He speaks!'

He turned to his brothers, who were listening to our conversation, and began to talk ardently to them. They talked long and seriously among themselves, nodding their heads approvingly. Then, with a gravely benevolent, that is, a purely Mussulman smile (which I love so dearly, precisely for its gravity), they turned to me and affirmed that Isa was God's prophet, His great and glorious prophet, and that He had worked great miracles: He made a bird of clay and breathed on it, and it flew . . . and that so it was written in their books. They were quite sure that in saying this they were giving me great pleasure by praising Jesus so highly, and Alcy was full of happiness because his brothers had wished to give me this pleasure.

Our writing also was extraordinarily successful. Aley procured paper (for which he would not allow me to pay), pens, and ink, and in some two months learnt to write excellently. He surprised even his brothers. Their pride and pleasure knew no bounds. They did not know how to thank me. At work, if we happened to be working together, they vied with each other in helping me, and thought themselves fortunate to do so. I do not even speak of Aley. He loved me perhaps as much as he loved his brothers. I shall never forget his leaving the prison. He led me behind the barracks, and threw himself on my neck and burst into tears. He had never kissed me, or wept, before. 'You have done so much for me, so much,' he said; 'even my father and mother would not have done so much: you have made me a man. God will reward you and I shall never forget you . . .'

Where, oh where is he now, my dear, dear, good Aley? . . .

Besides the Circassians we had in the barracks a whole group of Poles, who formed a completely separate clan, holding hardly any communication with the other prisoners. I have already said that, because of their exclusiveness and their hatred of the Russian convicts, they in their turn were hated by everybody. They were sick and harassed creatures. There were half a dozen of them. Some of them were educated; I shall say more of them, with greater particularity and detail, later. Sometimes, during my later years in prison, I had books from them. The first of these books that I read produced a strange, powerful, and peculiar effect on me. I shall speak of these impressions at some other time. They seem very curious to me, and I am certain that they will be quite incomprehensible to many. Some things are impossible to judge without personal experience of them. I will say one thing: moral deprivations are harder to bear than any physical sufferings. A man of the people, sent to penal servitude, enters a society like his own, or perhaps even more developed. He has, of course, lost much—his country, his family, everything—but his surroundings remain the same. The educated man, condemned by the law to the same punishment as the common people, often loses incomparably more. He must suppress all his wants and all his habits and transfer himself into surroundings quite inadequate for him; he must learn to breathe a different air . . . He is a fish pulled out of the water on to the sand . . . And frequently the punishment, prescribed by the law as identical, becomes ten times as painful for him . . . This would be true . . . even if all that were involved were the material conditions to which he must submit.

But the Poles constituted a special, integral group. There were half a dozen of them and they were together. Of all the prisoners in our barrack they liked only a Jew, and him, perhaps, only because he amused them. Even the other prisoners, however, liked our Jew, although absolutely all of them, without exception, laughed at him. He was unique, and even now I cannot remember him without laughing. Every time I looked at him I was reminded of Gogol's little Jew, Yankel, in *Taras Bulba*,* who, when he undressed to betake himself with his Jewess to some closet for the night, looked dreadfully like a chicken. Our Jew, Isaiah Fomich, was as like as two peas to a plucked chicken. He was a man no longer young, about fifty years old, small and puny, cunning and yet distinctly stupid. He was impudent and insolent, and at the same time terribly cowardly. He was covered with wrinkles and had brands, inflicted on the scaffold, on his forehead and cheeks. I could never understand how he had been able to endure sixty lashes. He had been accused of murder. He kept, in concealment, a prescription conveyed to him by other Jews from his doctor immediately after his punishment. It was for a salve to make his brands disappear in about two weeks. He did not dare to use this salve in the prison and was waiting for the end of his twenty-year term, after which, when he was sent to a Siberian settlement, he was firmly determined to make use of it. 'Or else I von't be able to get married,' he said to me once, 'and I vant to get married vithout fail.' I was great friends with him. He was always in excellent spirits. Prison life was easy for him; he was a jeweller by trade and was overwhelmed with orders from the town, where there was no jeweller, and thus was spared heavy work. He was, of course, a money-lender at the same time and supplied all the prison with money at interest and on pledges. He was in the prison before me, and one of the Poles told me of his arrival in detail. This is a highly amusing story, which I will tell later; I shall have something to say of Isaiah Fomich more than once.

The remaining inmates of our barrack consisted of four Old Believers, old men, with the usual fanatical literal belief in their religious books; two or three Ukrainians, dismal people; a young convict with a thin little face and thin little nose, about twenty-three years old, who had already committed eight murders; a group of coiners, one of whom was the clown of the barrack; and finally, several sullen and gloomy personages, shaven and disfigured, taciturn and envious, looking with frowning hatred at everything around them, and prepared to go on looking askance, frowning, hating, and holding their tongues for long years more—all the term of their sentences. All this only passed before my eyes on that first desolate evening of my new life—spinning past amid the smoke and soot, amid oaths and inexpressible sneers, in the mephitic atmosphere, to the jangle of fetters, curses, and shameless guffaws. I lay down on my bare boards, with my clothes under my head (I had as yet no pillow), and covered myself with my sheepskin coat, but for a long time I could not sleep, although I felt exhausted and broken by all the monstrous unexpectedness of my first impressions. But my new life was only just beginning. Much still lay before me which I had never conceived of, of which I had had no forebodings . . .

5. The First Month (1)

THREE days after my arrival in the prison I was ordered to go out to work. The first day of work was memorable, although nothing that occurred during its course was very out of the ordinary, not at least if one takes into consideration everything else that was extraordinary in my situation. But it, too, belongs to my first impressions, and I still continued to observe everything with avid curiosity. I had passed those three days full of the most oppressive feelings. 'Here is the end of my pilgrimage: I am in prison!' I constantly repeated to myself; 'here is my anchorage for many long years, the corner to which I have come with such feelings of pain and misgiving . . . But who knows? Perhaps when, after many years, the time comes for me to leave it, I shall be sorry to go! . . .' I added, not without a tinge of that enjoyment of misfortune which is sometimes carried to the length of an irresistible desire to reopen one's wounds—as though one could be in love with one's own pain, as though one found true pleasure in the realization of the full extent of one's unhappiness. The idea that I might in time come to regret this corner struck me with horror; even then I foresaw to what monstrous degree man is a creature of habit. But this still lay in the future and meanwhile everything around me was hostile and—terrible . . . or, if not everything, it all, naturally, seemed so to me. The savage curiosity with which my new companions regarded me, their reinforced harshness with the newcomer from the nobility, who had suddenly appeared in their corporation, a harshness which sometimes went as far as hatred—all this had been so harassing to me that I longed to be sent to work as quickly as possible, only to know and savour as soon as might be all my poverty, to begin living like all the rest, to get into the same rut as all of them as soon as I could. Of course, I did not notice or suspect many things that lay under my nose; I did not guess at the kindliness in the midst of the enmity. Meanwhile, the few kind, friendly faces I encountered even during those three days greatly heartened me. The most friendly and kindest was Akim Akimovich's. Among the sullen and hostile faces of the other convicts I could not help but notice some that were cheerful and good. 'There are bad people everywhere, but there are good ones among them as well,' was the thought I was quick to console myself with. 'Who knows? Perhaps these men are not so very much worse than those, *the others*, who remain there, outside the prison.' I thought this, and nodded my head in approval, but all the same—good God, if only I had known then how true it was!

There was one man, for instance, whom I only came to know completely after many, many years, and yet he was with me, and constantly near me, almost all the time of my sentence. This was the prisoner Sushilov. As soon as I mentioned just now the convicts who were *no worse* than other men, I involuntarily thought of him. He acted like a servant to me. I had another, also. At the very beginning, during the first few days, Akim Akimovich recommended one of the prisoners—Joseph—to me, telling me that for thirty copecks a month he would cook special food for me, if that officially supplied was too distasteful and if I had the means to buy my own. Joseph was one of the four cooks, nominated for our two kitchens by the prisoners, although they were perfectly at liberty to refuse the nomination or, having accepted it, to decline it again on the morrow. These cooks did not go out to work, and their sole duties consisted in baking bread and making cabbage soup. We called them not cooks but kitchen-maids (maids, not men), not, however, because we despised them (indeed, those selected for the kitchen work were efficient and as far as possible honest), but in good-natured jest, which did not offend the cooks in the slightest. Joseph was almost always chosen and for several years almost without intermission he remained a kitchen-maid, sometimes refusing, but only for a time, when his homesickness came to a head, and with it the desire to smuggle vodka. He was a man of rare honesty and gentleness, although he had been sent to Siberia for running contraband. He was that same smuggler, the tall, strong young man I have mentioned before, faint-hearted about everything, especially the rods, peaceable, mild, gentle with everybody, *never* quarrelling with anybody, but unable to refrain from running vodka, in spite of all his cowardice, out of sheer passion for smuggling. Together with the other cooks, he also traded in vodka, though not, of course, on the same scale as Gazin, for example, because he had not the daring to run great risks. With Joseph I always got along very well. As for the means of paying for one's own food, very little was needed. I shall not be far wrong if I say that my outgoings amounted to one silver rouble a month in all on food, besides bread, which was supplied, and sometimes if I was very hungry cabbage soup, in spite of my loathing for it, which, however, subsequently almost completely disappeared. I usually bought a piece of beef, a pound for each day. In winter, our beef cost half a copeck. It was brought from the bazaar by an old soldier, of whom we had one in each barrack to keep order. These voluntarily took on themselves the daily duty of going to the bazaar to shop for the prisoners, taking practically no payment for it, except perhaps some small trifle. They did it for their own peace of mind and because otherwise their lives would have been made impossible. In this way they brought in tobacco, brick tea, beef, white bread, and all sorts of things—with only one exception, vodka. They were not even asked for vodka, although they were sometimes treated to a drink. Joseph cooked for me for several years together, always the same joint of roast beef. How well it was roasted is another question, and that was not what mattered. It is remarkable that for several years I hardly said two words to Joseph.

I began to talk to him many times, but he seemed somehow incapable of sustaining a conversation; he used to smile or answer 'yes' or 'no', and that was all. It was very strange to see this Hercules with the nature of a seven-year-old child.

Besides Joseph, one of the people who helped me was Sushilov. I had not sought him out or made any overtures to him. He seemed to find me for himself, and attached himself to me; I cannot even remember when and how it happened. He began by doing my washing. Behind the barracks a pit had been dug for this purpose, and the prisoners' washing was done in troughs standing above this pit. Besides this, Sushilov invented a thousand different duties for himself to please me; he put the kettle on for my tea, ran various errands, sought out things for me, took my jacket to be mended, greased my boots about four times a month, and did all this with assiduous zeal, as though he were under God knows what obligation; in a word, he completely bound up his lot with mine and took all my affairs on himself. He never said, for example, 'You have so many shirts; your jacket is torn', and so on, but always '*We* have so many shirts now; *our* jacket is torn.' He was always trying to put himself in my place and apparently accepted this as the principal assignment of his whole life. He had no trade or, as the prisoners say, handiwork and, I think, it was only from me that he ever got a penny. I paid him as much as I could, that is, in farthings, and he was always meekly satisfied. He could not do without somebody to serve and apparently chose me in particular because I was politer than the others and more scrupulous about paying. He was one of those who could never grow rich or get themselves set on the path of success and who with us undertook to keep guard for the *maidans*, standing whole nights together in the passages in the freezing cold, listening for every sound in the yard lest it be the duty-officer, receiving for this five copecks in silver for practically the whole night and, in the event of discovery, losing everything and paying with their backs. I have already spoken of them. It is characteristic of these people to suppress their own personalities always, everywhere and before almost everybody, and to play not even a secondary but a tertiary role in matters of common import. All this is inborn in them. Sushilov was a very pitiful young man, meek and humble, even downtrodden, although none of us had trampled upon him; he was simply downtrodden by nature. I was always sorry for him, for some reason. I could not even look at him without this feeling, but why I was sorry I could not have told anybody. I could not talk to him, either; he was another who was incapable of carrying on a conversation and it was obviously a heavy labour to him to try; he only brightened up when, to end the conversation, you gave him something to do or asked him to fetch something or run some errand. I was even convinced, in the end, that I was affording him positive pleasure by this. He was neither tall nor short, neither handsome nor plain, neither stupid nor intelligent, neither young nor old, moderately pock-marked and medium fair in colouring. There was never anything very definite to be said about him. There was one thing: it seemed to me, as far as I could judge, that he belonged to the same fellowship as Sirotkin, and belonged to it solely because he was meek and downtrodden. The other prisoners sometimes laughed at him, principally because he had *changed places* on the march to Siberia in a convoy, and changed in return for a red shirt and a rouble in silver. It was because of the insignificant price for which he had sold himself that the prisoners laughed at him. To 'change places' means to exchange names, and consequently destinies, with somebody. However fantastic this may seem, it is a fact, and in my day it still flourished in Siberian prisoners' convoys, hallowed by tradition and defined by settled forms. At first I could not believe it, but in the end I had to accept the evidence of my eyes.

This is how it was done. A party of prisoners is being

escorted into Siberia. They are of every kind: some are
going to convict prisons, some to factories, some to settlements; they march together. Somewhere on the way, say in
the Government of Perm, one of the convicts wishes to
change places with another. For example, a certain Mikhaylov, convicted of murder or some other major crime, finds
it inconvenient to go to penal servitude for many years.
Let us suppose he is a shrewd fellow and worldly-wise,
and knows what he is doing: he looks for one of the same
party who is much simpler, meeker and more downtrodden,
and who has been condemned to a comparatively light
punishment—either to a few years in a factory, to simple
exile, or even to penal servitude, but for a much shorter
term. Finally he finds Sushilov. Sushilov has been a house-
serf and he is being sent to a settlement. He has already
marched fifteen hundred versts, of course without a copeck,
because Sushilov never can have a copeck—he trudges
along, tired, worn out, on regulation rations, without so
much as a taste of anything extra, with only the clothing
issued to him, performing services for everybody for a few
miserable coppers. Mikhaylov enters into conversation with
Sushilov, cultivates him, makes friends with him, and finally,
at one of the halts, treats him to vodka. Lastly, he makes his
suggestion; wouldn't Sushilov like to change places? 'I,'
says he, 'Mikhaylov, and so on and so on, I am going to
penal servitude that is not exactly penal servitude but some
sort of "Special Class". Although it's penal servitude, it is
something special and therefore better.' Not all the authorities, even in St. Petersburg, knew of the Special Class during
its existence. It was so special and so separate a class (in my
time there were not more than seventy men in it), that one
was unlikely to come across any trace of it. I afterwards met
people who had served in Siberia and knew it well, who
heard from me for the first time of the existence of the
'Special Class'. In the statute book there are altogether six
lines about it: 'There shall be set up in such and such a

prison a Special Class for the most serious criminals, pending the establishment in Siberia of heavy penal labour undertakings.' Even the prisoners in this 'Class' did not know whether it was meant for life or for a term of years. No term was specified, what was said was 'pending the establishment of heavy penal labour undertakings', and that was all; so it was 'while it lasts'. Nobody in the party, least of all Sushilov, knows this, not excluding Mikhaylov himself, who can hardly have more than an inkling of what the 'Special Class' is, based on the very serious nature of his crime, which has already brought him some three or four thousand versts. Consequently, it cannot be a good place he is being sent to. Sushilov, though, is simply being deported to a settlement; what could be better? 'Wouldn't you like to change places?' Sushilov is slightly drunk, he is a simple soul, full of gratitude to Mikhaylov, who has been so kind to him, and therefore he does not like to refuse. Besides, he has already heard among the party that it is possible to change, and that others do it, and consequently there is nothing extraordinary or unheard-of about it. They come to an agreement. The shameless Mikhaylov, taking advantage of Sushilov's unusual simplicity, buys his name from him for a red shirt and a silver rouble, which he gives him on the spot, before witnesses. On the next day Sushilov is no longer drunk, but he is again given drink, and besides, it is a bad thing to go back on one's word. The silver is already drunk, and soon the red shirt is too. 'If you won't do it, give the money back.' But where is Sushilov to get a silver rouble? If he does not give it back, the *artel* will make him: the *artel* watches such points strictly. Besides, if one has given one's word, one must keep it—the *artel* insists on this too. Otherwise, they will make his life impossible or perhaps simply kill him, and at the least he will be bullied.

Indeed, if the *artel* were once to tolerate any leniency in such a matter, the practice of exchanging names would come to an end. If it is possible to go back on a promise and upset a bargain once made after taking the money, who will fulfil one afterwards? This, in short, is the concern of the *artel*, of the community, and therefore the convoy of prisoners is very strict about it. At last Sushilov sees that there is no hope of begging himself off and decides to submit. An announcement is made to the whole party; anybody else who must be bribed receives his present and, if need be, is treated to vodka. To them, of course, it is all one whether Mikhaylov or Sushilov is to rot in hell; the vodka is drunk, they have been treated—and so their lips also are sealed. At the next halt, for example, the roll is called; Mikhaylov's name is reached: 'Mikhaylov!' and Sushilov answers 'Here!'; 'Sushilov!' and Mikhaylov calls 'Here!'—and they pass on. Nobody ever speaks of it again. At Tobolsk the convicts are sorted out; Mikhaylov is directed to the settlement and Sushilov, under reinforced guard, sent on to the Special Class. No further protest is possible; indeed, what proof can there be? For how many years would such a case not drag on? What further punishment could there be for it? Finally, where are the witnesses? If there were any, they would deny it. The upshot is that Sushilov lands in the 'Special Class' for a silver rouble and a red shirt.

The other prisoners laughed at Sushilov, not because he had changed places (although there is a general feeling of contempt for those who have exchanged a light sentence for a heavier, as for any fool who has got into a mess), but because he got only a red shirt and a rouble in silver, altogether too paltry a price. Usually the sums exacted for exchanging are large, again judging comparatively. They may even amount to thirty or more roubles. But Sushilov was so mild, such a nonentity, and so despicable to everybody, that somehow even to laugh at him seemed unsuitable.

I lived a long time with Sushilov, several years altogether. Little by little he grew extraordinarily attached to me, as I could not help but see, so that I also got very used to him. Once, however—I can never forgive myself for this—he failed to do something I had asked him to do, when he had just taken money from me, and I had the cruelty to say to him: 'Look, Sushilov, you take my money, but you won't do things for me.' Sushilov said nothing and went off about my business, but something had made him suddenly sad. Two days passed. I thought, 'This can't be because of what I said.' I knew that another prisoner, Anton Vasilyev, was pressing him for a trifling debt. He probably had not the money and was afraid to ask me for it. On the same day I said to him: 'Sushilov, I believe you wanted to ask me for money, because of Anton Vasilyev. Here, take it!' I was sitting on my planks and Sushilov was standing in front of me. He seemed thunderstruck that I had myself remembered his difficulties and offered him the money, all the more so because, in his opinion, he had recently taken so much money from me that he could not even hope that I would give him more. He looked at the money and then at me, then suddenly turned and went out. I was taken aback by all this. I followed him and found him behind the barracks. He was standing by the prison stockade, leaning against it with his face turned towards it and his head buried in his arms. 'What is the matter, Sushilov?' I asked him. He did not look at me and to my extreme astonishment I saw that he was on the edge of tears. 'You think . . . Alexander Petrovich . . .,' he began in a broken voice, still trying not to look at me, 'that I . . . that it is for money . . . that I . . . but I really . . . I . . . o-o-oh!' Here he turned towards the stockade again so abruptly that he bumped his forehead on it, and fairly burst into sobs . . . It was the first time that I had seen a man weep in the prison. It was almost impossible to console him and, although from that time he began to serve and look after me, if possible, even more zealously, yet I could see, from almost imperceptible signs, that in his heart he could never forgive me for reproaching him. And yet others laughed at him, snubbed him at every opportunity, sometimes swore at him abominably—and he lived in peace and harmony with them and never took offence. Yes, it is very difficult to know a man thoroughly, even after long years.

That is why the prison could not at first sight appear to me in the same light of reality in which it presented itself later. That is why, too, I said that, even though I looked at everything with such earnest and avid attention, I yet could not distinctly see much of what lay under my very nose. Naturally, what struck me at first were the more sharply outstanding aspects, those on a large scale, but even these, perhaps, produced a mistaken impression on me, and they left behind in my soul only a feeling of oppression and hopeless melancholy. My meeting with Aristov, another convict who had arrived in the prison not long before me, and who gave to my first days in the prison a particularly painful colouring, largely contributed to this effect. I had known even before my arrival in the prison that I should meet Aristov there. He poisoned all this first difficult period for me, and greatly enhanced my mental tortures. I cannot pass him over in silence.

He was the most loathsome possible example of the depths of infamy to which a human being can descend and the degree to which he can kill, with remorseless ease, every kind of moral feeling in himself. Aristov was the young man from a noble family to whom I have already referred in passing as acting as an informer for our major of all that went on in the prison, and as being friendly with his batman, Fedka. This is his story in brief: without finishing his education he quarrelled with his relatives in Moscow, who were horrified by his depraved conduct, and made his appearance in St. Petersburg. In order to obtain money he perpetuated a despicable act of informing: that is, he sold the lives of ten men to ensure the immediate gratification of his insatiable thirst for the coarsest and vilest pleasures, to which, seduced by St. Petersburg and its coffee-houses and brothels, he had become so addicted that he, an intelligent man, had run the risk of this hare-brained and senseless undertaking. He was soon found out; his denunciation involved innocent people and made false allegations and for this last he was sent to Siberia, to our prison, for two years. He was still very young; life was just beginning for him. One would have thought that such a terrible turn of fate ought to have been enough of a shock to his nature to make it check and change course. But he accepted his new lot without the least distress or even repugnance, suffered no moral disturbance and feared nothing in it, unless it was, perhaps, the inevitable necessity of leaving behind the coffee-houses and the brothels. It even appeared to him that the name of convict gave him more licence for even greater vice and filth. 'A convicted criminal is a convicted criminal; if I'm a convict, I need not be ashamed of acting basely.' This was literally his opinion. I remember this disgusting creature as something phenomenal. I lived for several years among murderers, rakes, and desperate scoundrels, but I can say positively that I have never in my life encountered such complete moral degradation, such absolute corruption, and such brazen vileness, as in Aristov. We had a parricide, of gentle birth, among us; I have mentioned him before; but I am convinced, from many signs and events, that even he had incomparably more nobility and humanity than Aristov. In my eyes, all through my prison life, Aristov was simply a lump of flesh, with teeth and a stomach, and with an insatiable thirst for the grossest and most bestial physical pleasures, for the satisfaction of the least and most capricious of which he was capable of the most cold-blooded violence, murder, or, in short, anything at all, provided he could hide his traces. I am not exaggerating anything; I knew Aristov well. He was an example of the lengths to which the purely physical side of a man could go, unrestrained by any internal standard or discipline. And how I loathed the sight of his smile of eternal mockery! He was a monster, a moral Quasimodo.* Add to all this that he was sly and clever, handsome, had even a certain amount of education and possessed some talents. No, better

fire, better plague and famine, than such a being in society!
I have already said that everybody in the prison had sunk so
low that spying and informing flourished and the convicts
regarded the fact without indignation. On the contrary, they
were all very friendly with Aristov and behaved incomparably more amicably with him than with us. Our drunken
major's indulgence towards him gave him weight and consequence in their eyes. Among other things, he had assured
the major that he could paint portraits (he used to affirm to
the other convicts that he had been an ensign in the Guards),
and the major ordered him to be sent to work in his (the
major's) own house, with the idea, of course, that he should
draw the major's portrait . . . There he met the batman
Fedka, who had an extraordinary influence on his master,
and consequently on everybody and everything in the
prison. Aristov spied on us on the major's own orders, but
he, when he was in his cups, used to slap his face and rail at
him as a spy and an informer. It often happened that immediately after one of these beatings the major would sit
down in a chair and order Aristov to go on with the portrait.
Apparently our major really believed that Aristov was a
remarkable artist, almost the equal of Brülow,* of whom he
had heard; but all the same, he considered that he had the
right to strike him across the face, because, said he, although
you may be an artist all right, now you're a convict, and if
you were Brülow himself, I am still your commanding officer
and accordingly I shall do as I please with you. He made
Aristov take off his boots, among other things, and carry
away various vessels from his bedroom, but all the same he
could not for long renounce the idea that Aristov was a great
artist. The portrait dragged on for a long time, almost a year.
At last the major realized that he was being bamboozled and,
fully convinced that the portrait would never be finished but
that it was, on the contrary, growing less and less like him
every day, he flew into a rage, thrashed the artist and sent
him back to do dirty work in the prison as a punishment.

Aristov plainly repined at this and found it hard to renounce his days of leisure, his pickings from the major's table, his friend Fedka and all the treats the two of them had contrived for themselves in the major's kitchen. But at least the major, on Aristov's removal, ceased to persecute Miretsky, a prisoner who was constantly being denounced by Aristov, for this reason: At the time of Aristov's arrival in the prison, Miretsky was alone. He was very miserable; he had nothing in common with the other prisoners and looked on them with horror and loathing, either did not notice or did not see all those things in them which might have had a reconciling effect on him, and was unable to get on a closer footing with them. They repaid him with the same hatred. Generally speaking, people like Miretsky are in a terrible position in prison. The cause which had brought Aristov to prison was unknown to Miretsky. Aristov, indeed, realizing the sort of person with whom he had to deal, immediately assured him that he had been sent there on a very different charge, almost the same as that for which Miretsky himself had been exiled. Miretsky was passionately glad to have found a companion, a friend. He looked after him, comforted him in his first days of penal servitude, which he supposed must be very painful to him, gave him his last money, fed him, shared his indispensable necessities with him. But Aristov at once began to hate him, precisely because he was honourable, because he regarded vileness with such horror, because he was completely different from himself, and he lost no time in reporting to the major everything that Miretsky had confided to him about the prison and the major during those first conversations. As a result, the major conceived a violent dislike for Miretsky, persecuted him and would have driven him to the last extremity if it had not been for the influence of the commandant. Not only was Aristov quite unblushing when Miretsky learned of his baseness, but he even seemed to like encountering him and sneering at him. This evidently gave him pleasure, as Miretsky himself several times pointed out to me. This foul creature later escaped in the company of another convict and a guard, but I shall speak of this escape later. At the beginning he tried to ingratiate himself with me, too, thinking that I had not heard his history. I repeat, he poisoned my early days in the prison with even greater anguish. I was horrified by the terrible filth and vileness into which I had been cast, and in the middle of which I now found myself. I thought that everything here was equally vile and filthy. But I was mistaken: I was judging everybody by Aristov.

During those three days I loitered miserably about the prison, lay on my planks, had shirts made, for payment, of course (a few farthings each), from the crash issued to me, by a trustworthy convict indicated to me by Akim Akimovich, and acquired, on Akim Akimovich's urgent recommendation, a folding mattress as thin as a wafer (made of felt covered with crash) and a pillow stuffed with flocks, dreadfully hard to my unaccustomed head. Akim Akimovich zealously concerned himself with the organization of all these things for me, and played some part in it himself, sewing together for me with his own hands a blanket of scraps of cloth collected from worn-out trousers and jackets, which I bought from other convicts. At the end of his term the things issued to him remained a convict's own property; they were immediately sold there, in the prison, and however worn a thing might be, there was always a hope of getting rid of it at some price. All this astonished me at first. It was now that I came into contact with the common people for more or less the first time. I myself had suddenly become as much one of the common people, as much a convict, as they. Their ways, their ideas, their customs, had become, so to speak, mine also, at any rate to outward seeming and in the eyes of the law, although I did not share them in reality. I was confused and bewildered, as though I had not even suspected or heard of any of this before, although I had in fact been told and knew of it. But reality produces a very different effect from hearsay knowledge. Could I, for example, have suspected at any previous time that such things as these old cast-offs could be reckoned as things at all?—but now I had sewn myself a blanket from these same old cast-offs! It is difficult even to conceive the sort of cloth that was allotted for the prisoners'·clothing. To look at it seemed very like real cloth, thick military stuff; but as soon as it began to wear, it turned into a kind of coarse netting and tore scandalously. The woollen garments issued, however, were to last only one year, but it was difficult to make them endure even for this time. A prisoner must work and carry heavy burdens; his clothes quickly got rubbed and worn. Our sheepskin coats, on the other hand, were issued for three years, and they usually served throughout that period as coats, blankets, and bedding. But the coats were strong, although it was no rarity to see, towards the end of the three years, some man wearing a sheepskin coat patched with sacking. In spite of this, at the end of their allotted term, they were sold, even in a very worn condition, for about forty copecks in silver. Some, in a better state of preservation, were sold for sixty or even seventy silver copecks, and in the prison this was a great deal of money.

Money, indeed—I have already spoken of this—had·a terrible significance and power. It can be stated positively that a prisoner who had even a little money suffered ten times less than one who possessed none at all, even though the latter was supplied with all the regulation property, and what use could money be to him?—so our authorities reasoned. I repeat once more that if convicts were deprived of all possibility of possessing their own money, they would either go out of their minds or die like flies (in spite of being supplied with everything they needed), or, finally, fall into unheard-of wickedness—some from boredom, others in order to be executed, annihilated, as soon as possible, or simply to 'change their lot' (a technical expression) by some means. And if the prisoner, after he has almost sweated blood to earn a few copecks or contrived extraordinary stratagems, often involving swindling or theft, to acquire them, then wastes them, this does not in the least show that he does not value them, however much it may appear so at the first glance. The prisoner is greedy for money to the point of sickness, of the obscuration of reason, and if he does indeed fling it away like chaff when he goes 'on the binge', he does so because there is one thing he values more highly than money. What is it that ranks higher than money for the convict? Freedom, or at any rate some illusion of freedom. Prisoners are great dreamers. I will speak of this later, but now I will say only one thing: will it be credited that I have known men sentenced to *twenty years* who have said to me, very calmly, such phrases as, for example: 'Just wait; God willing, I shall finish my stretch, and then . . .'? The whole idea of the word prisoner postulates a man without free will; but when he flings away money the prisoner is acting *of his own free will*. In spite of all brands, fetters, and odious prison walls shutting him away from God's world and confining him like a wild beast in a cage— he can still obtain vodka, that is, a strictly forbidden pleasure, enjoy women, and sometimes, though not always, even bribe the authorities nearest to him, old soldiers and even non-commissioned officers, who will turn a blind eye to the fact that he is violating law and discipline; more, he may even swagger a little with them, and the prisoner dearly likes to swagger—that is, to pretend to his fellows (and even to convince himself, *for however a short time*) that he has more will-power and authority than he appears to have. In a word, he may play the rake and the bully, crush whomever he chooses into the dust with a single word, and prove that he *can* do all this, that it is all 'in our own hands', that is, reassure himself of what a pauper cannot even dream of. This, by the way, is perhaps why convicts in general, even the staidest of them, manifest such an inclination to swaggering and boasting, and to a comical and very simple-minded puffing-up of their own personalities. Finally, all this excess has its risks, which means that it has some illusion of life, an illusion, however far-fetched, of liberty. And what would one not give for liberty? What millionaire, with his neck in a noose, would not give all his millions for a mouthful of air?

Sometimes the authorities were astonished when some convict, who had jogged along for several years in so tame and exemplary a fashion that he had even been made a 'trusty' for his meritorious conduct, suddenly, without rhyme or reason—as if a devil had entered into him—ran off the rails, 'went on a binge', grew violent, or sometimes simply plunged headlong into criminal conduct: either open insolence to the highest authorities, or murder, or rape, or something else of the same kind. He would be watched with amazement. Yet perhaps the whole cause of this violent break in a man from whom it was not in the least to be expected, was a mournful desire for an abrupt display of personality, a longing to be his own self, a wish to declare himself and his own lowly personality, appearing suddenly and developing into fury, insanity, the eclipse of reason, paroxysm, and convulsion. So, perhaps, one buried alive and awakening in his coffin, hammers on its lid and struggles to wrest it off, although, of course, reason might persuade him that all his efforts are vain. There, indeed, lies the point, that reason does not enter into this: it is the convulsion of madness. We must take into consideration that almost any manifestation of will in a prisoner is accounted a crime, and, that being so, it is naturally all the same to him whether the manifestation is great or small. A binge is a binge, to risk anything is to risk everything, even murder itself. And of course it is only the beginning that counts; afterwards a man grows intoxicated and nothing will stop him. Therefore it is best to avoid driving anybody to this point. It is more peaceful for everybody. Yes, but how?

6. The First Month (II)

WHEN I entered the prison I had a little money; I carried hardly any on my person, for fear it should be taken away, but I had hidden, that is, pasted into the Testament that we were permitted to take into the prison, a few roubles for emergencies. The book, with the money pasted into it, had been given to me in Tobolsk by others who were also suffering exile, measured in tens of years, and who had long been accustomed to see a brother in every unfortunate. There is in Siberia, and the supply is practically never exhausted, a number of people who seem to have assigned to themselves as their mission in life a brotherly care of the unfortunate and a disinterested and holy sympathy and compassion for them, as if they were their own children. I cannot refrain from briefly mentioning one encounter of mine. In the town in which our prison was situated there lived a certain lady, Nastasya Ivanovna,* a widow. Needless to say, none of us was able to know her personally during our stay in the prison. She had apparently chosen as her vocation the helping of exiles, but most of her care was devoted to us. Perhaps there had been a misfortune in her own family, or one of those nearest and dearest to her heart had suffered for some crime; at any rate, she seemed to find particular happiness in doing everything she could for us. She could not, of course, do very much; she was very poor. But we in the prison felt that there, outside, we had a most devoted friend. Among other things, she often conveyed to us news, of which we were sorely in need. When I left the prison and was sent off to another town, I managed to call on her and make her personal acquaintance. She lived somewhere in a suburb, with one of her near relatives. She was neither young nor old, neither pretty nor plain; it was even impossible to tell whether she was intelligent or well educated. All that you noticed in her, at every moment, was simply her infinite goodness, her invincible desire to gratify you, to make things easier for you, to do something that would be sure to please you. All this was revealed in her tranquil, warm-hearted regard. With others of my fellow prisoners I passed most of the evening with her. She looked at everything through our eyes, laughed when we laughed, hastened to express her agreement with everything we said; she busied herself with offering us what refreshments she could. We were given tea, *zakuski*, and sweetmeats, and I think that if she had had thousands of roubles she would have rejoiced only because she could have offered us more and done more to relieve those who still remained in the prison. When we said goodbye, she gave us each a cigarette-case to remember her by. These cases she had made for us herself out of cardboard pasted together somehow and covered with coloured paper just like what is used for binding little primers of arithmetic for infant schools (and perhaps some calculation had had to go into the making of those covers). Round the cases was pasted, for ornament, a narrow border of gold paper, for which she had perhaps had to go specially to the shops. 'You do smoke cigarettes, so perhaps this will be of some use to you,' she said, as though making timid excuses for her present . . . Some people say (I have heard it said and seen it written) that the most exalted love for one's neighbour is at the same time the greatest egoism.* What egoism there could be here is more than I can understand.

Although I had not very much money when I entered the prison, I somehow could not be seriously vexed with those convicts who, in almost my first hour of prison life, after they had already cozened me out of some of it once, came with immense *naïveté* a second, a third, or even a fifth time to borrow money from me. But I will freely confess one thing: I was very much annoyed that all these folk, with their simple-minded cunning, must certainly, I thought, consider me a fool and a dupe, and be laughing at me simply because I gave them money for the fifth time. They must inevitably think that I was taken in by their cleverness and trickery; if, on the other hand, I were to refuse them and send them away, I was sure they would have incomparably more respect for me. But however annoyed I might be, all the same I could not refuse them. I was put out, though, because I was seriously and anxiously concerned, during these first days, about how and on what footing I should establish myself in the prison, or rather on what footing I ought to stand with them. I knew with both my heart and my mind that this environment was new to me, that I was all at sea, and that one cannot live for so many years in that state. I had had to prepare myself. Needless to say, I had resolved that I must first of all act in direct accordance with the dictates of my feelings and conscience. But I knew also that, after all, this was only theoretical and that in practice the most unexpected things lay before me.

And so, in spite of all the little preoccupations of my installation in the prison, which I have already mentioned, and into the major part of which it was Akim Akimovich who enticed me, and in spite of the fact that they distracted me to some extent, I suffered greater and greater pangs of a terrible, corroding anguish. 'The house of the dead!' I would say to myself sometimes, watching from the steps of our barrack the prisoners, returned from work, lazily slouching about the prison yard, from the barracks to the kitchens and back again. Watching them, I tried to discover from their faces and their movements what sort of people they were and what their characters were like. They lounged before my eyes with scowling brows or excessively cheerful faces (these two expressions are those most frequently met with and are almost characteristic of penal establishments), wrangled or simply talked together, or, lastly, walked about alone, with quiet, measured steps, as if they were deep in thought, some with a weary and apathetic look, others (even here!) with an air of arrogant superiority, their caps pushed back and their sheepskin coats slung over their shoulders like capes, their faces expressing impudent mockery. 'All these make my surroundings, my world, henceforth,' thought I, 'and willy-nilly I must live with them' . . . I used to try to cross-question Akim Akimovich about them, when I was drinking tea with him, as I very much liked to do, so that I should not do so alone. In parenthesis, tea, during this first period, was almost my sole nourishment. Akim Akimovich did not refuse my tea, and would himself set up our comical little home-made tin samovar, lent to me by Miretsky. Akim Akimovich would usually drink one glass of tea (he even possessed tumblers) in sedate silence, return it to me, thank me, and immediately apply himself to working on my blanket. But he was unable to tell me what I wanted to know, and could not even understand why I was so interested in the characters of the prisoners around us, especially those nearest to us, and he used to listen to me with a sly little smile, which I remember very well. No, evidently I must find out for myself and not ask questions, thought I.

On the fourth day, just as on the occasion when I went to have my fetters changed, the prisoners were drawn up in two rows, early in the morning, on the square in front of the guardroom, near the prison gates. In front facing them, and at the rear, stretched two lines of soldiers with loaded rifles and fixed bayonets. A soldier has the right to fire at a prisoner who is attempting to escape, but at the same time he is answerable for firing, if he shoots except in circumstances of the most extreme necessity; the same applies in the event of open rebellion by the convicts. But who would think of trying to escape openly? An officer of Engineers appeared, who was in charge of the work, and also noncommissioned officers and men, overseers of the work in progress. The roll was called; a section of the prisoners, going to the sewing workshops, left first; the Engineers were not concerned with them; they worked apart, inside the

prison, and supplied it with clothes. Then others went off
to the workshops and others again to the ordinary rough
work. With about twenty other prisoners I too was sent off.
Beyond the fortress, on the frozen river, there were two
government barges which, because they were no longer
serviceable, were to be broken up so that the old timber, at
least, should not be entirely lost. All this old material, however, seemed to be worth very little, perhaps nothing at all.
Firewood was sold in the town at trifling prices and there
was much forest land round about. The prisoners were
directed to this labour solely in order that they should not
be idle, and they understood this very well. They always
applied themselves to such work indolently and apatheti-
cally, while it was almost always a different matter when the
work had some meaning and value in itself, and especially
when it was possible to arrange for a set task to be done.
Then, as if something had inspired them, and although there
could be no advantage to themselves, they exerted their
utmost efforts to perform it as quickly and well as possible;
their self-esteem was somehow involved. But in the present
labours, performed more *pro forma* than of necessity, it was
difficult to arrange a set amount of work and we must go on
working right up to the drum-beat that called us back home
at eleven o'clock. The day was warm and cloudy; it was all
but thawing. All our group turned our steps out of the
fortress to the river bank, with a slight chinking of chains,
which although they were concealed beneath our clothing,
gave out a thin, sharp metallic sound at every step. Two or
three men went off separately to the armoury for the necessary tools. I walked among the others and felt more cheerful;
I was eager to find out as soon as possible what kind of work
it was, what this penal labour was like and how I should acquit
myself, doing manual work for the first time in my life.

I remember everything, down to the smallest details. On
the way we met one of the townspeople, a bearded man who
stopped and thrust his hand into his pocket. A prisoner

promptly left our group, took off his cap, received the alms
—five copecks—and immediately returned to us. The man
crossed himself and continued on his way. The five copecks
were spent that morning on white loaves, which were equally
divided among the party. Among the group some were, as
usual, morose and silent, others indifferent and sluggish,
and others talked idly among themselves. One seemed
terribly pleased and cheerful about something and sang
and almost danced as he went along, clinking his fetters
with every skip. He was the same short, thickset prisoner
who, on my first morning, had had an argument with
another near the water-buckets while we were washing,
because the latter had made the rash and reckless assertion
that he was a great crested grebe. This high-spirited fellow
was called Skuratov. Finally, he began to sing a dashing
song, of which I remember the refrain:

> I wasn't there when they married me off,
> For I was down at the mill.

All we lacked was a balalaika.

His unusually cheerful frame of mind, of course, immediately aroused the displeasure of some of our party and was
almost taken as a personal affront.

'What caterwauling!' reproachfully said one prisoner,
although it was no business of his at all.

'The wolf has one song and he imitates it! But then he
comes from Tula!' remarked another, one of the gloomy
ones, in a Ukrainian accent.

'Suppose I do,' retorted Skuratov at once. 'In your Poltava
you used to choke yourselves with dumplings!'

'That's a lie! And what did you eat yourself? You ate
cabbage soup with a bast shoe for a spoon. I suppose the
devil feeds you with walnuts now,' added a third.

'Well yes, lads, it's true I'm pampered,' answered Skuratov with a slight sigh, as if he regretted it, addressing the
whole group rather than any one of us in particular. 'I've

been tortured' (he meant 'nurtured', but Skuratov always deliberately distorted words) 'on prunes and puff pastry ever since I was a babby. My own brothers own a stall in Moscow to this day—selling wind in the street market. Rich merchants they are, rolling in money.'

'And what did you sell?'

'Oh, we had various specialities. It was there, my lads, that I got my first two hundred . . .'

'Not roubles!' interrupted one curious listener, who had positively jumped at the notion of so much money.

'No, my lad, not roubles, but a beating with sticks . . . Luke, hi, Luke!'

'Luke Kuzmich to you!' growled a thin little convict with a sharp little nose.

'All right then, Luke Kuzmich, if you like.'

' "Uncle" to you!'

'Oh, the devil take it and you too! It's not worth while talking to you. And I had something nice to say to you, too. Well, that's how it was, mates; as it happened I didn't stay in Moscow very long; in the end I got fifteen lashes and got put away. So I . . .'

'What did they put you away for? . . .' interrupted one, who had been following the story attentively.

'Well, it was all—keep out of quod, don't drink moonshine, don't have any sort of good time, so I couldn't get rich in Moscow, lads, not nohow. And I was so keen to make a lot of money, I simply can't tell you, so . . .'

Many of them burst out laughing. Skuratov was evidently one of those self-appointed jesters, or rather clowns, who seemed to consider themselves bound to try to cheer up their sullen comrades and who, of course, got nothing in return but abuse. He belonged to a special and remarkable type of whom I may have to speak again.

'Now you'll have them trapping you instead of sables,' remarked Luke Kuzmich. 'Why, the clothes alone would fetch a hundred roubles.'

Skuratov had on an extremely ancient, extremely shabby sheepskin coat, which was conspicuously patched all over. He looked himself over from head to foot, calmly and carefully.

'My head's worth a lot, though, mates,' he answered. 'When I said good-bye to Moscow, it was a comfort to me that my head was going with me. Good-bye, Moscow, thanks for the birching; you made the bath hot for me; my hide got famously striped! And you needn't look at my coat, my lad . . .'

'I suppose I ought to look at your head?'

'His head! It isn't his at all, but one he was given in charity,' Luke chimed in again. 'He was given it in Tumen when he was going through with the convoy.'

'Well, Skuratov, I suppose you had some sort of trade?'

'A fine one! He used to lead blind beggars about, and street-singers, and pull them by the shirt-tails,' remarked one of the scowlers. 'That was his only trade.'

'Yes, I did actually have a shot at stitching boots,' Skuratov answered, completely ignoring these caustic remarks. 'But I only stitched one pair.'

'Why, did someone want to buy them?'

'Yes, someone turned up who obviously didn't fear God or honour his father and mother. God punished him—he bought them.'

Everybody round Skuratov rocked with laughter.

'And I worked once after that, as well, here,' went on Skuratov with enormous coolness. 'I sewed on some uppers for Lieutenant Stepan Fedorovich Pomortsev.'

'Was he pleased?'

'No, lads, he wasn't satisfied. He cursed me up hill and down dale, and besides that he kicked my behind. He was very annoyed. Ah,

> Half a minute afterwards,
> Akulina's man walks out . . .'

Unexpectedly he was off again, stamping and skipping along.

'Look at him; what a sight!' grumbled a Ukrainian who had come up beside me, scowling at him with angry contempt.

'He's no use!' remarked another in a serious and conclusive tone.

I decidedly could not understand why they were annoyed with Skuratov, or why, in general, all the cheerful ones, as I had already noticed during those first days, were held in some degree of contempt. The anger of the Ukrainian I put down to personal reasons. But it was not so much those as annoyance because Skuratov had no self-restraint, none of that assumed air of stern personal dignity worn with such pedantic accuracy by the whole prison, because, in a word, he was, in their phrase, 'no use'. It was not, however, every cheerful man who aroused anger or was treated like Skuratov and others of his kind. The man who allowed himself to be treated without ceremony, the good-natured man without artifices, was instantly subjected to humiliation. I found this somewhat disconcerting. But some of the cheerful ones were both able and willing to defend themselves, and gave no quarter, and they were perforce respected. Even here, in our group, there was such a man, well able to look after himself, but essentially good-humoured and good-natured (although I did not get to know this side of him until later), a tall, striking-looking young fellow with a large wart on his cheek and a highly comical expression on his face, which was, however, quite handsome and intelligent. He was called the Pioneer, because he had once served in the Pioneers; now he was in the Special Class. I shall have to speak of him again.

Not all the 'serious' ones, however, were as expansive as the Ukrainian who had expressed his displeasure at high spirits. There were some men in the prison who had aimed at pre-eminence, knowledge of everything that went on in the prison, resourcefulness, character, and wisdom. Many of them had actually attained their aim, that is, pre-eminence and a considerable influence over their fellows. These clever ones were often very hostile to one another, and each of them had many enemies. They treated the other convicts with dignity and even condescension, never entered into needless wrangles, stood well with the authorities, at work acted as foremen, as it were, and not one of them would have cavilled over a little singing; they did not condescend to such trifles. With me all such men were remarkably courteous all through my term, but not very communicative; this also appeared to be from considerations of dignity. Of these also I shall speak in greater detail.

We came to the river bank. Below, on the river, frozen into the water, was the old barge which was to be broken up. On the farther side of the river stretched the blue steppe; the prospect was wild and sombre. I expected that they would all set to work at once with a will, but they did not dream of doing so. Some sat down on beams of wood lying about on the bank; almost all drew out of their boots pouches of native tobacco, bought in the leaf at the bazaar at three copecks a pound, and short chibouks of willow-wood, with small, crude, home-made wooden bowls. The pipes were lighted; the guards stood round us in a line and set themselves, with an air of the greatest boredom, to keep watch.

'And who had the bright idea of breaking this barge up?' said one, as if to himself, not addressing anybody in particular. 'Did they want some match-wood or something?'

'It must have been somebody who doesn't care anything about us,' remarked a second.

'Where are those peasants off to?' asked the first, after a short silence, and without, of course, taking any notice of the answer to his previous question, pointing to where, in the distance, a group of peasants were making their way in single file through the untrodden snow. Everybody turned in that direction, and, for want of something to do, began to mimic them. One of the peasants, the last, was walking in an extraordinarily comical fashion, waving his arms, and with his head, on which was a peasant's tall fur cap, lolling sideways. His whole figure was clearly defined against the white snow.

'There now, friend Petrovich, how you've bundled yourself up!' remarked one of us, mimicking a peasant's accent. It was noticeable that the convicts in general somewhat looked down on the peasants, although half of them were peasants themselves.

'The one at the back walks as if he was planting radishes, lads . . .'

'He's worried, he's got a lot of money,' remarked a third.

Everybody laughed, but still lazily and as it were reluctantly. Meanwhile, a seller of white loaves, a pert and lively peasant woman, had come up.

The five-copeck piece we had been given was laid out on loaves and they were equally shared out on the spot.

The young fellow who had sold white bread in the prison took about a score of loaves and began a vehement argument, trying to get three loaves as his commission instead of two, according to the usual arrangement. But the woman would not agree.

'Well, so you won't give me it?'

'Why should I?'

'To keep the mice from eating it.'

'Be off with you!' screeched the woman, laughing.

At last our overseer, a non-commissioned officer with a stick in his hand, appeared.

'Hi, you, what are you sitting about for? Get on with it!'

'Well but, Ivan Matveich, give us a stint,' said one of our 'foremen', slowly getting up.

'Why didn't you ask before, when the work was given out? Break that barge up, that's your stint.'

At last, in a shiftless fashion, everybody got up and went down to the river with dragging feet. It immediately appeared that there were 'organizers', at least in talk, among the group. It seemed that the barge ought not to be chopped up haphazard but the beams and especially the ribs, fastened to the keel along the whole length of the barge with wooden nails, should be preserved, as far as possible—a long and tiresome job.

'Well, first of all we shall have to pull out this big beam here. Come on, lads!' remarked one, no organizer or foreman, but simply a labourer, a quiet and silent lad who had said nothing up to that point, and, stooping down, he embraced the beam with his arms and waited for helpers. But nobody went to help him.

'Yes, you'll pick it up, I don't think! You can't pick it up, and if your grandfather, the bear, came, he wouldn't be able to pick it up, either!' muttered somebody through his teeth.

'Well, what are we to begin with then, mates? I don't know . . .,' said the one who had thrust himself forward, bewildered, as he let go of the beam and straightened himself.

'What, can't you rearrange the whole job? . . . Why did you push yourself in? . . .'

'He couldn't share out the feed for three hens without making a mess of it, and here he's the first to . . . A fine fellow he is!'

'But I didn't mean anything, mates,' apologized the bewildered man. 'I only . . .'

'Well, am I supposed to keep you in dust-covers, or something? Or do you expect to be salted down for the winter?' shouted the overseer again, looking doubtfully at this crowd of some twenty men who did not know how to set about the work. 'Get on with it, and quick!'

'Saying quick doesn't make it quick, Ivan Matveich.'

'But you aren't doing anything at all! Savelyev! You

windbag! I said, why are you standing there, twiddling your thumbs? . . . Get to work!'

'What can I do all by myself?'

'Give us a stint, Ivan Matveich.'

'I've told you there's not going to be a stint. Break up the barge and then you can go home. Get on with it!'

We set to work at last, but sluggishly, unwillingly, clumsily. It was even irritating to see this crowd of strong, sturdy workmen who seemed determined to be puzzled how to go about the work. They were no sooner on the point of getting out the first and smallest rib than it became clear that it was breaking, 'breaking of itself', they said to the overseer by way of excuse; consequently it was impossible to do the work that way and it must be tackled differently. There followed a long discussion on how to tackle it differently and what to do. Needless to say, little by little the discussion became a wrangle and threatened to go even further . . . The overseer began to shout and wave his stick again, but once more the rib broke. Finally, it turned out that there were not enough axes and that some other tools must be brought. Two men were at once detailed to go to the fortress, under guard, for the tools, and while they waited all the rest calmly sat down on the barge, took out their pipes and again lit up.

At last the overseer spat.

'Well, the work you do won't bring any profit! Oh, these common people!' he grumbled angrily, waved his arms and went off to the fortress, brandishing his stick.

An hour later, the officer in charge appeared. He quietly heard the convicts out and then declared that he would allot us the task of taking out four more ribs, so long as they were got out whole and without breaking, and in addition we must take to pieces a considerable part of the barge, and only then would it be possible to go home. It was a big task, but, good heavens, how they set about it! What had become of all the laziness and doubts? Axes began to ring and wooden nails to be wrenched out. The rest pushed thick poles underneath the ribs and, setting twenty hands to a pole, briskly and skilfully levered the ribs out; and now, to my astonishment, the ribs broke away quite whole and undamaged. The barge seethed with activity. Everybody seemed suddenly to have become strikingly more intelligent. No unnecessary words, no oaths; each one knew what to say, what to do, where to go, what to recommend. Exactly half an hour before the drum beat, the allotted task was completed and the prisoners went back home, tired but completely content, although they had gained only some half hour from the regulation time. But as regards myself, I noticed one peculiarity: no matter where I went to help during the work I was everywhere in the way, everywhere a hindrance, and everywhere I was driven away almost with oaths.

The lowest ragamuffin of all, who was himself a very bad workman, and who did not dare to open his mouth in front of other cleverer, more efficient, prisoners, thought he had the right to shout at me and drive me away, if I stopped near him, on the pretext that I was hindering him. Finally one of the brisk ones said, with crude directness: 'Where do you think you're pushing to? Clear out! Why push in where you're not wanted?'

'You're out of your depth,' immediately chimed in another.

'You ought to go and pass round the hat,' said a third, 'to build a church, or to start a tobacco-fund for us; you're no good here.'

I had to stand aside, but it feels shameful to stand aside while everyone else is working. But when I really did move away from them to the other end of the barge, they immediately began to cry out:

'Look what sort of workmen we get sent to us! What can you do with them? Nothing at all!'

All this, of course, was done deliberately, because it

amused them. They felt the need to crow over former noble-men, and of course they were glad of this chance. It is easy now to understand why, as I said before, my first problem when I entered the prison was how to conduct myself, on what footing to place myself with these people. I had fore-seen that I should often have such collisions with them as I now experienced at work. But whatever collisions there were, I was determined not to alter my plan of action, which I had already partly worked out by this time; I knew that it was the right one. I was determined, namely, to bear myself as simply and independently as possible, and by no means to display any particular striving after friendship with them, but also not to repulse them if they themselves wished to be friends. By no means to fear their menaces and hatred and, as far as possible, to pretend that I did not notice them. By no means to be reconciled to some specific points and to show no indulgence to some of their habits and customs. In a word, not to allow myself to be thrust into complete fellowship with them. I realized from the very beginning that they would be the first to despise me if I did. According to their ideas, however, I ought (as I subsequently knew for a fact) even to have cherished and respected my noble origins in front of them; that is, I should have pampered myself, given myself airs, been disdainful with them, sniffed at every step, acted the fine gentleman, refused to soil my hands with work. That was their understanding of nobility. Needless to say, they would have abused me for this, but all the same they would have respected me in their hearts. Such a role was not for me: I had never been a gentleman in their understanding of the word; but on the other hand I promised myself never by any action to debase in their eyes either my education or my way of thinking. If, to please them, I had begun to pander to them, acquiesce in their opinions, be over-familiar with them, and lower myself to the level of their 'quality' in order to win their favour, they would immediately have supposed that I did it out of fear and cowardice and would have treated me with contempt. Arıstov was not an example: he had access to the major, and they themselves were afraid of him. On the other hand, I had no desire to lock myself up in chilly and inaccessible courtesy, as the Poles did. Now I could see very well that they despised me for wanting to work as they did, and for not being soft or putting on airs with them, and although I knew for certain that they would be obliged to change their opinion of me later, nevertheless the idea that they had, as it were, the right to despise me because they thought I was trying to ingratiate myself with them over the work—this idea greatly chagrined me.

When I returned to the prison, weary and worn out, in the evening, when the after-dinner work was finished, a terrible anguish again took possession of me. 'How many thousands of days like this one still lie before me,' I thought, 'and all alike, all exactly alike!' Silent and alone, I wandered in the already gathering twilight behind the barracks, along the outer palisade, and suddenly saw our Sharik bounding straight towards me. We had a prison dog, Sharik, just as they have company, battery, or squadron dogs. He had been in the prison from time immemorial and lived on scraps from the kitchen. He was a fairly big dog, black with white markings, a mongrel, not very old, with wise eyes and a bushy tail. Nobody ever made a fuss of him, nobody ever paid the slightest attention to him. From my very first day I had stroked him and given him bread from my hand. When I stroked him he stood quietly, looking lovingly at me and gently wagging his tail in token of pleasure. Now, when he had not seen me for some time—me, the first for years who had ever thought of petting him—he would run and look for me among the others, and this time, having found me behind the barracks, he yelped and ran to meet me. I don't know what came over me, but I flung my arms round his head and kissed him; he jumped up with his front paws on my shoulders and began to lick my face. 'So this is the friend fate sends me!' thought I, and after this, every time I returned from work during that first heavy and grievous period, before I went anywhere else I hurried first of all behind the barracks, with Sharik bounding along before me with yelps of joy, put my arms round his head and kissed him again and again, and my heart ached with a feeling that was at once somehow sweet and agonizingly bitter. And I remember that I even took pleasure, as though I were boasting to myself of my own misery, in thinking that here was the only creature now remaining in the whole world who loved me and was attached to me, my sole friend—my faithful dog Sharik.

7. New Acquaintances. Petrov

BUT time passed, and little by little I grew accustomed to my surroundings. With every day the common scenes of my new life became less and less disturbing to me. The events, the surroundings, the people—my eyes had somehow grown accustomed to them. To reconcile myself to this life was impossible, but it was long past time for me to accept it as an accomplished fact. All the misapprehensions that still remained in me I buried as deep inside myself as I could. The fiercely curious glances of the other convicts no longer rested on me so frequently, nor followed me with such deliberate impudence. They also, apparently, had grown used to the sight of me, and I was very glad of it. Already I went about the prison as though I were at home, knew my place on the planks, and had even, so it seemed, grown accustomed to things I had thought I should never get used to in a lifetime. Regularly every week I went to have half my head shaved. Every Saturday, during the rest period, we were called out in turn from the prison to the guardhouse for this purpose, and anyone who was not already shaved had to suffer for it, since there barbers from the battalions soaped our heads with cold water and pitilessly scraped them with the bluntest of razors; my blood still runs cold when I remember what torture it was. A remedy was soon found, however: Akim Akimovich pointed out to me a prisoner in the Military division who made it his trade to shave anybody who wanted it with his own razor for a copeck, and in this way made a little money. Many of the prisoners went to him in order to escape the official barbers, and yet they were not over-soft. Our prison barber was called 'the major', I do not know why, and I am quite unable to say in what way he could remind anybody of the major. Now, as I write this, the figure of this 'major' rises before me, a tall, lanky, silent fellow, rather stupid, always pre-occupied with his calling and invariably with a strop in his hand, on which day and night he was always setting his razor, already whetted to an impossible degree; he seemed completely absorbed in his occupation and obviously accepted it as his life's work. He was, indeed, highly delighted when his razor was keen and somebody came to be shaved: his lather was warm, his hand light, his shave velvety. He evidently enjoyed and was proud of his art, and carelessly accepted the copeck he had earned as though it were indeed a question of art and not of copecks. Aristov once caught it hot from the major when, sneaking to him about the prison, he mentioned the name of our prison barber and carelessly called him 'major'. The real major was wild with fury and most bitterly affronted. 'Don't you know, you miserable rascal, what a major is?' he shouted, his lips flecked with foam, as he settled accounts with Aristov in his usual way; 'don't you understand what a major is? Now along comes some scoundrel of a convict and you dare call him major to my face, in my presence! . . .' Only Aristov could ever have got on with such a man.

From the very first day of my life in prison I had begun to dream of freedom. Calculating when my term would come to an end became my favourite occupation, in a thousand different forms and applications. I could not even think of anything under a different aspect, and I am sure that every-one deprived of liberty for a fixed term must behave in the same way. I do not know whether the other convicts thought and made calculations as I did, but the astonishing levity of their hopes struck me from the first. The dreams of the man who is caged and deprived of freedom are quite differ-ent from those of the man who is alive in the real sense. The free man has his hopes, of course (for a change in his lot, for instance, or the successful completion of an enterprise), but he lives and acts; real life with all its chances and changes wholly engrosses him. It is different for the prisoner. He also has, let us concede, a life—prison life, convict life; but whoever he is and for whatever term he has been confined, he is definitely and instinctively unable to accept his fate as something positive and final, as a part of real life. Every convict feels that he is *not in his own home*, but as it were on a visit. He looks on twenty years as if it were two, and is quite confident that even at fifty-five, when he emerges from prison, he will still be the youth he is now, at thirty-five. 'I can still live!' he thinks, and obstinately banishes all doubts and other tiresome thoughts. Even those sent away for an indefinite term, those of the Special Class, even they sometimes calculated that at any moment, suddenly, there might come an order from St. Petersburg: 'Send him to Nerchinsk, to the mines, for a fixed number of years.' That would be capital: to begin with, it was practically six months' march to Nerchinsk, and marching in a convoy was infinitely to be preferred to sitting in prison!; and after-wards to serve out one's term in Nerchinsk, and then . . . And such calculations would be made by a grey-headed old man!

In Tobolsk I saw men who were chained to the wall. They sat there at the end of a chain some seven feet long; their bunks were there too. They had been chained for some exceptionally horrible deed, committed after they had come to Siberia. They were there for five years, or some of them for ten. For the most part they were cut-throats and bandits. I saw only one of them who seemed to be a gentleman; he had been at one time in one of the services. His speech was a softly submissive lisp; he had a rather sweet smile. He showed us his chain and what was the most comfortable way to lie down on the bunk. A caged bird must be exactly like him, in its own way. The behaviour of all of them was generally tame and subdued, and they seemed content; nevertheless, each one of them was anxious to complete his term as soon as possible. And why? For this reason: that then he would emerge from the foul and stifling cell with its low brick vaulting and walk about the prison yard, and . . . that is all. He would never be allowed to leave the prison again. He himself knew that a man released from the chain is kept in prison ever after, until he dies, and in fetters. He knew it, and yet he was painfully eager to finish his time on the chain as quickly as might be. Indeed, without that desire, could he stay five or six years chained up without dying or going out of his mind? Would any man endure it?

I felt that work might be my salvation, improve my health and strengthen my body. Constant mental unrest, nervous exasperation and the suffocating air of the barrack might completely destroy me. Let me be more often in the open air, get tired every day, grow used to carrying heavy weights —and at least I shall save myself, thought I, I shall grow strong, I shall come out healthy, lively, well, not old. I was not mistaken; work and activity were very beneficial to me. I watched, horrified, one of my fellow prisoners (a gentleman) wasting away in the prison like a candle. He had entered it with me, still young, brisk and handsome, and he left it broken down, grey-haired, crippled, and asthmatic. No, thought I, as I looked at him, I want to live, and I will live. On the other hand, at first I aroused the wrath of the other convicts by my liking for work, and for a long time I suffered their jeering contempt and mockery. But I took no notice of anybody, but set off briskly for the place, for example, where I could calcine and grind gypsum—one of the first crafts I learned. It was easy work. The Engineer authorities were ready as far as possible to lighten the labours of the gentlemen, which was not an indulgence, however, but mere justice. It would be a strange thing to exact from a man with only half the strength, who had never done any manual work, the same task as was allotted to a real labourer. But this 'pampering' was not invariable, or was carried out as it were by stealth; it must be kept strictly from the direct notice of the authorities. Fairly often heavy work had to be done, and then, of course, the gentlemen suffered twice as much fatigue as the other workers. There were usually assigned to the gypsum three or four men, the old or the weak, among whom we, of course, were num-bered; and in addition a real worker who knew the trade was attached to the party. For many years together it was usually the same one, Almazov, a dour, lean, swarthy man, no longer young, unsociable and morose. He had a deep contempt for us. He was, besides, a man of few words, so few that he could not even be bothered to grumble at us. The shed in which the gypsum was burnt and ground also stood on the waste land of the steep river bank. In winter, especially when the day was overcast, the river and the distant opposite bank were a depressing sight. There was something mournful and heart-rending in the wild and desolate landscape. But it was almost more melancholy when the sun sparkled on the endless white sheet of snow; oh, only to flee away into that steppe that began on the other side of the river and stretched in an unbroken carpet fifteen hundred versts to the south! Almazov usually set about the work grimly and silently; we felt a sort of shame at not being able to give him any real assistance, and he purposely managed alone, purposely did not ask us for any help, as if he wanted us to feel the full extent of our guilt and suffer remorse for our uselessness. But it was only a matter of firing the furnace to calcine the gypsum which was put inside it, and quantities of which we used to cart for him. On the next day, when the gypsum was thoroughly calcined, we began to unload it from the kiln. Each of us took a heavy beetle, filled his own trough with gypsum, and set about pounding it. It was very pleasant work. The brittle gypsum was quickly converted into a shining white dust, crumbling with great neatness and ease. We flourished our heavy beetles and made such a crackling as our ears found delightful. We would grow very weary at last, and at the same time we felt easier; our cheeks flushed and our blood coursed faster. Even Almazov would begin to regard us leniently, as one looks at little children; he would light his pipe with an indulgent air, and yet if he were forced to speak he could not help grumbling. He was always like that, however, but I think that in reality he was a kind man.

Another kind of work to which I was assigned was turning the lathe in the carpenters' workshop. The lathe was large and heavy. It required no small effort to turn it, especially when the turner (one of the Engineer tradesmen) was making something in the nature of a banister or the legs of a big table for the furniture of some government official, which needed wood almost as thick as a beam. In such a case, it was beyond one man's strength to turn the lathe and two were usually sent, I and another former nobleman, Boguslavsky. For many years, whenever there was anything to be turned, the work was always entrusted to us. Boguslavsky was a man still young, of puny and feeble physique, with a weak chest. He had come to the prison about a year before me, together with two of his friends—an old man, who throughout all his prison term was constantly praying to God, day and night (for which he was greatly respected by the convicts), and who died while I was there, and another, still very young, fresh, strong, ruddy, and hardy, who had supported Boguslavsky (whom half a stage exhausted) for seven hundred versts together on the march. The friendship between them was a sight to see. Boguslavsky was a man of excellent education and noble and generous character, but spoiled and ravaged by illness. We tackled the lathe together and it took both of us to manage it. This work gave me splendid exercise.

I also particularly liked clearing away snow. This usually took place after a storm and was of fairly frequent occurrence in the winter. After a snow-storm lasting all day and all night, one building would be covered half-way up the windows and another might be almost completely buried. Then, when the storm had ceased and the sun had come out, we would be driven out in large numbers, sometimes everybody in the prison, to clear away the snow from the government buildings. Each man was given a spade, and all of us together a task, which was sometimes of such magnitude that one must marvel that it could be accomplished at all, and everybody set to work amicably. The powdery, newly fallen snow, lightly frozen on top, was easily lifted by the spade in great lumps, which changed into sparkling powder as we flung them into the air. The spades cut into the white mass, glittering in the sun. The prisoners were nearly always merry over this work. The fresh winter air and the movement excited them. Everybody became more cheerful; there were laughter, shouting, witticisms. Games of snowball were started; not, of course, without bringing outcries against the mirth and high spirits from the solemn and disapproving ones, and the general gaiety usually ended in oaths and curses.

Little by little I began to enlarge the circle of my acquaintances. I was not, however, even thinking of making acquaintances: I was still uneasy, depressed, and mistrustful. My acquaintanceships began of their own accord. One of the first who began to visit me was the prisoner Petrov. I say *visit*, and I lay particular stress on the word: Petrov lived in the Special Class in the barrack farthest removed from mine. There could have been, on the face of it, no links at all between us: we had, and could have, positively nothing in common. Yet, nevertheless, during this first period, Petrov seemed to consider it his duty to drop in on me in my barrack practically every day or to stop me when, in leisure hours, I used to make for the back of the barracks where I could be as far as possible from all eyes. At first I found this disagreeable. But soon he managed to make his visits pleasant to me, in spite of the fact that he was not a particularly talkative or communicative man. In appearance he was rather short, strongly built, neat, fidgety; he had a rather pleasant, pale face with wide cheekbones, a bold glance, small white teeth set close together, and a perpetual pinch of snuff inside his lower lip. Many convicts had this habit of putting tobacco inside their lips. He seemed younger than he was. He was forty, but he did not look more than thirty. He talked to me with extraordinary lack of constraint and behaved in every respect as to an equal, that is with extreme decency and delicacy. If he noticed, for example, that I was seeking solitude, he would at once leave me, after talking for a minute or two, and he always thanked me for listening to him, a thing which it is needless to say he never did with anybody else in the whole prison. It is curious that our relations continued the same, not only during the first days but for several years, and hardly ever became closer, although he was really devoted to me. Even now I cannot decide exactly what he wanted from me or what made him come to me every day. Although later he did occasionally steal from me, yet his thefts were always somehow inadvertent; he scarcely ever asked me for money; therefore it was not for money or from any interested motive that he came.

I do not know, either, why it always appeared to me that he was not living in the prison with me at all, but somewhere else a long way away, in the town, and that he had merely dropped in to the prison in passing, to learn the news, pay me a visit, and see how we were getting on. He was always in a hurry, as though he had left somebody somewhere who was still waiting for him, or as though there were something he had not finished doing somewhere. For all that, he did not give the impression of being flustered. His glance, also, seemed strange: it was intent, with a shade of boldness and some mockery, but he seemed to gaze into space through the object he was looking at, as if he were trying to distinguish something else in the distance, beyond what was in front of his eyes. This gave him an absent-minded look. Sometimes I made a point of looking to see where Petrov went when he left me; where was it he was being waited for? But he hurried away from me into one of the barracks or a kitchen, sat down beside one of a group who were talking together, listened carefully to them, sometimes joined in the conversation himself, quite warmly, even, and then suddenly broke off and was silent. But whether he talked or sat silent, it was plain that it was merely in passing; somewhere he had something to do, they were waiting for him. The strangest of all was that he never did have anything to do, of any kind; he lived in utter idleness (except for the compulsory work, of course). He did not know any trade and almost never had any money. But neither did he trouble much about money. And what did he talk to me about? His conversation was as strange as himself. He would see, for example, that I was going somewhere behind the barracks, alone, and would suddenly turn sharply in my direction. He always walked quickly and turned abruptly. He would walk up to me, but would somehow give the effect of running.

'Good evening.'

'Good evening.'

'Am I disturbing you?'

'No.'

'Well, look, I wanted to ask you about Napoleon.* I suppose he's a relative of that other one in 1812?' (Petrov had been to a school for soldiers' sons and was literate.)

'Yes, he is.'

'Then how is it he's a President, as they say?'

He always asked his questions in a quick, abrupt manner, as though he must find out the answers as soon as possible. It was as if he were inquiring about some very important matter which would not brook the least delay.

I explained the President's position and added that he might perhaps soon be Emperor.

'How is that?'

I explained this also, as well as I could. Petrov listened attentively, even inclining his ear in my direction, and with ready comprehension and complete understanding.

'Hm . . . And here is something I wanted to ask you, Alexander Petrovich: is it true, as they say, that there are apes whose arms hang down to their heels and who are as big as the tallest man?'

'Yes, there are some.'

'What are they like?'

I explained as much as I knew of this, also.

'And where do they live?'

'In warm countries. There are some on the island of Sumatra.'

'That's in America, isn't it? Don't they say that the people there go about head downwards?'

'Not head downwards. And you are talking about the antipodes now.' I explained what America was and, as far as I could, what the antipodes were. He listened as attentively as though he had come running to me on purpose to learn about the antipodes.

'Ah! But last year I read about the Countess Lavallière;* Arafeyev brought back the book from the adjutant's. Is that all true or just—made up? It's a book by Dumas.'

'It's made up, of course.'

'Well, good-bye. Thank you.'

And Petrov disappeared; practically speaking, we never talked in any other way than this.

I made some inquiries about him. Miretsky, when he learnt of this acquaintanceship, tried to put me on my guard. He told me that many of the convicts inspired him with horror, especially at first, during his early days in the prison, but not one of them, not even Gazin, produced so dire an effect on him as this Petrov.

'He is the most desperate and fearless of all the prisoners,' said Miretsky. 'He is capable of anything, and nothing can stop him if he has taken some whim into his head. He would cut your throat, if the fancy took him, just cut your throat, without scruple and without remorse. I really don't think he is in his right mind.'

This unfavourable judgement strongly interested me. But Miretsky did not seem able to account for this feeling on his part. And it is a strange thing: after this I knew Petrov for several years, and talked to him nearly every day; all this time he was sincerely attached to me (although I decidedly do not know why),—and all through those years, although he behaved very prudently and did nothing at all that was terrible, yet every time I looked at him or talked to him, I was convinced that Miretsky was right, and that Petrov might very well be the most desperate, the most fearless of men, and one who knew no restraint. But I also am unable to account for thinking so.

I will remark, however, that this Petrov was the same man who planned to kill the major, once when he was summoned for corporal punishment, and the major 'escaped by a miracle', as the convicts said, leaving just before the punishment began. Another time, before he was sent to prison, his colonel struck him during drill. He had probably been beaten many times before, but this time he refused to put up with it and stabbed the colonel, openly, in broad daylight, before all the troops drawn up in their lines. (I do not, however, know all the details of his history; he never told it to me.) All these, of course, were simply explosions or eruptions in which the whole of his nature revealed itself in a flash. They were, all the same, extremely rare. He was really sensible and even meek. There were passions hidden in him, and they were hot and violent, but the glowing coals were kept covered with ashes and only smouldered quietly. I never saw any hint of bombast or vanity in him, for example, as I did in others. He rarely quarrelled, but on the other hand he was not particularly friendly with anybody, except perhaps Sirotkin, and with him only when he needed him. Once, however, I saw him seriously angry. There was something or other he had not been given; he had been the victim of some unfairness in sharing out. A powerfully athletic prisoner from the Civil division, Basil Antonov, a tall, bad-tempered, quarrelsome, sarcastic person, and no coward, was arguing with him. They had been shouting at one another for some time, and I thought the matter would most probably end in the exchange of a few punches, since Petrov sometimes, though very rarely, would brawl and scuffle like the lowest convict. But this time it happened differently: Petrov suddenly went pale, his lips trembled and turned bluish, he began to breathe heavily. He stood up and slowly, very slowly, with his quiet, barefooted walk (he liked to go barefoot in the summer), went over to Antonov. There was an instant hush all over the noisy, shouting barrack; you might have heard a fly buzz. Everybody was waiting to see what would happen. Antonov sprang up to meet him; he was quite white . . . I could not bear it and went out of the barrack. I expected to hear, before I reached the foot of the steps, the cries of a murdered man. But this time, also, the affair came to nothing: Antonov, before Petrov could reach him, hurriedly flung him the disputed article without a word. (It had all been a question of a few pitiful rags.) I need not say that for a couple of minutes Antonov grumbled a few curses, to relieve his mind and for the sake of the proprieties, in proof that he was not completely cowed. But Petrov paid no attention to the oaths and did not trouble to answer them: the affair had not been a contest of bad language, and it had been decided in his favour; he took up his rags and was quite satisfied. A quarter of an hour later he was wandering round the prison as before, with his air of having nothing at all to do, and seemed to be trying to find a conversation of special interest so that he could stick his nose in and listen. Everything seemed to attract his interest and yet somehow he remained for the most part untouched by anything, and simply slouched idly about the prison, drifting to and fro. He might have been compared to a worker, healthy and ready to make the sparks fly, but for the time being without any work to do, who meanwhile sits there waiting and playing with children. Another thing I could not understand was why he stayed in the prison and did not escape. He would not have hesitated to run away if he had had a strong wish to do so. Reason sways people like Petrov only so long as they do not strongly desire something. Then no obstacle on earth can stand between them and their desires. I have no doubt that he could have made a clever escape, baffled all his pursuers and gone without food for a week while he lay hidden somewhere in the forest or among the river-reeds. But he had evidently not yet stumbled upon this idea, or *wholeheartedly* wished it. I never saw any particular power of judgement or any great common sense in him. People like him are born with one idea, which they unconsciously allow, all their lives, to move them hither and thither; thus they drift throughout their lives, until they come across something which wholly answers their desires; then their heads are no more use to them. I wondered sometimes how a man who had killed his commanding officer for striking him could submit so unprotestingly to beatings with us. He was sometimes flogged, when he was caught with vodka. (Like all the other convicts without a trade he sometimes undertook the smuggling of vodka.) But he submitted to the beatings as though he fully consented to them, as though, that is, he recognized that he deserved them; otherwise nothing would have made him submit, even if his life had been at stake. I was astounded, too, when he robbed me, in spite of his obvious attachment to me. This weakness came upon him in fits and starts, as it were. Thus, he stole my bible, which I had given him simply to carry from one place to another. It was only a few steps, but he managed to find a purchaser on the way, sold it, and immediately drank the money. Probably he badly wanted a drink, and whatever he badly wanted *must* be procured. Here was a man who would murder somebody for twenty-five copecks to buy half a pint of vodka, although another time he would let him pass even if he had a thousand roubles. In the evening he himself told me of the theft, without either embarrassment or remorse, quite calmly, as though it were the most ordinary occurrence. I made an attempt to scold him soundly; I was grieved about my bible. He listened patiently and indeed meekly, agreed that the bible was a very useful book, was sincerely sorry that now I no longer had one, but showed no regret at having taken it; he looked so calm that I immediately stopped scolding him. He had put up with the scolding, arguing, probably, that since he could not commit such an action without being rated for it, he had better (he thought) allow me to relieve my feelings and have my fun by abusing him, but that in reality it was all nonsense, such nonsense that a serious man would be ashamed even to say such things. It seemed to me that in general he treated me like a child, almost like a baby, incapable of understanding the very simplest things. If I talked to him, for instance, of anything but the sciences or books, he indeed answered me, but only, as it were, out of politeness, and confining himself to very short replies. I often asked myself what there could be for him in all those bookish subjects about which he usually questioned me. It sometimes happened that I caught myself stealing a sidelong glance at him to see whether he was not poking fun at me. But no; he usually listened seriously and attentively, though only fairly so, and this last sometimes annoyed me a little.

He put his questions definitely and precisely, but he seemed to accept the information I gave him without surprise and even absent-mindedly . . . It seemed to me, too, that as far as I was concerned he had decided, without troubling his head much about it, that it was impossible to talk to me in the same way as to other people, that I should not understand anything at all outside books, and indeed that I was incapable of doing so, so that there was no point in worrying me with it.

I am convinced that he was even fond of me and I found this very surprising. Whether it was that he looked on me as somebody immature, not fully grown-up, or whether he felt for me that special sort of sympathy which every strong creature instinctively feels for a weaker (having accepted me as such), I do not know. And although it did not prevent him from robbing me, yet I am certain that even in the act of stealing from me he was sorry for me. 'Well, well!' thought he, perhaps, with his hand in my pockets, 'what a man! He can't even take care of his own things!' But I think he liked me for it, too. He himself said to me once, out of the blue, that I was 'too good-hearted', and: 'You are so very innocent, so innocent that it's pitiful. Only don't take offence, Alexander Petrovich,' he added after a minute; 'I only said it out of kindness, you know.'

With such people it sometimes happens that they stand out large and clear in their true colours at the moment of some sudden general movement or upheaval and thus attain their full activity at one bound. They are not orators and cannot be instigators or leaders; but they are the chief executives and the first to act. They begin simply enough, without any special fuss, but on the other hand they are the first to overleap the main obstacle, without hesitation or fear, rushing straight into danger—and the others rush after them, blindly, to the last ditch, where they usually lose their very heads. I do not believe that Petrov will come to a good end; he will perish all in a moment, and if he has not yet gone down to destruction it is because his hour has not struck. Who knows, however? perhaps he will live to be grey-haired and die peacefully of old age, still drifting aimlessly hither and thither. But I think Miretsky was right when he said Petrov was the most desperate man in the whole prison.

8. Desperate People. Luke

IT is difficult to say much about desperate characters; in prison, as elsewhere, there were rather few of them. One man, perhaps, would be terrible in appearance, and you might have regard to the tales told about another and keep out of his way. Some unaccountable feeling made me at first avoid all these people. Later, my way of looking at even the most terrible murderer changed in many respects. One man who had not committed murder might be more terrible than another who had been sent to exile for six murders. It was difficult to form even the most elementary idea of some crimes, there was so much that was strange in their execution. I say this because among our common people some murders derive from the most astonishing causes. There exists, for example, and in very large numbers, the following type of murderer: this man lives quietly and meekly. His lot is bitter but he endures it. Let us suppose he is a peasant farmer, a house serf, a tradesman, or a soldier. Suddenly something snaps inside him; he can stand it no longer and sticks a knife into his enemy and persecutor. Now begins the strange part: the man suddenly runs temporarily amok. His first killing was of his enemy, his persecutor; that was criminal but understandable: there was a motive; but afterwards he kills not enemies but chance passers-by, kills for amusement, because of a harsh word or a look, for a string of beads, or, simply: 'Get out of the way and don't let me catch you; I'm coming!' It is as if the man were intoxicated or in the grip of a raging fever. As if, having once transgressed the boundary that has been sacred for him, he begins to revel in the fact that for him there is no longer anything sacred; as if he had been carried away by overleaping at one bound all the restrictions of legality and authority, tasting the sweets of the most unbridled and infinite liberty, and knowing the pleasure of those pangs of terror of himself which it is impossible for him not to feel. He knows, in addition, that a terrible punishment awaits him. All this resembles, perhaps, the feeling of a man who, from a high tower, strains his eyes into the depths beneath his feet until finally he would gladly fling himself down, as soon as possible, and there an end! And all this may happen to the tamest and hitherto most unremarkable of people. Some of them even make a parade of this state. The more subdued they were previously, the more strongly they are moved to swagger and try to inspire terror now. They relish the terror and enjoy even the disgust they arouse in others. They affect a kind of *desperation*, and a man so 'desperate' is sometimes eager for punishment, eager to have *his fate decided*, because at last it becomes difficult for him to bear the weight of this assumed *desperation*. It is curious that this mood, this affectation, endures right to the scaffold and then is sharply cut off, just as though this stage were formally appointed, with specific rules laid down beforehand to this effect. Now the man suddenly becomes humble, effaces himself, goes as limp as an old rag. On the scaffold he whimpers and begs the people for forgiveness. He loses all control, and looking at him you see such a snivelling, slavering, and abject figure that you are astounded: 'Can this really be the same man who murdered five or six people?'

Some, of course, are slow to grow tame even in prison. They still preserve a certain swagger, a certain braggadocio: 'Look,' they seem to say, 'I am not at all what you suppose; I'm a "six-victim" man.' But in the end they become tame enough. Sometimes, indeed, they will distract themselves by recalling their daring exploit, the intoxication they knew once in their lives, when they were 'desperate'; and they dearly love, if only they can find a simpleton, to preen themselves before him, boasting and recounting their deeds and pretending to be unaware that he is aching to tell his own story. 'Look,' they say, 'what sort of man I was!'

And with what subtlety they preserve their self-esteem, how indolently off-hand their story sometimes is! What studied conceit is manifested in the tone, in every word of the narrator! And where did these simple people learn all this?

Once during these first days, lying, unoccupied and mournful, on my planks throughout one long evening, I listened to one of these stories and, through inexperience, took the teller for some terrible giant of evil, some incredible man of iron, and this at a time when I was almost ready to laugh at Petrov. The theme of the story was how he, Luke Kuzmich, for no other reason than his own amusement, had *laid out* a certain major. This Luke Kuzmich was that same young, thin little prisoner from our barrack, with the sharp little nose, the Ukrainian, whom I have already mentioned. He was really a Russian, but he had been born in the south; he was, I think, a house serf. There was really something sharp and overbearing about him: 'the bird is small, but his talons are sharp.' But prisoners instinctively see through people. Very few had any respect for him, or, as they say in the prison, 'very few had any respect to him.' He was terribly conceited. This evening he was sitting on a bunk sewing a shirt. Making shirts was his trade. Near him sat a young fellow of dull and limited mind, but good-natured and amiable, his neighbour on the plank-shelf, a tall and thickset prisoner named Kobylin. Because of their proximity, Luke often quarrelled with him, and generally treated him despotically and with mocking condescension, which Kobylin in his simplicity hardly even noticed. He was knitting a woollen stocking and listening unemotionally. Luke was telling his story in a rather loud and penetrating voice. He was anxious for everybody to hear him, although he pretended that, on the contrary, he was talking for Kobylin's ear alone.

'So, brother, they sent me away from our parts', he began as he stitched away, 'to K——,* for vagrancy, I mean.'

'When was that, a long time ago?' asked Kobylin.

'Well, it will be two years come next pea-harvest. Well, when we got to K——, they shoved me in jail there for a bit. Well, I looks around, and there was about twelve others in there with me, all Ukrainians, tall, strong, strapping chaps like bullocks. And so soft: the grub was bad, and the major did what he liked with them, just to suit his lordship's *pervenience*' (Luke mangled the word on purpose). 'I sits there one day, and then another, and I sees they're a cowardly lot. "Why", says I, "do you give in so easy to that fool?"

' "Just you try talking to him yourself!" says they, sniggering like. I says no more. And there was one fair comic Little Russian there, mates,' he added suddenly, abandoning Kobylin and addressing us at large. 'He was telling us all about his trial, and what he said to the judge, and crying fit to break his heart; said he'd left a wife and kids at home. And him a grown man, a big fatty as grey as a badger! "I says to 'im," he says, "no, I never! And that there old devil just goes on writing and writing. Ah, says I to myself, and if he never draws breath again, I'd be fair glad! And there he sits, writing away; and what he were writing! . . . And that were the finish of I!" Give me a bit of thread, Vasya; this prison stuff 's rotten . . .'

'This is from the bazaar,' answered Vasya, giving him the thread.

'Ours from the prison sewing-shop is better. The other day we sent our old soldier for some, and which wretched woman do you think he got it from?' went on Luke, threading his needle in the light.

'His old friend, of course.'

'Of course, his old friend.'

'Well, what next, what about the major?' asked the completely forgotten Kobylin.

This was all Luke needed. He did not, however, resume his story at once, and even seemed not to be favouring Kobylin with his attention. Calmly he straightened his thread, calmly and lazily crossed his legs beneath him, and at length began to talk.

'Well, at last I got my Little Russians worked up and they asked to see the major. First thing in the morning I had borrowed a knife from my neighbour and hidden it, just in case. The major was in a furious temper. Along he comes. "Now," says I, "don't funk it, mates!" But their hearts were in their boots and they were simply shaking with fright. In runs the major; he was drunk. "Who is it? What's all this? I'm tsar here, and I'm God as well!"

'When he says, "I'm the tsar and I'm God," I steps out,' went on Luke, 'and I had the knife in my sleeve.

' "No," says I, "your honour"—and all the time I was getting closer and closer,—"how can you possibly be," says I, "your honour? How can you be tsar and God?"

' "Ah, so it's you, it's you, is it?" shouts the major. "Trouble-maker!"

' "No," says I (closer and closer all the time)—, "no," says I, "your honour, as may be known and familiar to you yourself, our God, the omnipotent and omnipresent, is one," says I. "And our tsar is one, appointed by God Himself to rule over us. He, your honour," says I, "is our sovereign. And you," says I, "your honour, are only a major yet, and in command of us, your honour, by the tsar's gracious mercy," says I, "and your own deserving."

' "How-how-how-how!" He was absolutely yapping, he couldn't talk, he was fair choking. He was thunderstruck.

' "Like this," says I; and I jumps on him sudden and

slides that knife right into his stomach. It was as easy as easy. He rolls over, and his legs jerk a bit, and that's all. I threw the knife away.

'"Look at him, mates," says I. "Pick him up now." ' . . .

Here I shall digress. Unfortunately, such expressions as 'I am tsar, and I am God as well', and many others like it, were in not infrequent use, long ago, among many commandants. It must be acknowledged, however, that there are very few such commandants left, and perhaps they have disappeared entirely. I must remark, also, that those who paraded such expressions, and took pleasure in parading them, were for the most part commandants who had risen from the ranks. Officer's rank seems to turn their inner selves, and their heads as well, upside down. After they have groaned under the yoke for a long time and worked through all the grades of subordination, they suddenly behold themselves officers, commandants, gentlemen, and from inexperience and in the first flush of triumph, they have an exaggerated notion of their own power and importance; but only, of course, in relation to the ranks subordinate to them. With their superiors they display as before a servility which is completely unnecessary and even distasteful to many superior officers. Some of these crawlers, almost with tears in their eyes, hasten to explain to their commanding officers that they have risen from the ranks, although they are officers now, and that 'they will always remember their place'. But in relation to inferior ranks they are almost absolute dictators. It is, of course, doubtful whether there now remain many, or indeed whether even one could be found, who would cry, 'I am tsar, I am God.' Nevertheless, I will observe that nothing so irritates prisoners, and all inferiors in general, as expressions of this kind coming from superiors. This self-glorification, this exaggerated opinion of their own impunity, breeds hatred in the meekest of men and exhausts his patience. Fortunately, all this is now almost entirely a thing of the past, and even in the old days offenders were sternly proceeded against by the authorities. Several instances of this are within my knowledge.

In general, every kind of contemptuous negligence or show of squeamish reluctance in dealing with them is exasperating to subordinates. Some people think, for example, that if a prisoner is well fed and well cared for, and everything is done according to the law, that is the end of the matter. This is another delusion. Every man, whoever he may be, and however low he may have fallen, requires, if only instinctively and unconsciously, that respect be given to his dignity as a human being. The prisoner is aware that he is a prisoner, an outcast, and he knows his position in respect to the authorities; but no brands, no fetters, can make him forget that he is a man. And since he is a human being, it follows that he must be treated as a human being. God knows, treatment as a human being may transform into a man again even one in whom the image of God has long been eclipsed. These 'unfortunates' must be treated in as human a way as possible. This is their joy and their salvation. I have met good and noble commandants. I have seen the effect they have produced on these fallen ones. A few friendly words—and for the prisoners it was almost a moral resurrection. They rejoiced like children and like children they began to love. I must mention one other strange thing: prisoners do not like too familiar and *too* kindly an attitude of the authorities towards them. They want to respect those in charge of them, and this somehow prevents them from doing so. It pleases the prisoner that, for example, his commandant should wear orders, that he should have a good presence, that he should be in the good graces of some higher authority, that he should be severe, imposing, and just, and that he should guard his dignity. Prisoners very much like a man of this kind; he both keeps his own dignity and does not offend theirs, and consequently all goes well and harmoniously.

. . . . .

'I suppose they scorched your hide for that?' remarked Kobylin unemotionally.

'Hm . . . Scorched it, mate, they scorched it all right. Aley, hand me the scissors! Why, mates, isn't there a *maidan* today?'

'All the money's gone on drink,' said Vasya. 'If it hadn't, perhaps there would have been one.'

'If! If costs a hundred roubles in Moscow,' remarked Luke.

'How many did they give you altogether, for everything?' began Kobylin again.

'They gave me, my dear friend, a hundred and five. And I'll tell you what, lads, they all but killed me,' observed Luke, again abandoning Kobylin. 'This is how that hundred and five turned out. They took me out in full parade. And until then I hadn't ever known the whip. People had rolled up in masses, the whole town had come running; they were going to punish a desperate criminal, a murderer, that was why! And how stupid all those people were, I simply don't know how to tell you. Timoshka took off my clothes and made me lie down and he shouts: "Hold tight, I'm going to flay you!" and I waits for what's coming. When he lays it on the first time, I tries to let out a yell, and I opens my mouth, but there wasn't a yell in me. My voice had got stuck in my throat. When he hits me the second time, well, believe it or not, I didn't even hear them count "two". And when I came to, I heard them counting seventeen. They took me down from the horse four times after that and gave me half an hour's rest; and they doused me with water. I looks at them, with my eyes bulging out of my head, and, thinks I, "I'm going to die this minute" . . .'

'But you didn't, did you?' asked Kobylin naïvely.

Luke looked him up and down with a glance of the utmost scorn. There was a burst of laughter.

'What a dummy!'

'He's weak in the top story,' remarked Luke, as if repenting of having talked to such a man . . .

'He's touched,' agreed Vasya.

Luke, although he had killed six men, never inspired fear in anybody in the prison, although he perhaps sincerely wished to pass as an awe-inspiring figure . . .

9. Isaiah Fomich. The Bath.
Baklushin's Story

THE feast of Christmas was drawing near. The prisoners looked forward to it with heightened feelings and, watching them, I also began to expect something out of the ordinary. Four days before the holiday we were taken to the bath. In my time, and especially in my first years, prisoners were rarely taken to the bath. Everybody rejoiced and began to make preparations. The time appointed was after dinner, and we no longer worked in these after-dinner periods. The one in our barrack who was most pleased and bustled about the most was Isaiah Fomich Bumstein, a Jewish convict, whom I have mentioned already, in the fourth chapter of my story. He liked to steam himself into a stupor, into insensibility, and now every time that, turning over old memories, I happen to remember our convict bath (which deserves not to be forgotten), there looms up before me in the very foreground of the picture the unforgettable and supremely blissful face of Isaiah Fomich, the companion of my servitude and inhabitant of the same barrack. Lord, how comical, how laughable, that man was! I have already said a few words about his little figure: fiftyish, puny, wrinkled, with horrible brands on his cheeks and forehead, with a skinny, feeble, white body like a plucked chicken's. The expression of his face revealed unwavering, unshakeable self-satisfaction and even beatific happiness. He felt apparently not the slightest regret at having fallen into prison. Since he was a jeweller and there was no other in the town, he was able to spend all his time on jeweller's work for the gentry and official circles of the town. He was even paid something, little though it might be. He wanted for nothing, lived *like a rich man* even, yet was able to save money and lend it, against security and at interest, to the whole prison. He had his own samovar, a good mattress, cups and dinner-ware. The town's Jews did not deny him their protection and friendship. On Saturdays he went, under guard, to the local synagogue (as the law permitted him to do), and he led a very comfortable life, except that he was impatiently awaiting the end of his twelve-year term 'to get married'. There was in him a most comical mingling of *naïveté*, stupidity, sharpness, impudence, artlessness, timidity, boastfulness, and effrontery. It was very strange to me that the other convicts did not laugh at him at all, except when they amused themselves by chaffing him. Isaiah Fomich evidently served as an entertainment and a perpetual diversion for them. 'He is the only one we've got, so hands off Isaiah Fomich,' said the prisoners, and Isaiah Fomich, although he understood what the point was, was plainly proud of his importance, which greatly amused the prisoners. His arrival in the prison had been a humorous affair (it was before my time, but I was told about it). Suddenly one day, towards evening, in a leisure period, the rumour spread through the prison that a Jew had been brought in and was being shaved in the guardroom, and would presently come in. At that time there was not a single Jew in the prison. The prisoners waited impatiently for him and surrounded him as soon as he·entered the gates. The prison sergeant led him into the civil barrack and showed him his place on the planks. In his hands Isaiah Fomich carried a sack which contained the things he had been issued with and his own possessions. He put down the sack, hopped up on to the planks, and sat down with his legs folded beneath him, not daring to raise his eyes to look at anybody. Round him there broke out laughter and witty sallies directed against his Jewish origin. Suddenly a young prisoner, carrying in his hands his extremely ancient, filthy, and torn summer trousers, with some other rags in addition, made his way through the crowd. He sat down beside Isaiah Fomich and tapped him on the shoulder:

'Well, my dear friend, this makes six years that I've been waiting for you. Will you give me a lot of money for them?'

And he spread out in front of him the rags he had brought.

Isaiah Fomich, who had been so overcome with timidity when he entered the prison that he dared not even lift his eyes to the mocking, mutilated, terrible faces crowding closely round him, and had not yet managed to utter a word, saw the pledge, pulled himself together, and began deftly turning the rags with his fingers. He even moved them nearer the light. Everybody waited to see what he would say.

'Well, I suppose you won't give me a silver rouble. But really they would be worth it!' went on the borrower, winking at Isaiah Fomich.

'A silver rouble I couldn't, but seven copecks I might.'

And those were the first words spoken by Isaiah Fomich in the prison. Everybody simply rocked with laughter.

'Seven! Well, give me seven, then; you've got a bargain! Mind you take care of my pledge; you'll answer for it with your head.'

'With interest at three copecks, that will be ten copecks,' went on the Jew jerkily and in a shaking voice, as he put his hand in his pocket for the money and looked fearfully at the prisoners. He was both horribly scared and at the same time eager to drive a hard bargain.

'By the year, is it, the three copecks interest?'

'No, not by the year, by the month.'

'You're very tight-fisted, Jew. What's your name?'

'Isaiah Fomich.'

'Well, Isaiah Fomich, you'll go a long way here! Goodbye.'

Isaiah Fomich looked the pledge over once more, folded it up, and carefully thrust it into his sack, to the accompaniment of the other prisoners' continuing laughter.

Everybody was really almost fond of him, and nobody was ever offensive to him, although everybody was in his debt. He himself was as unaggressive as a hen, and when he saw the general attitude towards him, even preened himself, but with such artlessly comical effect that he was promptly forgiven. Luke, who had known many Jews in his time, often teased him, quite without malice and simply for fun, exactly as one amuses oneself with a dog, a parrot, a trained animal, or something of that kind. Isaiah Fomich knew this very well, was not in the least offended, and, very skilfully, joked his way out.

'Hi, Jew, I'll run you through!'

'You hit me once, and I'll hit you ten times,' spiritedly answered Isaiah Fomich.

'Scabby Jew!'

'What if I am?'

'Dirty Jew!'

'Perhaps I am. I may be dirty, but I'm rich; I've got money!'

'You sold Christ.'

'So you say.'

'Famous, Isaiah Fomich, you're a brick! Hands off him, he's the only one we've got!' shouted the other prisoners, laughing.

'Hi, Jew, you'll get knouted and sent to Siberia.'

'I'm in Siberia as it is.'

'You'll get sent still farther away.'

'Well, is God there?'

'Of course He is.'

'Well, that's all right; if *Pan* God is there, and money, it's all right anywhere.'

'Bravo, Isaiah Fomich; good for you!' would come the shouts from all round, and Isaiah Fomich, although he could see that they were laughing at him, would brisk up; the general applause gave him evident pleasure and he would begin to sing in a thin little falsetto to the whole barrack: tra-la-la, la-la!—a funny, foolish little tune, the only song (without words) he ever sang during his prison sentence. Afterwards, when he knew me better, he swore to me that it was that same song, to the self-same tune, that the Israelites sang, all six hundred thousand of them, from the greatest to the least, as they crossed the Red Sea, and that every Jew was commanded to sing that tune in the moment of triumph and victory over his enemies.

On the eve of every Sabbath, on Friday evening, people used to come into our barrack from the others in order to watch Isaiah Fomich setting up his 'Sabbath'. Isaiah Fomich was so innocently vain and conceited that this general curiosity also gave him pleasure. With forced and pedantic solemnity he covered his tiny table in a corner, unrolled his scroll, lighted two candles and, muttering some mysterious words, began to invest himself in his ephod ('evod', as he called it). This was a varicoloured garment of woollen material, which he kept carefully put away in his box. On both his arms he fastened phylacteries and on his head, right on his forehead, he bound a certain little wooden box, which made him look as though he had some sort of queer horn projecting from his forehead. After this his prayers began. He read them in a sing-song voice, shouted, spat, turned himself round, made sweeping and comical gestures. All this, of course, was prescribed by his ritual and there was nothing intrinsically comical or strange in it; what was funny was that Isaiah Fomich was, as it were, deliberately acting a part for our benefit and showing off his ritual. Now he would suddenly cover his head with his hands and begin to sob as he read. The sobbing increased and, exhausted, almost with a howl, he stooped his head, crowned with the phylactery, down to his book; but suddenly, in the midst of the most violent sobs, he would begin to laugh and read in a sing-song drawl and a voice now movingly triumphant, now weak from excess of joy. 'Look, he's all worked up!' the other prisoners used to say. I once asked Isaiah Fomich what was the meaning of the sobs and the sudden transition to happiness and bliss. Isaiah Fomich dearly loved such questionings from me. He hastened to explain that the weeping and sobbing represented the idea of the loss of Jerusalem and that the Law prescribed the most violent possible sobbing and beating of the breast at this idea. But at the moment of the very bitterest lamentations he, Isaiah Fomich, must *suddenly*, and as it were unexpectedly, remember (this *suddenly* is also prescribed by the Law) that the return of the Jews to Jerusalem had been prophesied. Then he must immediately give vent to rejoicing, songs, laughter, and recite the prayers in such a way that his voice expressed the greatest possible happiness and his face the greatest triumph and nobility. This *sudden* transition and the absolute necessity of making the transition pleased Isaiah Fomich extremely; he saw in it a particularly clever stroke of art and it was with a boastful air that he told me of this ingenious provision of the Law. Once, at the height of his prayers, the major came into the room, accompanied by the officer on duty and escorted by guards. All the prisoners sprang to attention beside their plank-beds, and only Isaiah Fomich redoubled his cries and grimaces. He knew that his prayers were permitted, that it was impossible to interrupt them and that, shouting thus in front of the major, he was, of course, risking nothing. But he found immense pleasure in pulling his faces in front of the major and playing a part for our benefit. The major went up to within a yard of him: Isaiah Fomich turned his back to his little table and began to chant his triumphant prophecy straight into the major's face, waving his arms meanwhile. Since he was enjoined to display in his face at this moment an extraordinary degree of happiness and nobility, he promptly did so, screwing up his eyes in a somewhat peculiar fashion, smiling and nodding his head towards the major. The major was dumbfounded; but at last, snorting with laughter, he called him a fool to his face and walked away, and Isaiah Fomich's cries were intensified. An hour later, when he was having supper, I asked him: 'What if the major had been angry, as his stupidity might have made him be?'

'What major?'

'How do you mean, what major? Didn't you see him?'

'No.'

'But he was standing straight in front of you, not two feet away.'

But Isaiah Fomich seriously assured me that he had positively not seen the major and that at that point in those prayers of his he fell into a kind of trance and saw and heard absolutely nothing of what went on around him.

I can see Isaiah Fomich as if he were here now, idling about the barracks on Saturdays without occupation, as he used to do, trying with all his might to do nothing, as the Law prescribes for the Sabbath. What impossible tales he told me every time he returned from the synagogue, what unlikely news and rumours from St. Petersburg he brought back with him, assuring me that he had them from his Jewish friends and that they had them at first hand!

But I have talked too much about Isaiah Fomich.

In the whole of the town there were only two public baths. The first, which was kept by a Jew, was divided into private rooms, for which the charge was fifty copecks each, and was intended for personages of the highest social circles. The other bath was principally for the common people; it was ancient, dirty, and cramped, and it was to this bath that our prison was taken. The day was frosty and sunny; the prisoners were overjoyed merely to be going outside the fortress and seeing the town. The joking and laughter were unceasing all the way. A whole platoon of soldiers escorted us with loaded rifles, to the wonder of all the town. In the bath we were divided into two relays; the second waited in the cold ante-room while the first bathed, as was inevitable owing to the smallness of the bath-house. But even so, the bath was so crowded that it was difficult to imagine how even half of us could find room in it. Petrov remained beside me; he had come hurrying up to help me, without any invitation from me, and he even offered to wash me. Together with Petrov, another prisoner volunteered to help me— Baklushin, from the Special Class, whom we called the Pioneer, and whom I have referred to before as being the most cheerful and good-hearted of the prisoners, as indeed he was. I was already slightly acquainted with him. Petrov even helped me to undress, since, not being used to it, I was taking a long time and it was cold in the ante-room, almost as cold as outside. It is, by the way, very difficult for a convict to undress, unless he has fully learnt the art. To begin with, he must be able quickly to untie his 'under-fetters'. These are made of leather, about six inches wide, and are put on immediately over the underclothes, under the iron ring which goes round the leg. A pair of under-fetters costs not less than sixty copecks in silver, yet nevertheless every convict procures them for himself, at his own expense, of course, because it is impossible to walk without them. The iron ring of the fetters does not closely encircle the leg, and a finger can be inserted between it and the leg; thus the iron strikes against the leg and rubs it, and in one day the prisoner without under-fetters would contrive to rub his skin into sores. But taking off the under-fetters is not really difficult. It is harder to take off the underclothes from beneath the fetters. This is quite an acrobatic feat. To take off the lower garment from, let us say, the left leg, one must first push it between the leg and the ring; then, when the leg is free of it, put it back through the same ring; then everything taken off the left leg must be thrust through the ring on the right leg;

and then everything that has been pushed down through the right ring must again be pulled through towards oneself. It is the same story again when it comes to putting on fresh garments. The novice has difficulty even in guessing how to set about it. We were first taught all this at Tobolsk by the prisoner Korenev, a former bandit chief, who had been confined five years on a chain. But the prisoners grew used to it and managed without the slightest trouble. I gave Petrov a few copecks to procure soap and wisps of bast; it is true that the prisoners were officially issued with soap, one piece to each man, a piece as big as a two-copeck coin, and about as thick as the slices of cheese served at evening parties as *zakuski* in middle-class households. Soap was sold there in the ante-room, together with *sbiten*,[1] white loaves, and hot water. Every convict was allowed, by arrangement with the owner of the bath, a single pailful of hot water; anybody who wanted to wash himself a little cleaner could get for two copecks a further pailful, which was handed into the bath itself through an opening in the wall from the ante-room specially made for the purpose. When I was undressed, Petrov guided me, even supporting me with his hand under my elbow, because he noticed that I found it very difficult in fetters. 'You must hold them up, on your calf,' he added, supporting me like a nurse: 'be careful here, there's a step.' I was even a little ashamed; I wanted to assure Petrov that I could go through by myself; but he would not have believed it. He treated me absolutely as though I were a child, a young and clumsy creature whom everybody was in duty bound to assist. Petrov was far from being a servant, anything rather than that; if I had offended him he would have known how to deal with me. I had not promised him money for his services, and he himself had not asked me for any. What then induced him to look after me so?

When we opened the door into the bath itself, I thought

---

[1] A kind of 'tea' made with berries, fruit, spices, &c., and sweetened with honey. [*Tr.*]

we had come into Hell. Imagine a room some twelve paces
in length and the same in breadth, into which was packed
what might perhaps be upwards of a hundred men, and was
certainly eighty at the very least, since the prisoners had
been divided into only two relays and something like two
hundred of us in all had come to the bath. Steam that half
blinded the eyes, soot, filth, a press so thick that there was
nowhere to put one's foot down. I took fright and would
have turned back, but Petrov encouraged me to go on.
Somehow, with enormous difficulty, we squeezed a way
through to the benches, over the heads of the men squatting
on the floor, so that we had to ask them to stoop to one side
to make it possible for us to get through. But all the places on
the benches were occupied. Petrov declared that we must
buy a place, and immediately began to bargain with a
prisoner whose place was near the opening in the wall. For
a copeck he relinquished his place, and at once received the
money from Petrov, who had had the foresight to bring it
with him into the bath and was carrying it clenched in his
fist; then he immediately whipped under the bench, directly
beneath my place, where it was hot and dirty and where the
sticky moisture accumulated to the depth of almost half
a finger. But even under the benches all the space was full;
people swarmed there also. On the whole floor there was
not a space as big as the palm of one's hand that was not
occupied by prisoners, sitting hunched up and splashing
water over themselves from their pails. Others stood upright
among them, holding their pails in their hands, and washed
themselves standing up; the dirty water trickled from them
straight on to the shaven heads of those who sat beneath.
On the shelf and all the steps leading up to it sat more men,
huddled together and stooped over, washing. But they
washed little. The common people do not wash much with
hot water and soap; they only steam themselves to a terrible
degree and then sluice themselves with cold water—that is
the whole extent of their bath. On the shelf fifty birch

switches rose and fell; they were all whipping themselves into a frenzy. More steam was added every moment. It was no longer merely hot; it was scorching. The whole place roared with shouting and laughter, to the accompaniment of a hundred chains dragging on the floor . . . Some, who wanted to pass through the mass, got tangled in the chains of others, caught their own against the heads of those sitting on the floor, and fell, swearing and dragging after them those whose heads they had snared. Dirt poured down from all sides. Everybody was in a state almost of intoxication, a kind of violent mental stimulation; there were shrieks and cries all about. Round the opening into the ante-room through which water was passed there was incessant cursing, crowding, and scuffling. The hot water got splashed all over the heads of those who were sitting on the floor before it could be carried back to its destination. At every moment the whiskered face of a soldier with his rifle in his hand would glance in through the window or the half-open door, looking for signs of disorder. The shaven heads of the convicts and their bodies, scarlet from the steam, seemed even more monstrously ugly. When a back is swollen with steam, the scars of blows inflicted at some time with whips or rods usually stand out clearly, so that now all the backs seemed newly injured. Terrible scars! A cold shiver ran over my skin when I looked at them. The steam was increased—and it spread in a thick, scalding cloud over the whole bath; everybody began to laugh and shout. Through the mist of steam glimmered scarred backs, shaven heads, crooked arms and legs; and as the crowning touch, Isaiah Fomich, on the very highest shelf, was roaring with laughter. He was steaming himself into insensibility, but apparently no degree of heat could satisfy him; for a copeck he hired another man to beat him with birch-twigs, but at last his attendant could endure it no longer, threw down the bundle of twigs and ran off to sluice himself with cold water. Isaiah Fomich was not discouraged but hired another, and a third; he had made up his mind beforehand that in such a cause he would not count the cost, but have as many as five bath attendants working in relays. 'You're a wonder to steam yourself; good for you, Isaiah Fomich!' cried the prisoners from below. Isaiah Fomich himself felt that at this moment he was higher than all the rest and outshone them all; he was in his glory, and in a strident, crazy voice he shrilled out his aria: Tra-la-la, la-la, drowning all the other voices. It came into my mind that if we should ever be all together in the fires of Hell, it would be very like this place. I could not forbear communicating this idea to Petrov; he merely looked all round and said nothing.

I had wanted to buy a place for him as well, next to me, but he squatted down at my feet and declared that he was very comfortable. Baklushin, meanwhile, was buying water for us and bringing it as it was wanted. Petrov declared that he would wash me from head to foot, so that 'you'll be nice and clean', and he tried hard to persuade me to steam myself. I would not venture on this. Petrov rubbed me all over with soap. 'And now I'll wash your little feet,' he added in conclusion. I should have liked to answer that I could wash them myself, but I did not want to cross him and allowed him to do as he would with me. In the diminutive 'little feet' there decidedly sounded no hint of servility; it was simply and solely that Petrov could not call my feet feet, probably because other people, grown-up people, had feet and I had as yet only 'little feet'.

Having washed me, he delivered me, with the same ceremony as before, that is, with the support of his arm and with elaborate precautions at every step, to the ante-room, and helped me to put on my underclothes, and only when he had quite finished with me rushed back into the bath to steam himself.

When we arrived home I offered him a glass of tea. He did not refuse, but drank it and thanked me. It occurred to me that I might spend a little money and treat him to a dram of vodka. The dram was found in our own barrack. Petrov was highly delighted, drank it, cleared his throat, and, remarking that I had put new life into him, hastily departed for the kitchen, as though there were something there that could not possibly be settled without him. In his place there appeared another companion for me, Baklushin (the Pioneer), whom I had also invited to have tea with me while we were at the bath-house.

I do not know a more amiable character than Baklushin. It is true that he gave no quarter to anybody, was indeed frequently involved in quarrels, did not like any meddling in his affairs—in a word, could stand up for himself. But his quarrels did not last long and I think all of us liked him. Wherever he went, people welcomed him with pleasure. He was even known in the town as the most amusing person in the world and as one who never lost his good humour. He was a tall lad, about thirty years old, with a spirited and simple-hearted face, quite handsome, but with a wart on it. He sometimes distorted this face so humorously in the course of impersonating anybody and everybody, that those who were near could not help guffawing. He was another of our clowns; but he did not afford our prison haters of laughter any pretext for reviling him as a 'frivolous and useless' person. He was full of fire and life. He made my acquaintance in my very first days in prison, and he had told me that he had gone to an army school and afterwards served in the Pioneers; he had even attracted the notice and liking of certain exalted persons and this, when he remembered old days, made him very proud. He at once began to question me about St. Petersburg. He was even something of a reader. Now, when he came to have tea with me, he first of all made the whole barrack laugh with the story of how one of the ensigns had scored off our major that morning and then, when he was seated beside me, he told me that he thought we were going to have some theatricals. We contrived to have a theatre in the prison on holidays. The actors had come forward and scenery was being constructed little by little. Some people in the town had promised to give clothes for the characters, even the women; there was even a hope of obtaining, through a batman, an officer's uniform with shoulder-cords. If only the major did not take it into his head to ban it, as he had the year before! But the year before, the major had been in a bad mood at Christmas: he had lost money at cards somewhere, and there had been some trouble in the prison besides, and so he had forbidden the plays out of spite; but now, perhaps, he would not want to interfere. In short, Baklushin was in a state of excitement. It was obvious that he was one of the leading spirits of the theatrical project, and I promised myself that I should certainly attend the performance. Baklushin's simple-hearted joy over the prospect of success went to my heart. One thing led to another and we had a long conversation. Among other things he told me that he had not served all his time in St. Petersburg but had committed some offence there and been sent to a battalion on garrison duty in R—,* as a non-commissioned officer, however.

'It was from there that I was sent here,' remarked Baklushin.

'And what was that for?' I asked him.

'What for? What do you suppose it was for, Alexander Petrovich? Actually it was because I fell in love!'

'Come, they don't send anybody here for that yet,' I objected, laughing.

'It is true,' went on Baklushin, 'it is true that in the course of the affair I shot a German who lived there, with a pistol. But really, judge for yourself, is a German worth sending men into exile for?'

'But how did it happen? Tell me; this is interesting.'

'It's a very funny story, Alexander Petrovich.'

'All the better. Do tell it.'

'Shall I? Well then, listen . . .'

What I heard was the story, not altogether comical, but odd enough, of a murder . . .

'It was like this,' began Baklushin. 'When they sent me to R——, I could see it was a fine big town, only there were a lot of Germans. Well, of course, I was still a young man, I was on good terms with my superior officers, I went about with my cap tilted over one ear, and in short I passed the time pleasantly. I winked at the German women. And there was one German girl, Luisa, who took my fancy. They were both laundresses, of the very whitest linen that ever was, she and her aunt. The aunt was old, and very fond of finery, and they were pretty comfortably off. At first I used to walk up and down past their windows and then I got to be really friends with them. Luisa spoke good Russian, only she made her *r*'s in her throat—a sweet little darling she was, I've never seen her like. I would have begun talking of one thing and another, but she said to me: "No, that can I not, Sasha, because I want to keep all my innocence, to be a fit wife for you," and she only wheedled me and laughed so loud . . . and she was so clean, I've never seen anybody like it, except her. And it was her that coaxed me to get married. Well, why not? think! So there I was getting ready to go and ask the colonel . . . Suddenly I looks—and Luisa didn't come out to meet me one time, and next time she didn't, and then the third time she wasn't there . . . I sends her a letter; there's no answer. "What's this?" thinks I. I mean, if she was only having me on, she would pretend and answer the letter and come to meet me. And besides, she didn't know how to lie; so, she had simply broken things off. "It's the aunt," thinks I. I daren't go to the aunt; although she knew about us, we'd kept it pretty dark all the same, I mean we'd been careful. I was going round like a madman and I wrote one last letter and said: "If you don't come I shall go to your auntie." That frightened her and she came. She was crying; she said there was a German called Schultz and he was a distant relation of theirs, a watchmaker, middle-aged and rich, and he had said he wanted to marry her—"so," says she, "that he can make me happy and he won't be left without a wife in his old age; and he loves me," says she, "and he's been meaning to do this for a long time, but he never said anything till he was ready. So there it is, Sasha," says she, "he's rich and this means my happiness; so you wouldn't want to take it away from me, would you?" I looks at her: she is crying, with her arms round me . . . Oh, thinks I, she is talking sense, you know! Well, where's the use of marrying a soldier, even if I have got my stripes? "Well," says I, "good-bye, Luisa, and God bless you; I couldn't deprive you of your happiness. And what about him; is he good-looking?" "No," says she, "he's so old, and he has a long nose . . ." and she even laughed. I left her; oh well, I thinks, it wasn't to be! Next morning I goes round by his shop, she had told me what street it was in. I looks through the window and the German is sitting there making a watch, forty-five he must have been, with a hook nose and goggle eyes, in a stand-up collar as high as this, very important. I just spit; I'd have liked to smash that window for him . . . but why? thinks I; no use crying over spilt milk! I went back to barracks in the twilight, laid down on my bed, and then, would you believe it, Alexander Petrovich? I cried . . .

'Well, that day passed, and the next, and the next. I didn't see Luisa. And meanwhile I had heard from a friend (she was an old woman, another laundress, and Luisa used to go and see her sometimes) that the German knew we loved each other and that was why he'd made up his mind to ask her as soon as possible. Otherwise he'd have waited another two years. It seems he'd made Luisa swear not to see me again, and meanwhile it seems he wasn't treating them, her and her auntie, at all well; and he said he might perhaps change his mind again and he wasn't at all sure yet what he would do. And she told me besides that two days afterwards, on Sunday, he had invited them to have coffee with him and there would be another relation there, an old man; he'd been a well-to-do merchant but now he was as poor as poor and was a watchman in a basement somewhere. When I heard that they would perhaps settle everything on the Sunday I got so wild that I couldn't control myself. And all that day and all the next day I did nothing but think about it. I could tear that German to pieces with my teeth, thinks I.

'On Sunday morning I still didn't know what I was going to do, but when Mass was over I jumped up, tightened up my greatcoat, and set off for the German's. I expected to find them all there. And why I went to the German's and what I was going to say when I got there, I don't know myself. But I put a pistol in my pocket just in case. I had this little pistol but it wasn't much use, it had an old-fashioned cock; I used to shoot with it when I was a little boy. You couldn't even fire it any more. But I loaded it with a bullet; I thought, they'll try to push me out and be rude to me; I'll pull out the pistol to scare them all. I got to the place. There wasn't anybody in the workshop; they were all sitting in the back room. There wasn't anybody there besides them—no servant. His only servant was a German woman, she was the cook as well. I went through the shop; I could see the door into there was fastened, and it was old, on a hook. My heart was thumping and I stopped and listened; they were talking German. I just shoved with my foot as hard as I could and the door came open. I looked and saw the table was laid. There was a big coffee-pot on it and the coffee was boiling over a spirit-lamp. There were rusks; on another tray there was a decanter of vodka and herrings and sausage and another bottle of some sort of wine. Luisa and her auntie, both dressed up, were sitting on the sofa. Opposite them the German himself on a chair, the bride-groom, with his hair combed, in his frock-coat and his collar sticking out in front. And beside him in a chair there was another German, quite old and grey and fat, not saying a word. When I went in, Luisa went white. Her aunt jumped

up and then sat down again and the German scowled. He
was very angry, he got up to meet me:

' "What do you want?" he says.

'I was bothered for a bit, but my temper took proper hold
of me.

' "What do I want?" says I. "Can't you welcome a visitor
and offer him some vodka? I've come to pay you a visit."

'He thought for a bit and then he says:

' "Sit."

'I sat down.

' "Well," says I, "give me some vodka."

' "Here is the vodka," says he, "please have some."

' "And you," says I, "give me good vodka." That meant
my bad temper was getting the best of me.

' "That is good vodka."

'I was very much offended that he should think so very
little of me. Most of all because Luisa was looking on. I
drank my vodka and then I said:

' "What makes you so rude, German? You ought to be
my friend. I came here in all friendliness."

' "Friends with you can I not be," says he. "You are a
common soldier."

'Well, then I got really wild:

' "You stuffed dummy!" says I; "you sausage-eater! Do
you know that at this moment I can do what I like with you?
Look, would you like me to shoot you with this pistol?"

'I pulls out my pistol, stands in front of him, and points it
straight at his head, point-blank. They all sat there, neither
alive nor dead; they dursn't say a word, and the old man,
he's shaking like a leaf and as white as a sheet, and not a
squeak out of him.

'The German was struck all of a heap, but he pulls himself
together.

' "I am not afraid of you," he says, "and I ask you, as an
honourable man, to drop this joke at once; but I am not a bit
frightened of you!"

' "Oh, you're a liar," says I; "you are frightened." Why, he dursn't move his head away from the pistol; he just sat there.

' "No," says he, "you it will not at all dare to do."

' "And why will I it not dare?" says I.

' "Because", says he, "it strictly forbidden is, and for it you severely punished will be."

'The devil knows what had got into that fool of a German. If he hadn't egged me on himself, he'd have been alive to this day, it would only have been a bit of an argument.

' "So I dursn't," says I, "according to you?"

' "No-o!"

' "I dursn't?"

' "You it will with me not at all dare to do . . ."

' "Well then, take that, sausage!" But when I grabbed at him, he sort of rolled over in his chair. The others yelled.

'I shoved the pistol in my pocket and cleared out, and when I got to the fortress, I threw the pistol in the nettles by the gate.

'I went to my barrack and laid down on my bed and, thinks I: they'll be coming for me straight away. One hour went by and then another—still they didn't come. And then just before it began to get dark, I got to feeling so anxious; I went out; I felt I absolutely had to see Luisa. I went past the watchmaker's. I looked and there was a crowd there, and the police. I went past the watchmaker's. I looked and there was a crowd there, and the police. I went to my friend: "Get hold of Luisa!" I'd hardly waited a moment when I sees Luisa come running and she just throws herself on my neck, and she's crying: "It's all my fault," she says, "for listening to auntie." She told me besides that her auntie had gone straight home after what happened, and she was so frightened that it made her ill, and—not a word: and she hadn't told anybody anything and she told me not to say anything; she was scared; let them do what they wanted there. "We," she says, Luisa, "weren't seen there by anybody just now." He'd sent the servant away because he was afraid of her. She'd have scratched his eyes out if she'd known he wanted to get married. None of the men from the workshop was at home either; he'd sent them all out. He'd made the coffee and got the *zakuski* ready himself. And the relation, he'd kept quiet all his life and never said anything, and when this affair happened he just took his cap and was the first to leave. "And probably he'll keep quiet too," says Luisa. That's just what happened. For two weeks nobody arrested me and nobody even suspected me. And in those two weeks, believe it or not, Alexander Petrovich, I was completely happy. I saw Luisa every day. And how she clung to me, how she clung to me! She cried and: "I'll follow you", says she, "wherever they send you; I'll give up everything for you!" I even thought I'd settle my life for good, I was so sorry for her. Well, after two weeks I was arrested. The old man and auntie had put their heads together and informed on me . . .'

'Wait a minute,' I interrupted Baklushin. 'For that they could only send you here for about ten years, or twelve at the outside, in the Civil division; and, you know, you are in the Special Class. How could that happen?'

'Well, that was something different,' said Baklushin. 'When I was taken before the judicial commission, the captain used bad language to me in the presence of the court. I wasn't going to stand that and I says to him: "What are you swearing for? Can't you see, you scoundrel, that you are in the presence of the law?" Well, then things went differently; I was tried again and sentenced for everything together; I got sent four thousand versts away, and into the Special Class here. But when I was taken out for my punishment, they took the captain as well; me to be sent along the green street,[1] and him to have his rank taken away and be sent to the Caucasus as a private . . . Good-bye, Alexander Petrovich. Come to our show . . .'

---

[1] i.e. to run the gauntlet. [*Tr.*]

10. The Feast of Christmas

AT last the holiday came. Even on Christmas Eve the prisoners did almost no work. Some went off to the sewing-shop and the other workshops; but the rest only attended at the parade and although they were assigned to various places, almost all of them immediately returned to the prison, singly or in groups, and after dinner nobody left it at all. Even in the morning the greater part of them went about their own business only, not the government's, some concerning themselves with the smuggling of vodka or the ordering of more, others seeing their pals, male and female, or collecting against the holiday the small sums owing to them for work they had done previously, Baklushin and the other participants in the theatricals going round among various acquaintances, predominantly officers' servants, and acquiring the necessary costumes. Some went about with harassed and preoccupied faces solely because others were harassed and preoccupied, and some, although they had no source from which they could anticipate receiving any money, yet looked as if even they were getting money from somebody; in short, everybody seemed to be expecting the next day to bring some change, something out of the ordinary run of things. Towards evening the old soldiers, who had been to the bazaar on the prisoners' errands, brought back with them many eatables of every conceivable kind: beef, pork, even geese. Many of the prisoners, even the most frugal and careful, scraping together their coppers all the year round, thought it their duty to be open-handed on a day like this and celebrate the feast-day in a worthy fashion. The morrow was a real holiday, to which the convicts had an imprescriptible right, formally recognized by the law. On that day the prisoner could not be sent to work, and there were only three such days in the year.*

And finally, who knows how many memories must be awakened in the hearts of these outcasts by the arrival of such a day? The major feasts are sharply imprinted in the memory of the common people from their earliest childhood. They are days of rest from their heavy labours, days of family gatherings. In prison they must be remembered with pain and longing. Among the convicts observance of the solemn festivals became something almost ceremonial; there were very few binges; everybody was serious and seemed occupied with something, although many of them had almost nothing at all to do. But even the idlers and revellers tried to preserve their dignity. It was as if laughter was prohibited. The general mood ran to a certain pedantry and irritable impatience, and anybody who disturbed the general tone, however inadvertently, was beset with yells and oaths, and they were angry with him as though he were showing disrespect to the holy day. This mood of the prisoners was remarkable and even touching. Besides his inborn reverence for the solemn religious festival, the prisoner was unconsciously aware that by this observance of the day he brought himself into contact with all the world, that consequently he was not altogether an outcast, a lost soul, a piece of flotsam, and that even in prison things were the same as among real people. They *felt* it; this was visible and understandable.

Akim Akimovich also made many preparations for the holiday. He had no memories of his family, for he had grown up an orphan in the house of strangers and had begun to work hard almost from reaching the age of fifteen; there had been no great joys in his life, because he had always lived regularly and monotonously, fearing to deviate by so much as a hair's breadth from what he deemed his duty. Nor was he particularly pious, because morality had apparently swallowed up all his human talents and particular qualities, all his passions and desires, both good and evil. In consequence of all this he prepared to meet the festival without flurry or agitation, undisturbed by yearning and altogether vain memories, but with calm, methodical seemliness of conduct, just as much as was required for the performance of his obligations and the ceremonies laid down once for all. Generally speaking, he did not like to have to do much thinking. He never troubled his head, apparently, about the meaning of any act, but he fulfilled a principle, once it had been shown to him, with religious accuracy. If on the next day he had been ordered to do the exact opposite, he would have done that too with the same submissiveness and exactness as he had done the opposite on the previous day. Once, and only once, in his life, he had tried to live by the light of his own intelligence—and he had landed in a convict prison. The lesson was not lost on him. And although he was not destined to grasp at any time exactly how he had come to grief, nevertheless he had deduced from what had happened to him a saving rule—never in any circumstances to try to reason, because 'his mind was not made for' reasoning, as the expression in use among the prisoners went. Blindly devoted to ritual, he regarded even his Christmas sucking-pig, which he had stuffed with *kasha* and roasted (with his own hands, because roasting was another of the things he could do), with a kind of anticipatory esteem, as though it were not an ordinary piglet, which might be bought and roasted at any time, but a special, Christmas one. Perhaps from his childhood he had been used to seeing a sucking-pig on the table on that day, and deduced that a pig was essential to the day, and I am sure that if he had ever once failed to eat pork on that day he would have felt a certain pang of conscience all his life for the obligation unfulfilled. Until the holiday he went about in an old jacket and trousers, which, although decently patched, were nevertheless quite worn out. It now appeared that he had carefully kept in his box the new suit issued to him a good four months before and, with a pleasurable idea of wearing it brand-new on the holiday, had not even touched it. And wear it he did. The evening before, he got out his new clothes, unfolded them, looked them over, brushed them, blew off the dust and, having set everything to rights, tried them on. It seemed they were an excellent fit; everything was in order, they buttoned up closely to the top, the collar propped his chin high as though it were made of cardboard, the waist was even nipped in something like that of a uniform, and Akim Akimovich almost simpered with pleasure and, not without swaggering, twirled in front of his tiny mirror, round which he had himself pasted a gilt border long ago in a free moment. Only one hook on the jacket collar seemed somehow not in the right place. Realizing this, Akim Akimovich decided to move it; he moved it and tried the jacket on again; this time it proved completely satisfactory. Then he folded the clothes again as before and put them away until the morrow with a quiet mind. His head was already satisfactorily shaved; but, examining himself closely in the mirror, he noticed that it did not seem quite smooth on top; there were some almost imperceptible bristles, and he went off at once to 'the major' to have himself suitably and properly shaved. Although nobody was going to inspect Akim Akimovich, he had himself shaved solely for the peace of his conscience, so that he should have fulfilled his duties for such a day. Pious respect for a button, a shoulder knot, a loop had been ineffaceably imprinted in his mind from his childhood as an incontestable obligation, and in his heart as the highest degree of beauty attainable by an honest man. Having set everything to rights, he, as the oldest prisoner in the barrack, arranged for straw to be brought in and carefully supervised its strewing on the floor. It was the same in the other barracks. I do not know why, but at Christmas we always strewed straw in the barrack. Afterwards, having completed all his labours, Akim Akimovich said his prayers, lay down on his bed and immediately fell into the quiet sleep of a baby, so that he should awake as early as possible in the morning. But then, all the prisoners acted in exactly the same way. In all the barracks they went to bed much earlier than usual. The usual evening work was forsaken; *maidans* were not so much as mentioned. Everybody was waiting for the morning.

It arrived at last. Early, before it was daylight, immediately tattoo was beaten, the barracks were opened, and the non-commissioned officer on duty, when he came in to number the prisoners, wished them the compliments of the season. They returned his greetings, returned them courteously and kindly. Having hastily said their prayers, Akim Akimovich and many others, who had geese and sucking-pigs in the kitchen, hurried there to see what was being done with them, how they were being roasted, where they had been put, and so on. Through the darkness we could see from the small windows of our barrack, plastered with snow and ice, that in both kitchens bright fires were blazing in all six stoves, where they had been laid before dawn. In the courtyard, in the darkness, prisoners were already walking about in their short sheepskin coats, worn either with the arms in the sleeves or slung round the shoulders; all this movement was setting towards the kitchens. But some, very few, however, had already managed to pay a visit to the 'tapsters'. These were the most impatient ones. But in general everybody behaved in a seemly and peaceable fashion, and with a kind of sedateness that was out of the ordinary. There were some who paid visits to other barracks to exchange greetings with a fellow countryman. Something like friendship made its appearance. I must remark in passing that friendly feelings between convicts were almost entirely unknown; I do not mean general friendliness—that was even less apparent—but private friendship, one prisoner making a friend of another. It hardly ever occurred among us, and this was a remarkable characteristic: things are not so among free men. Among us the relations between one man and another were generally dry and cold, with very rare exceptions, and this produced a formal tone, which once adopted had become established. I also left the barrack; it was just beginning to grow light; the stars were fading; a thin frosty vapour floated upwards. Pillars of smoke billowed out of the kitchen stove-pipes. Several of the prisoners, when our paths crossed, wished me the compliments of the season in a friendly way, without prompting. I thanked them and returned their good wishes. Some among them had not exchanged a word with me all through that month, until then.

A prisoner from the Military division, with his sheepskin coat slung round his shoulders, overtook me when I was close to the kitchen. While he was still in the middle of the yard he had seen me and called out: 'Alexander Petrovich! Alexander Petrovich!' He was making for the kitchen and hurrying. I stopped and waited for him. He was a young fellow with a round face and a quiet look in his eyes, who had little to say to anybody and had not said a word to me or paid me any attention from the time of my arrival in the prison until that moment; I did not even know his name. He ran up to me, out of breath, and stood close in front of me, looking at me with a somewhat stupid and yet at the same time blissful smile.

'What is it?' I asked, not without surprise, seeing him stand in front of me smiling, gazing hard at me, and yet not beginning to speak.

'Why, it's Christmas . . .,' he murmured, and understanding that there was no more to be said, hurried away into the kitchen.

In passing, let me say that even after that we never came any closer together, and hardly spoke a word to each other until the day I left the prison.

In the kitchen, round the stoves heated to redness, there was bustling and jostling, a regular crush. Each was looking after his own property; the 'kitchen-maids' had begun to prepare the prison food, since on this day dinner was fixed earlier. Nobody, however, had yet begun to eat, and although some might have wanted to, they preserved decorum before the others. The priest was being waited for, and the pre-Christmas fast was not supposed to be broken until after his visit. Meanwhile, it was still barely daylight when the shouted summons of the corporal: 'Cooks!' began to resound from outside the prison gates. These cries sounded almost continuously for nearly two hours. The cooks were summoned from the kitchens to receive the gifts which had been carried to the prison from every quarter of the town. They were brought in extraordinary quantities and took the form of white loaves, black bread, cheese-cakes, cakes, buns with sour cream, pancakes, and other pastries baked for the feast. I think there did not remain one house-wife in the upper and lower middle-class houses in the town who had not sent food as a Christmas greeting to the 'un-fortunates' shut up in the prison. There were rich gifts—bread made of the finest flour, with butter and eggs, and sent in large quantities. There were also very poor gifts—a cheap little white loaf and two black buns of indifferent quality barely smeared with sour cream: a gift to a beggar from a beggar out of his last small store. All were received with equal gratitude, without any distinction of gifts or givers. The prisoners to whom they were handed took off their caps, bowed, gave Christmas greetings, and carried the gift to the kitchen. When a great heap of this charitable food had been collected, the elders of each barrack were sum-moned and they divided everything equally between the different barracks. There were no disputes or quarrels; the affair was handled honestly and fairly. What was allotted to our barrack was shared out when it came to us; Akim Akimovich and another prisoner did the sharing out: they divided the food with their own hands and with their own hands distributed it to each of us. There was not the smallest objection, not the least sign of jealousy from anybody; everybody was content; there could not be even a suspicion that any alms might be concealed or unfairly distributed.

Having concluded his business in the kitchen, Akim Akimovich proceeded to array himself, dressed with all due seemliness and solemnity, leaving not the smallest hook unfastened, and when he was dressed, immediately set about his real prayers. He prayed for a fairly long time. Many other prisoners, for the most part elderly, were already at their prayers. The young men did not pray a great deal; it was much if one crossed himself as he got up, even on a holy day. When he had prayed, Akim Akimovich came up to me and with some ceremony offered me the compliments of the season. I at once invited him to tea, and he me to his sucking-pig. A little later Petrov too came running to greet me. He seemed to have been drinking already, and although he came running in out of breath he did not say much but only stood a short time in front of me in some kind of expectation, and soon left me to go to the kitchen. Meanwhile, preparations were being made in the Military barrack for the reception of the priest. This barrack was not arranged like the others; in it the planks stretched along the walls, not down the middle of the room, as in all the other barracks, so that this was the only room in the prison that was not encumbered in the middle. Probably it was arranged in this fashion so that, in case of necessity, all the prisoners might be collected in it. A little table was placed in the middle of the room and covered with a clean towel; on this they put an ikon and lighted a lampada. At last the priest arrived with the cross and holy water. When he had prayed and sung the service before the ikon he stood before the prisoners and all of them began to go up to kiss the cross with genuine piety. Then the priest walked round all the barracks and sprinkled them with holy water. In the kitchen he praised our prison bread, renowned for its flavour in the town, and the prisoners instantly decided to send him two fresh, newly baked loaves; one of the old soldiers was at once pressed into service to convey them. The cross was escorted to the gate with the same devotion with which it had been welcomed, and almost immediately afterwards the major and the commandant arrived. Our commandant was liked and even respected. He went round all the barracks in company with the major, wished everybody the compliments of the season, and called in the kitchen to taste the prison cabbage soup. The soup proved excellent; in honour of the day almost a pound of beef had been issued for each prisoner. Besides this, millet porridge had been prepared and butter was freely distributed. As he accompanied the commandant away, the major gave the order to begin dinner. The prisoners tried not to come under his eye. We did not like the ill-natured glance through his glasses which he directed right and left even now, looking for some disorder or for a man guilty of something or other.

We began dinner. Akim Akimovich's sucking-pig was excellently cooked. And now, although I cannot explain how it happened, when the major had left, indeed within five minutes of his departure, an unusually large number of drunken men appeared; and yet five minutes before they had all been almost completely sober. Many red, beaming faces made their appearance, and balalaikas were produced. The little Pole with the violin was already in attendance on one reveller who had hired him for the whole day, and was scraping out gay dance-tunes for him. The talk was growing louder and more tipsy. But dinner came to an end without any great disturbance. Everybody had eaten his fill. Many of the older or staider men immediately went off to lie down, as did Akim Akimovich, supposing, apparently, that a sleep after dinner was essential on great festivals. The little old man who was an Old Believer from Starodubov, after a short nap, climbed up on the stove, opened his book, and went on praying far into the night, almost without intermission. It was painful to him to see the 'shame', as he called the general merry-making. All the Circassians settled down on the barrack steps and watched the drunkards with curiosity, and with disgust as well. Nurra greeted me: 'Bad, bad!' he said, shaking his head with pious displeasure; 'oh, bad! Allah will be angry!' Isaiah Fomich proudly and wilfully lighted a candle in his corner and began to work, plainly demonstrating that he did not consider it a holiday at all. Here and there in the corners *maidans* were set up. Nobody was afraid of the old soldiers, but in case of the appearance of a non-commissioned officer (who, however, would try to notice nothing), sentries were posted. The officer of the watch looked into the prison only about three times in all the day. But the drunkards hid and the *maidans* were removed on his appearance and he had apparently decided not to pay any attention to minor breaches of discipline. On that day even a drunken man was accounted a small breach. Little by little people began to grow merry. Quarrels sprang up, too. By far the greatest number, nevertheless, remained sober and there was somebody to keep an eye on the intoxicated. Those who were on the binge, on the other hand, were drinking heavily. Gazin was in his glory. He prowled with a self-satisfied air about his place on the planks, underneath which he had boldly put his vodka, which had been kept until that time in the snow somewhere behind the barracks in a secret hiding-place, and he chuckled slyly as he saw his customers approach. He himself was sober and had not touched a drop. He intended his own celebrations for the end of the holiday, when he had, as a preliminary, whistled all the money out of the other prisoners' pockets. Songs resounded through the barracks. But the fires of intoxication were already dying into heady fumes, and from the songs it was not a long step to tears. Many men were wandering about with their balalaikas, with sheepskin coats slung round their shoulders, and strumming on the strings with a dashing air. In the Special Class a chorus of some eight voices had even been organized. They sang wonderfully well, to the accompaniment of balalaikas and guitars. Very few purely popular songs were sung. I remember only one, rendered with spirit:

> Last night as a bride
> I sat at the feast.

And here I heard a new version of the song, which I had not met before. At the end of the song there were several additional lines:

> The house of this bride
> Is garnished and swept:
> The spoons were well washed,
> The slops made the soup;
> Cobwebs swept from the walls
> Went into the pies.

But most of the songs they sang were special prison songs, all well known. One of them, 'Once upon a time . . .', was humorous, describing how a man used to make merry and live like a lord in freedom, but now he had fallen into prison. It told how he used to liven up his 'blancmange with champagne', but now

> Cabbage they give me, cabbage and water,
> And I wallow in it like a pig.

This, also very well known, was much in vogue:

> The life I lived was gay, lad,
> I'd capital of my own;
> I threw it all away, lad;
> Now I must reap what I've sown,

and so on. But among us the pronunciation was not 'capital' but 'copital'—as though 'capital' were derived from the word 'kopit'.[1] Sad songs were sung, too; one was a typical prisoners' song and also, I think, well known:

> The light of heav'n begins to shine,
> The drum beats in the day,
> The prison doors stand open now,
> The roll-call goes its way.

[1] To lay by, save up. [*Tr.*]

> Who knows or cares what life we lead
> Behind this prison wall?
> One watches us and keeps us still,
> The God who made us all, &c., &c.

Another, even sadder, was, however, sung to a beautiful melody; it was probably the work of some exile, and the words were sentimental and rather illiterate. I can now remember only a few of them.

> My eyes will never see that land,
> The land where I was born.
> Condemned to torment without end,
> Guiltless I lie forlorn.

> Above the roof the screech-owl calls,
> The woods the echoes hear;
> My sad heart aches, my spirit falls—
> I never can be there.

This song was often sung in the prison, but never in chorus, always by a single voice. In an idle hour somebody would go out on the steps of the barrack, sit down in a thoughtful mood, with his cheek propped in his hand, and strike up the song in a high falsetto. You would listen, and somehow it would rend your heart. We had some fairly good voices among us.

Meanwhile it was growing dusk. Melancholy, nostalgia, hazy stupefaction, began to loom up through the drunken merriment. Some who had been laughing an hour before were now, having far exceeded the limits of their capacity, sobbing somewhere in a corner. Others had already come to blows a couple of times. Others again, pale and hardly able to keep their feet, were staggering about the barracks and trying to provoke quarrels. Those who were of a melancholy turn in their cups looked in vain for friends to whom they could pour out their souls, weeping away their drunken sadness. All these poor creatures had wanted to enjoy themselves and spend the great festival in rejoicing—and Lord!

how heavy and dreary the day had been for almost every one of them. Each had passed it as though hope had cheated him. Petrov hurried in to see me once or twice more. He had drunk very little all day and was almost completely sober. But up to the very last hour he was still waiting for something which must inevitably happen, something extraordinary, festive and joyous. Although he said nothing about this, it could be seen in his eyes. He scurried tirelessly from barrack to barrack. But nothing special happened or came under his eyes except drunkenness and senseless brawling and heads aching with the fumes of drink. Sirotkin was also wandering about round all the barracks in a new red shirt, looking handsome and well washed, and he also seemed to be quietly and naïvely expectant. Little by little the barracks became disgusting and unbearable. There was, of course, much that was comical, too, but somehow I felt full of sadness and pity for all of them, and oppressed and stifled among them. Yonder two convicts were arguing over which should stand the other a drink. It was plain that they had been disputing for a long time and had even quarrelled violently. One in particular had some long-standing grievance against the other. He was complaining and endeavouring, though with feeble control of his tongue, to prove that the other had dealt unfairly with him: some sheepskin jacket had been sold, and some money had been concealed, during the previous Shrovetide. There was something more besides . . . The accuser was a tall and muscular young fellow, peaceable and not stupid, but when he was drunk he craved for a friend to whom he could pour out his sorrows. He was abusive now, and was vehemently airing his grievance as if with the intention of making peace even more heartily afterwards with his adversary. The other was a short, stout, stocky man with a round face, crafty and sly. He had drunk perhaps more than his comrade, but he was only slightly tipsy. He was an ill-natured man, reputed to be rich, but for some reason he thought it best not to annoy his expansive friend this time, and he took him to the tapster; the other went on asserting that he was bound and obliged to offer him something 'if there is any honour in you at all'.

The tapster, with some deference to his customer and a shade of scorn for the expansive friend because the latter's drunkenness had been achieved not at his own expense but by being treated, brought out and poured a cup of vodka.

'No, Stepka, you ought to do it,' said the expansive friend, still obsessed with his grievance, 'because it's your duty.'

'I'm not going to wear my tongue out for nothing, talking to you!' answered Stepka.

'No, Stepka, you're a liar,' insisted the first, taking the cup from the tapster, 'because you owe me the money; you've got no conscience. Even your eyes don't belong to you, they're only borrowed! You're a rotter, Stepka, that's what you are; in one word, you're a rotter!'

'Well, what are you whining about? You've splashed the vodka all over the place! Somebody does you the honour to give it you, so drink it!' shouted the tapster. 'I can't stand here waiting till tomorrow! . . .'

'I'm drinking it, no need to yell! Merry Christmas, Stepan Dorofeich!' And, holding the cup in his hand, he turned politely, with a slight bow, to Stepka, whom half a minute before he had been calling a rotter. 'May you flourish a hundred years, not counting what you've lived already!' He drank, cleared his throat, and wiped his mouth. 'Before, mates, I used to put down a lot of vodka,' he remarked with solemn dignity, addressing not anybody in particular but all of us, 'but now, it seems, I'm getting on a bit. Thanks, Stepan Dorofeich.'

'Don't mention it.'

'So now, Stepka, I am going on talking about you know what; and apart from having been a dirty rotter to me, I want to tell you . . .'

'I'll tell you something, you ugly drunken soak,' interrupted Stepka, losing his patience. 'Listen, and don't miss a single word: we'll divide the world into two halves; you can have one half and I'll have the other. Go away and don't let me see you again. I'm sick of you!'

'But aren't you going to pay me back that money?'

'How much more money do you want, you drunk?'

'Eh, you'll bring that money to me of your own accord in the next world, and I won't take it! We get our money with hard work and sweat and blisters. You'll suffer for my five copecks in the next world!'

'Oh, go to the devil!'

'Don't try to gee me up; I'm not a horse.'

'Get out, get out!'

'Rotter!'

'Dirty convict!'

And the wrangling recommenced, worse than before.

Here on the planks, aloof from one another, sat two men, one tall, corpulent, fleshy, a real butcher to look at; his face was red. He was so deeply moved that he was on the point of tears. The other was thin, feeble, wizened, with a long nose from which a drop seemed about to fall, and little pig's eyes turned to the floor. He was a man of some little education and polish, who had once been a clerk; he treated his friend with a kind of condescension, which secretly very much displeased the other. They had been drinking together all day.

'He violated me!' cried the beefy friend, violently rocking the clerk's head, which he had encircled with his left arm. 'Violated' meant struck. The beefy one, who had been a non-commissioned officer, was secretly jealous of his skinny friend and therefore vied with him in the choice of far-fetched words.

'I tell you that you are in the wrong . . .' began the clerk dogmatically, obstinately refusing to raise his eyes but continuing to look at the ground with a pompous expression.

'He violated me, do you hear?' interrupted the other, still

more violently tousling his dear friend. 'You are the only person left to me on earth now, do you hear that? That's why you are the only one I am telling, he violated me . . .'

'And I say again, such a sour excuse, my dear friend, constitutes merely a disgrace to your head!' replied the clerk in a thin, polite little voice, 'and you had better admit, my dear friend, that all this drinking comes of lack of thinking . . .'

His beefy friend recoiled a little, looked dully with his drunken eyes at the self-satisfied little clerk and suddenly, without warning, struck the little face as hard as he could with his enormous fist. This was the end of the friendship for that day. The dear friend fell senseless under the planks . . .

Here was an acquaintance of mine from the Special Class coming into the barrack—an infinitely good-natured and cheerful fellow, intelligent, inoffensively amusing, and unusually simple in appearance. He was the one who, on my first day in the prison, had been inquiring at dinner-time in the kitchen where the rich peasant lived, had announced that he 'had his pride' and had drunk tea with me. He was a man of about forty, with an extraordinarily thick lip and a big fleshy nose sprinkled with blackheads. In his hands was a balalaika, on which he was negligently strumming. After him trailed a hanger-on, an extremely small prisoner with a big head, whom I had known very little until now. Nobody, however, paid any attention to him. He was an odd person, mistrustful, eternally silent and serious; he worked in the sewing-shop and evidently tried to live a solitary life and have nothing to do with anybody. Now, however, he was drunk and had attached himself like a shadow to Varlamov. He was following him in a state of dreadful agitation, waving his arms, beating his fist against the walls and planks, and almost weeping. Varlamov seemed to take no more notice of him than if he were not there at all. It is remarkable that before this time these two men had had hardly any dealings with each other: they had nothing in common either in occupation or in character. They belonged to different divisions and lived in different barracks. The little prisoner was called Bulkin.

Varlamov, seeing me, grinned. I was sitting on my planks near the stove. He stopped opposite me at some distance, seemed to have an inspiration, staggered and, making his way towards me with unsteady steps, struck a bold, gay attitude and, lightly touching the strings, said in a recitative, with a barely perceptible tapping of his heels:

> She's a round face, a white face,
> Croons a song like a tom-tit,
>   Does my darling;
> In a dress made of satin
> With beautiful trimming
>   She's so pretty.

This song seemed to drive Bulkin crazy; he waved his arms and shouted to everybody there:

'He's a liar, mates, he's always lying! Not a single word of truth will he speak; it's all lies!'

'To Gaffer Alexander Petrovich!' said Varlamov, looking me in the eyes with a mischievous smile, and he all but came up and kissed me. He was a little tipsy. The expression 'to Gaffer So-and-so', that is, 'my respects to so-and-so', is used by the simple people all over Siberia, even in reference to a man of twenty. The word 'gaffer' has an honorary, respectful, even flattering, meaning.

'Well, Varlamov, how are you getting on?'

'Oh, from one day to the next. But everyone who is glad of a holiday gets drunk early; so please excuse me!' Varlamov talked in rather a drawling voice.

'He keeps on lying, he's lying again!' cried Bulkin, banging the boards with his hands in a kind of despair. But it was as if Varlamov had taken an oath not to pay the slightest attention to him. There was a great deal of humour in all this, for Bulkin had attached himself to Varlamov without rhyme or reason since early morning, simply because he had somehow got it into his head that Varlamov 'kept on lying'. He followed him like a shadow, cavilled at every word he spoke, wrung his hands, hammered at the walls and planks with them until he almost drew blood, and suffered, visibly suffered, from his conviction that Varlamov 'kept on lying!' If he had had any hair on his head he would probably have torn it with vexation. It was just as though he had taken on himself the duty of being responsible for Varlamov's actions, as though all Varlamov's shortcomings lay heavy on his conscience. But the funny part was that Varlamov did not even glance at him.

'He keeps on lying, he lies all the time, he's lying! There's not a word of truth in anything he says,' cried Bulkin.

'What's it matter to you?' answered the prisoners with a laugh.

'I must tell you, Alexander Petrovich, that I used to be very good-looking, and the girls all liked me very much . . .' began Varlamov, quite irrelevantly.

'He's a liar, he's lying again!' interrupted Bulkin with a kind of scream. The prisoners guffawed.

'And I used to make a show for them: I'd have a red shirt and velveteen trousers: I would lie on a couch like some Count Bottle, as drunk as a lord, and in short—anything you like!'

'He's lying!' insisted Bulkin.

'In those days I had a house from my dad, a two-story one, made of stone. Well, in two years I'd got rid of my two stories and I had nothing left but the gates, without the gate-posts. Well, what of that? Money is like pigeons; it flies in and it flies away again! . . .'

'He's lying,' Bulkin asserted still more vigorously.

'So when I came to my senses I sent my family a tearful letter from here; I thought they might send me a bit of money. Because, you see, they said I'd gone against my family. I had not honoured my father and mother. It's over six years since I sent it . . .'

'And haven't you had an answer?' I asked, laughing.

'No, I haven't,' he answered, suddenly beginning to laugh himself, and advancing his nose nearer and nearer to my face. 'And I've got a girl here, Alexander Petrovich . . .'

'Have you?—a girl?'

'Onufriev said not long since: "Mine may be pockmarked, and she's not pretty, but then she's got such a lot of clothes; and yours is pretty, but she's a beggar and goes about with a sack!"'

'And is that true?'

'It's true that she's a beggar!' he answered, and he began to shake with noiseless laughter; the others in the barrack laughed too. Everybody knew that he really had taken up with some beggar-woman, and that in six months he had given her only ten copecks altogether.

'Well, what then?' I asked, wishing to get rid of him at last.

He said nothing for a moment, but looked at me coaxingly and then pronounced in a wheedling tone:

'Well then, wouldn't you perhaps give me enough for half a pint, because of all that? You know, Alexander Petrovich, I've been drinking nothing but tea all day,' he added with emotion, 'and I've swallowed so much of that that it's given me asthma, and it's slopping about in my belly like in a bottle . . .'

While he was taking the money, Bulkin's mental disturbance apparently surpassed all bounds. He waved his arms wildly, like one desperate, almost weeping:

'Good people!' he cried, addressing the whole barrack in a frenzy, 'look at him! . . . He keeps on lying! Whatever he says, it's always, always, always lies!'

'And what's it got to do with you?' shouted the other prisoners, astonished at his raging fury. 'You funny little man!'

'I won't let him lie!' shrieked Bulkin, with flashing eyes,

thumping his fist on the planks with all his force. 'I won't have him lying!'

Everybody roared with laughter. Varlamov took the money, bowed his farewells to me, and hurried, grimacing, out of the barrack, to the tapster, needless to say. And now, apparently, he noticed Bulkin for the first time.

'Well, come on!' he said to him, stopping on the threshold, as if he really needed him for something. 'A knob on a stick!' he added, scornfully letting the exasperated Bulkin pass before him, and again beginning to strum on his balalaika . . .

But why describe this inferno? At last the heavy day comes to an end. The prisoners fall heavily asleep on their plank-beds. They talk and wander in their sleep even more than on other nights. Some still sit over their cards. The long-awaited holiday is over. Tomorrow is another week-day, we must work again . . .

11. Theatricals

THE first performance in our theatre took place in the evening of the third day after the holiday. There had probably been a good deal of preliminary bustle over its organization, but the actors had taken everything on themselves, so that the rest of us did not even know what was the state of affairs or what was actually being done; we did not even know properly what was to be presented. Throughout those three days the actors, as they went about their work, were trying as hard as they could to obtain costumes. Baklushin, when we met, simply snapped his fingers with pleasure. Apparently the major also happened to be in a fairly good mood. We, however, were completely ignorant of whether he knew anything about the theatre. If he knew, had he given formal permission? or had he simply decided to say nothing and shrug his shoulders at this enterprise of the prisoners, while insisting, of course, that everything should be kept in order as far as possible? I think he knew about the theatre, he could not help knowing; but he did not wish to interfere, understanding that worse might happen if he prohibited it; the prisoners would begin to make trouble and drink heavily, so that it was much better for them to have something to keep them occupied. I only suppose some such course of reasoning in the major, however, because it is the most natural, probable, and judicious. One might even say that if the prisoners had not had their theatre at the holiday season, or some occupation of the same sort, the authorities themselves would have had to invent one. But since our major was distinguished by a way of thinking exactly opposite to that of the rest of mankind, it is very probable that I have fallen into grievous error in supposing that he knew about the theatricals and permitted them. A man like the major must always have somebody to oppress, something to take away from somebody, somebody to deprive of his rights, in short, an opportunity to wreak havoc. In this respect he was well known throughout the town. What did it matter to him that his oppressions might be the specific cause of disorder in the prison? There are punishments for disorder (argue people like our major) and with these desperate ruffians of prisoners severity and the relentless application of the letter of the law are all that is required! These advocates of the application of the law definitely do not understand, and are incapable of understanding, that the mere literal fulfilment of the law, without reason or comprehension of its spirit, leads straight to disorder and has never led to anything else. 'The law says so; what more do you want?' they say, and are sincerely astonished that anybody should demand of them, in addition to the letter of the law, sound judgement and sober heads. These last in particular seem to many of them a superfluous and shocking luxury, an intolerable restraint.

But, however that might have been, the senior sergeant did not cross the prisoners, and that was all they needed. I can positively state that the theatre, and gratitude that it had been permitted, were the reasons that during the holiday period there was not one serious disturbance in the prison, neither a malignant brawl nor a theft. I myself was a witness of how their associates calmed down certain revellers or brawlers with the plea that the theatre would be forbidden. The sergeant had obtained the prisoners' word that everything should be peaceful and everybody conduct themselves properly. They were glad to agree, and the promise was faithfully kept: it was flattering, besides, that their word was accepted. I must, however, remark that permitting these theatrical performances cost the authorities nothing and involved them in no kind of sacrifice. There was no need to fence off any space beforehand; the stage could be erected and dismantled in about a quarter of an hour. The performances lasted an hour and a half, and if an order had suddenly come from higher up to stop the proceedings, it could have been done in an instant. The costumes were hidden away in the convicts' boxes. But before I describe the construction of the stage and the nature of the costumes, I will say a word about the programme, that is, about what it was proposed to perform.

There was no regular written programme. One did, however, make its appearance at the second and third performances; it had been written out by Baklushin for the officers and other distinguished visitors who had honoured our theatre with their presence even at the first performance. From among the officers, the officer on duty usually came in, and their commanding officer himself looked in once; we had one visit also from the Engineer officer. It was in case of such visitors that the programme was produced. It was anticipated that the fame of the prison theatre would resound far and wide through the fortress and even the town itself, especially since there was no theatre there.* It was said that a group of amateurs had once got up a single performance, but that was all. The prisoners rejoiced like children in their smallest success and even grew quite puffed up. 'Why, who knows,' they thought to themselves or said to one another, 'perhaps the very highest authorities may get to know of it; they will come and watch; then they will see what convicts are like. This is no simple soldiers' production, with some sort of puppets, and boats on the waves, and walking bears and goats. These are actors, playing a comedy like in the real theatre; there is no such theatre even in the town. There was once a performance, they say, at General Abrosimov's, and there will be again; well, as far as costumes go they can beat us; but when it comes to *dialogue*, who knows if they are any better than us? It will reach the Governor's ears, perhaps, and—what tricks can't the devil play?—maybe he will want to come and see us himself. There isn't a theatre in the town' . . . The prisoners' fancy, in short, especially after the success of the first night, went to the greatest lengths during those holidays, even as far as the thought of rewards or shortened terms of penal servitude, although at the same time they almost immediately began to laugh good-naturedly at themselves. In one word, they were children, absolute children, even though some of them were children forty years old.

In spite of the fact that there were no programmes I already knew, in outline, the contents of the proposed production. The first piece was *The Rivals Philatka and Miroshka*.* A full week before the performance, Baklushin had been bragging to me that the part of Philatka, which he had undertaken himself, would be so played that the like had not been seen even in the St. Petersburg theatre. He wandered about the barracks, boasting unmercifully and shamelessly but altogether good-naturedly, and sometimes suddenly letting fly with some 'acting', that is, with a bit of his part—and everybody would guffaw whether what he came out with was funny or not. I must, however, admit—and here the convicts showed that they knew how to control themselves and preserve their dignity—that those who went into ecstasies over Baklushin's sallies and his tales of the coming performances were either the very youngest and rawest new-comers or else the most important convicts, whose authority was unshakably established, so that they had no need to be afraid of the open expression of their feelings, whatever these might be, even if they were of the most simple-hearted (that is, according to prison ideas, the most unseemly) character. The others heard the rumours and gossip in silence, without criticism or contradiction, it is true, but with a most determined effort to treat the talk with indifference and even condescension. Only at the very last, practically on the day of the performance itself, did everybody begin to express interest: what will it be like? how are our lads doing? what about the major? will it be as good as the year before last? &c. Baklushin assured me that all the actors had been magnificently 'chosen for their parts'. That there would even be a curtain. That Philatka's fiancée would be played by Sirotkin—'and you will see for yourself what he looks like in women's clothes!' he said, screwing up his eyes and clicking his tongue. The Lady Bountiful would have a dress with flounces, and a pelerine, and carry a parasol, and the benevolent squire would appear in an officer's frock-coat with shoulder-cords and a cane. After this would come another piece, a drama: *Kedril the Glutton*.* The title very much interested me, but however many questions I asked, I could learn nothing about this play beforehand. I found out only that it had not been taken from a book but was 'copied out', and that they had obtained it from a certain non-commissioned officer in the suburbs, who had probably taken part in a performance of it in some soldiers' theatre. We, in our remote towns and provinces, have indeed such plays, unknown, it would seem, to anybody and perhaps never printed anywhere, which have appeared of their own accord from somewhere and constitute an indispensable appurtenance of every popular theatre in a certain region of Russia. By the way, I spoke of the 'popular theatre'. It would be an extremely good thing if one of our researchers would occupy himself with new and more careful investigations than previously into the popular theatre, which exists and flourishes and is not perhaps entirely without merit. I refuse to believe that everything I subsequently saw in our prison theatre had been devised by our own convicts. There must inevitably be a heritage of traditions, once-accepted modes of behaviour and conceptions, handed down from one generation to another from time immemorial. They must be sought among private soldiers and workers in industrial towns and even among the artisans and tradespeople in some unknown, poverty-stricken little towns. They have been preserved also in the country and in provincial towns among the servants of the great landowning houses. I think, indeed, that many old plays have been propagated in manuscript copies throughout Russia through no other medium than that of these great landowners' households. The landed gentry of former times and the great Moscow nobles used to have their own private theatrical companies of artists from among their serfs. And there are unmistakable indications that it was in those theatres that our popular dramatic art had its beginnings. As for *Kedril the Glutton*, however much I tried, I could learn nothing of it beforehand, except that evil spirits appeared on the scene and carried Kedril off to Hell. But what was the significance of 'Kedril' instead of Cyril?; was it of Russian or foreign provenance? I could not arrive at the answer. In conclusion, it was announced that a 'pantomime with music' would be presented. All this, of course, aroused great curiosity. There were some fifteen actors, all bold and confident spirits. They bustled about, held rehearsals, sometimes behind the barracks, concealed themselves and kept their own counsel. In short, they intended to surprise us all with something out of the ordinary and unexpected.

On working days the barracks were locked early, as soon as night fell. During the Christmas season an exception was made: locking-up was deferred until it was quite dark. This privilege was granted specifically for the theatre. While the festival lasted, before the evening of every day, there was usually sent out from the prison a humble request to the officer on duty 'to permit the theatrical performance and not to lock the prison for some time', with the additional remark that on the previous day also there had been a performance, that the locking-up had been postponed for a long time and that there had been no disorder. The officer reasoned thus: 'there were indeed no disorders yesterday and since they give their word that there will be none today, it means that they will see to it themselves, and this is the strongest of all safeguards. Besides, if I don't allow the performance, perhaps (who knows?—they are convicts) they will be deliberately troublesome and make difficulties for the sentries.' Finally, there was another point: sentry-duty is always boring, and here was a theatre, not a mere soldiers', but a convicts' theatre, and convicts are interesting people: it would be pleasant to watch. And the officer on duty has always the right to watch.

The orderly officer might come along: 'Where is the officer on duty?' 'He's gone into the prison to number the prisoners and lock the barracks'—a straightforward answer and a satisfactory excuse. In this manner, every evening during the holiday the officer on duty gave his permission for the performance and postponed locking the barracks until it was almost time for 'Lights Out'. The prisoners had known beforehand that there would be no obstacles raised on the part of the guard, and on that score their minds were easy.

Before seven o'clock Petrov came for me, and we went to the performance together. Nearly everybody from our barrack went, except the Old Believer from Chernigov and the Poles. The Poles did not make up their minds to visit the theatre until the very last performance on the fourth of January, and then only after they had been assured that it was good and amusing, and that there was no risk in going. The Poles' fastidiousness did not in the least disturb the other convicts and they were very courteously received on the fourth of January. They were even admitted to the best places. As for the Circassians and Isaiah Fomich, especially the latter, our theatre was a real joy to them. Isaiah Fomich gave three copecks every time and at the last performance put ten copecks in the plate, and his face was a picture of bliss. The actors had settled to collect from those present what each chose to give, for expenses and for their own *refreshment*. Petrov assured me that I should be allowed to occupy one of the best places, crowded to suffocation though the place might be, on the grounds that as I was richer than the others, I might be expected to give more, and besides I was more of a connoisseur than they. And so it turned out. But I must first describe the room and the arrangement of the theatre.

Our military barrack, in which the theatre had been constructed, was about fifteen yards long. From the courtyard one mounted the steps, then went into an entrance-lobby and thence into the barrack. This long room, as I have already said, was arranged in a special manner: the planks stretched like a shelf along the walls, so that the middle of the room was left free. The half of the room which was nearer the entrance from the porch was given up to the audience; the other half, which communicated with another barrack, was occupied by the stage. The first thing that impressed me was the curtain. It stretched, ten yards wide, right across the barrack. A curtain was such a luxury that the mere existence of one gave some excuse for wonderment. In addition, it was painted in oils; the design represented trees, arbours, ponds, and stars. It was made of canvas, some old and some new, one man giving so much here, another sacrificing so much there; made of old prison sheets and leg-wrappings cobbled together into a large sheet, it had one part, for which there had not been enough canvas, made simply of paper, which had also been begged, piece by piece, from various offices. Our painters, including our distinguished 'Brülow', Aristov, had charged themselves with drawing and colouring it. The effect was astonishing. Such splendours rejoiced the hearts of even the gloomiest and most carping prisoners, who, when the time of the performance came, without exception proved to be just as much children as the most fiery and impatient ones. Everybody was well satisfied, even complacent. The lighting consisted of a few tallow candles cut in pieces. In front of the curtain stood two benches from the kitchen, and in front of them two or three chairs which had been found in the non-commissioned officers' room. The chairs were intended, if the need arose, for the very highest personages of officers' rank. The benches were for non-commissioned officers, Engineer clerks, guards, and others who, although in positions of authority, were not of officers' rank, in case they looked in at the prison. So, indeed, they did; we were never without visitors from outside all through the holiday; one evening there would be more of them and another fewer, but at the last performance not a single place on the benches remained unoccupied. Finally, behind the benches again, came the convicts, standing, bare-headed in deference to the visitors, and wearing their jackets or short sheepskin coats in spite of the close steamy atmosphere of the room. There was, of course, far too little space for the prisoners. Besides the fact that some were literally sitting on top of others, especially in the back rows, the planks and the wings were all filled and there were even some devotees, constant frequenters of the theatre, in the other barrack, watching the performance from beyond the back of the stage. There was an unnatural crowding in the front half of the barrack, perhaps equal even to the thronging and crushing that I had so recently seen in the bath. The door into the entrance-lobby was open and there also, where there was twenty degrees of frost, the people stood in throngs. We, Petrov and I, were at once let through to the front, almost up to the benches, where it was much easier to see than in the back rows. This was partly because they saw in me the critic, the connoisseur, the frequenter of different theatres; they had seen Baklushin consulting me frequently and treating me with respect; now, therefore, I must be accorded all honour, and a good place. Let us concede that the convicts were in the highest degree vain and frivolous, but this was all affectation. They might laugh at me when they saw that I was useless to them as a helper at work; Almazov might regard us aristocrats with scorn and parade his skill at calcining gypsum before us. But there was something else mingled with their persecution and ridicule of us: we had once been gentry, we belonged to the same class as their former masters, of whom their remembrances could not be good. But now, in the theatre, they made way for me. They recognized that in this matter I might be a better judge than they. Those among them who were least well disposed towards me now (as I know) desired my commendation of their theatre and, without the least self-abasement, yielded me the best place. This is my present judgement, based on my impressions at the time. It seemed to me then, I remember, that their just estimate of themselves had nothing servile in it, but only a sense of personal dignity. A high and most characteristic trait of our common people is their feeling for justice and their thirst for it. The cocky habit of putting oneself in front everywhere *at whatever cost* and whether one is worthy of the first place or not, is not found among the people. One need only remove the outer husk and scrutinize the grain within attentively, closely and without prejudice, to see things in the people of which he had never even dreamed. Our wiseacres cannot teach the people very much. I will even maintain that, on the contrary, they ought themselves to learn from them.

Petrov had naïvely told me, while we were preparing to

go to the theatre, that I should be admitted to the front
rows for the additional reason that I should give more
money. There were no fixed prices: everybody gave what
he could or what he wished. Almost everybody put in something, even if it was only half a copeck, when a collection
was taken on a plate. But if I was let through to the front
partly because of the money, on the supposition that I would
give more than others, how much sense of personal dignity
there nevertheless was, even in this! 'You are richer than me,
so come to the front, for, although we are all equal here, yet
you will give more; consequently, a visitor like you is more
welcome to the actors; the first place is for you, because none
of us owes his place here to money but to respect and so we
ourselves ought to sort ourselves out.' How much truly
noble pride there is in this! It shows not respect for money,
but respect for oneself. Generally speaking there was no
respect for money in the prison, especially if one considers
the prisoners as a whole, in the mass or in their *artels*. Even
if I had to review each one singly, I do not recollect that
there was one who seriously debased himself because of
money. Scroungers indeed did exist, and they begged money
from me. But there was more of swindling and cheating than
of real begging in this procedure; it was more simple-hearted
and humorous. I do not know whether I make myself understood . . . But I was forgetting about the theatre. To
business.

Before the curtain was raised, the whole room presented
a strange and lively picture. To begin with, there was the
crowd of spectators, jammed, crushed, and squeezed together,
waiting patiently and with blissful faces for the performance
to begin. In the back rows the people clustered one on top
of the other. Many of them had brought with them from
the kitchen thick billets of wood; fixing one end of one of
these somehow against the wall, a man would clamber up
on it, propping himself with both hands against the shoulders
of those standing in front, and would stand thus for two

hours without changing his position, thoroughly pleased with himself and his place. Others buttressed themselves with their legs on the lower step of the stove and, leaning on those in front, stood all the time in this posture. This was in the rearmost rows near the wall. Along the side, perched on the planks above the musicians, stood another solid crowd. These were good places. Five or six men had planted themselves on the stove itself, and lay looking down from it. How they beamed with joy! On the window-sills along the other side clustered a throng of late-comers or those who had not been able to find good places. Everybody behaved quietly and decorously. Everybody wished to display himself in the best light before the officers and visitors. Every face reflected the most simple-hearted expectation. All of them were red and drenched with sweat from the heat and stuffiness. What a strange gleam of childlike happiness, of pure and delightful pleasure, shone on those seamed and branded foreheads and cheeks, in the glances of those men, always so sullen and gloomy, in those eyes which could sometimes glitter with a terrible flame! Everybody was bareheaded and from the right side every head presented a shaven surface to me. But listen, you can hear noise and bustle on the stage! The curtain is on the point of rising. The orchestra has just begun to play . . . This orchestra is deserving of mention. Along the side of the room, on the planks, some eight musicians had taken their places: two fiddles (one was already in the prison, the other had been borrowed from somebody in the fortress, but the player had also been found in the prison), three balalaikas, all crudely home-made, two guitars, and a tambourine in place of a double bass. The violins merely squeaked and whined, the guitars were atrociously bad, the balalaikas on the other hand were extraordinary. The nimbleness of the fingers strumming on the strings was certainly the equal of that required for the cleverest sleight of hand. The tunes played were all dances. In the liveliest passages the balalaika-players drummed with their fingers on the sounding-boards of their instruments; the tone, the taste, the execution, the way of handling the instruments, the character of the interpretation—all were in a class of their own, original, peculiar to convicts. One of the guitarists was also magnificently familiar with his instrument. This was that same former nobleman who had killed his father. As for the tambourinist, he simply performed miracles; now the tambourine spun on his finger, now his thumbs thrummed on its skin; now there came loud, rapid, even beats, now the heavy staccato suddenly dissolved, as it were, into a pattering murmur of innumerable tiny whispering, rattling notes. Finally there were two concertinas. Upon my word, I had never until that moment guessed what could be done with such simple popular musical instruments; the blending of tones, the skill of the playing, and, most of all, the feeling, the understanding and reproduction of the very essence of the music, were quite astounding. For the first time I completely understood exactly what there is of infinite revelry and audacity in the festive and reckless Russian dancing-songs. At length the curtain rose. There was a general stir; everybody shifted his weight from one foot to the other, those at the back raised themselves on tiptoe, some man slipped from his billet of wood; without exception, all mouths were open, all eyes were fixed, and the most complete silence reigned . . . The performance began.

Near me stood Aley among a group of his brothers and the other Circassians. They had all become passionately devoted to the theatre and went nearly every evening. All Mussulmans, Tartars, and so on, as I have more than once observed, are passionate lovers of every kind of spectacle. Beside them crouched Isaiah Fomich as well, apparently transformed, from the moment the curtain rose, into nothing but eyes and ears and a naïve and avid expectation of wonders and delights. It would have been lamentable indeed if his expectations had been disappointed. Aley's charming face shone with such beautiful, childlike joy that I confess it made me immensely happy to look at him, and I remember that every time an actor on the stage made some droll or clever sally and the room resounded with laughter, I would immediately turn and glance at his face. He did not see me; he was not concerned with me! Not very far away on my left stood another prisoner, an elderly man, always scowling, always grumbling and dissatisfied. He also noticed Aley, and I saw him turn several times to look at him with a half-smile; he was so delightful! 'Aley Semënovich', he used to call him, I don't know why. The performance began with *Philatka and Miroshka*. The Philatka (Baklushin) was really magnificent. He had an astonishingly clear-cut conception of the part. It was plain that he had studied every speech and every gesture. To every least word, to every movement, he succeeded in giving a sense and significance that were entirely in keeping with the character he was playing. Add to this study and the pains he had taken his astounding, unquenchable high spirits, his simplicity and lack of sophistication, and you would certainly, had you seen Baklushin, have agreed that he was a genuine actor born, with great talent. I had seen *Philatka* on the stages of Moscow and St. Petersburg, and I assert positively that both actors who played the part in the capitals played it worse than Baklushin. In comparison with him they were stage peasants and not real moujiks. They were over-anxious to present the moujik. Baklushin, moreover, had been stimulated by rivalry: everybody knew that the role of Kedril in the second play was to be taken by the prisoner Potseykin, an actor who was for some reason generally considered better and more gifted than Baklushin. Baklushin, like a child, was hurt by this. How many times he had come to me during the past few days and poured out his feelings! For two hours before the performance he was shaking with fever. When the crowd laughed and called out to him, 'Fine, Baklushin! Bravo, bravo!' his whole face was radiant with joy and true inspiration shone in his eyes. The kissing-scene with Miroshka, when Philatka shouts at him beforehand, 'Wipe your face!' and wipes his own, proved side-splitting. Everybody simply rolled with laughter. For me, however, the greatest interest lay in the audience: in this place everybody was unbuttoned. They had unreservedly surrendered to their enjoyment. Shouts of approval came thicker and thicker. Here one man nudged his neighbour in his haste to communicate his impressions, not caring, and perhaps not even seeing, who was standing next to him; another, at some funny point, would turn in an ecstasy of appreciation to the crowd, embrace them with a rapid glance as though exhorting them to laugh, wave his arm, and at once turn back eagerly to the stage, greedy for more. A third simply clicked his tongue and snapped his fingers; he found it impossible to remain still in his place and as there was nowhere to move to had to content himself with shifting from one foot to the other. Towards the end of the play the general mood of merriment had attained its highest point. I am not exaggerating in the slightest degree. Picture the prison, the fetters, the servitude, the long sad years to come, the monotonous existence, like drops of rain on a grey day in autumn—and then suddenly all these herded and captive men are allowed for one brief hour to relax and enjoy themselves, to forget the troubled dream of their lives, to construct a complete theatre—and in what a fashion! to the pride and astonishment of the whole town; as if to say, 'Look, now you know what we are like, we prisoners!' Everything, of course, was engrossing to them, the costumes, for example. It was terribly interesting to see some Vanka Otpety, for example, or Netsvetaev or Baklushin, in clothes so completely different from those in which they had seen them every day for so many years. 'Why, here's a convict, a convict whose fetters go jangle-jangle, and now he appears in a frock-coat and a round hat and a cloak—just like a civilian! He has fixed moustaches on his face and hair on his head. Look there, he has taken a red handkerchief from his pocket and is fanning himself with it; he plays the gentleman for all the world as if he were a gentleman himself!' Everybody is delighted. The 'benevolent squire' appeared in an adjutant's uniform (a very old one, it is true), epaulettes and a cockaded cap, and looked extraordinarily effective. There had been two aspirants for this part and—will this be believed?—they had quarrelled like little children over who should play it: they both longed to display themselves in an officer's uniform with shoulder-cords. The other actors had separated them and decided, by a majority of votes, to give the part to Netsvetaev, not because he was more dashing and handsome and therefore would more closely resemble a gentleman than the other, but because he assured everybody he would come on with a walking-cane and would flourish it and trace designs on the ground with it like a real gentleman and the prince of dandies, which Vanka Otpety could not do, because he had never even seen real gentlemen . . . And, in fact, when Netsvetaev entered with his lady he did nothing but draw freely and rapidly on the ground with the tip of a thin little rattan cane he had procured from somewhere, probably considering this the mark of the greatest gentility, the height of elegance and fashion. At some time in his childhood, as a barefooted little boy in a family of domestic serfs, he had probably chanced to see an elegantly dressed gentleman with a walking-stick, and been captivated by his skill in twirling it—and lo, the impression had ever since remained ineffaceable in his mind, so that now, at thirty-five years old, he remembered everything just as it had been, for the delight and fascination of the whole prison. Netsvetaev was so absorbed in his occupation that he did not look at anybody or anything, and did not raise his eyes even when he spoke, but only followed the movements of the tip of his cane. The Lady Bountiful was also remarkably striking, in her own way; she appeared in an old, worn muslin dress which looked like a veritable rag, with bare arms and neck, her face horribly daubed with red and white, wearing a calico nightcap tied under her chin; she had a sunshade in one hand and in the other a painted paper fan with which she fanned herself incessantly. A volley of laughter saluted the lady; the lady herself, indeed, could not contain herself and several times gave way to mirth. She was played by the convict Ivanov. Sirotkin, dressed as a girl, was charming. The songs also went off well. In a word, the play was concluded to the complete general satisfaction. There was no criticism; how could there be?

The overture was played through again and once more the curtain rose. This was *Kedril*. *Kedril* is something like *Don Juan*; at any rate, both the hero and his servant are carried off to hell by devils towards the end of the play. A whole act was performed, but this was evidently only a fragment; the beginning and end had been lost. There is not the slightest reason or logic in the whole thing. The action takes place in an inn, somewhere in Russia. The innkeeper leads into a room a gentleman in a greatcoat and a battered round hat. After him comes his servant Kedril, carrying a trunk and a chicken wrapped in blue paper. Kedril wears a short sheepskin coat and a lackey's cap. He is a great glutton. The convict Potseykin, Baklushin's rival, played Kedril; the gentleman was acted by the same Ivanov who had taken the part of the Lady Bountiful in the first play. The innkeeper (Netsvetaev) warns them that the room is haunted by devils and goes off. The gentleman, morose and preoccupied, mutters to himself that he has long known it, and orders Kedril to unpack and prepare supper. Kedril is a coward and a glutton. When he hears about the devils he turns pale and trembles like a leaf. He would run away, but he is afraid of his master. Besides, he is very hungry. He is lustful, stupid, cunning in his own way, and cowardly; he cheats his master at every step and yet fears him at the same time. This remarkable study of a servant, in which the features of Leporello are somewhat faintly and distantly discernible, was really excellently played. Potseykin had a decided talent and I thought him an even better actor than Baklushin. Of course, when I met Baklushin the next day, I did not fully reveal my opinion to him: that would have distressed him too much. The prisoner who played the gentleman did not act badly, either. His speeches were the most appalling rubbish, unlike anything on earth, but they were correctly and briskly spoken and his gestures were suitable. While Kedril busies himself with the luggage, his master walks moodily about the stage and declares for all to hear that the present evening sees the end of his wanderings. Kedril listens inquisitively, grimaces, utters 'asides', and makes the audience laugh with every word. He has no pity for his master; but having heard devils spoken of he wants to find out what it all means and now he begins talking and asking questions. His master finally explains that at one time, in a tight corner, he turned for aid to the powers of darkness, and the devils helped and rescued him; but today his time is up and perhaps this very night they will come for his soul, in accordance with the bargain he made. Kedril begins to grow terrified. His master, however, has not lost heart and bids him prepare supper. At the word supper Kedril cheers up, takes out the chicken and the wine and, in a twinkling, nips off a piece of the chicken and eats it. The audience guffaws. Now the door creaks, the wind rattles the shutters; Kedril shudders and hastily, hardly conscious of what he is doing, crams a huge piece of chicken, too big to swallow, into his mouth. Another roar of laughter. 'Isn't it ready yet?' cries the gentleman, as he walks about the room. 'At once, sir; . . . I am . . . getting it ready,' says Kedril, sits down at the table and calmly begins to devour his master's supper. The audience was evidently delighted with the servant's dexterity and cunning and with the fact that the gentleman was made a fool of. It must be acknowledged that Potseykin was really deserving of praise. The words: 'At once, sir; I am getting it ready' were excellently spoken. Seated at the table, Kedril begins to eat greedily, starting up at every step of his master's, in order that he shall not notice his tricks; as soon as his master turns round, he hides under the table and takes the chicken with him. At last he has blunted the edge of his hunger; it is time to think of his master. 'Kedril, will you be long?' cries that gentleman. 'Ready, sir,' briskly announces Kedril, suddenly realizing that almost nothing is left. In fact, only one chicken leg remains in the dish. The master, gloomily preoccupied and noticing nothing, sits down at the table and Kedril stations himself behind the chair with a napkin. Every word, every gesture, every grimace of Kedril's when, turning towards the audience, he motioned towards his nincompoop of a master, was greeted with uncontrollable laughter by the spectators. But now, as soon as the master begins to eat, the devils appear. Here everything became quite incomprehensible, and the devils themselves seemed altogether too fantastically impossible; a door in the wings opened and there entered something in white, and in place of its head there was a lantern containing a candle; another apparition, also with a lantern on its head, held a scythe in its hand. Why the lanterns, why the scythe, why devils in white, it was impossible for anybody to explain to himself. Nobody, however, stopped to consider this. I suppose it was all taken for granted. The gentleman turns sufficiently boldly to the devils and cries that he is ready for them to take him. But Kedril is as timid as a hare; he creeps under the table, not forgetting, in spite of all his fright, to seize the bottle as he goes. The devils go off for a moment; Kedril crawls out from under the table; but no sooner has the gentleman addressed himself again to the chicken than three devils burst once more into the room, seize him from behind, and carry him off to the nether regions. 'Kedril, save me!' cries his master. But Kedril has other fish to fry. This time he has taken the bottle and a plate and even the bread as well under the table. But now he is alone, the devils have gone and so has his master. He creeps out and looks round and a smile lights up his face. He screws up his eyes with knavish cunning, sits down in his master's place and, nodding to the audience, says in a half-whisper:

'Well, now I am alone . . . without a master! . . .'

Everybody laughed because he had lost his master; but now he adds in the same tone, confidentially addressing the audience and winking more and more cheerfully:

'The devils have taken my master! . . .'

The spectators' delight knew no bounds. Besides the fact that devils had carried off his master, it was said with such a comically triumphant grimace, that it was really impossible not to applaud. But Kedril's luck does not last for long. As soon as he has laid hands on the bottle and poured some wine into a glass, and just as he is on the point of drinking, the devils reappear, steal up behind him on tiptoe, and pounce on him from each side. Kedril yells with all the power of his lungs; he is too faint-hearted to dare turn round. Neither is he able to defend himself; in his hands are the bottle and glass, which he cannot find the strength to put down. Gaping with fright he sits for a moment, goggling at the audience with such a comical expression of lily-livered terror that he might positively pose for a picture of it. Finally he is lifted up and carried off; still holding the bottle he screams and kicks and screams again. His screams still resound from the wings. Now the curtain fell; everybody was laughing and delighted . . . The band struck up a Cossack dance.

They began quietly, only just audibly, but the tune swelled and swelled, the tempo increased, the balalaika-players' fingers rattled dashingly on the bellies of their instruments . . . This was the gopak in its full glory and really Glinka* would have learned a great deal if he had chanced to hear it in our prison. The pantomime to music was beginning. The gopak was kept up all through it. The scene represented the interior of a peasant hut. On the stage were a miller and his wife. The miller was mending his harness in one corner, while in another his wife was spinning flax. Sirotkin played the wife, Netsvetaev the husband.

I must remark that our scenery was very poverty-stricken. In this scene, as in the preceding play and all the other scenes, one supplied the deficiencies from one's own imagination rather than saw with one's eyes. Instead of a back-cloth some sort of rug or horse-cloth had been stretched across; at the sides were ragged screens. The left side was not screened off at all, so that the plank-beds were visible. But the spectators were not looking for defects and were content to supplement the actuality with their fancy, especially since prisoners are well versed in doing this. 'This is called a garden, so take it as a garden; a room—then it's a room; a hut, then it's a hut; it doesn't matter, and there's no need to make a great fuss about it.' Sirotkin looked very nice in the costume of a young peasant woman; a few complimentary remarks were whispered among the audience. The miller finished his work, took his hat, seized his whip, went up to his wife, and explained to her by signs that he must go out, but that if she received anybody in his absence, then . . . and he pointed to his whip. His wife listened and nodded her head. That whip was probably very familiar to her: this young woman's ideas were apt to stray from her husband. The husband went off. As soon as he was outside the door, his wife shook her fist after him. But now there came a knock; the door opened and a neighbour appeared, another miller, a bearded peasant in a caftan. He bore a gift in his hand, a red kerchief. The woman smiled; but as the neighbour was just on the point of embracing her, there was another knock on the door. Where could he go? She hastily hid him under the table and applied herself again to her spindle. Another suitor entered: this was a clerk in military uniform. Up to this point the pantomime had been faultless, the miming irreproachably correct. One might even have been astonished, watching these untrained actors, and reflected involuntarily on how much energy and talent goes to waste in our Mother Russia, sometimes almost fruitlessly, in bondage and the bitter lot of the unfortunate. But the prisoner who played the clerk had at one time probably been in a provincial or domestic theatre, and he imagined that all our actors, without exception, lacked understanding of the matter and could not even walk on to the stage in the proper way. He, therefore, now entered as they say the classical heroes used to enter in the old days: he took one long stride and, before he had moved the other leg, halted abruptly, threw back his head and his whole body, looked haughtily round, and—took another step. If such a gait was funny in classical heroes, it was even funnier in a regimental clerk in a comic scene. But our audience thought that this was probably all as it should be and took the lanky clerk's long strides for granted, without special criticism. Hardly had the clerk managed to reach the middle of the stage than another knock was heard; again the hostess was in a panic. Where could she put the clerk?—In the chest, which fortunately stood open. The clerk crept into the chest and the woman lowered the lid on him. This time the visitor was a singular one—another lover but of a peculiar kind. He was a Hindu and he even had the right dress. An irrepressible shout of laughter went up from the audience. Convict Koshkin played the Hindu and played him excellently. He looked like a Brahmin. In sighs he expressed the whole extent of his love. He raised his hands to heaven and then laid them on his breast, above his heart; but no sooner had he reached the tenderest point of his declaration—than there came a mighty blow on the door. The very sound revealed that this was the master of the house. The wife was beside herself with fear, the Hindu hopped about like a scalded cat, imploring her to hide him. Hastily she pushed him behind the cupboard and herself, forgetting to open the door, rushed back to her yarn and began spinning away, deaf to her husband's knocking, twisting in panic at a thread which

was not in her hands, and turning the spindle she had forgotten to pick up from the floor. Sirotkin's acting of this
panic was very good and convincing. But the master of the
house kicked in the door and went up to his wife, whip in
hand. He had been keeping watch and had seen everything,
and he made signs to her that he knew she had three persons
hidden. Then he looked for them. The first he found was
the neighbour and him he escorted from the room with
blows. The faint-hearted clerk, intending to run away, lifted
the lid of the chest with his head and thus betrayed himself.
The miller urged him on his way with a taste of the whip,
and this time the lovelorn clerk's gait was not in the least
classical. There remained the Brahmin; the husband sought
him for a long time and at last found him in the corner,
bowed to him politely, and dragged him into the middle of
the stage by the beard. The Hindu tried to defend himself
and yelled 'Accursed, accursed!' (the only words that were
uttered in the pantomime), but the husband did not heed
him and took his revenge in his favourite fashion. The wife,
seeing that her turn was coming, abandoned her yarn and
her spindle and ran out of the room; the spindle tumbled
to the ground and the convicts laughed aloud. Aley, without
looking at me, plucked me by the arm and cried: 'Look, the
Hindu, the Hindu!' and helplessly abandoned himself to
laughter. The curtain fell. Another scene began . . .

But I cannot describe all the scenes. There were two or
three more. They were all funny and unaffectedly gay. If
the convicts had not written them themselves, they had at
least made their own contributions to each of them. Practically every actor improvised freely, so that on the next
night one and the same man played one and the same part
rather differently. The last pantomime, of a fantastic nature,
ended with a ballet. A corpse was being buried. The Brahmin, with a numerous following, performed various con-
jurations over the grave but to no effect. At last 'The Setting
Sun' was played, the corpse revived, and everybody began

to dance with joy. The Brahmin danced with the corpse, and danced in a very peculiar manner, like a Hindu. This was the end of the performance, until the following evening. All our people, expressing gratitude to the sergeant and praising the actors, dispersed in a happy mood, well content. No wrangling was heard. Everybody was somehow unusually pleased, what might almost be called happy, and they all went to sleep, not as on any other night, but almost with a quiet spirit—and whence did it come? It was, nevertheless, no dream of my imagination. It was true and real. These poor creatures had only to be allowed to live for a tiny space in their own way, to enjoy themselves as ordinary people do, to pass one little hour free from prison routine—and their moral nature was changed, even if only for a few minutes . . . But now it was deep into the night. Some chance made me start awake; the old man was still muttering his prayers on top of the stove and would continue to do so until daybreak; next to me Aley was quietly sleeping. I remembered that even as he fell asleep he still laughed and chattered to his brothers about the theatre, and I found myself watching his peaceful, childish face with involuntary pleasure. Little by little I remembered everything, the past day, the holiday, all this month . . . and I lifted my head in terror and looked round at my sleeping companions by the dim wavering light of the cheap prison candle. I looked at their pale faces, their wretched beds, at all that hopeless misery and beggary, peering as closely as though I must make certain that all this was not the continuation of an ugly dream, but the real truth. But it was the truth: now I heard a groan from somewhere and somebody heavily flung out an arm with a clash of fetters. Another started in his sleep and began to talk, and the old man on the stove prayed for all 'Orthodox Christians'; I could hear his quiet, rhythmical, long-drawn-out 'Oh Lord Jesus Christ, have mercy upon us!'

'I am not here for ever, but only for a few years, after all!' I thought, and again laid my head down on my pillow.

PART II

1. The Hospital (i)

SOON after the holiday I fell ill and was removed to our military hospital.* It stood in isolation half a verst from the fortress. It was a long building of one story, painted yellow. In summer, when repair work was done, an extraordinary amount of yellow ochre was expended on it. In its enormous courtyard were situated the offices, the houses of the medical staff, and other buildings serving it. The main structure, however, contained only wards. There were many of these but only two for the prisoners, which were always well filled, especially in summer, so that the beds had often to be moved closer together. Our wards were filled with 'unfortunates' of every kind. Our convicts came there and various kinds of military criminals, classified into various categories —sentenced, awaiting sentence, and in transit; men came also from the correctional company, a strange institution to which soldiers from the battalions whose conduct was unsatisfactory or who were considered hopeless material were sent for reformatory discipline, and from which they usually emerged, after two years or more, finished scoundrels such as are rarely encountered. Those of our convicts who fell ill usually reported their illness to the corporal in the morning. They were at once listed in a book and sent under guard, with the book, to the military infirmary. There the doctors saw all the sick men from all the military commands distributed through the fortress, and those whom they found to be really ill were sent to the hospital. I was entered in the book, and some time after one o'clock, when everybody was leaving the prison for the afternoon's work, I went into the hospital. A sick prisoner usually took with him as much money as he could, bread (because he could not expect any rations in the hospital that day), a tiny pipe and a pouch containing tobacco and a flint and steel. These last objects were carefully hidden in the boots. I entered the precincts of the hospital not without some curiosity about this new aspect, as yet unknown to me, of our prison existence.

The day was warm, overcast, and dreary—one of those days when institutions like the hospital take on a particularly drab, sour, and sullen aspect. Together with my guards I went into the reception room, where stood two copper bath-tubs and where two other sick men, under arrest, were already waiting, with their guards. An orderly entered, looked us over in an indolent and lordly fashion, and went off even more indolently to inform the doctor on duty. The doctor soon appeared, examined us, treating us very kindly, and gave us 'charts' bearing our names. The further diagnosis of our illnesses, the prescription of medicines, diet, and so on, were the business of the house-surgeon in charge of the prison wards. I already knew that the prisoners thought no praise high enough for their doctors. 'They're as good as a father to you!' they said in answer to my questions, when I was about to go into the hospital. Meanwhile, we changed our clothes. The shirts and outer garments in which we had come were taken away and we were put into hospital shirts; in addition we were given long stockings, slippers, night-caps, and thick brown cloth dressing-gowns, lined with some kind of coarse, thick, hard material, almost like sticking-plaster. The dressing-gown was, to put it bluntly, absolutely filthy, but it was not until later that I realized the full extent of its uncleanness. Then we were taken to the prison wards, which were situated at the end of a very long, high, clean corridor. The surface cleanness everywhere was very gratifying; everything which met your eyes positively shone. This, however, may only have seemed so after the prison. The two men awaiting trial went to the ward on the left, I to the one

on the right. By the door, which was fastened with an iron
bolt, stood a sentry with a rifle, and next to him was another
guard. A corporal (one of the hospital guard) ordered me
to be let through and I found myself in a long narrow room
with beds standing along both sides; there were about
twenty-two of them and three or four were unoccupied.
The beds were those wooden ones, painted green, which
each and every one of us in Russia knows only too well—
those beds which, by some kind of predestination, can
never be free of bugs. I established myself in a corner on
the window side.

As I have already said, some of our convicts from the
prison were here. Several of them already knew me, or had
at least seen me before. There were far more men awaiting
trial or the execution of their sentences, and men from the
correctional company. There were not very many who were
seriously ill, unable, that is, to get out of bed. The others,
less seriously ill or convalescent, were either sitting on their
beds or walking up and down the room, where a space big
enough for this purpose remained between the two rows of
beds. The ward had an extraordinarily suffocating hospital
smell. The air was tainted with various unpleasant emana-
tions and the smell of medicaments, in spite of the fact that
the stove in the corner was lighted nearly all day long.
My bed was covered with a striped quilt. I took this off.
Under it appeared a woollen blanket lined with coarse
crash, and a thick sheet of very doubtful cleanness. A little
table, on which were a jug and a tin cup, stood beside the
bed. All this was decently covered by the small towel which
had been issued to me. Underneath the table was a shelf; on
this those who drank tea kept their teapots, pitchers of kvass,
and so on; but there were very few even among the sick who
drank tea. The pipes and pouches, though, which nearly
everybody, not excluding the consumptives, possessed, were
hidden under the beds. The doctor and other officials hardly
ever inspected them and if they caught anybody with a pipe

they pretended not to notice. Even the very sick, however, were nearly always careful to go near the stove to smoke. Very occasionally at night somebody might smoke in bed; but at night nobody went round the wards, except perhaps an officer sometimes, the commander of the hospital guard.

Until then I had never been a patient in any hospital; all my surroundings, therefore, had an exceptional novelty. I noticed that I aroused some curiosity. They had heard of me and they inspected me very unceremoniously and even with a shade of condescension, as though I were a new boy at school or a petitioner in a public office. Next to me on the right lay a prisoner awaiting sentence, the natural son of a retired captain. He had been convicted of counterfeiting money, and had already been in hospital about a year, but I do not think there was anything wrong with him, although he had convinced the doctors that he was suffering from an aneurism. He attained his object; he avoided corporal punishment and hard labour and, a year later, was sent away to T—,* to be kept in a hospital. He was a stocky, thickset fellow of about twenty-eight, a great swindler and an amateur lawyer, far from stupid, an extremely cheeky and confident young man, morbidly vain and quite seriously convinced that he was the most honest and upright person in the world, and even that he was completely innocent of all wrongdoing, a conviction in which he remained absolutely and for ever unshakable. He addressed me first, asked many inquisitive questions and informed me in some detail of the internal arrangements of the hospital. It goes without saying that the first thing he told me was that he was the son of a captain. He was immeasurably anxious to pass for a nobleman, or at least as 'well born'. After him I was approached by a patient from the correctional company, who told me that he was acquainted with many exiled noblemen, to whom he referred by their Christian names and patronymics. He was an old soldier; I could see from his face that he was lying. He was called Chekunov. He was evidently trying to make up to me, probably because he suspected that I had some money. Having seen that I had a little packet of tea and sugar, he immediately offered his services to procure a teapot and make tea for me. Miretsky had promised to send me a teapot the next day from the prison by one of the convicts who came to the hospital to work. But Chekunov took the whole matter into his own hands. He procured an iron pot and even a cup, boiled the water and made tea and, in short, took such uncommon pains to serve me that one of the patients was moved to make some bitter and pointed observations on the subject. This patient was a consumptive in the bed opposite mine, a soldier under sentence, Ustyantsev by name. He was the man I have mentioned before, who, in terror of flogging, had drunk a jug of vodka in which a great deal of tobacco had been steeped, and thus contracted tuberculosis. Until now he had lain silent, breathing with difficulty, watching me intently and seriously, and following Chekunov's actions with indignation. His indignation was given a peculiarly comical effect by its extraordinary, rancorous intensity. At last, unable to restrain himself:

'Look at the slave! He's found himself a master!' he said haltingly, panting with weakness. He was already in the last days of his life.

Chekunov turned indignantly on him.

'Who's a slave?' he demanded, looking scornfully at Ustyantsev.

'You are!' answered the other, in a tone so confident that it conveyed that he had every right to scold Chekunov, or even that he had been specially attached to him for the purpose.

'I'm a slave?'

'Yes, you are! Listen, good people, he doesn't believe it! He's surprised!'

'What's the matter with you? Look, by themselves they have no hands. They're not used to being without servants, everybody knows that. So why not help them, you shaggy-faced fool?'

'Who's shaggy-faced?'

'You are!'

'I'm shaggy-faced?'

'Yes, you are!'

'And I suppose you're a beauty? You've got a face like a crow's egg . . . if I'm shaggy-faced.'

'Well, so you are, shaggy-faced! After all, if God sees fit to kill you you ought to lay down and die. But no, you have to keep on struggling. Why don't you give up?'

'Why? No, I'd rather kowtow to a boot than a clog. My father never humbled himself, and he told me not to. I . . . I . . .'

He would have gone on, but he was seized by a terrible fit of coughing and spitting blood which lasted for some minutes. Soon a cold sweat of exhaustion beaded his narrow forehead. The cough prevented him or he would have gone on talking; you could tell from his eyes how much he longed to keep up the wrangle, but in his weakness he could only wave him away . . . Thus towards the end Chekunov had quite forgotten about him.

I felt that the consumptive's spite was directed against me rather than Chekunov. Nobody would be angry with Chekunov or despise him for wanting to do me a service and so earn a copeck. Everybody knew that he was doing it simply for money. In this respect the common people are not over scrupulous and they know what's what. What Ustyantsev really disliked was myself; he did not like my tea or the fact that even in fetters I was still a gentleman and unable to dispense with servants—although in fact I was quite unused to being waited on and did not want it. Indeed, I always wanted to do everything for myself and was particularly anxious not even to seem to put myself forward as a soft-handed and womanish creature playing the fine gentleman. In fact, to be honest, some part of my self-esteem depended on this attitude. But—and I decidedly do not understand why this always happened—I could never shake off the various servitors and hangers-on who attached themselves to me and finally got me completely in their power, so that in reality they were my masters and I was their servant; somehow it always seemed to turn out that my outward appearance showed that I was indeed too lordly to do without servants and acting the fine gentleman. I found this, of course, very vexatious. But Ustyantsev was a consumptive and irritable. The other patients preserved an air of indifference, with a tinge even of condescension. I remember that they were all concerned with one special circumstance: from prison gossip I had learned that a man under sentence, who was at that very moment running the gauntlet, would be brought to us that evening. The prisoners awaited the new-comer with some curiosity. They said, however, that the punishment would be light—only *five hundred* altogether.

Little by little I surveyed everything around me. As far as I could see the really sick were principally sufferers from scurvy and diseases of the eye—which were endemic in that part of the world. There were several of these in the ward. The other genuine cases were ill with fevers, various sores, and diseases of the chest. This ward was not like the others: here all diseases, including even the venereal, were gathered together in one swarm. I say *genuine cases* because there were some who had *just come*, without any illness, 'for a rest'. The doctors admitted them willingly, from sympathy, especially when there were many empty beds. Conditions in the guardrooms and prison were so bad compared with those in the hospital that many convicts were delighted to come there as patients, in spite of the stifling air and the fact that the ward was locked. There were even some who really liked lying in bed and hospital life generally; most of these, however, were from the correctional company. I looked round curiously at all my new companions, but I remember that one aroused my particular interest—a dying man from our prison, another consumptive, also in his last days, who lay in the next bed but one to Ustyantsev and was thus almost opposite me. He was called Mikhaylov; only two weeks before I had seen him in the prison. He had been ill for a long time and ought to have gone for treatment long before; but with a kind of obstinate and unnecessary patience he had steeled and conquered himself and had come to hospital only at the holiday season, to die in three weeks of a terrible consumption which ate him up like a fire. I was struck now by the terrible alteration in his face—one of the first I had noticed when I entered the prison: it had somehow seemed to catch my eye. Next to him lay a 'correctional' soldier, who was already an old man and horribly and revoltingly sluttish . . . But I cannot go through the complete list of patients . . . I remember this nasty old man solely because he produced an impression on me and in one minute managed to give me a fairly complete understanding of some peculiarities of the prison ward. I remember that this old horror had a most violent cold in the head at the time. He was always sneezing, and all the next week he sneezed, even in his sleep, in regular volleys, five or six times together, punctually adding every time: 'Lord, what an affliction to have to bear!' At this moment he was sitting on his bed and greedily stuffing his nose with snuff from a twist of paper, so as to sneeze more violently and clear his head more thoroughly. He sneezed into a check cotton handkerchief, his own property, which had been washed a hundred times and was faded to the last degree, while his little nose wrinkled up in a peculiar fashion, falling into innumerable tiny lines, and the blackened old stumps of his teeth and his red, slobbery gums were revealed. When he had finished sneezing he immediately spread out his handkerchief, carefully inspected the abundant moisture which had accumulated in it and quickly smeared it on his prison dressing-gown, so that all the moisture remained on the dressing-gown and the handkerchief was left only very slightly damp. This he went on doing all the week. This painstaking and miserly care for his own handkerchief to the detriment of the government dressing-gown did not call forth any protest from the other patients, although one of them would have to wear the same dressing-gown after him. But our simple people are careless and unsqueamish to an extraordinary degree. But I shrank with revulsion and immediately, filled with curiosity and disgust, began an involuntary inspection of the dressing-gown I had just put on. I now realized that it had been attracting my notice for some time by its strong smell; it had by now had time to get warm on my body and smelt more and more powerfully of medicines, plasters, and, I thought, some kind of pus—which was not to be wondered at, since it had not left the shoulders of sick men for countless years. Perhaps the coarse lining in the back of it had been washed through occasionally, but I cannot be certain of this. On the other hand this lining was now impregnated with every conceivable kind of fluid, lotions, the water from broken blisters, and so on. Besides all this, the prison ward often received men who had just run the gauntlet, their backs covered with wounds; they were treated with wet dressings and thus the dressing-gown, put on straight over the wet shirt, could not but suffer, with all this left on it. And all the time I was in the prison, all those years, whenever I happened to be in the hospital (and that was fairly often), I always put on my dressing-gown with fearful mistrust. I particularly disliked the lice which were sometimes met with in them, huge and remarkably fat ones. The other convicts took pleasure in killing them; when one of the creatures cracked under a thick, clumsy thumb it was possible to judge from the very sight of the hunter's face what degree of satisfaction he had received. The bugs were also very unpopular with us and sometimes in the long dull winter evenings the whole ward would get out of bed in order to exterminate them. And although, in spite of the oppressive smell, everything in the ward seemed as clean as possible on the surface, we could not boast of inner or, so to

speak, *underneath*, cleanliness. The patients were used to
this state of affairs and even considered it inevitable; and
indeed the hospital rules did not tend to particular cleanliness. But of the rules I shall speak later.

As soon as Chekunov had served my tea (made, I may
remark in passing, with the ward water, which was brought
in once every twenty-four hours and only too quickly became
tainted in our atmosphere), the door was opened somewhat
noisily and there was led in, under reinforced guard, the
soldier who had just undergone the punishment of running
the gauntlet. This was the first time I had seen a man in this
condition. Subsequently I was to see many brought, and
some (whose punishment had been too severe) even carried
in, and every time the incident constituted a great distraction for the patients. These men were usually received
among us with expressions of intense sternness and even
with a certain amount of forced solemnity. The reception,
however, depended to some extent on the seriousness of the
crime and consequently on the amount of punishment. A
very badly beaten and, by reputation, desperate criminal
enjoyed more respect and attention than, for example, some
poor little recruit who had deserted, like this one who had
been brought in now. But in the one case as in the other no
particular sympathy was expressed, nor were any tactless
remarks made. The unfortunate man was helped and cared
for in silence, especially if he could not manage without aid.
The orderlies themselves knew that they were giving the
victim into the care of experienced and skilful hands. The
help usually consisted in the constant and necessary
changing of sheets or shirts wrung out of cold water which
were applied to the lacerated back, especially if the victim
was in no fit state to look after himself; and, in addition, of
the adroit plucking out from the wounds of splinters from
broken rods, which frequently lodged in the back. This last
operation was usually very painful for the sufferer. But
generally speaking I was always very surprised at the forti-

tude in enduring pain of these victims. I saw many of them, sometimes cruelly beaten, and hardly one of them uttered a groan! Only the face would be transformed; it would be pale, the eyes were inflamed, the look was wandering and uneasy, the lips quivered so that the poor wretch was obliged to bite them almost until the blood came. This time the soldier who had come in was a lad of about twenty-three years old, of strong and muscular build, tall, well-made and swarthy-skinned, with a handsome face. His back, however, had been fairly badly hurt. The upper part of his body was naked to the waist; a wet sheet had been thrown on his shoulders, making him shudder in every limb as though he had fever; and for an hour and a half he walked ceaselessly up and down the ward. I studied his face; he seemed not to be thinking of anything, but his eyes had a strange, wild look and his fleeting glance plainly could not rest on any object without laborious effort. I thought he looked hard at my tea. It was very hot and a cloud of steam rose from the cup, while the poor wretch was chilled to the bone and shivering, with chattering teeth. I offered him the tea. He turned silently and abruptly towards me, took the cup and drank the tea standing, without sugar and very hastily, while he seemed to be making a determined effort not to look at me. When he had drunk it all he put down the cup, still silently, and without so much as a nod of the head, resumed his pacing up and down the ward. But he had other things to occupy him than words or nods. As for the other convicts, at first all of them for some reason avoided all conversation with the man who had been punished; on the contrary, after they had first done what they could to help him, they seemed to force themselves not to pay him any further attention, perhaps because they wanted to leave him in peace as soon as possible and not pester him further with questions or 'sympathetic concern'; and he seemed well content with this state of affairs.

Meanwhile dusk had fallen and the night lamp was lighted.

Some of the prisoners, although very few, even produced their own candlesticks. Finally, after the doctor's evening visit, the non-commissioned officer of the guard came in and ticked off all the patients, and the ward was locked, when the night bucket had first been carried in . . . I was astonished to learn that this bucket would remain there all night, though there were proper lavatories just outside, in the corridor, not more than a couple of yards from the door. But such was the established rule. In the day-time a prisoner might be let out of the ward for not more than one minute, but not at night under any pretext. Prison wards were not like the ordinary ones and the prison patient must continue to undergo his punishment even when he was ill. Who first established this rule I do not know; I only know that there was no true regard for the regulations in it and that the fruitless aridity of red tape was never more clearly demonstrated than in cases like this. The rule did not, of course, originate with the doctors. I repeat, the convicts could not praise their doctors too highly; they looked on them as their friends and honoured them. Each one experienced kindness and heard friendly words from them; and the convict, rejected by all men, valued that kindness and those friendly words because he felt they were sincere and unfeigned. It could have been otherwise; nobody would have called them to account if the doctors had behaved differently, that is, more roughly and inhumanly: consequently the kindness came from real love of their fellow creatures. And naturally they knew that every patient, whoever he was, whether a convict or not, needed the same fresh air, for example, as every other patient, even of the highest rank. The patients in other wards, when they were convalescent, might walk freely about the corridors, take more exercise and breathe air less vitiated than the close atmosphere of the wards, always unavoidably filled with suffocating exhalations. It is terrible and nauseating to picture now to what extent our already poisonous atmosphere must have been further poisoned at night when that wooden bucket was carried in, with the warmth of the ward and the presence of certain diseases which were intolerable without some outlet. If I said just now that the convict had to bear his punishment even when he was ill, I did not of course suggest, and I do not now suggest, that the rule was framed simply and solely for the purpose of punishment. Needless to say, that would have been a ridiculous aspersion on my part. There is no need to punish the sick. And if that is so, it follows as a matter of course that it was probably some strict and drastic necessity that forced the authorities to take measures so harmful in their consequences. What then was it? The trouble is that there is only one possible reason which could even partially explain the necessity of this measure and of many others besides, which were so incomprehensible that it seemed impossible to explain them or even so much as guess what the explanation might be. How could such useless cruelty be accounted for? Only by supposing that a prisoner was prepared to go into hospital, deliberately feign illness, deceive the doctors, go out to the lavatory, and take advantage of the darkness to run away. It is almost impossible to discuss seriously the whole absurdity of this idea. Where could he escape to? how could he escape? what could he escape in? By day prisoners were allowed out of the ward one by one; it could have been just the same at night. A sentry with a loaded rifle stood by the door. The lavatories were literally two paces from the sentry and, in addition, a second guard accompanied the patient and did not take his eyes off him all the time. There was only one window, with double frames for the winter and an iron grating. Under the window, in the yard, close to the windows of the prison ward itself, another guard was on sentry-duty all night. To get out of the window, the frame and grating would have to be knocked out. Who was going to let that be done? But let us suppose that the escaper could kill the guard beforehand, in such a way that he would not be able to utter a sound or be heard by anybody. Even if we accept this absurdity, it would still be necessary to break the window and the iron bars. Note that the ward guards slept close by, near the sentry, and that ten paces away, by the other prison ward, stood another armed sentry and another 'second guard', and yet others near by. And where could anybody run to in winter, in stockings, slippers, a hospital dressing-gown, and a night-cap? And if this was so, if there was as little danger as this (which really amounts to no danger at all), why such serious overburdening of sick men, perhaps in the last days or hours of their lives, sick men, to whom fresh air was even more necessary than to the healthy? What was the purpose? I never could understand it.

But since the question 'what for?' has once been asked, and since I have already broached the subject, I cannot refrain from mentioning another doubt which has remained with me for so many years, a mysterious question to which also I have never contrived to find any answer. I cannot help saying at any rate a few words about it, before I resume my description. I am talking of the fetters, from which no illness releases the convicted criminal. I have watched even consumptives die in chains. Everybody was quite used to it and thought of it as being part of the order of things and unquestionable. I doubt whether anybody so much as considered it, when it never occurred even to one of the doctors, during all those years, to intercede with the authorities to have the irons struck off a prisoner who was seriously ill, especially with consumption. Let us concede that the fetters are not in themselves insufferably heavy. They weigh between eight and twelve pounds. A healthy man can carry ten pounds without being overburdened. I was told, however, that after several years the legs begin, as it were, to wither from wearing the irons. I do not know whether this is true, although there is certainly some probability in it. A weight, even a small one, even no more than ten pounds, fastened to the leg for ever does after all constitute an abnormal addition to the weight of the limb and may produce a certain degree of harmful effect after a long time . . . But let us suppose that all this does not matter to a healthy man. Is it the same for a sick one? Let us suppose that it is nothing even for an ordinary sick man. But what about those who are grievously ill, what, I repeat, about the consumptives, whose arms and legs wither in any case, so that every straw becomes a burden to them? I earnestly maintain that if the medical authorities had successfully sued for the relief of even one consumptive, this in itself would have been a great and true kindness. We may assume that it will be said that the convict is an evil-doer and unworthy of kindness; but must we really aggravate the sufferings of one who has already been touched by the finger of God? It is indeed impossible to believe that the only object of this evil was punishment. The consumptive is spared corporal punishment by the courts. It follows that here too we must have some measure of mysterious importance, taken as a salutary precaution. But what it can be, it is impossible to understand. Certainly nobody could really be afraid that the consumptive would run away. Who could entertain such an idea, especially with a certain stage of the development of the disease in mind? To feign consumption and deceive the doctors in order to escape is moreover impossible. It is not that kind of disease; it can be detected at the first glance. And, by the way, is a man really put in fetters solely for the purpose of preventing or hampering his escape? Not at all. Fetters constitute a stigma, a disgrace, a physical and moral burden. Or so, at least, it is supposed. But they can never hinder anybody's flight. The clumsiest and most unskilful of convicts could without great difficulty very soon file them through or break their rivets with a stone. Fetters definitely do not guard against anything; and if this is so, if they really are assigned to the condemned criminal only as punishment, then I ask again: does one punish dying men?

Just now, at the moment of writing, I recall very clearly

one dying man, a consumptive, that Mikhaylov, in fact, whose bed was almost opposite mine, not far from Ustyantsev's, and who died, I remember, on my fourth day in the ward. It is possible that in talking now of consumptives I have been involuntarily reproducing those impressions and ideas which came into my head at that time about his death. Mikhaylov himself, however, I did not know well. He was still a very young man, about twenty-five years old, no more, tall, thin, and unusually comely to look at. He was in the Special Class and was taciturn to a singular degree and always rather quiet and mildly sad. He seemed to 'shrivel up' in prison. That, at least, was the expression used afterwards by the prisoners, among whom he was kindly remembered. I can recall only that he had very fine eyes, and I honestly do not know why I remember him so distinctly. He died at about three in the afternoon of a clear, frosty day. I remember how the sun's strong, slanting rays pierced through the greenish panes, lightly covered with frost, of our ward windows. A flood of light poured over the unhappy man. He was unconscious when he died, and for several hours his life continued to ebb slowly and painfully away. Even in the morning his eyes no longer recognized those who went near him. They wished to do something to relieve him; they could see that things were going hard with him; his breathing was laboured, deep and hoarse; his breast rose and fell profoundly as though he could not get enough air. He threw off the blanket and all the bedclothes and finally began to tear off his shirt; even that seemed too heavy for him. They helped him to remove his shirt. It was terrible to see that long, long body with its arms and legs wasted to mere bone, its fallen stomach, projecting breast-bone, and ribs as distinctly defined as a skeleton's. Nothing at all remained on his body but a wooden cross and a reliquary and his fetters, through which he could by now have pulled his wasted leg. Half an hour before his death everybody in the ward seemed to grow quiet and began to speak almost in whispers. If anybody moved about, he tried to make his steps noiseless. There was little conversation among us, and that on indifferent subjects, but occasionally glances would be directed at the dying man, whose breathing grew harsher and harsher. Finally, with his aimless, nerveless hand he groped for the reliquary on his breast and tried to tear it away, as though even it were too great a burden. Some ten minutes later he died. They knocked on the door and informed the sentry. The sentry came in, looked dully at the dead man, and went for the orderly. The orderly, a nice young fellow, a little too preoccupied with his appearance, which, however, was fairly prepossessing, soon came in; he approached the dead man, his rapid steps ringing loudly through the hushed ward, and with a peculiarly detached air, which seemed specially adopted for the occasion, took his arm and felt the pulse, shrugged his shoulders, and went out. The guard was immediately informed; this was an important criminal from the Special Class and his death must be recognized with due ceremony. While they waited for the guard, one of the prisoners opined in a hushed voice that it would be a good thing to close the dead man's eyes. Another listened to him attentively, silently walked over to the corpse, and closed the eyes. Seeing the cross lying there on the pillow he took it up, looked at it, and silently restored it to Mikhaylov's neck; when he had put it on, he made the sign of the cross. Meanwhile the dead face was stiffening; a ray of sunlight played over it; the mouth was half open and two rows of white, young teeth gleamed between the thin lips curled back against the gums. At last the sergeant of the guard came in, wearing his short sword and a helmet, and behind him came two sentries. He approached, with steps that grew slower and slower, looking doubtfully at the prisoners, who were silently and grimly watching him from all sides. One pace away from the dead man he stood stock-still, as though overcome by shyness. He seemed struck by the sight of that wasted body, completely naked except for the fetters, and suddenly he unbuttoned the strap, took off his helmet, quite unnecessarily, and crossed himself with great care ... He had a grim, grey, soldierly face. I remember that Chekunov, another grey-headed old man, was standing there at that moment. All the time, without speaking, he intently watched the sergeant's face, gazing straight into his eyes, and following every gesture with a strange attentiveness. But their glances met and something made Chekunov's lower lip tremble. It curled strangely, baring his teeth, and suddenly, almost involuntarily, he gestured towards the corpse and said:

'He must have had a mother, too!'—and walked away.

I remember that the words seemed to pierce through me. Why should he say that? what brought it into his head? But now they were lifting the corpse, raising it together with the bed; the straw rustled, the fetters clanked loudly against the floor, in the midst of the general stillness . . . Somebody picked them up. They carried away the body. Suddenly everybody began to talk loudly. You could hear the sergeant, outside in the corridor, sending somebody for the smith. The dead man must have his irons struck off . . .

But I have digressed . . .

2. The Hospital (II)

THE doctors went round the wards in the morning between ten and eleven; they all appeared in a group, escorting the head physician. About an hour and a half before them our house-surgeon visited the ward. At that time the house-surgeon was a young doctor who knew his job and was kind and friendly; the prisoners were very fond of him and found in him only one shortcoming to criticize: he was 'too meek'. He was, indeed, rather uncommunicative and even seemed shy of us, almost bashful; he would change the patients' diet almost as soon as he was requested to do so and even seemed prepared to prescribe the medicines they asked for. It must be said that many doctors in Russia enjoy the love and respect of the common people; this, as far as my observations go, is quite true. I know that my words may seem paradoxical, especially in view of the general mistrust of all the Russian common people for medical science and outlandish drugs. Indeed, the simple people, when they are suffering from serious illnesses, would rather go to the village wise woman to be cured or treat themselves with their own home-made popular remedies (which are not to be despised) for years together, than go to a doctor or enter hospital. There is another extremely important circumstance, not connected with medicine at all, namely the general mistrust of the masses for everything that bears the stamp of the administration, for all uniforms; besides this, the people have been terrified of and prejudiced against hospitals by various frightening stories, often absurd but sometimes not without foundation. Most of all, they are frightened by the Prussian routine of the hospital, the strangers all round one all the time one is ill, the strict regulations about food, tales of the persistent severity of orderlies and doctors, of the cutting-up and disembowelment of corpses, and so on and so forth. Besides, so the people reason, it is the gentlefolk who are cured, because after all the doctors are gentlemen themselves. But on closer acquaintance with doctors (not all without exception, but the great majority) their fears very quickly disappear, a fact which, in my opinion, redounds greatly to the honour of our doctors, especially the younger ones. The greater part of them are capable of earning the respect and even the love of the ordinary people. I am writing of what I, at least, have seen and experienced, more than once and in many different places, and I have no reason to think that in other places things were often very different. There are, of course, some benighted spots where doctors can be bribed, make a large profit out of their hospitals, neglect their patients, and even forget their medicine altogether. Things like this still exist, but I speak of the majority, or rather of the spirit, the tendency, which is being realized today. Those others, traitors to their profession, wolves in the sheep-fold, whatever they may urge in their own defence, even if, for example, they say it is the *environment* which has ruined them in their turn, can never be justified, especially if, in addition, they have lost all love of humanity. For loving-kindness, gentleness, human sympathy, are often more important to the patient than any medicine. It is high time for us to stop our apathetic complaining that our environment has ruined us. Grant that it is true that our environment swallows up much of what is in us, it still does not devour everything, and a clever and accomplished rogue will often use the influence of his environment to cover and excuse not only his weakness but his evil-doing as well, especially if he has the gift of fine speech or writing. However, I have again digressed from my subject; I merely wished to say that the simple people's mistrust and hostility are for official medicine rather than for the doctors themselves. When they learn what these are really like, they quickly lose many of their prejudices. To this day the other circumstances of our hospitals fail in many ways to correspond to the temper of our common people and are incapable of gaining their trust and respect. Such at least is my opinion, based on some of my own impressions.

Our house-surgeon usually stopped by each bed and seriously and extremely carefully examined the patient, questioned him, and prescribed his treatment and diet. Sometimes he could not help seeing that the patient had nothing wrong with him; but since the prisoner came for a respite from his labour, or to sleep for a short time on a mattress instead of bare boards, or, finally, to be at any rate in a warm room and not in a damp guardhouse where numbers of men under arrest, all pale and wasted, were crowded together (men awaiting trial or sentence, throughout Russia,

THE HOSPITAL (II) 219

are almost always pale and wasted—a sign that their conditions and moral state are worse than those of the convicts themselves), our house-surgeon calmly diagnosed some *febris catarrhalis* or other and left them to lie there, sometimes for a whole week. All of us used to smile about that *febris catarrhalis*. We knew very well that it was a formula adopted by mutual agreement between doctor and patient to signify a case of swinging the lead: 'prison colic' was how the prisoners themselves translated the term. Sometimes a patient would take undue advantage of the doctor's tender-heartedness and stay in the hospital until he was driven out by force. At such times our house-surgeon was a sight to see; he almost blushed and seemed unable for shame to say bluntly to a patient that he was getting well and ought to ask for his discharge very soon, although he had the absolute right to discharge him himself, without any beating about the bush or attempts at persuasion, simply by writing on his chart *sanat. est*. First he would hint, then he would almost plead: 'Isn't it nearly time for you to leave?' he would say; 'after all you are almost well, and the ward is overcrowded', and so on, until the patient grew ashamed and himself asked for his discharge. The senior physician, although he was both a humane and an honest man (the patients were very fond of him also), was incomparably stricter and more resolute than the house-surgeon and on occasion even displayed a sternness which earned for him our special respect. He appeared, with the rest of the medical staff, after the house-surgeon had made his rounds, and he also examined each man individually, stopping especially by the beds of the seriously ill, for whom he could always find the kindly, the encouraging, frequently indeed the intimate word, and left behind him a general feeling of approval. He did not reject or send back men who entered the hospital with 'prison colic'; but if a patient lingered too stubbornly, he simply discharged him. 'Come, old man, you've been here long enough and had a good rest; now you must go; fair's fair.' Those who turned stubborn were usually either lazy workers (especially in summer when the work was heaviest) or prisoners awaiting corporal punishment. I remember that particularly severe measures, almost amounting to cruelty, were used against one of these to persuade him to leave the hospital. He had entered with eye trouble: his eyes were inflamed and he complained of violent stabbing pains in them. He was treated with blisters, leeches, spraying the eyes with some sort of caustic fluid, and so on, but the disease showed no tendency to disappear and the eyes grew no clearer. Gradually the doctors realized that the illness was not genuine; the inflammation was always equally slight and neither grew worse nor improved, but remained stationary, a suspicious sign. The other prisoners had known for a long time that the patient was shamming and contriving to deceive people, although he himself did not admit it. He was a young fellow and quite good-looking but he made a somewhat unpleasant impression on all of us: he was furtive, suspicious, lowering, unwilling to talk to anybody, and always scowling; he seemed to be concealing himself from all the world, as though he suspected everybody. I remember that it even occurred to some of us that he might do something desperate. He was a soldier, had been caught thieving, convicted, and sentenced to receive a thousand strokes of the rods and be sent to a corrective company. Men who had been condemned to corporal punishment, as I have mentioned before, sometimes had recourse to terrible expedients in order to postpone the moment of punishment: on the eve of its execution they would stick a knife into some officer or into a convict like themselves, and have to be tried again; their punishment was postponed for some two months and their object was attained. It mattered little to them that in two months' time the punishment would be twice or thrice as severe, if only they could put off the fatal minute for a few days, at whatever cost—so completely had the spirit of some of these unhappy creatures failed them. Some of us even whispered among ourselves that we ought to be on our guard against this patient: he might do somebody an injury during the night. This, however, was only talk, and nobody took any special precautions, not even those whose beds happened to be next to his. He was seen, however, to rub his eyes at night with lime from the plaster and something else, so that in the morning they would again have become red. Finally the head physician threatened to insert a seton. In obstinate and long-continued diseases of the eye, when all other remedies have been tried, the doctors decide on a drastic and painful measure to save the sight: they insert a seton, just as though the patient were a horse. In this instance the poor wretch still refused to recover. What obstinacy of character—or was it extreme cowardice? A seton, after all, although certainly not the same as a flogging, was also extremely painful. A handful of skin was gathered up at the back of the patient's neck and a knife was thrust right through, producing a long wide wound from side to side of the nape of the neck; into this wound was inserted a fairly wide, coarse tape, about the breadth of a finger, and every day at a certain time this tape was dragged backwards and forwards so as to break the wound open again; thus the wound discharged continuously and did not heal up. The poor wretch bore this torture, although the pain was excruciating, for several days, until at last he agreed to be discharged. In the course of one day his eyes became quite well, and as soon as his neck healed he went back to the guardhouse, to go out again and face his thousand strokes the next day.

The minute before punishment is, of course, a grievous one, so hard to bear that perhaps I do wrong to call the fear of it faintheartedness and cowardice. It must indeed be dreadful, when men will incur punishment that is two or three times as heavy, if only it is not carried out immediately. I have, however, also mentioned those who ask to be discharged as soon as possible, even with backs still not healed from the first blows, so as to undergo the remainder of their punishment and escape finally from their position 'under judgement'; conditions for all those awaiting the execution of their sentence in the guardhouse are, of course, incomparably worse than penal servitude. Apart from differences in temperament, the ingrained habit of suffering punishments and beatings plays a large part in the resolution and fearlessness of some of these men. Both the back and the spirit of a man who has been repeatedly beaten become, as it were, fortified, and at length he comes to look on punishment philosophically, almost as a minor inconvenience, and no longer fears it. This is, generally speaking, true. One of our prisoners from the Special Class, a Kalmuck Christian, Alexander, or as we called him Alexandra, by name, a strange fellow, full of mischief, fearless and at the same time very good-natured, used to tell me how he had taken 'his four thousand', and tell it laughing and joking; but he would also swear, with great seriousness, that if he had not been brought up from childhood under the lash, from the weals of which his back was literally never free throughout his life with his tribe, he would most certainly not have endured those four thousand blows. When he talked of it, he almost blessed his upbringing under the whip. 'I was beaten for everything, Alexander Petrovich,' he told me once, sitting on my bed one afternoon before the lights were lit, 'for anything and everything, everything that ever happened; I was beaten for fifteen years, from the very first day I can remember; everybody used to beat me who felt like it; so in the end I got quite used to it.' How he came to be a soldier I don't know; he may have told me but I do not remember; he was always a fugitive and a vagabond. I remember only his story of how terribly afraid he had been when he was sentenced to four thousand strokes for the murder of an official. 'I knew they would make it as hard for me as they could and I mightn't live through it. I'm used to beatings all right, but after all four thousand is no joke!—

and besides, all the important people were so angry with me!
So I knew, I knew for certain, that I should have to pay for
it; I didn't expect to pull through; they'd beat me to death.
To begin with I thought I'd try being converted, because
I thought, perhaps they will let me off, and however much
my own people told me that it wouldn't be any good, they
wouldn't let me off, I still thought, "I'll try it all the same;
after all, they'll be sorrier for a Christian." Well, so I was
baptized, and they christened me Alexander. But all the
same, the beating was still the same beating. They might
have let me off at least one! I thought I had something to
grumble about. But I thought to myself: "Just you wait, I'll
cheat the lot of you yet." And what do you think, Alexander
Petrovich, I did! I was terribly good at shamming dead, not
quite dead, I mean, but as if I was going to kick the bucket
at any minute. They took me out; they laid on the first
thousand; it stung and I yelled; they laid on the second and
"well," thinks I, "this is the end of me"; it sent me clean off
my head and my legs just crumpled up under me. I fell flat
on the ground, with my eyes rolled up and my face all blue
and not breathing, only foaming at the mouth. The doctor
came: "He's going to die this minute," says he. So they
carried me into the hospital and I came round straight away.
So afterwards they took me out twice more, and they were
annoyed with me, they were frightfully annoyed, and I
fooled them twice more; when it came to the third thousand
I could only stand one before I fainted, and as for the fourth,
every stroke went through me like a knife, and every single
one was as bad as three, they laid them on so hard! They
were furious with me. That miserable last thousand (blast
it to hell!) was as bad as the first three put together, and if I
hadn't been practically dead before they finished (there was
only a couple of hundred left), they would have beaten me
to death then and there; but I wasn't going to have that
without putting up a bit of a fight. I fooled them again,
because I fainted again, and they were taken in again, and

why not? The doctor was. So for the last two hundred they laid it on so hard that two thousand hadn't been as bad the other time; but no, they were fooled again, they didn't kill me, and why didn't they kill me? All because I was brought up on the whip from a baby. That's why I'm alive today. Oh, I've been beaten all right, I've been beaten in my time!' he added as he finished his story, with a sort of sad hesitancy, as though he had to force himself to remember all the times he had been beaten. 'But no,' he added, breaking a momentary silence, 'there's no telling how many times I've been thrashed: and where's the use of trying to count them? I can't count up so far.' He glanced at me and laughed, so good-humouredly that I could not help smiling in reply. 'Do you know, Alexander Petrovich, even now if I dream at night it's always about getting a licking; I never have any other kind of dream.' He did, in fact, often cry out at night, and he used to yell with all the power of his lungs, so that the other prisoners would immediately nudge him awake: 'What the devil are you shouting about?' He was a robust fellow of about forty-five, not very tall, fidgety, cheerful, able to get on well with everybody; and if he was incorrigibly light-fingered and was often beaten for it, which among us was not sometimes caught stealing, and which among us had not been beaten for it?

I will add one further point: I was always astonished at the extraordinary good nature and lack of malice with which men who had been flogged spoke of their beatings and of those who had inflicted them. Very often it was impossible to detect the slightest shade of resentment or hatred in narratives which sometimes made my heart rise into my throat and begin to thump heavily and violently. But they used to tell their stories and laugh like children. I remember Miretsky's telling me about his punishment; he was not a nobleman and had received five hundred strokes. I had heard this from others and I asked him whether it was true and what it had been like. He answered somewhat briefly and like a man suffering from some internal pain; he seemed to try not to look at me and his face flushed; after a few moments he did look at me and his eyes were glittering with the fires of hatred, while his lips trembled with indignation. I felt that he could never forget that page of his past. But our prisoners, almost all of them (I will not swear that there were no exceptions), looked on the matter quite differently. It could not be, I sometimes thought, that they considered themselves guilty and deserving of punishment, especially if their violence had been directed not against their own class but against the authorities. The majority of them did not blame themselves at all. I have already said that I saw no evidence of remorse, even when the crime had been against one of their own class. Crimes against the ruling class were not even worth mentioning. It sometimes seemed to me that in such cases they had their own special, so to speak, practical, or rather, realistic way of looking at things. They took into account fate, hard facts, and their attitude was not so much reasoned as unconsciously, as it were, adopted, like some sort of faith. A prisoner, for example, although always inclined to feel justified when any crime against the authorities was concerned, so much so that it would never even occur to him to question the idea, nevertheless in practice realized that the authorities must regard his crime from quite a different standpoint, and that consequently he must be punished and cry quits. It was a sort of duel. The criminal knows besides that, without any doubt, he is acquitted by the court of his own class, the common people, which will never, as he also knows, finally condemn him and will usually exonerate him completely, so long as his crime is not against his own kind, his brothers, the common people to whom he belongs. His conscience is at peace and he is strong in the power of his conscience and morally undisturbed, and this is for him the main thing. He feels as it were that he has something to lean upon and therefore feels no hatred but accepts what comes to him as an ineluctable fact, which he did not initiate and cannot end, and which will continue unchanged for a long, long time, a part of the established, passive, but desperate struggle. What soldier feels personal hatred for the Turk with whom he is at war?—yet the Turk cuts him down, thrusts him through, or puts a bullet into him.

Not all the tales, however, were quite so indifferently and cold-bloodedly told. They spoke of Lieutenant Zherebyatnikov, for example, with a shade, though faint, of real indignation. I became acquainted with this Lieutenant Zherebyatnikov when I was first in hospital, only, of course, through the talk of the prisoners. Later I saw him in the flesh, when we had him on guard duty. He was a tall, fat, gross man, not yet thirty, with bloated red cheeks, white teeth, and a loud, coarse laugh. It was evident from his face that he was the most unreasoning man in the world. His pleasure in floggings and beatings with rods, on the occasions when he was put in charge of executions, amounted to a passion. I hasten to add that even then I regarded Lieutenant Zherebyatnikov as a monstrous exception among his own kind, and so did the other prisoners. There were others besides him in the old days, those old days of which 'the memory is fresh but hardly to be believed', who delighted in fulfilling such duties with diligent zeal, but for the most part the procedure was carried out simply and without special enthusiasm. The lieutenant, however, was something of a refined connoisseur of executions. He loved, passionately loved, the art of the executioner, loved it purely as an art. He relished it highly and, like some jaded patrician of imperial Rome, sated with pleasures, invented various refinements and unnatural variations in order to provide some small stimulus and pleasurable titillation for his soul, lapped in its layers of fat. Here now is a prisoner brought out for the execution of his sentence; Zherebyatnikov is in charge; one glance at the long rows of men drawn up with thick sticks in their hands, and he is inspired. Smugly he walks down the ranks and earnestly insists that each man shall fulfil his duty with zeal and devotion, or else . . . But the soldiers already know what that *or else* means. Now the criminal is led out, and if he has until this moment been unacquainted with Zherebyatnikov, if he has not yet learnt all about him from A to Z, here is an example of the kind of trick Zherebyatnikov will play upon him. (Needless to say, it is only one of a hundred such tricks; the lieutenant is inexhaustible in invention.) Every prisoner, in that moment when he is stripped and his arms are bound to the stocks of the rifles by which non-commissioned officers will drag him the whole length of the 'green street' (that double line of soldiers)—every prisoner, following a universal custom, begins in a tearful, plaintive voice to implore the officer in charge to make his punishment lighter, not to aggravate it by excessive severity: 'your honour,' (cries the wretch), 'spare me, be a father to me, make me remember you in my prayers for a thousand years, don't destroy me, have mercy on me!' Zherebyatnikov is only waiting for this; he immediately stops the proceedings and, with a sentimental air, begins to talk to the prisoner:

'My dear friend,' says he, 'what am I to do with you? the law punishes you, not I.'

'Your honour, everything depends on you. Be merciful!'

'Do you think I am not sorry for you? Do you think it will be a pleasure for me to watch you being beaten? After all, I, too, am a man! What do you think, am I a man, or aren't I?'

'Certainly, your honour, it's a well-known fact; you are our father, we are all your children. Be a father to me!' cries the prisoner, already beginning to hope.

'Yes, my friend, judge for yourself; after all, you have got a mind to judge with: I am quite well aware that I must, in all humanity, look with compassion and even indulgence on you, sinner though you are . . .'

'It's Gospel truth you're speaking, your honour!'

'Yes, with indulgence, however sinful you are. But this is a matter for the law, not for me! Think! After all, I serve God and my country; I should be taking a grievous sin on myself if I weakened the law. Think of that!'

'Your honour! . . .'

'Well, why not? All right, since it is for you! I know I am doing wrong, but so be it! I will spare you this once, your punishment shall be light. But what if that is just the way to do you harm? If I take pity on you now and punish you lightly, you will hope that it will be the same next time, and you will commit another crime, and what then? It will be on my conscience . . .'

'Your honour! I will tell my friends and my enemies! As though before the throne of the Creator in heaven . . .'

'Well, all right, all right! Will you swear to me that you will be well behaved in future?'

'May the Lord strike me dead, and in the other world may I never . . .'

'Don't swear, it's sinful. I will take your word for it; do you give me your word?'

'Your honour!!!'

'Well, listen to me: I spare you because of your orphan tears; are you an orphan?'

'Yes, your honour, I'm all alone in the world, neither father nor mother . . .'

'Well then, because of your orphan tears; but mind, it's the last time . . . Take him,' he adds in such a tender-hearted tone that the prisoner hardly knows how he can best remember such kindness in his prayers. But now the ominous procession moves and he is led away; the drum thunders, the first rods are raised . . . 'Let him have it!' yells Zherebyatnikov at the top of his voice. 'Scorch him! Lay on, lay on! Flay him! Again, again! Give it him hot, the orphan, the sneak-thief! Cut him down, beat him down!' And the soldiers lay on for all they are worth, sparks flash before the eyes of the poor wretch, he begins to cry out, and Zherebyatnikov runs after him along the column, laughing, laughing, helpless with laughter, holding both his sides, so doubled up with laughter that in the end one must be sorry for the kind-hearted creature. He is full of glee and finds it all very funny, and only occasionally are his loud healthy peals of laughter interrupted and one hears again: 'Lay on, lay on! Flay him, the thief, flay the orphan! . . .'

Here is another variation he invented: preparations would be made for a flogging; again the prisoner would begin to beg for mercy. This time Zherebyatnikov would not pull sorrowful faces, but be open and frank:

'You see, my dear fellow,' he would say, 'I shall punish you as I ought, because you deserve it. But I tell you what I might perhaps do for you; I will not have you bound to the rifle-butts. You shall go alone, in a different way. Run as fast as you can through the whole line! Every stick will still strike you, but the whole thing will be quicker, you know. What do you think? Would you like to try?'

The prisoner would listen doubtfully, mistrustfully, and consider it. 'Well, why not?' he would say to himself. 'Perhaps it really would be better to be free, and if I run with all my might, the torture will be over five times as quick, and perhaps not every blow will reach me.'

'All right, your honour, I agree!'

'Well, I agree too, so off with you! Mind you don't go to sleep!' he would yell to the soldiers, knowing very well, however, that not one blow would fail to reach the culprit's back; any soldier who missed also knew what he would suffer for it. The prisoner would begin to run with all his might along the 'green street', but of course he could not run through fifteen columns: the sticks would come crashing down all at once on his back, like a drum-beat, like a stroke of lightning, and the poor wretch would fall with a cry, as though he had been cut down or had stopped a bullet. 'No, your honour, the regulation way is best' he would say, slowly raising himself from the ground, pale and shocked, and Zherebyatnikov, who had known all about it before-hand and what the result would be, would roar with laughter. But there is no describing all his amusements, or re-telling all the tales that were told about him!

The other prisoners talked in rather a different fashion, in another tone and another spirit, of a certain Lieutenant Smekalov who had fulfilled the duties of commandant of our prison before our major was appointed to the position. Although Zherebyatnikov was talked of fairly indifferently, without special bitterness, nevertheless his exploits were not admired and he was not commended, but quite plainly loathed. He was even rather looked down on and despised. But Lieutenant Smekalov was remembered with pleasure and delight. The fact is that he was not at all a lover of flogging; there was not a trace in him of the pure Zherebyat-nikov quality. Nevertheless he was far from having any objection to flogging: the fact was that his very floggings were remembered among us with a kind of indulgent liking, so great was this man's power of pleasing the convicts. How was it done? How did he earn such popularity? It is true that we prisoners, like perhaps all the Russian people, were ready to forget any torments for one kind word: I mention the plain fact, without analysing it one way or the other. It was not difficult to please these people and gain their liking. But Lieutenant Smekalov won *special* favour, so much so that even his way of flogging was referred to almost affectionately. 'He was as good as a father to us,' the prisoners used to say, and they would sigh, comparing their former temporary commandant Smekalov with the present major. 'He was a treasure!' . . . He was a simple man and perhaps, in his own way, even a good man. But sometimes a man in authority not only is good but has great generosity of spirit, and yet what happens?—nobody likes him, and sometimes they simply laugh at a man like that. The point was that Smekalov somehow contrived to make all our prisoners accept him as a man *of their own kind*, and this is a great accomplishment or, to speak more exactly, inborn talent, which even those who possess it hardly ever stop to consider. It is strange, but there are among them some people quite without good qualities, who yet sometimes enjoy great popularity. They are not fastidious about their company, not easily disgusted—and that, I think, is the reason. They neither look nor sound like fine gentlemen but have about them, as it were, the special flavour of the common people, which is born in them, and, good God, how sensitive the people are to that flavour! What will they not put up with for it? They are prepared to exchange the most compassionate of men for the most severe, if the latter has their own particular homespun flavour. What if this man with the right flavour has also a genuinely good heart, even if only in his own way? Then he is without price! Lieutenant Smekalov, as I have already said, inflicted cruel punishments on occasion, but he somehow contrived that nobody should bear him any grudge; more, in my time, when all these events were ancient history, his *little tricks* were even remembered with amusement and pleasure. He had not had many of these tricks, however: he had not enough artistic invention. In fact, he had one joke and one alone, with which he entertained himself for almost a whole year; and perhaps it seemed amiable simply because it was the solitary one. There was a great deal of *naïveté* in it. For example, a prisoner who had committed some crime would be brought out. Smekalov himself would come to the execution with a smile and a joke, and he would ask the culprit a question about something, something irrelevant, something about his personal, private, prison affairs, and this not with any ulterior motive, not in order to curry favour with him, but quite simply—*because he really wanted to know*. The rods would be brought, and a chair for Smekalov; he would sit down and even light his pipe. He had one of those very long pipes. The prisoner would begin to beg for mercy . . . 'Oh no, brother, lie down; what is the use? . . .' Smekalov would say; the prisoner would sigh and lie down. 'Now, my dear fellow, do you know such-and-such verses by heart?' 'Of course I do, your honour; we are Christians and we learnt them as children.' 'Say them, then.' The prisoner already knew what to recite, and he also knew what would happen when he did so, because the same jest had already been repeated thirty times before with others. And Smekalov himself knew that the prisoner knew; he knew that even the soldiers, standing with their sticks raised above the prostrate victim, were tired of hearing the same joke, but all the same he repeated it again, for it was an eternal delight to him, perhaps because he was the author of it. The prisoner began to recite, the men with the rods waited, and Smekalov leaned forward, raised his hands, and, forgetting to smoke, waited for the well-known words. After the first of the familiar verses the prisoner came at last to the words 'as it is *in heaven*'. That was all that was wanted. 'Stop!' cried the lieutenant, blazing with excitement, turned like a flash, with a gesture of inspiration, to the man with his stick raised, and shouted: 'Give him seventy times seven!'

And he roared with laughter. The soldiers standing round grinned too; the man with the rod grinned, even the victim almost grinned, although at the word '*seven*' the rod was already whistling through the air and in an instant would bite like a razor into his guilty back. And Smekalov exulted, exulted because he had been so happily inspired and himself had put together 'in heaven' and 'seventy times seven'— which both rhymed and was so apt. And he would leave the scene of the punishment thoroughly pleased with himself, and the man who had been flogged would also go away almost pleased with himself and with Smekalov, and lo, in half an hour he would be telling the prison how the joke, already repeated thirty times before, had now been repeated for the thirty-first time. 'No two ways about it, the man's a jewel! What a sense of humour!'

Sometimes the reminiscences of this best of lieutenants even had a smack of sentimentality.

'You'd be going past, mates,' one prisoner would say, his face all smiles at the remembrance, 'you'd be walking along and he would be up and sitting there at his window in his dressing-gown, drinking his tea and smoking his pipe. You'd take off your cap. "Where are you going, Aksenov?" ' "To work, of course, Mikhail Vasilyevich. I have to go to the workshop first of all." He would laugh to himself . . . Oh, he was a jewel, no two ways about it!'

'We shall never get another like him!' one of his hearers would add.

3. The Hospital (III)

I HAVE begun discussing corporal punishment and various people who carried out these interesting duties at this point because it was only now, when I was removed into the hospital, that I achieved a full and graphic understanding of all these things. Into our two wards were brought all those who had undergone the punishment of running the gauntlet, from all the battalions, correctional companies, and other military commands stationed in our town and all the surrounding countryside. In those first days, when I was still so eagerly absorbing all that happened round me and all those conditions which were so strange to me, the men who had undergone or were awaiting corporal punishment naturally produced a very powerful impression on me. I was agitated, disturbed, and afraid. I remember how I suddenly began to probe eagerly into all the details of these new phenomena, listen to the talk and stories of other prisoners, ask them questions, and try to arrive at a conclusion. I wanted, among other things, to acquire a firm grasp of all the degrees of sentence and execution, all the shades of difference in the executions, and the prisoners' own point of view on all this; I was trying to picture to myself the state of mind of a man going to his punishment. I have already said that hardly anybody is entirely unmoved just before an execution, not excluding even those who have been often and severely beaten. At this point there descends on the condemned man an agonizing and purely physical terror, involuntary and irresistible, which completely overwhelms his moral nature. Even later, and throughout my years in prison, I could not help watching those condemned men who, having spent some time in hospital after the execution of the first part of their sentence, were discharged with their backs healed, to undergo on the following day the remainder of their strokes. Such a division of the punishment into two parts is always ordered by the doctor who is present at the execution. If the number of strokes prescribed for the crime in question is very great, so that the prisoner cannot endure them all on one occasion, they are divided into two or even three parts on the advice of the doctor, given at the actual time of the punishment, as to whether the victim is able to continue his progress through the lines or whether this will endanger his life. Usually five hundred, a thousand, or even fifteen hundred strokes will be inflicted at one time; but if the sentence is of two or three thousand, it will be carried out in two or even three parts. Those whose backs had healed after the first part of their punishment and who were leaving the hospital to undergo the second half, were extremely dismal, sullen, and silent. There was to be observed in them a kind of stupor of the mind, an unnatural vacancy. A man in this state would never start a conversation, and for the most part did not speak at all; the most curious thing was that the other prisoners did not talk to him and tried to avoid all reference to what was awaiting him. There was not one unnecessary word and no attempt to offer comfort; there was, in general, a definite effort to avoid taking much notice of him. This, of course, is the best for the condemned man. There are exceptions, like Orlov, for example, whom I have talked of before. After the first part of his punishment there was only one thing that annoyed him—that his back took a long time to heal and he could not obtain his discharge as quickly as he would have liked, so as to undergo the remainder of his sentence as soon as possible, be sent off in a convoy to the place to which he was to be exiled, and escape on the way. But this intention kept him cheerful, and God knows what he had in his mind. He had a passionate nature, tenacious of life. He was highly pleased with himself and in a very exalted state, but he stifled his emotions. The fact was that before the first part of his punishment he had thought that he would not be allowed to survive the rods but must die. While his fate was still undecided, various rumours had reached him of the measures taken by the authorities against him, and even then he had prepared himself to die. But when he survived the first part of his strokes he took heart. He came to the hospital half dead from the beating; I had never before seen such sores; but he came with joy in his heart, full of hope that he would remain alive and that the rumours had been false; and since he had survived the rods this time, he was by now beginning to dream of the road and of escape, freedom, the forests and the plains . . . Two days after his discharge from hospital, he died in the same hospital, and indeed in the same bed; the second half of his punishment had been too much for him. But I have mentioned this before.

Yet those same prisoners whose days and nights were so troubled before their punishment bore the execution of it manfully, even the most pusillanimous of them. I rarely heard a groan even from men who were very seriously injured; the people are generally able to endure pain. About the pain I asked many questions. I wanted to know definitely how great this pain was and what it was really like. I honestly do not know why I tried to learn this. I remember only that it was not from idle curiosity. I repeat that I was agitated and shaken. But whomever I asked, I could not get an answer that satisfied me. It burns, it scorches like fire—this was all I could learn, the only answer I received. It burns, that's all. Also during this early period, when I came to know him better, I asked Miretsky. 'It is very painful,' he answered, 'and it feels like fire; it is as if your back were being roasted over a very hot fire.' Everybody, in short, expressed it in the same word. I remember, however, that I made one strange observation, although I will not vouch for its accuracy; but the general judgement of the prisoners themselves strongly supports me: it is that the birch, if a large number of strokes are inflicted, is the severest of all the punishments in use among us. This would seem, at first sight, absurd and impossible. But a man may be flogged to death with five hundred or even four hundred strokes of the birch, and with more than five hundred it is almost a certainty. No man, even of the strongest constitution, could endure a thousand strokes at one time. Five hundred strokes of the rods, however, can be borne without the slightest danger to life, and even a man who is not strong can be given a thousand without risk. Even two thousand will not kill a man of moderate strength and with a healthy constitution. The prisoners all said that the birch was worse than the rods. 'The birch,' they said, 'bites more; the pain is worse.' The birch is certainly more painful than the rods. It stings more, has a more powerful effect on the nerves, which it excites beyond bearing. I do not know how things are now, but in the recent past there were gentlemen to whom the power of flogging a victim gave a satisfaction resembling that of the Marquis de Sade* or Madame de Brinvilliers.* I imagine that there was something in those sensations, at once sweet and painful, that made these gentlemen's hearts swoon with pleasure. There are people who, like tigers, thirst for blood. Any man who has once tasted this dominion, this unlimited power, over the body, blood, and spirit of a human creature like himself, subject like himself to the law of Christ, any man who has tasted this power, this boundless opportunity to humiliate with the deepest degradation another being made in the image of God, becomes despite himself the servant instead of the master of his own emotions. Tyranny is a habit; it has the capacity to develop and it does develop, in the end, into a disease. I maintain that the best of men may become coarsened and degraded, by force of habit, to the level of a beast. Blood and power are intoxicants; callousness and perversity develop and grow; the greatest perversions become acceptable and finally sweet to the mind and heart. The man and the citizen perish eternally in the tyrant, and a return to human dignity, to remorse and regeneration, becomes almost completely impossible to him. Besides this, example and the possibility of such arbitrary power act like a contagion on the whole of society; such despotism is a temptation. A society which contemplates such manifestations calmly is already corrupted at its roots. In short, the right given to one man to inflict corporal punishment on another is one of the ulcers of society, one of the most powerful destructive agents of every germ and every budding attempt at civilization, the fundamental cause of its certain and irretrievable destruction.

Society sickens at the professional executioner, but not at the gentleman amateur. It is only recently that the contrary view has been expressed, and then only in books and in the abstract. Even then not all of those who express it have yet succeeded in stifling the lust for power in themselves. Every manufacturer and employer must inevitably take pleasure in the fact that his workmen and their families are sometimes wholly and solely dependent on him. This must be so: a generation does not so quickly uproot what has been implanted in it by heredity, a man does not so soon repudiate what has entered into his blood, so to speak, with his mother's milk. Revolutions are not so speedily accomplished. It is too little, far too little, to recognize one's own guilt and ancestral sin; one must wean oneself completely from it. And this cannot so soon be done.

I have spoken of the executioner. The executioner's nature is found in embryo in almost every contemporary man. But the feral characteristics do not develop equally in all men. If in one their development reinforces all his other qualities, that man will of course become terrible and monstrous. There are two kinds of executioner; some are executioners of their own choice, the others because it is their job. The voluntary executioner is of course in all respects inferior to the professional, whom the people nevertheless abominate with a loathing compounded of horror, nausea, and unconscious, almost mystical, terror. Whence comes this almost superstitious fear of one executioner, combined with such indifference to and near approval of another? There are some very strange examples: I have known people who, good, honourable, and respected by society though they were, yet could not endure it with calmness if a culprit did not shriek under the rods and beg and pray for mercy. A man who is being punished absolutely must shriek and beg for mercy. That is taken for granted— it is considered both seemly and indispensable; and when the victim refused to shriek one officer whom I knew, and who in other respects might perhaps be considered a kindly man, took it as a personal affront. At first he might have meant to make the punishment light, but when he did not hear the usual 'your honour, my own father, spare me and I will pray for you for ever' and so on, he grew furious and inflicted about fifty extra strokes, in the desire to elicit shrieks and prayers—and he got them. 'People can't behave like that; he's a brute,' he explained to me very seriously. As for the real executioner, the forced, unwilling one, it is well known that he is a condemned prisoner, sentenced to exile and retained as an executioner; to begin with he acts as an apprentice to another executioner and when he has learnt the art he is kept in a prison for life, where he lives apart in a room of his own, even doing his own housekeeping, but nearly always under guard. Of course a living man is not a machine; he flogs because he must, but he also may be carried away sometimes; nevertheless, although the flogging may give him satisfaction, he hardly ever feels any personal hatred for his victim. The skill of his hand, his knowledge of his art, the desire to impress his fellows and the public, all stimulate his vanity. He takes pains for the sake of his art. He is well aware, besides, that he is an outcast and that superstitious terror meets and follows him everywhere, and it is impossible to swear that this has no influence on him and does not intensify his ferocity and likeness to the beasts. The very children know that he has 'renounced his father and mother'. It is a strange thing that all the many executioners I have come across have been fairly highly developed people with common sense, intelligence, and unusual vanity or even pride. Whether this pride had developed as a reaction from the general contempt for them, and whether it was intensified by their consciousness of their power over their victims and the terror they inspired in them, I do not know. Perhaps even the very showiness and theatricality of the circumstances in which they appear before the public on the scaffold facilitate the development of some haughtiness in them. I remember that once, during a short period, I often came into contact with a certain executioner and watched him closely. He was a fellow of middle height, about forty years old, lean and muscular, with quite a pleasant and intelligent face and curly hair. He was always extraordinarily grave and sedate; he bore himself like a gentleman and always answered my questions briefly, sensibly, and even amiably, but with a somewhat arrogant amiability, as though he looked down on me. The officers of the guard often talked to him in my presence and, as I can testify, with a kind of respect. He was aware of this and when anybody in authority was present deliberately redoubled his politeness, dryness, and conscious dignity.

The more graciously a superior spoke to him the more stiff-necked he seemed, and although he did not abandon the most exquisite courtesy I am sure that at that moment he considered himself immeasurably above the man he was talking to. This feeling was depicted in his face. It sometimes happened that he was sent out under guard on a hot summer's day to destroy the town's dogs with a long thin stick. There was an extraordinary number of dogs in the little town, dogs which did not belong to anybody and which bred with extreme rapidity. In the heat of the summer they became dangerous and the authorities arranged for the executioner to be sent to destroy them. But even this degrading task evidently did not humiliate him. It was worth seeing with what dignity he went about the streets, in the company of his weary guards, frightening all the women and children by his mere appearance and turning a calm and even condescending eye on everybody he met.

The executioner's is a good life. He has money, good food, and vodka. The money comes from the bribes he takes. The civilian who has been arrested and given a sentence of corporal punishment will take care to give the executioner a present beforehand, even if it takes his last penny. But from some sentenced men, the rich ones, the executioners themselves demand a named sum, fixed in accordance with the prisoner's apparent means; they may take as much as thirty roubles and sometimes even more. There may even, with very rich men, be a great deal of bargaining. The executioner cannot, of course, make his blows very light; he would answer for it with his own back. On the other hand, in return for a bribe, he promises his victim that he will not make the punishment excessively painful. Almost always his proposal is accepted; if it is not, he will make the punishment really barbarous, and this is entirely within his power. It may happen that he sets a considerable price even on a very poor victim; relatives come to him, try to bargain, humble themselves, and woe to the victim if they cannot

satisfy the executioner. In such cases the superstitious terror
he inspires is a great help. What wild unbelievable tales are
told of executioners! The prisoners themselves assured me
that an executioner could kill a man with one blow. But,
first of all, when did this ever actually happen? It may have
done so, however. It was said with great conviction. Indeed,
one executioner swore to me that he could do it. It was said
also that an executioner could give a swinging blow full on
the criminal's back without leaving any weal behind, and
that the criminal would not feel the slightest pain. However,
there are already too many stories about all these tricks and
subtleties. But even if the executioner does receive a bribe
to make the punishment light, yet the first blow is always
violent and given with all his might. This has even grown
into an invariable rule with them. He may soften the following blows, especially if he is paid in advance, but the first,
whether he has been paid or not, is hellish. I really do not
know why this should be so. Is it in order to prepare the
victim for further strokes, with the idea that after that one
terrible blow the others which are less painful will seem
quite trivial, or simply a desire to show off before his victim,
strike terror into him, stun him in the first moment and
make him realize whom he is dealing with—in short, to
show his quality? In any case, before the beginning of the
punishment the executioner is in a state of great exaltation,
conscious of his strength and knowing himself to be supreme;
at that moment he is an actor; his audience is filled with
wonder and dismay and it is certainly not without some
pleasure that he cries out to his victim, before the first
stroke, the familiar and ominous words: 'Hold tight, I'm
going to flay you!' It is difficult to conceive to what extent
human nature may be perverted.

In those early days in the hospital I listened eagerly to all
these prisoners' tales. Lying there was terribly boring for all
of us. Every day everything was the same, every day was just
like every other. In the mornings the doctor's visit, and

dinner soon afterwards, supplied some distraction. Food, of course, was a major diversion in our monotonous existence. The diets, determined by the nature of the patients' illnesses, were varied. Some had only soup with groats, some only gruel, and others only a semolina porridge, which many were very pleased to have. The prisoners grew soft from long lying in bed and developed a taste for dainties. Those who were improving or almost well were given a piece of boiled beef, or 'bull', as we called it. The best rations were for patients with scurvy—beef with onions, horse-radish, and so on, and sometimes a mug of vodka. The bread was black or brown, again according to the nature of the illness, and was well baked. The formalism and nicety in the prescription of diet amused the patients. In some illnesses, of course, the patient did not want to eat. On the other hand, those patients who had an appetite could eat what they liked. Some exchanged their food, so that a diet suitable for one kind of illness might go to a case of quite a different kind. Others, who were on a low diet, bought beef or the food prescribed for scurvy and drank kvass or the hospital beer, buying it from those who had it. Some even ate two men's rations. These rations were sold and resold for money. The portions containing beef were very expensive; they cost five copecks in paper money. If there was nobody in our ward to buy from, the guard used to be sent into the other prison ward, and if he drew a blank there, then into one of the soldiers' wards, the 'free' wards, as we called them. Somebody willing to sell was always found. They were left with nothing but bread to eat, but on the other hand they were coining money. Poverty, of course, was universal among us, but those who had a few coppers would send as far as to the market for white rolls and even for various dainties. Our guards ran all these errands quite disinterestedly. After dinner the really boring time set in: some would sleep for want of something to do, some would gossip, some wrangle, some tell stories aloud. If no new patients were brought in things were even duller. The arrival of a new-comer almost always created some stir, especially if he was not known to anybody. He was scrutinized carefully and efforts were made to find out who and what he was, where he came from, and what his crime had been. Men who were on their way to other prisons were particularly interesting; they always had something to tell which was not merely their own personal affairs; if a man did not himself speak of these he was never questioned about them, but was asked where his convoy had come from, who was in it, by which route it had come, where it was going, and so on. Some, as they listened to these new travellers' tales, were reminded, as it were by the way, of something from their own past, various prisoners' convoys, journeys into exile, executioners, and officers in charge of convoys. Men who had run the gauntlet used also to be brought in about this time, late in the afternoon. As I have already said, their arrival always had a fairly marked effect on the patients; but they were not brought in every day and a day when there were none of them seemed somehow very slack; everybody seemed to get terribly on everybody else's nerves, and there were even quarrels. We were glad to see even lunatics who were brought in for examination. The ruse of feigning madness in order to escape punishment was occasionally resorted to by condemned men. Some were quickly unmasked, or rather they themselves decided to change their policy and, after acting like Bedlamites for two or three days, they would suddenly become sensible, calm down, and gloomily ask for their discharge. Neither the prisoners nor the doctors reproached these men or shamed them by alluding to their recent tricks; in silence they were discharged and led away, to return to us two or three days later after their punishment. Such cases were, however, on the whole rare. But the genuine lunatics who were brought in for observation were a real plague to the whole ward. Some of them, lively and talkative, given to shouting and weeping and singing, were received by the prisoners at first almost enthusiastically. 'Here's fun!' they would say, watching some newly arrived Tom of Bedlam. But for me it was terribly painful and oppressive to see these unhappy wretches. I could never look at lunatics unmoved.

Soon, however, the endless grimaces and restless antics of the lunatic who had been greeted with laughter grew decidedly tiresome to all of us and in a day or two finally deprived everybody of patience. One of them was kept in the ward for about three weeks, and it seemed there was nothing to do but run away. During this time, as if to make things worse, another madman was brought in. This one made a particularly deep impression on me. All this was in my third year in the prison. In my first year, or rather in the very first months of my prison life, in the spring, I used to go with a party to work in a brick-yard two versts away, as a labourer for the kiln-setters. The kilns had to be repaired in readiness for making bricks in the coming summer. The first morning Miretsky and Boguslavsky introduced me at the works to the resident overseer, Sergeant Ostrozhsky. He was a Pole, an elderly man of about sixty years of age, tall and lean, extraordinarily handsome and even majestic in appearance. He had been in the army in Siberia for a very long time, and although he was of peasant origin (he had come to Siberia as a private soldier after the Polish rising of 1830), yet Miretsky and Boguslavsky liked and respected him. He was always reading the Catholic bible. I talked with him, and he spoke very pleasantly and sensibly, had extremely interesting things to say, and looked at you honestly and with great goodness of heart. After that I did not see him for two years, but only heard that he had been arrested for some offence, and now all of a sudden he was brought into our ward, a madman. He came in shrieking and laughing wildly and began to dance round the ward with the most uncouth and obscene gestures. The prisoners were delighted, but I felt very sad. After three days we did not know what to do with him. He was constantly wrangling, fighting, shrieking, and singing, even at night, and he incessantly made gestures so disgusting that they made everybody feel sick. He was afraid of nobody. He was put into a strait-jacket but this made things even worse for us, although without it he had picked quarrels with and attacked practically everybody. Sometimes during those three weeks the whole ward begged the chief physician with one voice to remove our affliction into the other prison ward. There, after a day or two, they in their turn petitioned for him to be sent to us. And since we happened to have two lunatics at the same time, both violent and both aggressive, our two wards went on exchanging madmen turn and turn about. But each seemed worse than the other. Everybody breathed more freely when at last they were taken away somewhere . . .

I remember also another strange madman. Once, in the summer, a prisoner awaiting the execution of his sentence, a robust and loutish-looking fellow of about forty-five, with a face disfigured by smallpox, little red eyes sunk in fat, and an extremely sullen and morose expression, was brought in. His bed was next to mine. He seemed a very quiet fellow, spoke to nobody and sat as though he were pondering over something or other. It began to grow dusk and suddenly he turned to me. Without preamble, but with the air of one confiding something extraordinarily secret, he began to tell me that he had been condemned to two thousand strokes, but that now he would never receive them because the daughter of a certain colonel was working for him. I looked doubtfully at him and answered that I did not think the colonel's daughter was in a position to do anything in such a case. I had not yet guessed his condition; he had been brought in not as a madman but as an ordinary sick man. I asked him what his illness was. He answered that he did not know, that he had been sent here for some reason but that he was quite well, and the colonel's daughter was in love with him; once, two weeks before, she had been driving past the guardhouse when he chanced to look out of his little barred window. As soon as she saw him she fell in love with him. And since then, on various pretexts, she had been three times to the guardhouse; the first time she came with her father to visit her brother, who was on guard duty at the time; another time she had come with her mother to distribute alms and had whispered to him as she went past that she loved him and would save him. It was strange to hear the minute detail in which he related all this balderdash, which was of course a pure figment of his poor disordered brain. He believed religiously in his escape from punishment. He spoke calmly and confidently of the young lady's passionate love for him, and in spite of the inherent absurdity of the story, it was uncanny to listen to this romantic tale of a lovelorn maiden from a man approaching fifty, with such a melancholy and dispirited look on his ugly face. It was strange what terror had accomplished in this timid soul. Perhaps he really had seen somebody from the window, and the madness born of his fear and growing with every hour had suddenly found its form and its outlet. This unhappy soldier, who had probably never once given a thought to young ladies in his life, had suddenly invented a complete romance, instinctively clutching at even this poor straw. I heard him out without saying anything more, and told the other convicts about him. But when they grew inquisitive he chastely held his peace. The next day the doctor questioned him at great length, and since he told the doctor that there was nothing wrong with him, and since the examination seemed to show this really to be so, he was discharged. But we did not learn that *sanat.* had been entered on his chart until after the doctors had left the ward, so that we were unable to tell them where the trouble lay. And we ourselves did not fully realize the true state of affairs. The whole business might be attributed to the error of the authorities who had sent him to us without explaining why. There had been some carelessness there. Or perhaps even those who sent him had only suspicions and were far from convinced of his madness, but acted on obscure indications and sent him to us to be kept under observation. However that may have been, the wretch had to undergo his punishment two days later. It appears that he was dumbfounded at the unexpectedness of this; up to the last moment he did not believe that he would be punished, and when they led him along the lines he began to yell, 'Help!' This time he was not put into our ward, because there was no bed in it, but into the other. But I inquired about him and learnt that for a whole week he did not speak a word to anybody, and that he seemed bewildered and extremely unhappy . . . Afterwards, when his back was healed, he was sent away somewhere. At least, I never heard anything more of him.

As for treatment and medicines in general, as far as I could see those who were only slightly ill neither followed the doctors' orders nor took their prescriptions, but those who were seriously ill, or indeed really ill at all, took great interest in their treatments and took their mixtures and their powders with careful regularity; but best of all they loved external remedies. Cupping-glasses, leeches, poultices, and blood-lettings, which our simple people so like and have such faith in, were suffered among us willingly and even with pleasure. One strange circumstance attracted my interest. These same men who were so patient in bearing the agonizing pain of the rod or the birch, quite frequently complained, writhed, and even groaned if they had to undergo a cupping. I do not know how to explain this, whether it was that they had really grown very soft or that they were simply playing up. It is true that our cuppings were of a special kind. The little instrument used to make incisions in the skin had been lost or broken in the distant past by the orderly, or perhaps it had simply got out of order, so that the indispensable scarification of the skin had to be done with a lancet. Something like twelve cuts are made for each cupping. With the little instrument it is not painful. The twelve little knives dart out like a flash and the pain is not felt. But making the incisions with a lancet is a different matter. A lancet cuts comparatively slowly; the pain is apparent; and since ten cuppings demand a hundred and twenty cuts, all of them together were, of course, very painful. I myself have experienced it, but although it smarted and was tiresome, still it was not so bad that one could not help groaning. It was even comical sometimes to watch a great sturdy fellow squirming and beginning to whimper. It might be compared with what happens when a man, who can be firm and even tranquil in a serious matter, mopes and behaves like a spoilt child at home if there is nothing for him to do, refuses to eat what is put before him and is quarrelsome and abusive; nothing suits him, everybody gets on his nerves, everybody is rude to him, everybody annoys him; in short, 'he doesn't know what he *does* want', as they say sometimes of gentlemen of this kind, who are to be met with, however, among the common people as well and who, in the sort of life we all must share, were all too frequently found in our prison. It happened more than once that when his companions in the ward began to tease one of these spoilt children and perhaps one of them to give him a downright scolding, he would stop at once, as though he had really only been waiting for a scolding to be quiet. Ustyantsev particularly disliked this sort of man and never missed an opportunity of wrangling with one of them. Indeed, he did not let pass any opportunity of falling foul of anybody. This was both a pleasure and a necessity for him, doubtless because of his illness, but also partly because of his dullwittedness. He would first gaze steadily and solemnly at his victim and then in a calm, assured tone of voice begin to read him a lecture. He meddled in everything; it was as though he had been appointed to keep an eye on the discipline or morals of all of us.

'He sticks his nose into everything,' the prisoners used to say, laughing. But they were kind to him and avoided

quarrelling with him, although they laughed at him sometimes.

'Well, he does talk our heads off! He's worse than a
wagon-load of monkeys . . .'

'Talk your heads off, indeed! Everyone knows you don't
take your cap off to a fool! Why should he yell over a lancet?
He must learn to take the rough with the smooth and put up
with things.'

'What's it got to do with you?'

'No, mates,' interrupted one of the prisoners; 'cupping's
nothing; I've tried it. But nothing hurts worse than having
your ear pulled.'

Everybody laughed.

'Did somebody pull yours for you?'

'Don't you believe me? Of course they did!'

'Well, your ears certainly do stick up a bit.'

This prisoner, Shapkin, certainly had extremely long,
prominent ears. He was a vagrant, still young, a quiet and
sensible fellow, who always spoke with a kind of straight-
faced, secret humour, that made some of his stories very
funny.

'How should I know whether you've had your ears pulled?
Why should it ever enter my mind, fathead?' Ustyantsev
intervened again, irritably addressing Shapkin, although the
latter had not been speaking to him at all, but to all of us.
Shapkin did not even look at him.

'Who pulled them for you?' asked somebody.

'Who? Why, a policeman, of course. That was when I was
on the road, mates. We'd got to K——, two of us, me and
another tramp called Efim; he hasn't got any other name.
On the way there we'd done pretty well out of a peasant at
a place called Tolmina. It's a little village, Tolmina is. Well,
we came to the town and had a look round to see if we
couldn't make a bit here as well, and then clear out. When
you're in the open, you're as free as air, but in the town you
feel uncomfortable, you know. Well, first of all we went into

a pub. We had a look round. A chap came up to us; he was down on his uppers and out at elbows, but he was wearing a town suit, not peasant's clothes. Well, we talked a bit. Then he says, "Do you mind telling me how you got here? Have you got papers?"

' "No," says we, "we came without papers."

' "Just so. Us as well. I've got a couple of pals here too," says he, "and they're in General Cuckoo's army, as well; we're all on the road. So you won't mind me asking you, because we've been on a bit of a binge here and of course we didn't make anything while it was going on. So stand us half a pint."

' "With the greatest pleasure," says we. So we had a drink. So then they told us about a job, cracking a crib, that's to say right in our line. There was a house there, on the edge of the town, and one of the townies lived there, with any amount of stuff, so we thought we'd pay him a visit at night. But as soon as the five of us got into the rich man's house that night they caught us. They took us to the police-station and then to the captain himself. "I'll do the questioning," says he. He comes out smoking his pipe, and they bring him a cup of tea, a big strong chap with whiskers. He sits down. And besides us they'd brought in three others, all tramps too. Well, a tramp's a funny person, you know, brothers: he never can remember anything and even if you was to hit him over the head with a club, he's forgotten everything, he doesn't know a thing. The captain comes straight up to me. He'd a big, booming voice, as if he was shouting into a barrel. "Who are you?" Well, of course, I just say the same as everybody else: "I don't remember nothing," says I, "your honour. I've forgotten."

' "Wait," says he, "I'll have something to say to you after; I know that mug of yours." And he was staring at me with his goggle eyes. But I'd never laid eyes on him before. Then he says to one of the others, "Who are you?"

' "Clear out, your worship."

' "Is that what they call you, Clear out?"

' "Yes, your worship, that's it."

' "All right, you're Clear out. And you?" That's to the next one, I mean.

' "I'm after him, your worship."

' "What's your name?"

' "That's my name, I'm after him! your worship."

' "And who called you that, you rascal?"

' "It was good people named me, your worship. There are *some* good people in the world, your worship, you know."

' "And who were these good people?"

' "I disremember, your worship. Please be kind enough to forgive me."

' "Have you forgotten all of them?"

' "Yes, your worship."

' "But surely you had a father and mother? . . . You remember them, at least?"

' "I suppose I must have had, your worship, but I disremember. Perhaps I had, your worship."

' "Where have you lived until now?"

' "In the woods, your worship."

' "In the woods all the time?"

' "Yes."

' "What about winter?"

' "I haven't seen winter, your worship."

' "Well, you; what do they call you?"

' "Axe, your worship."

' "And you?"

' "Sharpen it and look slippy, your worship."

' "And none of you remembers anything?"

' "Not a thing, your worship."

'He just stood there and laughed, and they were looking at him and grinning. But another time he might push your teeth in, it all depends. A lot of great big fat fellows they were too. "Put 'em in the clink," says he, "and I'll deal with 'em later. But you"—it was me he was talking to—"stop here. Come here and sit down!" I sees there's a table and some paper and a pen. Thinks I, now what's he trying to do? "Sit down on that chair," says he, "and pick up that pen and write," and he grabs me by the ear and pulls it. "I can't," says I, "your worship." "Write!"

' "Have a heart, your worship!" "You can write, so write!" He was still pulling my ear, and he goes on pulling it and twisting it. Well, I tell you, lads, I'd rather he'd given me three hundred of the best; I saw stars. "Write and have done with it!" '

'Why, was he cracked or something?'

'No, it wasn't that. But there was a clerk in Tobolsk had been up to some little games: he'd pinched some government money and made off, and his ears stuck out, too. Well, his description had been sent out everywhere. And it seems it fitted me down to the ground, so he was trying to find out if I could write, and how well.'

'That explains it, mate! And did it hurt?'

'I can tell you it did.'

There was a general laugh.

'Well, did you write?'

'How could I? I pushed the pen about, backwards and forwards on the paper, and then he gave up. Well, of course he had to give me a dozen slaps in the face, but with that he lets me go—only to the prison, I mean.'

'And can you write, really?'

'I used to be able to, but when they began writing with pens I forgot how to . . .'

It was, then, with tales like this, or rather with gossip like this, that we sometimes passed our weary hours. Lord, what boredom! Long, stifling days, each one exactly like every other in every way. If we could only have had a book of some kind! Nevertheless, I often went into hospital, especially at first, sometimes because I was ill, sometimes simply to stay in bed and get away from the prison. It was hard to bear there, even worse than in hospital, morally burdensome. Malice, hostility, wrangling, envy, perpetual nagging at us gentlemen, spiteful, menacing faces! Here in the hospital, at least, we were all on a more or less equal footing and lived more amicably. The heaviest time of the whole day was the evening, after the candles were lit, and the early hours of the night. We settled down early. A feeble night-light made a spot of brightness in the distance by the door, but our end of the ward was dim. The air grew fetid and stifling. Somebody, unable to sleep, would get up and sit for an hour and a half on his bed, with his night-capped head bent as if in thought. In an effort to kill the time somehow, you would watch him for an hour together, trying to guess what he was thinking of. Or you would begin to dream and remember the past and great broad, vivid pictures would form in your mind's eye; details would come back to you which at another time you would hardly remember or feel with such intensity as this. Or you would wonder about the future: shall I ever get out of prison? where shall I go? when will that time come? shall I ever go back to my own country? The thoughts would go on and on, and hope would begin to stir in your soul . . . Or another time you would simply begin to count: one, two, three . . . and so on, hoping to fall asleep somehow while you counted. Sometimes I counted up to three thousand without going to sleep. Now somebody would begin to toss and turn. Ustyantsev would cough his diseased, consumptive cough, groan feebly and add, each time, 'O Lord, I have sinned!' The sound of that sick, whining voice was strange in the universal stillness. Somewhere in a corner others, also unable to sleep, would begin to talk to one another from their beds. One would begin to tell of his past life, far away and long ago, of tramping the roads, of his children, of his wife, of how things used to be. You would feel, from the mere sound of that remote whisper, that nothing of all he spoke about would ever return to him, and that the speaker himself had floated away from it all like a piece of driftwood; the other would listen.

All you would hear would be a quiet, monotonous whisper, like water murmuring far away . . . I remember a story I heard, one long winter night. From the first it seemed to me like a feverish dream, as though I lay burning with fever and this were the creation of my delirium . . .

4. Akulka's Husband (A Story)

IT was already late, after 11 o'clock. I had dropped asleep, but suddenly I was awake. The small, dim flame of the night-light scarcely relieved the darkness of the ward. Almost everybody was asleep. Even Ustyantsev slept, and in the stillness his laboured breathing could be heard, and the way the phlegm rattled in his throat with every breath. All at once, far away in the corridors, the heavy tread of the relief guard resounded. The stock of a rifle clashed on the floor. The door of the ward opened; the corporal, stepping cautiously, counted over the patients. A minute later the ward was locked, the new guard was posted, the picket retreated, and the earlier stillness reigned again. It was only now that I noticed that not far away on my left two men who were not asleep seemed to be whispering together. It used sometimes to happen in the wards that men who had lain side by side for months together without exchanging a single word would suddenly begin to talk under the evocative influence of the night, and one would lay bare all his past to the other.

These two had evidently been talking for a long time. I had missed the beginning and even now I could not hear all that was said; but little by little I grew used to it and began to follow everything. I could not sleep: what was I to do, how could I help listening? . . . One was talking with feverish intensity; he was half lying in bed, with his head raised and his neck stretched out towards his companion. He was evidently violently excited and eager to tell his story.

His hearer was sitting up in bed, morose and completely indifferent, occasionally growling something in answer or as a mark of sympathy, but apparently more out of politeness than from any real interest, and continually stuffing his nose with snuff from a horn. This was Cherevin, a soldier from the correctional company, a man of about fifty, a sullen, pedantic, coldly moralizing creature, stultified with self-satisfaction. Shishkov, who was telling the story, was still a young man, not yet thirty, a civil prisoner, who worked in the tailor's shop. I had paid little attention to him previously, and even after this, throughout my life in prison, I somehow did not feel drawn to take any interest in him. He was an empty, silly creature. Sometimes he would be silent and sulky, behave very uncivilly and go for weeks without speaking. Sometimes he would suddenly get mixed up in some affair or other and begin to tattle, grow heated over trifles, and scurry from barrack to barrack, carrying the latest gossip, backbiting and losing his temper. Somebody would give him a thrashing and he would relapse into one of his silent fits. He was a cowardly, milk-and-water creature. Everyone seemed to treat him with disdain. He was rather short and spare, with eyes that seemed shifty or at times vacantly mooning. Sometimes when he had something to tell he would begin to talk with hot excitement, waving his arms about—and break off abruptly or wander off on to something else, be carried away by the details of the new subject and forget what he had begun to speak about. He frequently got involved in disputes and when he did he invariably used to find something to reproach the other man with, some wrong done to himself, of which he would speak with feeling, almost weeping . . . He was a fair performer on the balalaika, and he liked to play; on holidays he even danced, and danced well, when he was made to . . . It was very easy to make him do anything . . . It was not that he was so very compliant, but he liked to be thought good company and make himself pleasant . . .

For a long time I could not fathom what he was talking about. I thought at first, too, that he was fighting shy of his subject and wandering off into side-issues. He had perhaps noticed that Cherevin could hardly have been less interested in his story, but he seemed to be deliberately trying to convince himself that his hearer was all attention, and perhaps he would have felt very much hurt if he had been forced to believe the opposite.

'. . . He used to go out into the market,' he went on, 'and everybody bowed and scraped, and, in short, he was a rich man.'

'Did you say he had a business?'

'Yes, he had. We workers were very poor. The women had to carry water ever such a long way from the river, up the high bank, to water the vegetables; they'd work like niggers, and in the autumn they wouldn't get enough out of it for cabbage soup. It was ruination. Well, he had a big farm and worked it with labourers, three he kept; then besides he kept bees and sold honey, and cattle as well, and in our parts that meant he was a very important person. He was terribly old, seventy at least, and he was beginning to feel his age—a great big grey-headed man. He'd go into the market in his fox-skin coat and everybody was very respectful. They knew how important he was, I mean. "Good morning, sir, Ankudim Trofimovich!" "Good morning to you, too," he'd say. He didn't think he was too good to talk to anybody. "Long life to you, Ankudim Trofimovich!" "And how are things with you?" he would ask. "Well, things are all right, just as soot is white. What about you, sir?" "We get along somehow, as well as poor sinners can expect; we're only smoking lamps." "Long life to you, Ankudim Trofimovich!" He wasn't too proud to talk to anyone and when he talked, every word was as good as a rouble. He liked reading—he knew how to read and write—and he was always reading holy books. He'd make his old woman sit down in front of him: "Now listen, wife, and try

to understand!" and he'd begin to explain it to her. The old
woman wasn't exactly old; he'd married again, because of
children—I mean he hadn't any with the first wife. But
with the second, this Marya Stepanovna, he had two sons
who weren't grown up and he was sixty when the youngest,
Vasya, was born, but this Akulka I'm talking about, the
daughter, was the oldest of all and she was eighteen.'

'That was your wife, was it?'

'Wait a bit. First Philka Morozov sticks his nose in here.
"You," he says, this Philka, to Ankudim, "you share out;
you give me back all my four hundred roubles; am I one of
your labourers? I'm not going to haggle with you, and I
don't want", says he, "your Akulka. I'm beginning to have
a good time now," says he. "My parents are both dead now,"
says he, "so I'm going to drink all my money and then hire
myself out, as a soldier, I mean, and in ten years I'll come
back to you a field-marshal." Ankudim did give him his
money and settled up with him for good—because his father
had been partners with the old man in the business. "You're
a bad lot," says he. So then he says: "Well, whether I'm
a lost soul or not, it was from you, you old greybeard, I
learned to skin flints. You want to scrimp and save over
a couple of farthings, and you scrape up all sorts of rubbish,
in case it might come in for porridge. I've had enough",
says he, "of all that sort of thing. You scrape and save and
scrape and save, and at last the devil is all you have. I'll do
what I choose," says he. "And anyhow I won't have your
Akulka: I've slept with her without the need of that . . ."

' "How dare you," says he, Ankudim I mean, "talk shame
of an honest father's honest daughter? When did you sleep
with her, you serpent's tallow, you pike's blood?" All
shaking with rage he was. Philka told me himself.

' "I won't marry her," says he, "and not only that, I'll
see that nobody else marries your Akulka. Nobody will
take her; even Mikita Grigoryevich won't have her now,
because now she's shamed. Her and me's been having our

fun ever since the autumn. I wouldn't have her now for a hundred crayfish. Go on, try it: offer me a hundred crayfish this minute—and I won't have her . . ."

'And what a regular roystering time he had, that lad! He made the earth groan, and the town was full of uproar. He collected a band of good pals and he had a pile of money; he was on the binge for three months on end, and then he'd lost everything. "When I've finished all my money", he used to say, "I'll let the house go, I'll let all my things go, and then I'll hire myself out to go as a soldier in someone else's place or else I'll take to the roads!" He used to be drunk from morning till night and he drove a pair of horses with bells on. And all the girls were terribly in love with him. He was pretty good at playing the bagpipes.'

'I suppose he'd had to do with Akulka before?'

'Stop, wait a bit. I'd just buried my father too, and my mother used to make ginger-bread. She worked for Ankudim and that's what we lived on. It wasn't much of a life. Well, we had a little farm, too, on the other side of the wood, and we used to sow a bit of corn, but after my father died it went to rack and ruin, because I was having a good time too, mate. I used to screw money out of my mother with my fist . . .'

'That's bad, to hit her. It's a great sin.'

'I used to be drunk, pal, from early morning to late at night. Our house was all right; it was our own, even if it was so old it was rotten, but it was as bare as the palm of your hand. We never got enough to eat, we used to have to chew a bit of rag by the week together. As for my mother, she used to jaw and jaw at me, but what did I care? . . . I was always with Philka Morozov in those days, mate. I was with him from morning to night. "Play your guitar for me", he'd say, "and dance, and I'll lie down and throw you money, because I'm a very rich man." And the things he did! But he wouldn't take stolen goods. "I'm no thief," says he, "I'm an honest man." "Let's go", says he, "and smear

Akulka's gate with tar, because I'm not going to have her marrying Mikita Grigoryevich. I've set my heart on stopping him now," he says. The old man had been wanting to get Mikita Grigoryevich for his daughter before. This Mikita, he was an old man as well, a widower, and he wore glasses. He had a business. When he heard that there were stories going round about Akulka, well, of course, "that", he says, "would bring great shame on me, and besides, I've no wish to get married, because of my age." So we smeared Akulka's gates, and so they gave her a thrashing for that, her folks gave her a good hiding . . . Marya Stepanovna shouted: "I'll make it hot for her!" And the old man says, "In the olden days," he says, "when the good patriarchs lived, I'd have chopped her up and burnt her at the stake, but now", he says, "the earth is all darkness and decay." All down the street the neighbours used to hear Akulka howling: they thrashed her from morning to night. And Philka would go shouting all over the market: "Akulka's a fine lass," says he, "she likes a good time. You're all dressed up today, who's your lover, pray? I've given them something there; they won't forget me in a hurry," he says. Just about then I met Akulka once, she was carrying some pails, and I shouts out, "Good morning, Akulina Kudimovna! Humble greetings to your ladyship! Where are you going to, my pretty maid? To live with my lover, sir, she said," and that's all I said, but she just looks at me, and those eyes of hers were so big, and she'd gone as thin as a shaving. So when she looked at me, her mother thought she was having a bit of fun with me and she shouts from the porch: "Why are you grinning there, you shameless hussy?" and the same day she thrashed her again. She used to thrash her for a whole mortal hour, sometimes. "I'll flog her to death," she says, "because she's no daughter of mine now." '

'I suppose she was a whore, then?'

'Just you listen, uncle. I was still getting drunk with Philka all this time, and then my mother comes to me, when

I was in bed. "Why are you in bed," she says, "you brute? You're a good-for-nothing waster," she says. She gave me a real dressing-down, I mean. "Get married," she says, "get married to that Akulka. They'll be glad to give her even to you now, and give you three hundred roubles into the bargain." So I says to her, "But you know," I says, "now she's been put to shame before everybody." "You're a fool," she says, "the marriage crown covers everything; besides, you'll have the whip hand of her if ever in all her life she turns out to have done you wrong. And we could do with their money. I've talked to Marya Stepanovna already," she says, "and she's very ready to listen." So I says, "Twenty roubles down," I says, "and then I'll marry her." Well, believe it or not, right up to the wedding I was drunk every minute of the time. Then Philka Morozov threatened me. Says he, "I'll break every rib in your body, Akulka's husband, and if I want to I'll sleep with your wife every blessed night." So I says, "You're a liar, you dog's carcass!" Well, there he'd insulted me in front of the whole street. I ran home and I says, "I won't get married unless they put down another fifty roubles!" '

'And would they let her marry you?'

'Marry me? Why not? We weren't nobodies, after all. My father was ruined by a fire only just before he died, or else we were richer even than them. That Ankudim did say to me, "You're a beggarly lot," he says, "no better than tramps." But I comes back at him, "You", I says, "got a lot of tar smeared on your gates." And he says, "What reason", he says, "have you got to give yourself airs? Try to prove that she's not honest! A lie may have no legs, but slander has wings! There's the icon," says he, "and there's the door. You needn't have her. But give back the money you had." So then I finished with Philka: I sent with Mitri Bykov to tell him I was going to shame him before the whole world, and right up to the wedding, pal, I was drunk all the time. Only I sobered up just in time. When they brought us back from the church, they sat us down and Mitrophan Stepanovich, her uncle, I mean, he says, "The knot may be tied in dishonour, but it's tied fast enough," he says; "the thing's done and finished with." The old man, Ankudim, was drunk too, and he began to cry—he sits there with the tears running down his beard. Well, mate, this is what I did: I took a whip with me in my pocket that I'd got ready beforehand, and I was meaning to have a bit of fun with Akulka now. "I'll teach you", I was going to say, "to get married by a nasty bit of cheating," and I meant to show people that I hadn't got married with my eyes shut . . .'

'Good for you! You mean, so she would feel from then on . . .'

'No, uncle. I wish you'd learn to keep your mouth shut. In our parts as soon as you're married they take you straight into the barn while they go on drinking. Well, they left me and Akulka in the barn. She sat there all white, without a drop of blood in her face. She was frightened, I mean. Her hair was as white as flax, too. She had big eyes. And she never used to say a word; you'd hear no more of her than if a dumb woman was living in the house. She was a queer one altogether. Well, brother, would you believe it; I got my whip ready and put it down by the bed and then, mate, she turned out to be as innocent as a babe unborn.'

'Never!'

'Absolutely innocent; as innocent as could be. Well, then why had she had all that to put up with? What had Philka Morozov shamed her before all the world for?'

'Yes.'

'I got down on my knees to her then, straight off the bed and I put my hands together and I says, "My dear," I says, "forgive me for being such a fool, Akulina Kudimovna, as to take you for that. Forgive me," I says, "I'm a brute!" And she sits there on the bed looking at me and she puts both her hands on my shoulders and laughs with the tears running down, crying and laughing both at once . . . Then I went to all of them. "Well," I says, "if I meet with Philka Morozov he won't have another hour to live!" And the old people, they didn't know where to turn to say how thankful they were: that mother of hers almost fell at her feet, and she howled. But the old man said: "If we had only known, we wouldn't have found you a husband like this one, our darling daughter." But when I went with her to church on the first Sunday, me in an astrakhan hat, a fine cloth caftan, and velveteen trousers, and her in a new hare-skin jacket and a silk kerchief—I mean I was a match for her and she was a match for me—well, you ought to have seen us then! The folk all admired us: I'm not so bad to look at, and Akulinushka, though you couldn't praise her up above everyone else, still you couldn't say anything bad about her; and out of a bunch of a dozen she wouldn't be the one you'd throw away . . .'

'Well, all right.'

'Well, listen. The day after the wedding I was drunk, but I ran away from the guests; I just slipped away and ran. "Let's have that lazy good-for-nothing, Philka Morozov," I said; "give him here, the blackguard!" I was shouting it all over the bazaar. Well, I was roaring drunk so they caught me just by the Vlasovs', and it took three men to get me back home by force. And there was a lot of talk in the town. The lasses in the market were saying to one another: "Girls! My dears! Do you know what? That Akulka turned out to be honest." And Philka, a bit after, says to me in front of people, "Sell your wife and you can get drunk. Our Yashka," he says, "the soldier, got married just for that: he never slept with his wife and he was drunk for three years afterwards." I said to him: "You're a dirty scoundrel!" "And you're a fool," he says. "After all, you weren't sober when you got wed. How could you tell about a thing like that if you were drunk?" I went home, and I shouts: "You married me off when I was drunk!" My mother tried to start an argument on the spot. "Your ears, mother," I says, "are stopped with gold. Give Akulka here!" Well, so then I began to knock her about, and I went on and on, mate, I went on for nearly two hours, till I couldn't stand up myself; she wasn't able to get up for three weeks . . .'

'Well, of course,' phlegmatically remarked Cherevin, 'if you don't beat them they'll . . . But had you caught her with a lover?'

'No, not to say caught,' said Shishkov, after a short silence, with a certain amount of effort. 'But I had taken offence, I felt very much offended, people had made a laughing-stock of me and the ringleader in it all was Philka. "You've got a wife", he says, "fit for people to take as a pattern." He invited us to visit him, and this was the first thing he offered us: "His wife", he says, "is a kind soul, a perfect lady, with good manners, who knows how to treat people and she's always nice, that's how things are with him now. Have you forgotten, my lad, that you smeared her gates with tar yourself?" I was sitting there drunk, and just then he sort of grabbed me by the hair, and while he was grabbing he was pushing me down and he says, "Dance," he says, "Akulka's husband. I'll hold you by the hair like this and you dance to amuse me!" I shouted, "You dirty rotter!" And he says to me, "I'm going to come and see you with a lot of pals and I'll beat your wife Akulka with sticks, under your very nose, as much as I like." So, believe it or not, after that I daren't go out of the house for a whole month: I thought he would come and put shame on me. And just because of that I began to beat her . . .'

'But why should you have? You can tie people's hands but you can't tie their tongues. It's not a good thing to beat them so much. You ought to punish them, teach them a lesson, and then be kind to them. That's what wives are for.'

Shishkov was silent for a time.

'I had taken offence,' he began again, 'and so I got into the habit again: some days I would beat her from morning till night; she couldn't do anything right.

'If I didn't beat her, I was bored. She used to sit and not say a word, and look out of the window and cry . . . She used to be always crying, and I used to be sorry for her but I beat her. My mother used to scold away at me because of her: "You great good-for-nothing lump of meat," she says, "you're only fit for Siberia!" "I'll kill her," I shouts; "and don't anybody dare to say anything to me, because I was tricked into getting married." At first the old man, Anku-dim I mean, tried to stick up for her, he'd come and say, "You", he'd say, "aren't up to much yourself. I'll have justice on you!" But afterwards he gave it up. And then that there Marya Stepanovna just ate humble pie. One time she came and begged with tears in her eyes: "I've come to ask you something, Ivan Semenovich," she says; "it's a little thing but it would be a great favour. Give us a bit of hope!" and then she bowed down to me. "Make up your mind to forgive her! Wicked people took away our daughter's good name: you know yourself she was honest when you married her . . ." She bowed down to the ground; she was crying. But I got on my high horse: "I won't even listen to you now! Now I shall do just as I want with all of you, because now I've lost control of myself; and Philka Moro-zov", I said, "is my pal and my best friend . . ." '

'That meant you'd taken up with him again, did it?'

'Not me. You couldn't even get near him. He'd turned into a regular soak. He'd chucked away everything he'd got and then hired himself out to go for a soldier instead of somebody's eldest son. In our parts, when you're a sub-stitute like that, up to the very last day when you're carted off everything in the house is yours and you're the boss of everything. The substitute gets the money in full when he reports and up till then he lives in the house, and sometimes it's as long as six months, and the things he does to the people of the house, it's enough to make them take the icons out for shame! "I'm going for a soldier in your son's place," they say; "that means I'm doing you a great favour, so you ought to worship me for it, or else I'll say no." So Philka was raising the devil there, sleeping with the daughter, pulling the father's beard after dinner every blessed day— and doing everything he'd a fancy to. Every blessed day he had to have a bath, and they had to throw vodka on the hot stones instead of water, and the women-folk had to carry him to the bath-house in their arms. He would go back to the house after a binge and stand outside in the street: "I won't use the gate; take the fence down!"—so they would have to pull down the fence in another place and he would go through that way. At last he came to the end, they took him off to report and got him sobered up. Crowds and crowds of people came out all down the street: "They're taking Philka Morozov off for a soldier!" He was bowing to everybody. And just at that moment Akulka was coming from the kitchen garden; when Philka saw her, close to our gate, he shouted "Stop!" and jumped out of the cart and bowed down to the ground. "My darling," he says, "my treasure, I have loved you for two years and now they're taking me off for a soldier, with a band. Forgive me," he says, "honest daughter of an honest father, because I've been a rotter to you, and it's all my fault!" And he bows down to the ground again. Akulka stood still at first, as if she was frightened, and then she makes him a low bow and she says, says she, "Forgive me, too, good young man; I bear you no malice." I followed her into the house. "What did you say to him, you bitch?" And believe me or believe me not she looked at me and said, "I love him now," she says, "more than all the world." '

'No!'

'Well, that day I never said a word to her all day . . . Only when it was nearly evening I said, "Akulka! I'm going to kill you now," I said. That night I couldn't get to sleep and I went out into the passage for a drink of kvass, and the dawn was just beginning to break. I went back into the house. "Akulka," I said, "get ready to go out to the farm." I'd been meaning to go before that and my mother knew we were going. "That's right," she says, "it's harvest time and they tell me the labourer's been in bed for three days with the stomach-ache." I put the horse in the cart and I didn't say anything. As you go out of our town there's woods for fifteen versts and our farm's on the other side of the woods. We went three versts into the woods, and then I stopped the horse. "Get up, Akulina," I says, "your end has come." She looked at me and she was frightened, and she stood in front of me and didn't say anything. "I've had enough of you," I says. "Say your prayers!" So I grabs her by the hair; her plaits were so thick and long and I twisted them round my hand and I squeezed her between my knees from behind and I took out my knife and bent her head back and I cut her throat like a calf . . . She screamed and the blood just spouted out and I threw my knife down and put my arms round her and I laid down on the ground with my arms round her and I yelled and roared over her; she was screaming and I was screaming; she was all wriggling and struggling out of my arms, and the blood was all on me, the blood—it was just pouring all over my face and over my hands as well, just pouring . . . I left her, all at once I was terrified and I left the horse and ran and ran, and ran home by the back ways and into the bath-house; we had a bath-house that was old and we didn't use it; and I hid under the bench and stayed there. I stayed there till it was dark.'

'And what about Akulka?'

'Well, seemingly she got up after I left her and she set out for home too. They found her afterwards a hundred yards from the place.'

'So you hadn't killed her, then?'

'No . . .' Shishkov paused.

'There's a vein,' remarked Cherevin, 'and if you don't cut right through it, this vein, at the first go, a person will go on struggling and however much blood runs out he won't die.'

'But she did die. They found her dead that night. They raised a hue and cry and began looking for me, and after it was dark they found me in the bath-house . . . I've been here over three years, I reckon,' he added after a pause.

'H'm . . . Of course, no good comes of it if you don't beat them,' remarked Cherevin, in a calm and formal tone, as he took out his snuff-horn again. He began taking long, deliberate sniffs. 'There again, my lad,' he continued, 'by your own account, you turned out very stupid. Once I caught my wife like that with a lover too. So I made her go into the shed and I doubled up my halter. "Who did you swear to be true to?" I says. "Who did you swear to be true to?" And then I thrashed her, thrashed her with the halter, I thrashed and thrashed for an hour and a half, till she screams: "I'll wash your feet," she screams, "and drink the water." They called her Avdotya.'

5. The Summer Time

BUT now it was the beginning of April, and Holy Week was already drawing near. Gradually the summer work began. With every day the sun was warmer and brighter; the air smelt of the spring and had a disturbing effect on the whole organism. Even a man in fetters was moved by the advent of the fine weather, which awakened even in him vague aspirations, strivings, and longings. I think men pine even more bitterly for freedom in the bright sunshine than in the grey days of winter or autumn, and this was noticeable among all the prisoners. They seemed to rejoice in the bright weather, yet at the same time a certain impatience and fretfulness in their natures was intensified. I certainly noticed that prison quarrels seemed to occur more frequently in the spring. Noise, shouting, and general uproar occurred more often and complicated disputes arose; at the same time you would suddenly come across a man whose musing gaze, as he worked, was fixed on the blue distance somewhere across the Irtysh, where begins the immense carpet, stretching for fifteen hundred versts, of the free Kirghiz steppe; you would hear the deep sigh, from the very bottom of the lungs, as though he pined to breathe that far-away air of liberty, and ease his crushed and fettered spirit. At last, with a sigh of grief that seemed to be shaking off his dreams and wandering thoughts, the convict would seize his spade or the bricks he must drag from one place to another with an abrupt and sullen impatience. A minute later he would already have forgotten the feeling which had suddenly descended on him and be laughing or cursing according to his nature; or he would fling himself on his task, if he had been set one, with extraordinary and quite disproportionate zeal and begin to work with all his strength, as if he were trying by dint of work to crush something inside himself that was oppressing and stifling him. All these were strong men, for the most part in the full flower of youth and vigour . . . Fetters weigh heavy at such times! I am not playing the poet now: I feel convinced of the truth of my observations. In the warmth of spring, when the sun is bright and you feel with your whole soul and being the reawakening of nature in all its boundless might, the confinement of the prison, the guards, the subjection to the will of others, become increasingly irksome; but besides all this, in this season of spring, all over Russia and all over Siberia, vagabondage begins with the appearance of the first lark: God's people escape from the prisons and lose themselves in the forests. After the foul air of the dungeon, the courts, the fetters, and the rods, they wander at their own sweet will wherever they wish, wherever the land looks pleasant and they can be free; they eat and drink what God sends wherever they find it, and at night they fall asleep tranquilly in the forest or in the open fields, untroubled by the major cares of life, delivered from the anguish of the prison, in God's keeping like the birds of the forest, and with only the stars of heaven to bid them good-night. It is certainly a hard, hungry, wearing life to 'serve in General Cuckoo's army'. Sometimes his soldiers never see bread for days together; they must remain hidden from all the world; sometimes they must steal and loot and even kill. 'An exile is the same as a baby: whatever he sees he wants', they say in Siberia of the convict-settlers. This saying may be applied with as much or more force to the wanderer. It is seldom that a tramp is not a highway robber and he is nearly always a thief, more of course from necessity than from inclination. Some men are born vagabonds. They will run away even from the settlement, after they have finished their prison term. One might expect them to feel happy and secure in the settlement, but no, something seems to draw them away, to call them to wander. The life of the forest, a poor and terrible life though free and full of adventure, has something seductive in it, a mysterious attraction, for anyone who has once experienced it: all at once a man will be off, even though he may sometimes be a modest sober man who has shown every promise of becoming a good settler and a capable farmer. Sometimes he may even have married and founded a family, and lived five years or more in one place, yet suddenly one fine morning he will disappear, leaving his wife, his children, and the whole neighbourhood perplexed and bewildered. One of these runaways was pointed out to me in the prison. He had not committed any particular crime, or at least I never heard his name mentioned in that connexion, but he was always running away; his whole life had been spent on the move. He had been in the southern-most regions of Russia, beyond the Danube, in the Kirghiz steppes, in eastern Siberia, and in the Caucasus—he had been everywhere. Who knows, perhaps in other circum-stances he might, with his passion for travelling, have made a Robinson Crusoe. It was other men who told me all this, however; he himself did not talk much in prison, and then only when he simply had to say something. He was a peasant, of very small stature, extremely quiet, and with a singularly calm, almost blank, expression, calm, indeed, to the point of idiocy. In summer he loved to sit in the sun, invariably humming a little song to himself, but so softly that he was inaudible at a distance of five yards. His features had a wooden look; he ate very little, chiefly bread; he never bought a single white loaf or a glass of vodka; indeed it is questionable whether he ever had any money, and doubtful whether he even knew how to count. His attitude to everything was one of complete calm. He used to feed the prison dogs sometimes, and nobody among us fed the prison dogs. Russians in general are not very given to feeding dogs. He was said to have been married, and more than once; he said he had children somewhere . . . How he came to be in prison I have no idea. Everybody expected him to give us the slip too, but either the time had not yet come or his day was over; he went on living quietly among us, seeming to regard in a contemplative fashion all his strange surroundings. One could not rely on him, however, although one might wonder what purpose he could have in running away, or what good it would do him. All the same, the life of a wanderer in the forest, taken as a whole, is paradise compared with prison. It is easy to understand this; indeed, there can be no comparison. It may be a hard lot, but one is one's own master. That is why every convict in Russia, wherever he may be, becomes a little restless in the spring, with the first kindly rays of the sun. Not everybody has any intention of running away, nevertheless; it may confidently be said that, because of the difficulties and for fear of the consequences, only one man in a hundred will make up his mind to it; the other ninety-nine, on the other hand, will indulge in dreams of how they might escape and where they might escape to, and get some comfort for their souls from the mere desire and the simple computing of the possibilities. One may remember how he did once run away . . . I am speaking now of men who are already serving their sentences. But of course it is those who are awaiting sentence who most frequently decide to escape. Convicts, if they run away at all, do so only at the beginning of their terms. When he has served two or three years the prisoner begins to value those years and little by little reconciles himself to the idea that it is better to finish his term of hard labour lawfully and join a settlement than run such a risk and suffer such a terrible fate in the event of failure. And failure is very possible. It is doubtful whether one in ten succeeds in *changing his lot*. Among the convicts it is most often men who have been condemned to extremely long terms who resolve to escape. Fifteen or twenty years seem an eternity, and the man condemned to such a term is always ready to dream of changing his lot, even when he has already undergone ten years of penal servitude. Finally, the brands are partly responsible for reluctance to run the risks of flight. *Changing one's lot* is a technical term. Thus, if he is caught while attempting to escape, a convict under interrogation will answer that he wanted to change his lot. This rather bookish expression is literally applicable here. Any fugitive envisages the possibility, not so much of gaining complete freedom—he knows this to be almost unattainable—as of landing in a different institution, being sent off to a settlement, or standing trial again for a new crime committed in his wanderings—in short of going no matter where, so long as it is not back to the old place which has grown so tiresome to him, not back to his former prison. All these fugitives, if in the course of the summer they do not find, by a lucky chance, some place in which to spend the winter—if, for example, they do not come across somebody who finds it to his advantage to offer asylum to such refugees, or if they do not procure (sometimes by means of murder) somebody else's passport, with which they can live anywhere—and if they have not been caught by autumn, mostly come flocking back to the towns and prisons of their own accord, as vagabonds, and spend the winter in prison, not of course without hopes of escaping again in the summer.

The spring had its effect on me also. I remember how sometimes I gazed hungrily through the gaps in the stockade, and how I used to stand for long periods leaning my head against the fence and looking obstinately and insatiably at the green grass on the fortress rampart and the sky whose blue grew deeper and deeper. My restlessness and longing increased with every day and the prison became more and more hateful to me. The hatred which I, as a gentleman, constantly experienced from the convicts during my first years in prison became unbearable and my whole life was poisoned with its venom. During those years I often went into hospital, without the excuse of illness, solely in order to be away from the prison and avoid that obstinate, unappeasable general hatred. 'You are iron beaks; you have pecked us to death,' the convicts told us; and how I used to envy the common people who came to the prison! They at once found friends everywhere. For these reasons the spring, the spectre of freedom, the general gladness in all nature, produced in me also a disturbing and melancholy effect. At the end of Lent, in the sixth week, I think, I had to prepare for Communion. During the first week the whole prison had been divided for this purpose, by the senior non-commissioned officer, into seven groups, one for each week of the fast. Thus each group consisted of upwards of thirty men. I liked the week of preparation very much. Those who were preparing were excused work. We went to the church, which was not very far from the prison, two or three times a day. It was a long time since I had been in church. The Lenten services, so familiar from my far-off childhood in my father's house, the solemn prayers, the deep reverences—all stirred up in my heart the far-distant past and recalled the impressions of the years when I was still a child; and I remember how pleasant I found it when we were taken by our guards, with loaded rifles, to the house of God in the mornings, over the ground still frozen from the night. The guards, however, did not go into the church. Inside the church we crowded together near the door, at the very back, so that we could only just hear the deacon's loud voice and catch a glimpse through the throng of the priest's black vestments and his bald head. I remembered how, standing in the church as a child, I used sometimes to look at the common people clustering thickly near the entrance and obsequiously making way for a pair of showy epaulettes, a stout landowner, or an overdressed but extremely pious lady, all of whom would pass through to the front and were ready at any moment to wrangle over the best places. At that time I thought that those who stood near the door did not pray in the same way as we did, but meekly, fervently, with humility and a full consciousness of their lowly state.

Now I myself had to stand in that place, and indeed in a worse one yet; we were fettered and stigmatized as criminals; everybody drew aside from us and even seemed afraid of us; we always had alms bestowed on us and I remember that this somehow even pleased me, and there was a peculiar subtlety in that strange feeling of satisfaction. 'If it must be so, so be it!' I thought. The prisoners were very zealous in their devotions and each of them always brought to the church his pitiful copeck for a candle or to put in the collection: perhaps as he gave it he thought, or rather felt, 'I too am a man, and in the sight of God all men are equal . . .' We partook of the sacrament at the early mass. When the priest, with the chalice in his hands, recited the words: 'Accept me, O Lord, even as the thief', almost all of them, apparently applying the words literally to themselves, bowed down to the ground, their fetters clanking.

Now Easter came. Each of us received from the authorities an egg and a slice of wheaten bread made with milk, butter, and eggs. Once again the townspeople heaped gifts upon the prison. Once again there was a visit from the priest with his cross, once again a visit from the Governor, once again our cabbage soup was made with meat, once again men got drunk and staggered about the prison—all was exactly as it had been at Christmas, with this difference, that now it was possible to walk in the courtyard and warm oneself in the sun . . . There seemed to be more light and space than in the winter, but also more sadness. The long endless summer days seemed especially unbearable on holidays. On working days our labour at least served to shorten the day.

The summer work proved to be really much heavier than the winter work. More and more engineering was done. Prisoners built, dug the ground, laid bricks; others were employed in the locksmiths', carpenters', and painters' workshops on the repair of government buildings. Others again were sent to make bricks. This last we considered the heaviest work of all. The brickworks were three or four versts from the fortress. Every day throughout the summer a large party of convicts, about fifty strong, set off at about six o'clock in the morning to make bricks. Labourers, men, that is, who were not craftsmen or skilled in any trade, were chosen for this work. They took bread with them, since because of the distance it was not convenient for them to return for dinner, which would have entailed an extra walk of some eight versts; so they dined when they came back to the prison in the evening. They were given a task for the whole day and it was so great that a prisoner could hardly get through it in a long working day. He must first dig and carry the clay, and bring water, and then trample the clay into pug in a pit, and finally make it into a great number of bricks, two hundred, I think, or perhaps even two hundred and fifty. I went to the brickworks only twice. The men, tired and exhausted, did not return from the brickyard until it was evening, and all the summer they were constantly reproaching the others with the fact that they had the heaviest work to do; this apparently afforded them some consolation. In spite of all this, some men went to the brickyard with a certain eagerness: to begin with, it was outside the town; the place was open and free, on the banks of the Irtysh. Here, at any rate, there was something more comforting to look round on than the official buildings of the fortress. It was possible both to smoke freely and even to enjoy the immense pleasure of lying down for half an hour. I, though, either went as before to the workshops or the gypsum kilns or was employed in the capacity of a brick-carrier on the buildings. I had at one time to carry bricks from the bank of the Irtysh to a barrack that was being built, a distance of about a hundred and sixty yards across the fortress rampart, and this work went on for about two months. I even liked doing it, although the rope with which the bricks had to be carried always chafed my shoulders. But I was pleased because the work was visibly developing my strength. At first I could carry only eight bricks at a time; each brick weighed twelve pounds. But afterwards I progressed to twelve and then to fifteen bricks, and this made me very content. Physical strength is no less necessary than moral in prison, for the endurance of all the material discomforts of that accursed life.

And I wanted to live again, after the prison . . .

I liked dragging bricks, however, not only because it strengthened my body, but also because the work took me to the bank of the Irtysh. I speak of that river-bank so often because that was the only place from which God's earth could be seen, the pure bright distance and the free, lonely steppes, whose wild emptiness had a strange effect on me. The bank was the only place where one might stand with one's back to the fortress and not see it. All the other places where we worked were either in the fortress or close to it. From the very first I hated that fortress and especially some of the buildings in it. Our major's house seemed to me an accursed, loathsome place and every time I went past it I looked at it with hatred. But on the river-bank you might forget yourself; you would look at that vast, solitary expanse as a captive gazes at freedom from the window of his prison. To me, everything there was dear and lovely: the bright hot sun in the unfathomable blue sky, the songs of the

Kirghiz tribesmen*carried from the farther bank. You would gaze for a long time and finally you would distinguish the beggarly, sooty tent of some nomad; you would see the wisp of smoke near the tent and the Kirghiz woman busy there with her two sheep. It was all poor and savage, but it was free. You would make out a bird in the clear blue translucent air and tenaciously follow its flight for a long time; now it skimmed the water, now it disappeared in the blue, now it reappeared, a scarcely discernible speck . . . Even the poor, sickly flower I found in the early spring in a cleft in the stony bank—even that arrested my attention in a rather painful way. The anguish of all that first year in prison was unendurable, and it made me irritable and bitter. Because of that anguish I did not notice many of the things around me. I covered my eyes and refused to look. Among my malicious and hostile prison comrades I did not see the good people, the people who were capable of both thinking and feeling, in spite of the repulsive crust that covered them on the surface. Among all the wounding words I never noticed the kind and affectionate word, which was all the dearer because it was spoken without any ulterior motive, and not infrequently from a heart that had borne and suffered more than mine. But why enlarge upon this? I was extremely glad if I found myself tired out as I returned home: perhaps I should sleep! For in summer trying to sleep was an agony, almost worse than in winter. It is true that the evenings were sometimes very pleasant. The sun, which all day had not left the prison courtyard, declined at last. Then it grew cool, and afterwards came the (comparatively speaking) almost cold night of the steppes. The prisoners, waiting for the time when they would be locked up, used to walk about the courtyard in groups. It is true that they crowded most thickly into the kitchen. There was always some urgent prison question under discussion there; this subject or that was talked over; sometimes they would canvass a rumour, often absurd but nevertheless awakening extraordinary interest among these men cut off from the world; once, for instance, the news was announced that our major was to be given the sack. Prisoners are as credulous as children; they themselves knew that the 'news' was nonsense and that the prisoner Kvasov who had brought it was well known as a chatterbox and a 'ridiculous' man, who they had long ago decided was not to be trusted and who, whatever he said, never told the truth—yet they seized upon the announcement, criticized it, embroidered it, diverted themselves with it, and ended by being angry with and ashamed of themselves for believing Kvasov.

'Who's going to turn him out?' cried one. 'He's got a solid neck, for sure; he'll be tough!'

'But after all there must be lots of people higher than him!' objected another, an impetuous fellow, not at all stupid, and with some experience of life, but disputatious beyond belief.

'One raven doesn't peck out another's eyes!' remarked a third sullenly, as though speaking to himself; this was a grey-headed man sitting alone in a corner to finish his cabbage soup.

'And I suppose the ones that are higher than him will come here and ask you whether to send him away or not?', casually added another, gently strumming on a balalaika.

'Why shouldn't they?' answered the second angrily. 'I mean all us poor people must ask for it. Everybody must give evidence if they begin to ask us. To be sure, we all shout loud enough, but when it comes to doing something, we back out.'

'What did you expect?' said the balalaika player. 'Prison is like that.'

'The other day', the argumentative one went on hotly, without listening to him, 'there was some flour left. We scraped it up and it was only the very last sweepings, and we sent it to be sold. But no, he got to hear about it; the foreman informed on us and they took it away; economy, that was. Well, was that right or wasn't it?'

'And who were you thinking of complaining to?'

'Who? Why, the inspector himself, what's coming.'

'Who do you mean, the inspector?'

'That's right, mates, the inspector's coming!' said a lively young fellow, who was literate—indeed he had been a clerk and had actually read *The Duchess de la Vallière* or something of the sort. He was always cheerful and waggish but he was held in respect because he had a certain amount of experience and knowledge of affairs. Paying no attention to the general curiosity he had aroused about the inspector's coming visit, he went up to the 'kitchen-maid' (the cook, that is) and asked him for some liver. Our cooks often traded in such things. They would buy a piece of liver, for example, with their own money, fry it and sell it in small pieces to the other prisoners.

'Half a copeck's worth, or a copeck?'

'Cut me a copeck's worth; I want to make people jealous!' answered the convict. 'It's a general that's coming, mates, a general from St. Petersburg; he's going to inspect all Siberia. It's true. The commandant's servants were talking about it.'

The news produced extraordinary excitement. The questions went on for a quarter of an hour: who exactly was he, what sort of general, what was his rank and was he senior to the generals here? Prisoners are very fond of talking about ranks, about the authorities, about which of them are superior to others, who can make whom do what he wants and who has to let himself be ordered about, and they even argue and dispute about generals and almost come to blows. One might wonder what good it can do any of them. But the degree of a man's knowledge of the world, his conversational powers, and his social standing before he came to prison are measured by his detailed information about generals and the other authorities. Generally speaking, the higher authorities are considered the most elegant and important subject of conversation in prison.

'So it turns out that our major really is going to be given the sack, mates,' remarked Kvasov, a little red-faced man, hasty and singularly lacking in common sense. It was he who had first reported the news about the major.

'He'll buy himself out of it!' abruptly objected the sullen grey-haired convict, who had by now finished his soup.

'Of course he will,' said another. 'He's fiddled a bit of money, he has! He was a battalion commander before he came here. It was only the other day he wanted to marry the priest's daughter.'

'He didn't marry her, though: they showed him the door; that means he's poor. A fine catch he is! When he stands up everything he's got stands up with him. He lost the lot playing cards at Easter. Fedka told me.'

'Yes. The lad's not a free spender; he just throws it away.'

'Ah, my lad, I've been married too. It's a bad thing for a poor man to get married: get married and you can't even lie in bed as long as you want to!' remarked Skuratov, thrusting himself into the conversation at this point.

'Of course it was you we were talking about,' observed the casual young fellow who had been a clerk. 'But you're a great fool, I tell you, Kvasov. Do you really think our major could give presents to a general like him, or that a general like him would come all the way from St. Petersburg on purpose to inspect the major? You're a fool, my lad, and so I tell you.'

'Why? Even if he is a general, do you mean he wouldn't take a bribe?' inquired one of the crowd sceptically.

'Of course he wouldn't, and even if he does, he'll want a thumping big one.'

'Of course; as big as he is.'

'A general will always take a bribe,' roundly declared Kvasov.

'I suppose you've bribed one?' said Baklushin, who had

just come in, contemptuously. 'Have you ever even seen a general?'

'Yes, I have!'

'Liar!'

'Liar yourself!'

'Well, lads, if he's seen one, let him say straight out, in front of everybody, which general he knows. Come on, tell us, because I know all the generals.'

'I've seen General Ziebert,' answered Kvasov, somewhat hesitatingly.

'Ziebert? There's no such general. He must have looked at you from behind, this Ziebert, and you were so scared you thought he was a general, when he was only a lieutenant-colonel or something.'

'No, you listen to me,' cried Skuratov, 'because I'm a married man! There was a general in Moscow, really, a Ziebert, and he was Russian, but his family was German. He used to confess to a Russian priest once a year, at the Feast of the Assumption, and he was always drinking water, like a duck. Every blessed day he drank forty glasses of water from the River Moscow. They said he did it to cure some illness; his vally told me himself.'

'And I suppose with all that water his belly got full of fish?' remarked the prisoner with the balalaika.

'That's enough from you! Here we're talking seriously, and they . . . What Inspector is this, then, mates?' anxiously inquired a fidgety prisoner, Martynov, an old man who had been in the Hussars.

'Really, what rot people talk!' remarked one of the sceptics. 'And where on earth do they get it from, eh? It's all nothing but rubbish!'

'No, it's not rubbish,' dogmatically asserted Kulikov, who had until then preserved a dignified silence. He was a ponderous fellow, something under fifty years of age, with an extraordinarily handsome face and a disdainfully majestic manner. He was aware of this and prided himself on it. He was part gipsy, made money in the town as a horse-doctor, and in the prison sold vodka. He was an intelligent man and had seen much in his time. He was as sparing of words as if they were roubles.

'It's right enough, mates,' he continued quietly. 'I heard about it last week; a general's coming, a very big one, and he's going to inspect all Siberia. Everybody knows he'll get his presents, only not from our Eight-eyes: *he* won't even dare go near him. Generals is all different from one another, lads. There's all sorts. Only I'll tell you one thing, our major will stop where he is, whatever happens. That's certain. We are folk without a tongue, and the bosses aren't going to tell tales on their own sort. The Inspector will just take a look into the prison and then go away and report that he found everything all right . . .'

'Quite right, lads, but the major's in a blue funk; you know he's drunk all day.'

'But in the evening he drives a different wagon. Fedka tells us.'

'You can't wash a black dog white. It's not the first time he's been drunk, is it?'

'Well, that's a fine thing, if even the general won't do anything! No, that's enough of copying their tomfoolery,' said the convicts to one another, growing excited.

The news of the Inspector's visit spread through the prison like wildfire. Men roamed about the courtyard, impatient to impart the information to one another. Others deliberately kept silent and cool, plainly endeavouring to increase their own importance in this way. Others again remained unconcerned. On the barrack-steps lounged prisoners with balalaikas. Some went on gossiping, others struck up songs. But generally speaking everybody was in a highly excited state that evening.

Between nine and ten o'clock we were all counted, herded into our various barracks and locked in for the night. The nights were short; we were awakened before five o'clock and it was at least eleven before everybody was asleep. Until that time there was always bustle and talking and sometimes there were *maidans* as well, as there were in winter. With the night came intolerable heat and airlessness. Although the coolness of the night flowed through the window with its raised sash, the prisoners tossed all night on their planks as though they had fever. Fleas swarmed in myriads. They throve among us in winter, too, and in quite sufficient numbers, but when spring came they bred in such quantities that, although I had heard of this before, I could not believe it until I had experienced it myself. And the nearer we drew to summer, the more vicious became their attacks. It is true that, as I have proved for myself, one can get used to fleas; all the same, they are a grievous affliction. They used to torment us to such an extent that at last one would lie as though in a fever, aware that one was not really asleep, but only dozing fitfully. Finally, when just before morning there was a lull and the fleas, so to speak, died down, and when you sank at last into real, sweet sleep in the fresh morning air—the sudden pitiless rattle of the drum struck up reveille from the prison gates. Huddled inside your sheepskin coat, you cursed as you listened to the loud, distinct strokes as though you were counting them, while through your dreams crept the unbearable thought that it would be the same again tomorrow, and the next day, and every day for years, until the moment of freedom came. But when would that be, you thought, and where was this freedom? Meanwhile you must wake up; the daily round was beginning, the throng of men jostling, dressing, hurrying to work. To be sure, you might sleep again in the middle of the day for about an hour.

The talk about the Inspector had been true. The rumours grew more positive every day and finally everybody knew for certain that an important general was coming from St. Petersburg to inspect all Siberia, then that he had already arrived, and then that he was in Tobolsk. Every day new rumours reached the prison. There were reports from the town as well: we heard that everybody had taken fright and was in a flutter, trying to put the best face on things. It was said that receptions, balls, and parties were being planned in the highest official circles. Crowds of prisoners were sent out to level the roads in the fortress, remove hillocks, repaint fences and posts, repair plaster, whitewash—in short an effort was made to set to rights in a twinkling everything that had to make a good showing. The prisoners understood all this very well and the talk among themselves grew steadily hotter and more animated. Their fancy went to extraordinary lengths. They even planned to put forward a *grievance* when the general asked if they were satisfied. Meanwhile they argued and disputed with one another. The major was in a state of agitation. He descended upon the prison more often, more often shouted at people, attacked them more often, sent them more often to the guardroom, and paid zealous attention to spit and polish. Just at this time, as luck would have it, an incident occurred in the prison which, instead of upsetting the major, as might have been expected, actually gave him satisfaction. One prisoner, in a scuffle, thrust an awl into another's ribs, close under his heart.

The prisoner who committed this crime was called Lomov, and the wounded man was one we called Gavrilka; he was an incorrigible vagabond. I don't remember whether he had any surname; among us he was always called Gavrilka.

Lomov was one of a well-to-do peasant family from the K— district of the Province of T—. They all lived together as a family: the old father, his three sons, and their uncle, the father's brother. They were rich peasants. It was said all over the province that they had as much as three hundred thousand roubles in paper money. They farmed the land, dressed hides, and dealt in various commodities, but their chief occupations were money-lending, sheltering vagabonds, receiving stolen goods, and other arts. The peasants of half the district were in their debt and found themselves in bondage to them. The Lomovs had the reputation of clever and cunning peasants, but at last their vanity began to get the better of them, especially when a very important personage of their parts began to spend the night at their house on his journeys, made the personal acquaintance of the old man and took a liking to him for his shrewdness and resourcefulness. They took it into their heads that they were above the law and took ever greater and greater risks in various illegal enterprises. Everybody grumbled about them, everybody wished the earth would open and swallow them up; but they went on giving themselves more and more airs. Police captains meant nothing to them. At last they came a cropper and were lost, not through their evil ways, not through their secret wrong-doing, but through a false accusation. They had a large farm, or what is called in Siberia an intake, some ten versts from the village. They had once, in late summer, six Kirghiz living and working there, who had been in bondage to them for a long time. One night all these Kirghiz labourers were murdered. An investigation began. It lasted for a long time. In the course of it many other misdeeds came to light. The Lomovs were accused of killing their labourers. They themselves had told the story and all the prison knew it; they were suspected of owing a great deal of money to their labourers and, since in spite of their great possessions they were miserly and greedy, of having murdered the Kirghiz in order to avoid paying them. During the inquiry and trial all their possessions went to rack and ruin. The old man died. The sons were sent to different places. One of them found himself, with his uncle, in our prison for twelve years. And what was the truth? They were completely innocent of the death of the Kirghiz. It was later that Gavrilka, a notorious rogue and vagabond, but a merry and dashing fellow, appeared here in the same prison, and it was he who bore the responsibility for the whole thing. I did not hear, however, whether he himself acknowledged it, but the whole prison was convinced that the murders were his work. Gavrilka had had some dealings with the Lomovs while he was on the road. He came to prison with a short sentence, as a runaway soldier and a tramp. He and three other tramps had murdered the Kirghiz; they thought they would do very well out of plundering the farm.

The Lomovs were not liked among us, I don't know why. One of them, the nephew, was a fine young fellow, intelligent and good-humoured, but his uncle, who had run the awl into Gavrilka, was a loutish and quarrelsome moujik. Even before this he had fallen foul of many of the men and had taken some sound drubbings. Everybody liked Gavrilka for his cheerful and easy-going nature. Although the Lomovs knew that Gavrilka was the criminal, and although they were in prison because of what he had done, they did not quarrel with him; they never, however, had anything to do with him and he for his part paid no attention to them. Then suddenly a quarrel brewed up between him and the Lomov uncle over a most repulsive wench. Gavrilka began to brag about her favours, the moujik grew jealous, and one fine afternoon he stabbed him with the awl.

Although the Lomovs had been ruined by their trial, they lived in the prison like rich men. They plainly had some money. They kept a samovar and had tea to drink. Our major knew this and conceived an extreme dislike of the two Lomovs. Everybody could see that he was always finding fault with them and generally trying to get at them. The Lomovs accounted for this by the major's desire to be bribed by them. But they did not offer him a bribe.

If Lomov had driven in the awl even a little further he would of course have killed Gavrilka. But in fact the affair ended in no more than a scratch. The matter was reported to the major. I remember how he came at the gallop, out of breath and obviously pleased. He treated Gavrilka with extraordinary kindness, as though he were his own son.

'Well, my boy, can you walk as far as the hospital, I wonder? No, it would be better to harness a horse for him. Harness a horse at once!' he shouted urgently to the sergeant.

'But I don't feel anything, your honour. It was only a little prick, your honour!'

'You don't know, you don't know, my dear boy; you will see . . . It's a dangerous place; it all depends on where the wound is; he got you just under the heart, the cut-throat! And you, you!' he yelled, turning to Lomov, 'well, now I'll show you! . . . To the guardroom!'

And he did, indeed, 'show' him. Lomov was tried and, although the wound proved to be the merest prick, the intention had been evident. The criminal's term of hard labour was increased and he was given a thousand strokes. The major was completely satisfied . . .

At last the Inspector came.*

On the day after his arrival in the town he came to the prison. For some days before everything had been washed and polished till it shone. The convicts were newly shaven. Their clothes were white and clean. In summer, by regulation, everybody wore coarse white linen jackets and trousers. On each back was sewn a black circle, about three inches in diameter. A whole hour had been spent in instructing the prisoners how to answer in case the great personage should speak to them. Rehearsals had been held. The major bustled about like one possessed. An hour before the general's appearance we were all standing at attention in our places like statues. At length the general arrived, at one o'clock in the afternoon. He was a very important general, so important that every official heart in western Siberia must have sunk at his arrival. He made a grim and majestic entrance; behind him flocked a large suite of local bigwigs escorting him, some of them generals or colonels. There was one civilian, a tall and handsome gentleman in a frock-coat and low shoes, who had also come from St. Petersburg and who bore himself with extraordinary independence and ease of manner. The general addressed him frequently and with extreme courtesy. This greatly mystified the prisoners: a civilian, and held in such esteem, and by such a general! Later we learned his surname and what he was, but there was a great deal of talk. Our major, crammed into a tight uniform with an orange collar, with bloodshot eyes and a blotchy crimson face, did not apparently make a very pleasant impression on the general. Out of special respect for the distinguished visitor he was without his glasses. He stood at some distance, as stiff as a ramrod, and his whole being quivered with feverish anticipation of the moment when his services would be required and he would fly to fulfil his excellency's behest. But he was not wanted for anything. The general silently walked round the barracks, glanced into the kitchen and, I believe, tasted the cabbage soup. I was pointed out to him: so-and-so, they said, a former nobleman.

'Ah!' answered the general. 'And how does he behave now?'

'Satisfactorily for the time being, your excellency,' was the reply.

The general nodded and about two minutes later left the prison. The prisoners, of course, had been dazzled and over-whelmed; nevertheless they were left rather at a loss what to think. Any mention of a grievance against the major had of course been quite out of the question. Indeed the major had all along been perfectly confident of this.

6. Prison Animals

THE purchase of a bay horse, which took place soon after-wards, occupied and entertained the prisoners much more pleasantly than the exalted visitor. We were supposed to have a horse to bring in water, remove refuse, and so on.

A prisoner was detailed to look after it. Needless to say, he was kept under guard while he drove it. There was plenty of work for our horse, both morning and evening. 'Sorrel' had been with us a very long time. He was a good little horse, but worn out. One fine morning, just before St. Peter's Day, Sorrel fell down as he was bringing in the evening's supply of water, and died within a few minutes. Everybody was grieved and collected round, discussing and arguing. The former troopers, gipsies, horse-doctors, and so on among us displayed on this occasion a great deal of specialized knowledge of horse-flesh and even wrangled with one another, but they could not resurrect Sorrel. He lay there dead, with a swollen belly which everybody felt bound to poke with his finger. This act of God was reported to the major and he decided that a new horse must be bought at once. On St. Peter's Day itself, in the morning after mass, when we were collected together in full force, horses for sale began to be brought in. It was taken for granted that the purchase should be entrusted to the prisoners themselves. We had some real experts among us and it would be difficult to take in two hundred and fifty men who had formerly devoted themselves exclusively to this interest. Kirghiz tribesmen, horse-copers, gipsies, and tradesmen from the town made their appearance. The prisoners impatiently awaited the arrival of each new horse. They were happy, like children. What most flattered their vanity was that here they were, as though they were free men buying a horse for *themselves*, as though the money really came from *their* pockets and they had a perfect right to make the purchase. Three horses were brought and taken away again before they settled on the fourth. The dealers looked about them with some wonder and a kind of timidity and sometimes even glanced back at the guards who had brought them in. A gang of a couple of hundred of these men, shaven, branded, in chains, and at home in their own prison den, whose threshold nobody ever crossed, imposed its own kind of respect. Our fellows exhausted all their cunning in testing each horse as it was led up. There was nothing that they did not examine, no part that they did not handle, and all, besides, with such businesslike seriousness of demeanour, such an air of worried concern, that the welfare of the prison might have depended on their efforts. The Circassians even leapt on to the horses' backs, their eyes blazed and they gabbled in their incomprehensible language, nodding their heads and baring the teeth in their swarthy hook-nosed faces. One of the Russians, his whole attention riveted on their discussion, looked as though he wanted to get inside their eyes. He could not understand one word they said and so was trying to divine from the expression of their eyes whether they had decided that the horse was suitable or not. To any stranger looking on such quivering attention would have seemed very odd. Why, one might wonder, should a prisoner, and such a very unremarkable prisoner, humble and subdued, who in the presence of certain of his own fellows did not even dare to open his mouth, why should he show such special concern over this question? It was as though he were buying the horse for himself, as though it were not, in fact, a matter of complete indifference to him which horse was bought. Except for the Circassians, it was the former gipsies and horse-dealers who were the most prominent: the others yielded them the first place and the first word. There even took place something in the nature of a knightly duel between two of these men in particular—the prisoner Kulikov, a former gipsy, horse-thief, and coper, and a cunning little Siberian moujik, a self-taught horse-doctor, who had only recently arrived in the prison and had already managed to oust Kulikov from all his practice in the town. The fact was that our self-taught prison farriers were very highly esteemed in the town, and not only the artisans and merchants but even the highest officials turned to the prison when their horses fell sick, although there were several real veterinary surgeons in the town. Until the arrival of Yolkin, the Siberian moujik, Kulikov had had a large practice and, of course, had received a monetary reward. He was a regular gipsy quack, and knew much less than he pretended. His income made him an aristocrat among us. He had long since inspired every convict in the prison with involuntary respect by his worldly wisdom, his intelligence, his daring, and his determination. He was listened to and obeyed. But he talked little: he spoke as though every word cost him a rouble, and then only on the most important occasions. He was a decided coxcomb, but there was in him a store of really genuine driving-force. He was already fairly well on in years, but very handsome and very sensible. With us gentlemen he behaved with a certain refinement and politeness, and yet at the same time with extreme dignity. I think that if one had dressed him smartly and introduced him in the guise of some count or other into a St. Petersburg club, he would not have been at a loss even there, but would have taken a hand at whist and talked remarkably well, speaking little but with weight, and perhaps throughout the evening nobody would have guessed that he was not a count but a tramp. I am speaking seriously: he was quite intelligent, resourceful, and quick-witted enough. In addition his manners were very good and elegant. He must have seen a great deal in his day. His past, however, was shrouded in a mist of obscurity. He was in the Special Class. But Kulikov's veterinary fame was tarnished by the arrival of Yolkin, who, although he was only a moujik, was a very astute moujik; he was about fifty and a schismatic. In about two months he had supplanted Kulikov with almost all his clients in the town.

He cured, and with great ease, horses that Kulikov had given up long before. He even cured some that had been despaired of by the town's veterinary surgeons. This moujik had been sent to our prison, with some others, for making counterfeit coins. He would go and get himself involved in a business like that in his old age! He himself used to tell us, laughing at himself, that from three real gold pieces they could turn out only one false one. Kulikov had taken his rival's veterinary successes rather badly; his fame even among the prisoners had begun to grow dim. He kept a mistress in the suburbs, and wore a velveteen tunic, a silver ring, ear-rings, and his own boots with fancy tops, and suddenly he was forced, for want of other income, to turn 'tapster'. Everybody therefore was afraid that the purchase of our new bay horse might be the occasion for open warfare between them. They waited curiously. Both men had their own supporters. The leaders of each party were already working themselves up and personalities were gradually beginning to be exchanged. Yolkin himself was ready at any moment to screw up his sly face into the most sarcastic of smiles. But things turned out differently. Kulikov had no thought of being abusive, but even without that he conducted himself in a masterly fashion. He began by being conciliatory and even listened respectfully to his rival's critical opinions but then, taking him up on one point, he modestly and firmly remarked that he was mistaken, and before Yolkin could collect his wits and correct himself, he showed that he had indeed been mistaken, and exactly how. In short, Yolkin was taken down a peg with extraordinary skill and unexpectedness, and although he nevertheless retained the upper hand, even the Kulikov party were left satisfied.

'No, mates, it seems it's not easy to put him down. He can stand up for himself all right!' said some of the prisoners.

'Yolkin knows more,' remarked others, but not assertively. Both parties had suddenly adopted an extremely conciliatory tone.

'It's not that he knows more, only he has a lighter hand. But when it comes to horses Kulikov will tackle anything.'

'That's right, mate!'

'Anything . . .'

At last the new Sorrel was chosen and bought. This was a famous little horse, young, strong, and good-looking, with an extraordinarily kind and cheerful face. In all other ways he was, naturally, beyond reproach. Bargaining began: thirty roubles was asked and our prisoners offered twenty-five. The haggling was keen and prolonged; the offers were slowly raised and the price lowered. At last they began to see the funny side of it.

'You're not taking the money out of your own purse, are you?' said some. 'Why higgle?'

'I suppose you're trying to save the Treasury money,' cried others.

'All the same, lads, all the same, it's . . . everybody's money . . .'

'Everybody's! Well, well, anyone can see there's no need to sow fools like us; we come up of our own accord . . .'

Finally the bargain was struck at twenty-eight roubles. The major was informed and the purchase was authorized. Needless to say, bread and salt were immediately carried out and the new Sorrel was conducted into the prison with due honour. I don't think there was a prisoner who did not take the opportunity of patting his neck or stroking his nose. The same day the bay was harnessed to the water-cart and everybody watched curiously to see how the new Sorrel would pull his barrel. Our water-carrier, Roman, looked at the new horse with enormous complacency. He was a peasant some fifty years old, of a sedate and taciturn nature. All Russian coachmen and drivers, indeed, have extremely sedate and taciturn natures, as if it were really true that constant association with horses gives a man a peculiar stolidity and even consequence. Roman was a quiet man, gentle with everybody and not much given to talking; he took snuff from a horn and from time immemorial had always been kept busy with the prison bays. The newly purchased one was the third. All of us were convinced that sorrel or bay was the right colour for the prison, that it was somehow natural. Roman, too, supported this idea. A roan or skewbald horse, for example, would not on any account have been bought. The office of water-carrier was, as if by some right, reserved in perpetuity for Roman and none of us would ever have thought of disputing his claim. When the last Sorrel fell down dead it never entered anybody's head, not even the major's, to blame Roman in any way; it was the will of God, that was all, and Roman was a good driver. The bay soon became the prison pet. Prisoners might be dour people but they often used to go and stroke him. Roman, returning from the river, used to stop to shut the gates opened for him by one of the corporals, and the bay, coming inside the prison, would stand still with the barrel and wait for him, rolling his eyes back towards him. 'Go on by yourself!' Roman would shout to him and the bay would begin to pull again, draw the barrel to the kitchen, and stand waiting for the cooks and latrine orderlies to bring their buckets for water. 'Clever little Sorrel!' they would call to him. 'He's brought it all by himself! . . . He does what he's told.'

'Yes, he does; he's nothing but a poor dumb beast, but he understands!'

'Good old Sorrel!'

Sorrel would shake his head and snort as though he did really understand and was pleased to be praised. And somebody would not fail to take him some bread and salt. The bay would eat it and again shake his head as though to say: 'I know you, I know you! I'm a nice horse and you're a nice man!'

I, too, used to like to take the horse bread. It was somehow pleasant to look at his handsome face and feel on my hand his soft warm lips skilfully picking up my offering.

Generally speaking, our prisoners were capable of loving animals, and if they had been allowed they would have delighted to rear large numbers of domestic animals and birds in the prison. And I wonder what other activity could better have softened and refined their harsh and brutal natures than this. But it was not allowed. Neither the regulations nor the nature of the prison made it possible.

Chance did bring, however, a few animals into the prison

at various times during my stay there. Besides the bay horse we had dogs, geese, and the goat Vaska, and for some time an eagle stayed with us.

As I have already said, our regular prison dog was Sharik, a wise and good-natured animal with whom I was always the best of friends. But since dogs in general are regarded by all peasants as unclean animals to whom no attention ought to be paid, hardly anybody among us took any notice of Sharik. The dog simply existed, slept in the yard, lived on scraps from the kitchen, and aroused no particular interest in anybody, but he knew everybody and regarded everybody in the prison as his master. When the prisoners were returning from work, as soon as the cry of 'Corporals!' sounded from the guardroom, he ran to the gates, affectionately welcomed every party, wagged his tail, and looked invitingly into the face of everybody who came in, in the hope of some sort of caress. But for many years all his efforts did not bring him a single pat from anybody except me. Because of this, he loved me best of all. I don't remember how it happened that another dog, Belka, afterwards turned up in the prison. The third, though, Kultyapka, I brought in myself, carrying him back with me from work when he was a puppy. Belka was a strange creature. Somebody had run over him in a cart, and his back was bent downwards, so that when he ran it used to look from a distance as though two animals joined into one were running. Besides this, he was all mangy, with suppurating eyes; his tail was almost denuded of hair and always carried between his legs. Thus abused by fate, he had plainly made up his mind to submit. He never barked or growled at anybody, as though he did not dare. He lived for the most part behind the barracks, on scraps; if ever he saw one of us he would immediately, while we were still some paces distant, turn over on his back in token of submission, as if to say, 'Do what you please with me; you can see I will not even think of offering resistance.' And every prisoner before whom he squirmed on his back would aim a blow at him with his boot, as though considering it his bounden duty. 'Look at that miserable cur!' the convicts used to say. But Belka dared not even howl, and if he felt the pain too much to be silent, would only utter a pitiful stifled yelp. In just the same way he would squirm before Sharik or any other dog whenever he ran out of the prison on his own affairs. He used to turn over on his back and lie there submissively whenever a big lop-eared mongrel rushed at him, barking wildly. But dogs like other dogs to be humble and submissive. The savage cur would be appeased at once, and would stand in a thoughtful kind of way over the humble animal lying there with his legs in the air and slowly and with immense curiosity begin to sniff him all over. What did the wriggling Belka think of during this time? 'Well, what now? Is this ruffian going to tear me to pieces?'; this was probably what came into his mind. But, after sniffing him carefully all over, the other dog, finding nothing particularly remarkable, would give it up. Belka would jump up at once and again, limping, attach himself to the end of a long string of dogs escorting some pampered bitch. And though he knew for certain that he would never be allowed to be on an intimate footing with the bitch, nevertheless to hobble along with them, although only at a distance—even that was some comfort to him in his misery. He had plainly long ago ceased to worry about honour. Having lost all chance of a career in the future, he lived only for food and was fully aware of it. Once I tried to stroke him; this was something so new and unexpected that he suddenly squatted close to the ground, began to tremble all over, and whined loudly with emotion. Out of pity I stroked him many times. After that he could not see me without whining. He would see me from a distance and give a plaintive and pitiable whine. The end came when he was torn to pieces by other dogs on the rampart outside the prison.

Kultyapka was of a quite different character. Why I carried him to the prison from the workshop, when he was still a blind puppy, I do not know. I enjoyed feeding and rearing him. Sharik at once took Kultyapka under his wing and slept with him. When Kultyapka grew a little bigger he allowed him to bite his ears and pull his hair, and played with him in the way full-grown dogs usually do play with puppies. It was strange, but Kultyapka grew hardly at all in height, but only in length and breadth. He had curly hair, of a mousy light-brown colour; one of his ears hung down and the other was pricked. He had an excitable and high-spirited disposition, like every puppy, who is usually so glad to see his master that he squeals, yelps, and clambers up to lick his face, and is ready to parade all his other feelings on the spot: 'Only let my enthusiasm be seen; decorum doesn't matter!' Wherever I might be, as soon as I shouted 'Kultyapka!' he would appear suddenly round some corner, as if he had shot out of a trapdoor, and rush towards me, squealing rapturously, bounding along like a little ball and tumbling head over heels as he came. I was terribly fond of this little monster. It looked as though fate had nothing in store for him but a life of contentment and happiness. But one fine day the prisoner Neustroev, whose occupation was tanning skins and making women's shoes, began to take particular notice of Kultyapka. Some idea had struck him. He called Kultyapka to him, felt his coat, and rolled him gently over on his back. Kultyapka, quite unsuspicious, squealed with pleasure. But next morning he had disappeared. I looked for him for a long time, but there was no sign of him anywhere; it was not until two months later that it was all explained: Neustroev had taken a great fancy to Kultyapka's coat. He had skinned him, tanned the skin, and used it to line a pair of velvet winter bootees, which the judge's wife had ordered from him. He even showed me the boots when they were finished. The lining was wonderful. Poor Kultyapka!

Many of our prisoners tanned skins, and they often used to bring in with them dogs with good coats, who immediately disappeared. Some had been stolen, some were even bought. I remember seeing two prisoners once behind the kitchen. They were laying their heads together and seemed very busy about something. One of them held on a rope a magnificent large black dog, evidently of an expensive breed. Some good-for-nothing manservant had stolen it from his master and sold it to our shoemakers for thirty copecks in silver. The convicts were preparing to hang it. This was a very convenient procedure: they stripped off the skin and flung the body into a big, deep cess-pit which was situated in the remotest corner of the prison yard, and which stank horribly in the heat of summer. It was rarely cleaned out. The poor animal seemed to understand the fate in store for it. It looked searchingly and uneasily from one to another of us three, and occasionally ventured on a slight wave of the bushy tail hanging between its legs, as if trying to soften our hearts by this sign of its trust in us. I moved away as quickly as I could and they, of course, brought their business to a successful conclusion.

The geese took up their quarters with us quite by chance. Who had bred them, and to whom they really belonged, I do not know, but for some time they provided a great deal of entertainment for the prisoners and they even became well known in the town. They had hatched out in the prison and were kept in the kitchen. When the brood was half-grown, the whole gaggle took to following the convicts to work. As soon as the drum began to rattle and the convicts made a move towards the gates, our geese would run cackling after us, flapping their wings, jump one after another over the high sill of the side gate, and invariably make for our right flank, where they would form up in line and wait for the end of the roll-call. They always attached themselves to the biggest party and while work proceeded they grazed at a short distance. As soon as the party moved off again back to the prison, they too got up to go. Rumours of the geese who went to work with the convicts spread through the town.

'Look, there are the convicts with their geese!' people used to say when they met us. 'How did you train them?' 'Here's something for your geese,' somebody would add, giving us money. But in spite of their attachment to us, the geese were all killed for some feast-day.

We would not have killed our goat Vaska, on the other hand, for anything in the world, if it had not been for one particular circumstance. I do not know where he came from, either, or who brought him to us, but we suddenly found we had a very pretty little white kid in the prison. In a few days he was a favourite with all of us and he became a diversion and even a consolation to us all. A pretext was found for keeping him: we must, since we had a stable, keep a goat in the prison. He did not live in the stable, however, but at first in the kitchen and then all over the prison. He was an extremely graceful and mischievous creature. He would come running when he was called and jump up on benches and tables; he playfully butted the prisoners and was always lively and amusing. One evening, when his horns were already a fair size, Babay, the Lezgian, who was sitting on the barrack-steps among a group of other prisoners, took it into his head to butt at him. They had been butting their foreheads together for some time—this was a favourite game with the goat among the convicts—when Vaska suddenly sprang to the topmost step and, as soon as Babay turned aside, reared up in a flash, hugged his little front feet close to himself, and launched himself full at the back of Babay's head, sending him flying head over heels down the steps, to the delight of everybody there and not least of Babay. In short, everybody was terribly fond of Vaska. When he began to grow up, a certain operation, which our veterinary surgeons performed very skilfully, was prescribed for him after earnest general consultation. 'Or else he will smell goaty,' said the prisoners. After that Vaska began to grow terribly fat. Indeed he was fed as if to fatten him for killing. At last he was full-grown, a beautiful big he-goat of terrific size and with enormously long horns. He used to waddle as he walked. He, too, formed the habit of going to work with us, to the amusement of the prisoners and the people who met us. Everybody knew the prison goat, Vaska. Sometimes, if they were working on the river bank, for instance, the prisoners would gather pliant willow-branches, leaves, and flowers from the ramparts and adorn Vaska with them; they twisted branches and flowers between his horns and hung him all over with garlands. Vaska, thus bedecked and beautified, always walked at the head of the convicts on the way back to the prison, and they marched behind, looking proudly at the passers-by. Their delight in the goat went so far that some of them, like children, took it into their heads: 'Why not gild Vaska's horns?' But they only talked of the idea, they did not carry it out. I remember, though, asking Akim Akimovich, our best gilder after Isaiah Fomich, whether it would really be possible to gild the goat's horns. He first looked very carefully at the goat, pondered the question seriously, and answered that it was perhaps possible, 'but it wouldn't last, and besides it would be quite useless.' That was the end of the matter. And Vaska would have gone on living in the prison for a long time and perhaps died from shortness of breath caused by his fatness, but on one occasion, as he was leading the prisoners back from work, adorned and bedecked, he came full into the path of the major, driving in a droshky. 'Stop!' he roared. 'Whose is that goat?' Somebody explained to him. 'What? A goat in the prison, without my permission? Sergeants!' A sergeant appeared and was forthwith ordered to kill the goat immediately. He was to skin it and sell the skin in the market, paying the money into the prisoners' fund, and to give the meat to the prisoners for soup. There was much talk in the prison and many regrets, but we dared not disobey. Vaska was killed over our cesspool. The carcass was bought by one of the prisoners, who paid a rouble and a half into the prison fund. With this money white loaves were purchased and the prisoner who had bought Vaska sold the meat cut up for roasting. The meat proved to be really extremely good.

An eagle, one of the small eagles of the steppes, also lived with us in the prison for some time. Somebody had carried him in injured and exhausted. The whole prison population surrounded him; he could not fly; his right wing trailed on the ground and one leg was dislocated. I remember the fierce rage with which he looked round at the curious crowd and opened his hooked beak, preparing to sell his life dearly. When everybody had done staring at him and began to move away, he struggled off lamely, hopping on one leg and flapping his sound wing, into the farthest part of the prison, where he retreated into a corner and crouched close to the palisade. There he lived for about three months and never once left his corner the whole time. At first men used to go up and look at him and set the dog on him. Sharik would rush fiercely at him but was plainly afraid to go too near, and this heartily amused the prisoners. 'What a fierce beast!' they said; 'he won't give in!' Later Sharik began to hurt him cruelly; his fear had passed and he got quite clever at catching the eagle by his injured wing when he was set on him. The eagle defended himself with all the strength of his beak and talons and, crouching in his corner, watched with the proud, fierce gaze of a wounded king the inquisitive crowd who had come to stare at him. At last, everybody grew bored with him; everybody left him to himself and forgot him, except that every day one might see scraps of fresh meat and a crock of water beside him. Somebody, then, must be looking after him. At first he refused to eat and ate nothing for some days; finally he began to take food, but never from anybody's hand or while people were there. More than once I watched him from a distance. Not seeing anybody and thinking that he was alone, he sometimes decided to come out of his corner and hopped along the fence for some twelve paces from his place; then he went back and again came out, as though he were taking exercise.

If he caught sight of me, he scrambled hastily back to his place with ungainly leaps and hops and, throwing back his head, with his beak open and his feathers bristling, instantly prepared for battle. I could not appease him with any caresses: he pecked and thrashed about, would not take meat from me and all the time, as I stood over him, stared fixedly into my eyes with his wicked piercing gaze. Solitary and vicious, mistrusting every man, implacably hostile, he waited for death. At last the prisoners seemed to recollect that he was there, and although nobody had troubled about him or even remembered his existence for two or three months, sympathy for him seemed suddenly to awaken in everybody. Men began to say that the eagle must be taken outside the walls: 'Let him peg out, only not in prison,' said some.

'That's right, he's a wild, free bird and you'll never get him used to prison,' others agreed.

'He's not like us, seemingly,' added somebody.

'That's a stupid thing to say! After all, he's a bird and we're men.'

'The eagle is the king of the forest, mates,' Skuratov was beginning, but this time nobody listened to him. After dinner one day, when the drum beat for work, they seized the eagle, somebody gripped his beak in his fist, for he began to struggle savagely, and he was carried out of the prison. The rampart was reached. The dozen or so men who made up this party watched curiously to see where the eagle would go. It was strange, but they all seemed content, as though they themselves had been given a measure of freedom.

'Look, the nasty brute! You do him a good turn and he goes on biting you!' said the man who was holding him, looking almost affectionately at the vicious bird.

'Let him go, Mikitka!'

'It's no good trying to put him off with anything but the real thing. Give him his freedom, real free freedom!'

They flung the eagle down from the rampart into the steppes. It was late in the autumn, a cold dark day. The wind whistled over the naked steppes and rustled the withered yellow tufts of steppe grass. The eagle took a straight course, flapping his injured wing, as if he were hurrying no matter where, only to get away from us. The prisoners' eyes followed him curiously, as his head appeared and disappeared again in the grass.

'Look at him!' said one thoughtfully.

'He won't even look round,' added another. 'He hasn't looked back a single time, mates; he just runs!'

'Did you think he'd come back to say thank you?' asked a third.

'Of course not; he's free!'

'Yes, deliveration, that is!'

'You can't see him any more, brothers . . .'

'What are you standing there for? March!' shouted the guard, and they trailed off to work in silence.

7. The Grievance

(HERE at the beginning of this chapter the editor of the late Alexander Petrovich Goryanchikov's Memoirs considers it his duty to make the following communication to his readers:

In the first chaper of 'Memoirs from the House of the Dead' something is said of a parricide, a former nobleman. He is cited, among other things, as an example of the unfeeling way in which the prisoners sometimes talked of their crimes. The author says also that the murderer had not confessed his crime in court but that, judging by the accounts of people who knew all the details of his story, the facts were so clear that it was impossible to doubt his guilt. These people told the author that the criminal's conduct had been thoroughly disreputable, that he was encumbered with debts, and that he had killed his father out of greed, to inherit his money. Everybody in the town where this parricide had formerly worked, moreover, told the same story; the editor of the 'Memoirs' has fairly reliable information on this last point. Finally, the 'Memoirs' state that in prison the murderer was always in most excellent spirits, that he was giddy, flighty, and irresponsible in the highest degree, although far from a fool, and that the author had never seen any sign of special cruelty in him. The author adds: 'I need not say that I did not believe in this crime.'

The editor of these 'Memoirs from the House of the Dead' has recently received information from Siberia that this criminal was in fact innocent and had suffered ten years of penal servitude unjustly. His innocence has been officially proclaimed by the courts. The real criminals have been discovered and have confessed, and the unhappy fellow has been released. The editor cannot doubt the authenticity of this information . . .

There is no more to add. There is no need for words or for enlarging on the full depth of the tragedy and on the young life ruined by this terrible accusation. The facts are in themselves too clear and too astonishing.

We thought also that if such a thing has proved to be possible, this mere possibility adds a new and extremely striking feature to the author's full and characteristic picture of the House of the Dead.

Now to continue:)

I have said before that I did finally grow accustomed to my situation in prison. But this 'finally' was reached with great pain and anguish, and by too small degrees. In fact it took me almost a year, and that year was the hardest of my life. It is for this reason that all of it is so firmly fixed in my memory as a whole. I think I remember every hour of that year in its proper sequence. I have said also that the other prisoners were no better able to get *used* to the life. I remember wondering many times during that year: 'What about them? How do they feel? Are they really used to it? Are they really resigned?' And these questions greatly interested me. I have already mentioned that all the prisoners lived there, not as though they were at home, but as though they were spending the night at a wayside inn, at the end of one stage of a long march. Men who had been sent there for life, even, were unsettled and full of longing to be gone, and each of them inevitably cherished in his heart a dream of something almost beyond possibility. This eternal restlessness, expressed plainly though silently, this strange fever and fret, these hopes, sometimes involuntarily given voice, although they were so utterly without foundation as to seem like delirium and yet (what was most striking of all) frequently managing to survive in men of apparently most realistic common sense—all this lent the place an unusual aspect and character, so much so that it perhaps constituted its most typical feature. Somehow one felt, almost from the first glance, that here was something that did not exist outside the prison. Everybody here was a dreamer, and the fact was obvious. It produced a painful effect, because the dreaming gave most of the prison population a sullen and dreary, somewhat unhealthy appearance. By far the greatest number of prisoners were taciturn and full of an ill will that amounted to hatred, and they disliked parading their hopes. Candour and simple-heartedness were despised. The more unrealistic the hopes, and the more the dreamer himself realized their unrealistic quality, the more obstinately he kept them hidden and inviolable in his own bosom, but he could not renounce them. Perhaps—who knows?—some were secretly ashamed of them. There is in the Russian character so much common sense and sobriety and so much inward mockery, of oneself first of all . . . Perhaps it was this constant hidden dissatisfaction with self that caused all the impatience displayed in the everyday relations of these men with one another, and all their incompatibility and deriding of one another. And if once one of them, simpler or more

impatient than the rest, came forward and expressed aloud
what was in everybody's heart, giving rein to his dreams and
hopes, he was at once roughly suppressed, snubbed, and
ridiculed; but to my mind his most zealous persecutors
were precisely those whose dreams and hopes went even
farther than his. I have already said that naïve and simple
men were generally looked on among us as the commonest
fools and treated with contempt. Every man had grown so
sullen and self-centred that he began to despise the good
and unselfish. Apart from the naïve and simple chatterers,
all the rest, the silent ones, were sharply divided into the
good-hearted and the ill-natured, the gloomy and the bright.
The sullen and ill-natured were incomparably more numerous; if some among them happened to be talkative by nature
they were inevitably untiring scandal-mongers and jealous
trouble-makers. They made everybody else's business their
own, although they revealed their own hearts and their own
affairs to nobody. That was not the fashion, it was not done.
The good-hearted—a very small handful—were quiet and
silent and nursed their hopes in secret, and they were, of
course, more disposed to be hopeful and to have confidence
that their hopes would come true. It seemed to me, however,
that there was yet another division in the prison, that of
those who were completely desperate. Such a one was, for
example, the old man from the Starodubsky Settlements.
There were, however, very few men in this category. The
old man (I have mentioned him before) looked tranquil, but
from certain indications I suppose that his mental state was
frightful. He had his salvation, though, his way of escape:
prayer and the idea of martyrdom. The prisoner whom I
have mentioned before, who had read his bible with so much
devotion and who went out of his mind and attacked the
major with a brick, was probably one of those deprived of
their last hope and abandoned to despair; and since it is impossible to live when one is completely without hope, he had
devised a solution for himself in the form of voluntary,

almost artificial, martyrdom. He declared that his attack on the major had been without malice, and made solely with the desire of accepting suffering. And who knows what psychological process had completed itself then in his soul? No living man can exist without some aim and the endeavour to attain it. A man who has lost his purpose and his hope not infrequently turns monster from misery . . . The purpose of all of us was freedom, release from prison.

Here I am, however, trying to classify the whole prison into types: but is this possible? Reality is infinitely diverse, compared with even the subtlest conclusions of abstract thought, and it does not allow of clear-cut and sweeping distinctions. Reality resists classification. We, too, had our own special life, poor though it may have been; nevertheless, we had it, and it was our own inward life, peculiar to us, not simply the official existence.

I have already made some mention of the fact that at the beginning of my stay in prison I did not penetrate into the inner depths of this life, and indeed was incapable of doing so, and therefore all its outward manifestations were then an unutterable torment and anguish to me. Sometimes I absolutely hated my fellow sufferers. I even envied them and cursed my own fate. I envied them because they, after all, were among their own kind, among companions whom they could understand, although in fact they were just as wearied and disgusted as I was by this companionship under the lash and the rod, this enforced association, and each one kept the eyes of his mind averted from the others. I repeat once more that the envy which visited me in moments of bitterness had its legitimate foundations. Those people are, in truth, decidedly wrong who say that a nobleman, an educated man, or the like, bears exactly the same hardship in our prisons and penal establishments as any peasant. I know this theory, I have heard it put forward recently and I have read of it. It is founded on an idea that is both true and humane: prisoners are all people, all human beings. But the idea is too abstract. It loses sight of a great many practical considerations, which only experience can enable us to understand. I do not say this because the feelings of the educated gentleman are more refined and sensitive or his development greater. It is difficult to apply any standard of measurement to the soul and its development. Education itself furnishes no criterion here. I am the first to admit that among these suffering men, in the midst of the coarsest ignorance and oppression, I met evidences of the most delicate inner feeling. It sometimes happened in prison that you knew a man for several years, thought of him as a brute and not a man at all, and despised him. Then suddenly a chance moment would reveal his soul in an involuntary convulsion and you saw in it such wealth, such feeling and heart, so clear an understanding of its own and others' suffering, that your eyes would be opened and in the first moment you would hardly be able to believe what you yourself had seen and heard. The opposite might also happen: education sometimes coexisted with such barbarism and cynicism that you were revolted, and however kind or favourably prejudiced you might be, you could find in your heart neither pardon nor excuse.

I say nothing, either, of the changes in habits, mode of life, food, and other things, which are of course harder to bear for a man from the higher strata of society than for a peasant, who when he was free not infrequently went hungry and who in prison at least eats his fill. We may assume that for a man of the least strength of will all this is trivial compared with other hardships, although in reality the change of habits is a matter not at all trifling or unimportant. But there are inconveniences before which all this pales, to such an extent that you pay no attention to the filthy surroundings, the restraints, or the scanty, disgusting food. The most delicate of fine gentlemen, the softest of molly-coddles, when he has worked all day in the sweat of his brow as he never worked when he was free, will eat black bread and cabbage soup with black beetles in it. You can even get used to it, as in the prisoners' comic song about the fine gentleman who went to prison:

> Cabbage they give me, cabbage and water,
> And I wallow in it like a pig.

No, the most important fact is that every new-comer to the prison, within two hours of his arrival, begins to be *at home*, a member of the prison fellowship of the same standing as every other. They all understand him and he understands them all, they all know him, they all think of him *as one of themselves*. It is different with the well-bred man, the gentleman. However upright, good, and wise he may be, he will be despised for years by the whole body of prisoners; they will not understand him and, most important, they will not trust him. He is not a friend, not a comrade, and although in the course of years he may finally come to the state of not being despised, nevertheless he will not be *one of them*, and he will be eternally tormented by the consciousness of his alienation and his solitude. Sometimes this alienation arises not from malice on the prisoners' part, but simply and unconsciously. He is not one of them, and that is all. Nothing is more terrible than to live outside one's own sphere. A peasant, transferred from Taganrog to Petropavlovsk, will find exactly the same Russian peasant there and at once come to terms and settle down with him, and two hours later, perhaps, they will be living peaceably together in the same hut. It is different for noblemen. They are divided from the common people by the profoundest of gulfs, and this fact is *fully* seen only when the *nobleman* is suddenly compelled, by the power of laws external to himself, to become one of the common people. Otherwise, you may associate all your life with the people, you may come into contact with them every day for forty years together, in the civil service, for example, in any of the accepted formal relationships, or even simply in a friendly way, as a benefactor and in a certain sense a father—you will never know the essence of them. It will all be an optical illusion, no more. I know, of course, that everybody, absolutely everybody, who reads this remark of mine will say I exaggerate. But I am convinced that it is true. My conviction was reached, not through books, not theoretically, but through reality, and I had quite enough time to verify my conviction. Perhaps in the future everybody will learn to what degree it is correct.

Events seemed to conspire from the first moment to confirm my observations and affect me nervously and painfully. During that first summer I wandered about the prison almost completely alone. I have already said that I was in such a state of mind that I could neither appreciate nor distinguish those prisoners who might have liked me, who did indeed like me in later days, although they never met me on an equal footing. There were others who, like me, were former noblemen, but this fact did not lift the burden from my soul. I longed to cut myself off from it all, but there was no refuge. Here, for instance, is one of those incidents which from the beginning gave me most cause to realize my isolation and the peculiarity of my position in the prison. Once, this same summer, not long before the beginning of August, between twelve and one o'clock of a hot bright weekday, when everybody was usually resting before the afternoon's work, all the prisoners suddenly got up as one man and began to line up in the prison yard. I had not known about anything until that very moment. At that time I was sometimes so wrapped up in myself that I hardly noticed what was going on around me. The convicts, however, had been deeply disturbed for a full three days. Perhaps the excitement had begun a great deal earlier still, as I thought later, when I involuntarily recalled some of the prisoners' talk and the sullenness and particularly bitter mood that had recently been noticeable in them. I had attributed this to the heavy work, the long slow summer days, the involuntary day-dreams of the forest and of being as free as air, and the short nights, in which it was difficult to sleep one's fill. Perhaps all of this had now combined to produce one outburst, but the pretext for the outburst was the food. During the past few days there had been loud grumbles and expressions of discontent in the barracks, and especially when we were together in the kitchen at dinner or supper; they were dissatisfied with the cooks and even tried replacing one of them, but immediately turned out the new one again and reinstated the old. In short, everybody was in an unsettled state of mind.

'The work's hard, and we get tripe to eat,' somebody would grumble in the kitchen.

'Well, if you don't like it, order blancmange,' retorted another.

'I'm very fond of tripe in my soup, mates,' a third would put in, 'because it tastes good.'

'But if you get nothing but tripe to eat all the time, does it still taste good?'

'There's one thing certain, now's the time when we ought to eat meat,' said a fourth; 'we slave away at the workshops, and when you've finished your work you want something to get your teeth into. And what sort of food is tripe?'

'If it's not tripe, it's awful.'[1]

'Yes, just look at that awful! Tripe and awful, it's either one or the other. Fine food that is! Is that right or isn't it?'

'Yes, the grub's rotten.'

'He's cramming his pockets for sure.'

'It's none of your business.'

'Whose is it then? It's my belly. If everybody was to make a complaint, that would settle it.'

'Make a complaint?'

'Yes.'

'Seemingly the beating you got last time for complaining wasn't enough for you, you great block!'

'That's right enough,' grumbled another, who had not

---

[1] i.e. offal, in the prisoners' sarcastic mispronunciation.

spoken before. 'Don't be in too much of a hurry. What are you going to say in your complaint? Tell us that first, clever!'

'All right, I'll tell you. If everybody was to go, I'd speak with all the rest. The poor ones, I mean. There's some that eats their own food and some sits down to nothing but prison grub.'

'There now, what sharp eyes jealousy has given him. It makes some people sore to see others well off.'

'Don't gape at someone else's bit, but get up and get some of your own.'

'Get some! I'll argue about this business with you till my hair turns grey. I suppose you're rich, if you want to sit tight and do nothing?'

'Eroshka's rich, he has a dog and a cat.'

'But really and truly, mates, why should we sit still? I mean, we've had enough of putting up with their tomfoolery. They're skinning us alive. Why shouldn't we go?'

'Why? I suppose everything's got to be put in words of one syllable for you; you have to be spoonfed. This is prison, that's why!'

'What it comes to is this—God send the poor people quarrel and the Governor will fill his belly.'

'That's right. Eight-eyes has got fat. He's bought a pair of greys.'

'Yes, and he doesn't half like a drink, does he?'

'The other day he had a fight with the vet at cards.'

'They'd been playing all night. Our man was fighting for two hours. Fedka told me.'

'That's why it's always "awful".'

'Oh, you're fools! It's not our place to make a complaint.'

'But if we all go out, we'll see what excuse he can make. We must stand firm on that.'

'Excuse! He'll push your teeth in, that's all!'

'And then we'll be tried besides.'

In short they were all extremely worked up. Our food at that time really was bad. Besides, one thing kept coming on

top of another. But most important was the general mood of
dejection and the endless concealed suffering. The convict is
by nature cantankerous and mutinous; but it is rare for all
or a large group to mutiny at once. This is because of their
habitual disagreements. Every one of them was aware of
this, and that is why there was more violent talk than action
among us. This time, however, the excitement did not come
to nothing. They began to collect in little clusters, they
discussed matters in the barracks, they grew abusive and
they balefully recalled all the major's reign; every smallest
detail was dragged out into the light. There were some who
were particularly heated. In every affair of this kind agitators
and ringleaders always make their appearance. The ringleaders in these cases—cases of grievances, that is—are
generally very conspicuous people, not in prison alone, but
in workshops, companies of soldiers, and so on. They are
a special type, everywhere very similar. They are hot-headed
men, eager for justice and quite simply and honestly convinced that it is inevitably, invariably, and above all immediately, possible. They are not more stupid than other people,
and some of them are even very clever, but they are too
passionate to be cunning and calculating. If there do indeed
exist men who in such cases can guide the people shrewdly
and win their cause, they constitute a different type of
popular leaders and natural commanders, a type very rare
among us. But those of whom I am now speaking, the
fomenters of grievances and ringleaders in complaints, nearly
always lose their cause and consequently people our prisons
and penal establishments. They lose because of their hot-
headedness, but their hot-headedness gives them their
influence over the masses. Men follow them willingly. Their
ardour and honest indignation impress everybody and the
most irresolute join them in the end. Their blind confidence
in success seduces even the most hardened sceptics, although
sometimes that confidence has such shaky and infantile
foundations that it is a wonder to the disinterested onlooker

that they are followed. The main thing is that they march in the van, and that they advance without fear. They rush forward like bulls, horns down, often without understanding the matter, without heed, and without that practical casuistry by means of which the most debased and abject creature not infrequently wins his cause, gains his ends, and emerges unscathed from the struggle. But *they* must always come to grief. In everyday life these people are peevish, irritable, touchy, and impatient. Very frequently they are terribly limited; but this constitutes part of their strength. The most vexatious thing about them is that often, instead of making straight for their object, they allow themselves to be diverted and fling themselves on trifles instead of the important things. It is this that brings them to disaster. But the masses can understand them; this is their strength ... But I must say a word or two on what constitutes a *grievance*.

In our prison there were several men who had come there for airing grievances. It was they who were the most agitated now. There was one in particular, Martynov, who had once served in the Hussars, a hot-headed, restless, suspicious man, but honest and upright. Another was Vassily Antonov, a man as it were cold-bloodedly irascible, with an insolent look, a smile of sarcastic superiority, and unusual intelligence, but equally honest and truthful. But I cannot enumerate them all; there were many of them. Petrov, among others, scurried to and fro, lent an ear to every knot of men, said little but was plainly full of excitement, and was the first to rush out of the barrack when the men began to form up.

The prison non-commissioned officer who acted as our sergeant-major came out at once in a fright. When the men were drawn up in lines they politely asked him to tell the major that the convicts wished to speak to him and ask him about some points. All the old soldiers had followed the sergeant out and were ranged on the other side, opposite the prisoners. The errand with which the sergeant had been charged was out of the usual run and filled him with dismay. But he dared not delay to inform the major. To begin with, if the prison had indeed mutinied, something even worse might come of it. All our authorities seemed to have an intensely cowardly attitude towards the convicts. Secondly, if nothing came of it and they all immediately reconsidered and dispersed, even then the sergeant was obliged to report to the authorities everything that went on. Pale and shaking with fright, he hurried away to the major, not even trying to interrogate or admonish the convicts himself. He could see that they would not even speak to him now.

Quite without knowing why, I too had lined up in the yard. I did not learn all the details of the affair until afterwards. Now I thought some sort of roll-call was proceeding, but not seeing the sentries who conducted the checks, I was surprised and began to look round. The men's faces were excited and angry. Some were even pale. They were all silent and apprehensive in the expectation of having to speak to the major. I noticed that many of them looked at me with extreme astonishment, but they turned away without saying anything. It evidently seemed strange to them that I too had lined up with them. They plainly did not believe that I also wanted to voice a grievance. Soon, however, almost all the men standing near me turned towards me again. They all looked questioningly at me.

'What are you here for?' Vassily Antonov, who was standing a little farther away from me than the others, asked me loudly and very rudely; until then his speech and behaviour to me had always been polite.

I looked at him in perplexity, still trying to understand what all this meant, and already divining that something out of the ordinary was happening.

'That's right, what do you want standing here? Get back into your barrack,' said a young fellow, one of the soldiers with whom I had been unacquainted until then; he was a quiet, decent lad. 'It's nothing to do with you.'

'Well, after all, everybody's getting into line,' I answered;
'I thought it was an inspection.'

'Look, he's come crawling out too,' shouted somebody.

'Iron beak!' said another.

'Fly-crushers!' said a third, with unspeakable contempt.
This new nickname raised a general guffaw.

'He condescends to share the kitchen with us,' added
somebody else.

'Everything's fine for them. This is prison, but they eat
white bread and buy sucking-pigs. You eat your own food,
don't you? Why come poking in here?'

'This is no place for you,' said Kulikov easily, coming up
to me; he took me by the arm and led me away.

He himself was pale, his black eyes flashed and he was
biting his lower lip. He could not wait for the major with
composure. I, by the way, very much liked to watch Kulikov
at all such times, on all those occasions, that is, when he was
forced to reveal himself. He showed off terribly, but he
played his part. I think he would have gone to execution
with a certain elegance and panache. Now, when the others
all addressed me rudely and reviled me, he redoubled his
politeness to me, with evident deliberation, but at the same
time his words seemed particularly, even overbearingly,
insistent, and allowed of no objection.

'We are here on our own business, Alexander Petrovich,
and it is nothing to do with you. Go away and wait . . . All
your lot are over there, look, in the kitchen; go to them.'

'Go and hide in a hole, with Old Nick himself!' put in
somebody.

Through the raised kitchen window I could indeed see
our Poles; it seemed to me, however, that there were many
others there as well. Embarrassed, I went to the kitchen,
pursued by laughter, oaths, and the catcalls which took the
place of whistling in the prison.

'He don't like us! Yah, yah, yah! Nobble him! . . .'

Never before in the prison had I been so insulted, and this

time I found it very distressing. But I had struck an un-fortunate moment. Tokarzewsky met me in the kitchen passage; he was one of the gentlemen, a young man of strong and generous character, not very highly educated and terribly fond of Boguslavsky. The convicts singled him out from the others and even rather liked him. He was brave, manly, and physically strong, as each of his gestures seemed to demonstrate.

'What are you doing, Goryanchikov?' he called to me. 'Come here!'

'But what is all that?'

'They are making a complaint; surely you know that? Of course they won't succeed: who will believe convicts? They'll begin looking for the ringleaders and if we're there, it goes without saying they'll put the first blame for the mutiny on us. Remember why we were sent here. They'll simply be flogged, but we shall be tried. The major hates all of us and he'll be delighted to ruin us. He'll use us to clear himself with.'

'And the convicts wouldn't be reluctant to give us up, either,' added Miretsky, as we entered the kitchen.

'Don't worry, they wouldn't spare us!' agreed Tokar-zewsky.

Besides the gentlemen there were many people, thirty in all, in the kitchen. They had all remained behind, unwilling to join in the complaint, some out of cowardice, some from definite conviction of the entire fruitlessness of any voicing of grievances. One who was there was Akim Akimovich, an inveterate and natural enemy of all such actions, which disturbed good conduct and the normal course of duty. He was silently and with extraordinary tranquillity awaiting the end of the affair, not in the least worried about its outcome, but on the contrary completely convinced of the inevitable triumph of order and the will of the authorities. Isaiah Fomich, too, was standing there in extreme perplexity and dejection, avidly and apprehensively listening to our talk.

He was painfully anxious. There also were all our lower-class prison Poles, who had joined their gentlemen. There were a few timid souls from among the Russians, people who were always silent and downtrodden. They had not plucked up enough courage to go out with the others and dejectedly waited to see what the end would be. Finally, there were some morose and always grim convicts who were fearless enough. They had stayed out of an obstinate and fastidious conviction that the whole thing was absurd and that nothing would come of it. But I am sure that they nevertheless felt somehow awkward; they did not look altogether sure of themselves. Although they knew that they were quite right about the grievance, as subsequently became clear, they were conscious all the same that they were renegades who had abandoned their comrades, as though they had betrayed them to the major. Yolkin was there, too—the sly little Siberian peasant who had been sent to us for coining and who had taken Kulikov's veterinary practice away from him. The old man from the Starodubsky Settlements was also there. Every single one of the cooks had stayed behind, probably in the belief that they also were part of the administration and that consequently it was not fitting for them to demonstrate against it.

'But', I began irresolutely, addressing Miretsky, 'almost everybody has gone out, except these here.'

'And what's that to us?' muttered Boguslavsky.

'We should have risked a hundred times more than them if we had gone out, and what for? *Je haïs ces brigands.* Surely you don't believe for one moment that this complaint will accomplish anything? Why should we want to thrust ourselves into their mess?'

'Nothing will come of it,' struck in one of the convicts, an obstinate and ill-natured old man. Almazov, who was there, was quick to express his agreement.

'Except that about fifty of them will get a flogging, nothing will come of it.'

'The major's come!' shouted somebody, and we all rushed eagerly to the windows.

The major had galloped in, seething with malice, wild with rage, crimson and bespectacled. Silently but resolutely he went up to the front rank. In these cases he really was bold and did not lose his head. But then he was nearly always half drunk. Even his greasy cap with its orange band and his dirty silver epaulettes had something sinister about them at that moment. Behind him walked his clerk, Dyatlov, an extremely important personage in our prison, possessing influence even over the major. He was a sly youth, and very cunning, but not a bad fellow. The prisoners quite liked him. Behind him came our sergeant, who had plainly had a most terrible dressing down and was expecting another ten times as bad; after him came three or four guards, not more. The prisoners, who had stood bareheaded all the time, I think, since the major had been sent for, now all straightened up and dressed their ranks; each of them shifted from one foot to the other and then they all froze where they stood and waited for the first word, or rather yell, of the supreme authority.

It followed at once; with his second word the major howled with all the force of his lungs and on this occasion even with something like a shriek; he was already beside himself. From the windows we could see him scurrying along the front row and hurling himself at prisoners to cross-question them. Neither his questions nor the prisoners' replies, however, were audible, owing to the distance. We could distinguish only his shrill squeals.

'Mutiny! . . . the gauntlet! . . . ringleaders! . . . You're a ringleader! You're a ringleader!' and he hurled himself at some man.

The answer could not be heard. But a minute later we saw the prisoner separate himself from the others and walk towards the guardroom. After another minute another followed him, and then a third.

'All under arrest! I'll show you! Who's that in the kitchen?' he squealed, seeing us through the open window. 'Everybody here! Drive 'em all out here at once!'

The clerk Dyatlov came to us in the kitchen. He was told that we had no grievance and immediately returned to the major.

'Oh, they haven't?' he said, two tones lower, evidently very pleased to hear it. 'It doesn't matter; everybody here!'

We went out. I felt that it was somehow shameful of us. Indeed, we all went with something of a hangdog air.

'Ah, Prokofyev! Yolkin as well . . . And you, Almazov . . . Stand here, stand close together,' said the major to us, hurriedly yet gently, looking kindly at us. 'Miretsky, you come here too . . . There, make a list, Dyatlov! Write down everybody immediately, those who are satisfied in one list, and those who aren't in another—everyone, down to the last man, and bring the paper to me. I'll put all of you . . . under arrest! I'll show you, scoundrels!'

The list had its effect.

'We're satisfied!' came in a sullen and rather hesitant shout from among the crowd of malcontents.

'Oh, you're satisfied? Who's satisfied? Anyone who is satisfied, step out!'

'We're satisfied, we're satisfied!' joined in several voices.

'You're satisfied! Does that mean you were led astray? Does it mean there were ringleaders and mutineers? So much the worse for them! . . .'

'Lord, what's this?' came somebody's voice from the crowd.

'Who shouted that? Who was it?' roared the major, rushing in the direction from which the voice had been heard. 'Was it you, Rastorguev? Did you shout? Guardroom!'

Rastorguev, a tall and rather bloated young fellow, stepped out of the crowd and slowly walked towards the guardroom. It was not he who had shouted at all, but since he had been singled out he did not protest.

'You're too well off, that's what's the matter with you!' the major howled after him. 'Look at your fat face! You've not — for three days! I'll find you all out, you'll see! All those who are satisfied, step forward!'

'We're satisfied, your honour!' several dozen voices said glumly; the rest were obstinately silent. But that was all the major needed. It was obviously best for him to end the matter as soon as possible, and to end it with some measure of consent.

'Ah, now you're all satisfied!' he said hastily. 'I could see it . . . I knew. It was agitators! Obviously there are agitators amongst them!' he continued, turning to Dyatlov. 'That must be more fully investigated. But now . . . it's time for work. Sound the drum!'

He was present himself as we were sent out. The prisoners dispersed to their work sadly and silently, pleased at any rate to get out of his sight as quickly as possible. But afterwards the major immediately visited the guardroom and dealt with the ringleaders, not, however, very harshly. Indeed, he seemed in a hurry to get it over. One of them, it was said afterwards, asked for pardon, and was at once forgiven. It was plain that the major was not quite himself, and perhaps he was even in a funk. In any case a grievance is a ticklish business, and although the prisoners' complaint could not really be called a grievance, because it had been made not to the highest authorities but to the major himself, it was all the same somewhat awkward, not very nice. It was particularly disconcerting that the rising had been so general. He had to stamp it out at whatever cost. The ringleaders were soon released. The very next day the food improved, although not for long. During the first few days the major took to visiting the prison more frequently and found fault more often. Our sergeant went about worried and perplexed, as though he had still not recovered from his shock. As for the prisoners, for a long time after this they could not settle down, though they no longer got excited as before, but fretted silently and seemed somehow puzzled. Some were crestfallen. Others grumbled over the whole business, but without many words. Many bitterly and openly laughed at themselves, as though to punish themselves for harbouring a grievance.

'Swallow it and like it!' one would say.

'If you want your little joke, you must pay for it!' added another.

'Where can you find a mouse to bell the cat?' asked a third.

'The likes of us aren't to be convinced without a club, that's well known. We were lucky we weren't all flogged.'

'In future you know more and talk less, and you'll be better off!' angrily remarked somebody.

'Do you think you can teach us, teacher?'

'Of course I can.'

'And who are you to poke your nose in?'

'Up to now I've always been a man, but who are you?'

'You're something the dog's chewed up, that's what you are!'

'You're another!'

'For goodness' sake, shut up! What do you want to make that row for?' everybody shouted at the disputants.

That evening, that is on the day of the complaint, I met Petrov behind the barracks as I returned from work. He had been looking for me. He came up and muttered two or three vague, disjointed words, but soon fell into an absent-minded silence and walked mechanically at my side. The whole affair still weighed painfully on me, and I thought Petrov could perhaps make something clear for me.

'Tell me, Petrov,' I asked him, 'your fellows are angry with us, aren't they?'

'Who's angry?' he asked, as though jerked back to reality.

'The prisoners with us, . . . the gentlemen?'

'Why should anyone be angry with you?'

'Well, because we didn't join in the grievance.'

'What was there for you to make a grievance about?' he asked, as though trying to understand me. 'After all, you have your own food.'

'Oh, good God! Some of you have your own food as well, but they joined in. Well, so ought we . . . out of comradeship.'

'But . . . but how can you be our comrades?' he asked, puzzled.

I glanced at him quickly: he definitely did not understand me, did not know what I was driving at. I, on the other hand, in that moment understood him completely. Now for the first time a certain idea, which had been obscurely stirring in me and haunting me for a long time, became finally clear to me and I suddenly understood what I had until then only vaguely divined. I understood that I should never be received into their company, even though I was a prisoner, even if it were for ever and a day, even if I were in the Special Class. But what remains clearest in my memory is Petrov's look at that moment. In his question: 'how can you be our comrade?' there sounded such unfeigned innocence, such simplehearted perplexity. I wondered whether there was not in those words some tinge of irony, of bitterness, of mockery. There was nothing. I was simply not a comrade, and that was all there was to it. You go your way and let us go ours; you have your own affairs, we have ours.

And really, I had been on the point of thinking that after the affair of the grievance they would simply fall on us like wolves and make life impossible for us. Not a bit of it: not the slightest reproach, not the merest hint of a reproach, did we hear, and there was no increase of malice towards us. They simply harried us a little on this occasion, as they had done before, and nothing more. However, they were not in the least angry, either, with all those who had refused to associate themselves with the grievance and remained behind in the kitchen, or with those who had been the first to shout out that they were satisfied with everything. Nobody, in fact, even referred to this. I found this last particularly difficult to understand.

8. Comrades

I, OF course, was most drawn to my own kind, that is to the 'gentlemen', especially at first. But of the three Russian former members of the nobility we had in the prison (Akim Akimovich, the spy Aristov, and the one who was supposed to be a parricide), I associated and talked only with Akim Akimovich. I must admit that when I approached him it was, so to speak, in desperation, in moments of the most intense boredom and when there was nobody else to turn to. In the last chapter I made an attempt to classify all our prisoners into types, but now, remembering Akim Akimovich, I think I might add another class. It is true that he alone constituted it. This was the class of completely indifferent convicts. Absolutely indifferent ones, those, that is, to whom it was all the same whether they lived in freedom or in prison, there were none, of course, nor could there be any, but Akim Akimovich seemed almost to constitute an exception. He had even settled himself in prison as though he were preparing to spend the rest of his life there: everything around him, beginning with his mattress and pillows and his household goods, had been arranged so solidly, so stably, so lastingly. Of the improvised, the temporary, there was no trace. He still had many years to spend in prison, but I doubt whether he even once thought of his release. But if he had reconciled himself to reality, it was not, of course, from inclination but perhaps from subordination, which, however, was for him the same thing. He was a good man and in the beginning even helped me with advice and did me some services; but sometimes, I confess, he involuntarily produced in me immeasurable dejection, especially in the early days, and intensified my already sufficiently wretched frame of mind. Yet it was that misery which had made me talk to him. I would be hungry sometimes for a living word of some kind, however jaundiced, however impatient, however bitter: we might even have only cursed our fate in unison: but he silently pasted his lanterns or told me how the regiment had been reviewed in such and such a year, and who commanded the division, and what his name and patronymic were, and whether he had been satisfied with his review, and how the firing signals had been changed, and so on. And all in a sedate, even tone, like water falling drop by drop. He hardly showed any enthusiasm even when he told me how the privilege of wearing a 'St. Anne' on his sword had been conferred on him for his part in some affair in the Caucasus. It was only that his voice took on an unusual importance and dignity; he even lowered it a little to a certain mysterious solemnity when he pronounced the words 'St. Anne', and after that, he became particularly silent and sedate for the next three minutes . . . In that first year I had sometimes stupid moments when (always quite suddenly) I began almost to hate Akim Akimovich, I don't know why, and silently cursed my fate for having placed me head to head with him on the planks. An hour later, I was usually reproaching myself for this. But this was only in the first year; afterwards I was completely reconciled to Akim Akimovich in my heart, and was ashamed of my former stupidity. Outwardly, as I remember, we never quarrelled.

Besides these three Russians, there were eight other gentlemen in the prison in my time. With some of these I associated fairly closely and even with pleasure, but not with all. The best of them were morbid, eccentric, and irritable in the highest degree. With two of them later I simply ceased to speak. Only three of them were men of culture: Boguslavsky, Miretsky, and old Zhokhovsky,* who had once been a professor of mathematics somewhere, a good, kind old man, a great eccentric and, in spite of his education, apparently extremely limited. Miretsky and Boguslavsky were quite different. I got on well with Miretsky from the first; we never quarrelled and I respected him, but I could never really like him or become attached to him. He was deeply mistrustful and embittered, but he could control himself surprisingly well. It was just this capacity in him that displeased me: one somehow felt that he would never open all his heart to anybody. Perhaps, however, I am mistaken about this. His was a strong and noble nature. His extraordinary and even somewhat Jesuitical skill and caution in his dealings with people betrayed his profound hidden scepticism. And yet his spirit suffered painfully from this very duality: scepticism and a deep, utterly unshakable belief in his own personal convictions and hopes. In spite of all his worldly shrewdness, however, he was irreconcilably at odds with Boguslavsky and his friend Tokarzewsky.* Boguslavsky was a sickly man, with some tendency to tuberculosis, irritable and nervous but essentially kind and even great-hearted. His irritability amounted at times to extreme intolerance and capriciousness. I could not endure these characteristics and later broke with Boguslavsky, but I never ceased to like him; with Miretsky I never even had words, but I never liked him. In breaking with Boguslavsky I found myself obliged to part also with Tokarzewsky, the same young man I mentioned in the previous chapter. I was very sorry to do this. Although Tokarzewsky was not an educated man, he was good-natured and manly—in short, a fine young fellow. The fact was that he so loved and respected Boguslavsky that he looked on anybody who had fallen out at all with Boguslavsky as almost his own enemy. I think he subsequently broke even with Miretsky on account of Boguslavsky, although not for a long time. All of them, however, were morally sick, jaundiced, irritable, and mistrustful. This is understandable: things were hard for them, even harder than for us. They were all far from their own country. Some of them had been exiled for long terms, ten years or twenty years, and, what was more important, they were deeply prejudiced against all those around them, saw in the convicts nothing but brutes and could not, indeed would not, discern in them one good feature, one sign of humanity. And this too was easy to understand: they had been driven to this unhappy point of view by the force of circumstances, by fate. It is clear that in prison they were stifled with misery. With the Cherkesses and Tartars, and with Isaiah Fomich they were pleasant and friendly, but they avoided all the other convicts with disgust. Only the Starodubsky Old Believer earned their full respect. It is remarkable, however, that throughout all the time I was in the prison not one convict ever reproached them with their origins, their creed, or their way of thinking, as may sometimes happen among our simple people with respect to foreigners, especially Germans, although only rarely. The Germans, however, they perhaps do no more than laugh at; to the Russian peasant the German is a figure of fun. But the convicts treated our foreigners even respectfully, much more so than us Russians, and did not *touch* them. But they never seemed to be willing to notice or take account of this. I have spoken of Tokarzewsky. It was he who, when they were being transferred from the place of their first exile to our prison, carried Boguslavsky in his arms almost all the way, when he, feeble in health and constitution, was almost exhausted by half a day's march. They had been exiled first to U—. There, they told us, they had been all right, much better, that is to say, than in our fortress. But they had entered into a correspondence, quite innocent, however, with exiles from another town, and for this it had been deemed necessary to send three of them to our fortress, where they would be more under the eyes of our highest authorities. The third was Zhokhovsky. Until their arrival Miretsky had been alone in the prison. How much misery he must have suffered in the first year of his exile!

This Zhokhovsky was the old man I have mentioned before, who was everlastingly praying. All our political criminals were young, and some of them very young; Zhokhovsky alone was over fifty. He was a man who was undoubtedly honest, but a little odd. His companions Boguslavsky and Tokarzewsky disliked him, indeed did not speak to him, and described him as mulish and quarrelsome. I do not know how far they were right. In prison, as in all other places where people are herded together not of their own will but by compulsion, it seems to me it is easier for them to quarrel and even to conceive hatred for each other, than in freedom. Many circumstances contribute to this. Zhokhovsky, however, really was a rather stupid and perhaps disagreeable man. None of the rest of his comrades could get on with him, either. Although I never quarrelled with him, I did not get on with him particularly well. I think he knew his own subject, mathematics. I remember that he was always trying to expound to me in his broken Russian some special system of astronomy he had invented. I was told that he had once published it, but the learned world had only laughed at him. I think his wits were a little deranged. He used to spend whole days on his knees, praying, and this won him the general respect of the prison, which he enjoyed until the day of his death. He died in our hospital, in my presence, after a severe illness. The respect of the convicts he had acquired at his very first step in the prison, after an encounter with our major. On the road from U— to our fortress they had not been shaved, and had grown beards, so that when they were taken straight to the major he was furiously angry at this breach of discipline, for which, however, they were not in the least to blame.

'What a state they're in!' he roared; 'they're tramps, they're brigands!'

Zhokhovsky, who did not then understand Russian well, and thought they were being asked which they were, tramps or brigands, answered:

'We are not tramps but political prisoners.'

'Wha-a-at? You're impudent, are you? Impudent!' roared the major. 'To the guardroom! A hundred this instant, this very moment!'

The old man was beaten. He lay down under the rods without protest, bit his hand and endured the punishment without a groan or a murmur and without moving a muscle. Meanwhile the others had already entered the prison, where Miretsky was waiting for them at the gates, and he absolutely fell on their necks, although he had never seen them before. Shaken by agitation at the major's reception of them, they told him all about Zhokhovsky. I remember Miretsky's telling me about it: 'I was beside myself,' he said. 'I didn't know what was happening to me; I was shaking as though I had a fever. I waited for him near the gate.' Zhokhovsky was to come straight from the guardroom, where he had been beaten. The side-gate opened: without looking at anybody, with a pale face and pale trembling lips, he walked past all the convicts, who had gathered in the yard when they learnt that a gentleman was being beaten. He went into the barrack and straight to his place where without a word he fell on his knees and began to pray. The convicts were astounded and even touched. 'When I saw that old man,' said Miretsky, 'with his grey head, who had left behind his wife and children in his own country, when I saw him on his knees, shamefully beaten and praying to God, I rushed away behind the barracks and for two whole hours I was quite distracted; I was frantic . . .' From that time the convicts conceived a great regard for Zhokhovsky, and always treated him respectfully. They particularly liked the fact that he had not cried out under punishment.

I must, however, tell the whole truth: it is far from possible to judge the attitude of the authorities in Siberia towards the gentlemen exiles, whoever they might be, whether Russians or Poles, from this instance. This example shows only that one may happen upon a hasty and evil man, and, of course, if that evil man were a senior commander in some remote place, the lot of an exile to whom that evil commander had taken a special dislike would be almost hopeless. But it must be acknowledged that the very highest authorities in Siberia, on whom depends the tone and temper of all other commanders, are very scrupulous with respect to prisoners of the educated class, and even disposed in some instances to treat them indulgently in comparison with the rest of the prisoners, the common people. The reasons for this are clear : to begin with, these highest authorities are themselves of the educated class; secondly, it had happened even before this that certain of the educated prisoners had refused to submit to corporal punishment and attacked their executioners, with dire results; thirdly, and I think most important, long before this, indeed thirty-five years earlier, a great mass of exiles from the upper classes had suddenly appeared in Siberia, and in the course of thirty years these exiles had succeeded so well in establishing and recommending themselves all over Siberia, that in my day the authorities, from old traditional habit, involuntarily looked on educated prisoners of a certain category with other eyes than on all other exiles. Following the example of the highest authorities, the lower officials had become accustomed to taking the same attitude, since of course they obediently and subserviently borrowed their attitude and tone from above. Many of these lower officials, however, took a stupid view, in their hearts criticized the disposition of their superiors and would have been immeasurably pleased if they had only been allowed to arrange things in their own way. But they were not allowed to have everything as they wanted it. I have firm grounds for thinking so and they are these: The Second division of convicts, to which I belonged, and which consisted of prisoners in fortresses under military command, was incomparably harder than the other two, the third category (serving in the workshops) and the first (in the mines). It was harder not only for the gentlemen but for all the other prisoners, simply because the command and organization of this category were all military, very like the penal battalions in Russia. The military régime was harsher, the discipline stricter, we were always in chains, always guarded, always under lock and key; and this is not true in the same degree of the two other categories. So, at least, all our prisoners said, and there were experts in this matter among them. They would all have been glad to get into the first category, which was considered by the law the hardest, and they often dreamed of doing so. All those who had been in them spoke with horror of the penal battalions in Russia, and asserted that in all Russia there are no harder places than the fortress penal battalions, and that Siberia was paradise compared with the life there. Consequently, if in conditions as severe as those in our prison, under military rule, under the eyes of the Governor-General himself, and, finally, in the face of instances (which sometimes occurred) when officious outsiders, from malice or zeal for the service, were prepared to report to the proper quarters that certain unreliable commandants were showing leniency to a certain class of criminals—if in such a place, I say, the educated prisoners were regarded in a somewhat different light from the other convicts, then they must have received favourable treatment in the first and third divisions. Consequently, I think I may judge of all Siberia, in this respect, from the place in which I found myself. All the rumours and tales on this subject which reached me from exiles of the first and third divisions confirmed my conclusions. In truth, in our prison the authorities treated all us gentlemen with greater consideration and circumspection. There was certainly no kind of indulgence in respect of work or living conditions: we had the same work, the same fetters, the same locks and bolts, and in short everything the same, as all the prisoners. Indeed, it was impossible to give us any relief from these. I know that in that town in *the not so remote past* there had been so many informers, so much intrigue, so much digging of pits for one another that the authorities were naturally afraid of being informed against. And what indeed could have been more terrible at that time than a report that a certain class of criminals was being treated leniently? So everybody was a little afraid, and we lived on the same footing as all the other convicts, but with respect to corporal punishment there were exceptions. It is true that we should have been flogged with great readiness if we had deserved it, committed, that is, some offence. Duty to the service and equality in respect of corporal punishment required it. But all the same we were not just beaten capriciously, for no reason; but that sort of capricious treatment was of course sometimes dealt out to the common prisoners, especially by some subordinate commandants who were eager to assert their authority and make themselves felt whenever the occasion offered. It was known to us that the commandant, when he heard the story of the old man Zhokhovsky, was very indignant with the major and impressed upon him that in future he must kindly keep himself in hand. So everybody told me. We also knew that the Governor-General himself,* who had trusted and to a certain extent liked our major, as an efficient and quite capable man, also reprimanded him when he learnt of the matter. And our major took notice. How much, for example, he longed to get at Miretsky, whom he hated because of Aristov's slanders, but he could find no way to have him flogged, although he was always seeking some pretext, harrying him and looking for a good excuse. The whole town soon learnt the story of Zhokhovsky, and the general opinion was against the major; many people reproached him and some even said very harsh things. I am reminded now of my first meeting with the major. We, that is, another gentleman exile and myself, who had entered the prison together, had been frightened while we were still in Tobolsk by tales of the unpleasant character of this man. The old exiles, educated men with twenty-five-year sentences, who were there at the time, and who had greeted us with proffered sympathy and kept in touch with us all the time we were in the transit quarters, put us on our guard against our future commander and promised to do all they possibly could, through the people they knew, to protect us from his persecutions. The three daughters of the Governor-General, who had come from Russia at that time to pay their father a visit, did indeed receive letters from them and, I think, spoke to their father in our favour. But what could he do? He simply told the major to be a little more careful. Between two and three o'clock in the afternoon we, my companion and myself, arrived in the town and our guards took us straight to our ruler. We stood in the hall waiting for him. Meanwhile the prison sergeant had been sent for. As soon as he appeared the major too came out. His crimson, pimply, ill-natured face produced an extraordinarily depressing effect on us: he was like a vicious spider pouncing on the poor fly that had fallen into its web.

'What's your name?' he asked my companion. He spoke rapidly, harshly, jerkily, and evidently wanted to make an impression on us.

'So-and-so.'

'Yours?' he went on, turning to me and glaring at me through his spectacles.

'So-and-so.'

'Sergeant! Take them at once to the prison and see that half their heads are shaved, immediately, as civilians; fetters to be changed tomorrow. What greatcoats are those? Where did you get them?' he asked abruptly, transferring his attention to the long grey coats with yellow circles on the back, which had been issued to us in Tobolsk, and in which we had appeared in his illustrious presence. 'That's a new uniform. It is probably some new uniform . . . Still experimental . . . comes from St. Petersburg . . .,' he said, making us revolve in turn. 'Have they anything with them?' he asked the guard who had accompanied us.

'They have their own clothes, your honour,' answered the escort, instantly jumping to attention, even with a slight quiver. Everybody knew the major; they had all heard of him and they were all afraid of him.

'Take it all away. Let them keep only underclothes, the white things, but if there is anything coloured, take it away. Put all the rest up to auction. Put the money in the prison funds. A prisoner has no possessions,' he went on, looking sternly at us. 'See that you behave well. Don't let me hear of you. Otherwise . . . cor-por-al pun-ishment! For the smallest offence—the r-r-rods! . . .'

All that evening I, being unused to that kind of thing, was almost ill from this reception. Its effect on me, moreover, was reinforced by what I saw in the prison; but I have already told of my introduction to it.

I mentioned just now that they did not, indeed dared not, show us any indulgence or give us any greater relief in our work than the other prisoners. Once, however, they tried to do so: for three months Boguslavsky and I were sent as clerks into the Engineers' office. But it was done by the Engineer officers, and done in strict secrecy—that is to say, perhaps everybody who needed to do so knew of it, but they pretended that they did not. This happened while commandant Kuplennikov was still in office. Lieutenant-colonel Kuplennikov seemed sent by heaven, but he remained with us for a very short time—not more than two months, if I am not mistaken, and perhaps even less than that, and when he went away to Russia he had made an unusual impression on all the prisoners. They not only liked him, they adored him, if such a word can be used here. How he did it I do not know, but he conquered them from the start. 'He's a father to us, a father! No need of any other!' the convicts were always saying, all the time he commanded the Engineers' department. He was, I believe, terribly dissipated. He was not tall and he had an arrogant, self-confident look. On the other hand he was amiable almost to tenderness with the convicts and really literally loved them like a father. What made him like them so much I am unable to say, but he could not see one without saying a friendly, cheerful word and exchanging a smile or a joke with him, and, most important, in all this there was nothing condescending, not a suggestion of superior station or purely official kindness. He was their friend, in the most real sense one of them. But in spite of all his instinctive democracy, the prisoners never once allowed themselves the slightest discourtesy or familiarity with him. On the contrary. But a prisoner's face would light up when he met the commander, and he took off his cap and began to smile even before he reached him. And if the commander spoke to him, it was received like the gift of a rouble. Such people do exist. He was a fine-looking man with an upright and gallant walk. The prisoners used to refer to him as an eagle. He, of course, could do nothing to make things easier for them; he superintended only the engineering work, which had, as under all the other commanders, the same unchanging course once officially appointed for it. Occasionally, at most, if he chanced to meet a working party and saw that they had finished their task, he would not keep them for the remaining time but allow them to go before the drum beat. But what was pleasing was his trust in the prisoners, the absence of petty fault-finding and peevishness, and his complete lack of certain offensive mannerisms of the rest of the official world. If he had lost a thousand roubles, I think the most hardened thief among us, finding them, would have taken them back to him. Yes, I am convinced that it would have been so. It was with the profoundest pleasure that the prisoners heard that their eagle of a commander had quarrelled with our hated major. This happened in the very first month after his arrival. Our major had once served with him. They met as friends after their long separation, and they used to enjoy a good time together.

But suddenly there was a violent break. They quarrelled, and became deadly enemies. We even heard that they had come to blows on one occasion, which was quite possible with our major: he was always fighting. When the prisoners heard this they were overjoyed. 'Fancy Eight-eyes trying to be friends with someone like him! He's an eagle, and our major's a —', and here usually followed a word unsuitable for print. We were terribly curious to know which had beaten the other. If the rumour of their fighting had proved false I think our prisoners would have been very disappointed. 'No, probably the commander won,' they said; 'he's a little 'un but a good 'un, and they say the major hid under the bed from him!' But soon the commander left, and the prisoners again fell into dejection. It is true that all our Engineers' commanders were good: during my time they were changed three or four times: 'All the same we shall never get another one like him,' the convicts said; 'he was an eagle, a regular eagle, and he stuck up for us.' This same officer had a great liking for all of us gentlemen, and towards the end he used sometimes to tell Boguslavsky and me to go to his office. By the time he left this arrangement had already been put on a more regular footing. Among the Engineers there were men (one in particular) who were very sympathetic to us. We used to go there and copy papers and our copying had begun to grow very good, when suddenly there came an order from the highest authorities that we must at once be sent back to our former work: somebody had informed on us.* This, however, was a good thing: the office work had begun to bore us both. Afterwards, Boguslavsky and I were sent almost always to the same work, most frequently in the workshops. We used to talk to one another a great deal about our hopes and our beliefs. He was a capital fellow, but some of his convictions were very strange and peculiar to himself. Very often among a certain highly intelligent type of people, quite paradoxical ideas establish themselves. But they have suffered so much in their lives for these ideas, and have paid so high a price for them that it becomes very painful, indeed almost impossible, for them to part with them. Boguslavsky received any objection with pain and answered me caustically. However, he was perhaps more in the right than I was about many things, I do not know. But finally we parted, and it was a great grief to me: we had shared so much.

Meanwhile, with the years Miretsky seemed to grow more and more gloomy and melancholy. Depression overwhelmed him. Earlier, at the beginning of my time in the prison, he had been more communicative, or at any rate his feelings more frequently and with greater force broke through to the surface. He had already been more than two years in the prison when I arrived there. At first he was interested in much that had happened in the world during those two years, of which, being in the prison, he had not known; he questioned me closely, listened to what I said, and grew excited. But as time went on, all his interest seemed to become concentrated inside himself, in his own heart. The hot coals were covered with ashes. His resentful bitterness grew greater and greater. 'Je haïs ces brigands,' he would often repeat to me, with hatred in the look he turned on the convicts, whom I had now learned to know better, and none of my arguments in their favour had any effect on him. He could not grasp what I was saying; sometimes, though, he would absent-mindedly agree with me, but the next day he would again be repeating: 'Je haïs ces brigands.' He and I, by the way, often spoke French to one another, and for this reason Dranishnikov, one of the Engineer privates who guarded us at work, nicknamed us the 'medicos', although I don't know what his idea was. Miretsky grew animated only when he remembered his mother. 'She is old and she is ill,' he told me; 'she loves me more than anything in the world, and here I am, not knowing whether she is alive or dead. It was enough to kill her knowing I had had to run the gauntlet . . .' Miretsky did not belong to the nobility and had undergone corporal punishment before he was exiled. Whenever he remembered this he used to clench his teeth and look the other way. Towards the end he began to go about more and more frequently alone. One morning, not long before noon, he was summoned to the commandant. The commandant came out to him with a cheerful smile.

'Well, Miretsky, what did you dream about last night?' he asked him.

'I absolutely jumped,' Miretsky told us. 'I felt as if I had been stabbed through the heart.'

'I dreamt I had a letter from my mother,' he had answered.

'Better still, better still!' replied the commandant. 'You are free! Your mother petitioned . . . Her petition has been granted. Here is a letter from her, and here is the order about you. You will leave the prison at once.'

Miretsky returned to us pale and still stunned by the news. We congratulated him. He pressed our hands with his own, which were cold and trembling. Many of the other prisoners also congratulated him and rejoiced in his good fortune.

He was released as a settler, and remained there in our town. He was soon given employment. At first he often came to the prison and he would tell us various items of news when he could. It was for the most part the political news that most deeply interested him.

Of the other four, besides Miretsky, Tokarzewsky, Boguslavsky, and Zhokhovsky, that is, two were still very young men serving short sentences; they had little education but were honest, simple and straightforward. The third was almost simple-minded and had nothing particular in him, but the fourth, an elderly man, left a very disagreeable impression on all of us. I don't know how he came to be classified with the former gentlemen, and indeed he denied that he was one. He was a coarse, petty-bourgeois creature, with the manners and principles of a shopkeeper who has grown rich by cheating over copecks. He was entirely without education and was not interested in anything outside his trade. He was a house-painter, but far above the common run, a magnificent painter. The authorities soon heard of his ability, and the whole town began to ask for him to paint their walls and ceilings. In the course of two years he painted nearly all the official residences. Their inhabitants paid him themselves, and thus he was not badly off. But the best of it was that some of his fellow prisoners began to be sent to work with him as well. Of the three who were always going with him, two learnt the trade from him and one of them began to paint as well as he. Our major, who also occupied a government house, claimed his services in his turn and ordered that all his walls and ceilings should be painted. The house was a wooden one, of one story, rather tumbledown and extremely shabby on the outside: but inside it was painted like a palace, and the major was delighted . . . He rubbed his hands and said that now he simply must get married: 'with such quarters it is impossible not to,' he added very seriously. He grew more and more pleased with the painter, and through him with the others who worked with him. The work lasted a whole month. In the course of this month the major quite changed his mind about all prisoners of our class and began to protect them. Things reached such a pitch that he once suddenly summoned Zhokhovsky from the prison.

'Zhokhovsky,' he said, 'I wronged you! I had you flogged for nothing, I know. I am sorry. Do you understand? I, I, I,—am sorry!'

Zhokhovsky answered that he understood.

'Do you understand that *I, I*, your commander, have sent for you to ask your forgiveness? Do you feel that? Who are *you* compared with me? A worm! Less than a worm: you are a convict! And I am a major, by the grace of God! A major! Do you understand that?'

Zhokhovsky answered that he understood that, too.

'Well, so now I am making my peace with you. But do you

feel this, do you feel it fully, do you appreciate it to the full? Are you capable of understanding this, and feeling it? Just think: I, I, a major . . .' and so on.

Zhokhovsky himself described all this scene to me. It showed that even in this drunken, quarrelsome, undisciplined man there was some feeling of humanity. Considering his mentality and education, this step could be counted almost generous. Perhaps, however, his being drunk was a contributory factor.

His dream did not come true: he did not marry, although he had indeed quite made up his mind to do so when the decoration of his quarters was finished. Instead of getting married he found himself in court, and he was ordered to send in his resignation. Now all his old sins came home to roost. Earlier, it will be remembered, he had been Governor of that same town . . . The blow fell on him unexpectedly. In the prison, rejoicing at the news knew no bounds. It was a festival, a celebration. The major, it was said, howled like an old woman and wept floods of tears. But there was nothing to be done. He went into retirement and sold his pair of greys, and afterwards all his estate, and he was even reduced to destitution. We used to meet him afterwards in a shabby civilian frock-coat and with a cockade in his cap. He would scowl at the prisoners. But all his impressiveness had vanished as soon as he took off his uniform. In uniform he was the thunder, he was God. In a frock-coat he suddenly became nothing, and looked like a lackey. It is wonderful how much a uniform does for people like him.

9. The Escape

SOON after the major's replacement a radical change took place in our prison. The penal servitude division was abolished and in its place there was founded a military penal company, based on the penal battalions in Russia. This meant that exiled convicts of the Second division were no longer brought to our prison. It began to be peopled from this time only by military prisoners, men, that is, who were not deprived of civil rights, soldiers like all other soldiers except that they had been convicted and sentenced to short terms (up to six years at the most), and who when they left the prison returned to their battalions as privates, as they had been before. Those of them, however, who were sent back to prison for a second offence were sentenced, as before, to twenty years. We had, indeed, had a Military division in the prison before this change was made, but they had lived with us because there was nowhere else for them. Now the whole prison was given over to this Military division. It goes without saying that the former convicts, the true civilian convicts, deprived of all rights, branded, and with half their heads shaved, remained in the prison until the expiration of their full sentences; no new ones arrived, however, and little by little those remaining completed their sentences and went away, until at the end of about ten years not one can have been left in our prison. The Special Class also remained and from time to time the worst military offenders continued to be sent there, pending the opening in Siberia of the heaviest forced-labour establishments. Thus life continued for us essentially as before, in the same conditions and with the same work and almost the same regulations; it was only the officials who changed and became more numerous. There were appointed a staff officer, the commander of the company, and four commissioned officers besides, who took turns on duty in the prison. The old soldiers too were abolished; in their place were installed twelve non-commissioned officers and a quartermaster-sergeant. Division into sections of ten men was introduced, with a corporal who was chosen from among the prisoners themselves, nominally, of course; and naturally Akim Akimovich at once became a corporal. All this new establishment, and the whole prison with all its officials and prisoners, remained as before under the command of the Commandant as the highest authority. That, then, is all that had come about. The prisoners, of course, were very excited at first; they discussed, speculated, tried to gauge their new masters; but when they saw that everything remained essentially the same as before, they calmed down at once, and our life resumed its old course. The main thing was that we were all rid of the major; everybody seemed to relax and take heart again. Their frightened look disappeared; everyone knew now that he could have things out with the authorities in case of need, and that it would only be by mistake if the innocent were punished instead of the guilty. Vodka even continued to be sold in the same way and on the same basis as before, in spite of our having non-commissioned officers in place of the old soldiers. The sergeants proved to be for the most part decent, intelligent men who understood their situation. Some of them, though, showed to begin with a tendency to bullying and, from inexperience, of course, thought they could treat the prisoners like soldiers. But soon even these realized how things were. To some, indeed, who were too slow to understand, the prisoners themselves pointed out the realities of the situation. There were some fairly sharp clashes: for example, a sergeant would be enticed to drink and then they would tell him, in their own way, of course, that he had drunk with them, and so . . . The end of it all was that the sergeants calmly looked on, or rather tried not to see, when bladders of vodka were carried in and sold. What is more, like the old soldiers earlier, they would go to the bazaar and bring the prisoners white bread, beef, and all the rest; anything, that is, that could be handled without loss of dignity. Why everything had been so altered, or why penal companies were established, I have no idea. This all happened during my last years in the prison. But I was destined to spend two years under these new conditions . . .

Ought I to describe all this life and all my years in prison? I think not. If I were to set down successively and in order everything that happened and that I saw and experienced during those years, I might of course write three or four times as many chapters again as I have written already. But such a description would of necessity finally become very monotonous. All the happenings would have too much of the same colouring, especially if the reader had already succeeded in acquiring, from those chapters which are already written, any kind of satisfactory understanding of the life of Second-division convicts. I have wished to present our prison and all I lived through during those years in one clear and vivid picture. Whether I have attained this end I do not know. Indeed, it is not altogether for me to judge. But I am sure it is possible to end here. Besides, sometimes all these memories fill me with depression. And perhaps I cannot even remember everything. The later years seem to have been half effaced from my memory. Many circumstances, I am convinced, have been completely forgotten. I remember, for example, that every year, essentially so like every other, passed sluggishly and drearily. I remember that those long dull days were as monotonous as drops of water falling from the roof after rain. I remember that nothing but passionate longing for resurrection, renewal, a new life, gave me the strength to wait and hope. And I did at length grow strong; I waited, counting every day, and in spite of the fact that a thousand still remained, I ticked them off one by one with delight, followed their funerals, buried them, and when the new day dawned I rejoiced that there now were left not a thousand but nine hundred and ninety-nine. I remember that all through this time, although I had hundreds of companions, I was terribly alone, and I came to love my solitude at last. In my mental isolation I reviewed all my former life, down to the last trifling detail, pondered over my past, judged myself sternly and inexorably, and at moments even blessed the fate that had sent me that solitude, without which there would have been neither the self-judgement nor the stern scrutiny of my earlier life. And what hopes made my heart beat high! I thought, I determined, I swore to myself that the mistakes and lapses of the past should never occur again in the future. I drew up a programme of my future and resolved to follow it strictly. A blind faith was born in me that I could and would fulfil it all . . . I waited for freedom, I cried for it to come quickly; I wanted to put myself to the test again, to renew the struggle. At times I was seized with feverish impatience . . . But it is painful for me now to recall my spiritual condition at that time. All this, of course, concerns nobody but myself . . . But I have set it down because it seems to me that everybody will understand it, since the same thing must happen to anybody who is sent to prison for a term in the flower of his years and strength.

But why talk of it? . . . Better tell something further, in order not to break off too abruptly.

It occurs to me that I may perhaps be asked whether it really was impossible for anybody to escape, and whether nobody did escape from our prison during all those years. I have already stated that when a prisoner had spent two or three years in prison he began to set a value on those years and to calculate involuntarily that it was better to endure the rest without trouble or danger and go out at length to the settlement in the legitimate way. But this calculation takes place only in the heads of prisoners whose term of penal servitude is not very long. The long-term convict might well be ready to take a risk . . . But this seemed not to be so in our prison. I do not know whether this was because of cowardice, the strict military supervision, or our situation in the open steppes, which was in many respects unfavourable—it is difficult to say. I think all these reasons had their influence. It was indeed rather difficult to run away from our prison. Nevertheless, there was one instance in my time: two men tried it, and they among our most important criminals.

After the major had been replaced, Aristov (who had been his spy in the prison) remained completely alone and without protection. He was still a very young man, but his character was growing stronger and more settled with the years. He was, generally speaking, a daring, resolute, and even very intelligent man. Although if he had been given his freedom he would have continued to spy and to live by various underhand activities, he would not have been so stupidly and imprudently caught as before, when he paid for his stupidity with exile. One of his occupations among us was fabricating false passports. I do not state this as a certainty, however; it is what I heard from some of the prisoners. They said he had been doing work of this kind even while he was still a frequenter of the major's kitchen and, of course, he made what profit he could from it. In short, I think he might have done anything to change his lot. I had the opportunity of learning something of his mind and heart; his cynicism went to the extreme of shocking impudence and the coldest mockery and aroused unconquerable repugnance. I think if he had craved a glass of vodka and if the only way of getting it had been to slit somebody's throat, he would certainly have done so, provided it could have been done in secret, without anybody's knowledge. In prison he had learnt prudence. This was the man who caught the attention of the Special-Class convict Kulikov.

I have spoken of Kulikov before. He was a man no longer young, but full of passion, vitality, and energy, and with unusual capabilities. There was strength in him and he still wanted to live; men like him still desire life even up to extreme old age. And if I had wondered why our prisoners did not run away, Kulikov would have been the first to arouse that wonder. But Kulikov did make up his mind to it. Which of them had the more influence, Aristov on Kulikov or Kulikov on Aristov, I do not know, but each was worthy of the other and both alike were well suited to such an enterprise. They became intimate. I think Kulikov counted on Aristov to prepare passports for them. Aristov was a gentleman, a man of good society—this promised some variety in their future adventures if only they could reach Russia. Who knows how they came together or what hopes they had ?; but quite certainly they hoped for something beyond the routine Siberian vagabondage. Kulikov was by nature an actor and capable of playing many and various parts in life; he could hope for much, or at least for variety. Prison is bound to oppress such men. They plotted to escape.

But escape was impossible without the connivance of a guard. They must persuade a guard to join them. In one of the battalions stationed in the fortress there was a Pole, a man of energy who perhaps deserved a better lot; he was no longer young, but earnest and full of spirit. In his youth, immediately after he came to Siberia as a soldier, he had deserted, out of a deep longing for his home. He was caught and punished, and kept for two years in a penal company. When he was sent back to his battalion, he was a changed man and began to serve with zeal and energy. He was made a corporal for his good service. He was ambitious, self-reliant, and conscious of his own value. He spoke and looked like a man who knew his own worth. Several times during those years I encountered him among our guards. The Poles, too, told me something about him. It appeared to me that his former homesickness had turned to a fixed, dumb, and secret hatred. He was a man capable of anything, and Kulikov made no mistake in choosing him as a comrade. His name was Koller. They came to an agreement and fixed a day. It was in the heat of June. The climate in that town is fairly equable: in the summer the weather is settled and the days are hot; this is just right for the tramp. They could not, of course, simply walk out of the fortress: the town stands on a hill, open on all sides. For a considerable distance round it there is no forest. They would have to change into the dress of ordinary townspeople and for this they must first get to the outskirts of the town, where there was a house which Kulikov had long frequented. I do not know whether his friends there were fully in the secret, but one must assume that they were, although afterwards, at the trial, the point was not entirely cleared up. That year, in a corner of the suburb, a certain very comely young woman, nicknamed Vanka-Tanka, was just beginning to practise her calling; she was a young woman of great promise, which she subsequently partly fulfilled. Another nickname they gave her was 'Fire'. I think she also played some part in this affair. Kulikov had been spending all his money on her for a whole year. Our two adventurers went into the yard one morning as work was assigned, and artfully contrived to be sent, with another prisoner, Shilkin, a stove-setter and plasterer, to plaster the empty military barracks, which the soldiers had quitted some time before to go under canvas. Aristov and Kulikov went as Shilkin's mates. Koller turned up as one of the guards, and as two guards were needed for three prisoners, Koller, as a senior man and a corporal, was readily entrusted with a young recruit, so that, by precept and example, he might teach him the duties of a guard. Koller must have been very much under the influence of our runaways, and have had great faith in them, if, after such long and, in the last few years, successful service in the army he, an intelligent, reliable, and prudent man, decided to follow them.

They went to the barracks. It was about six o'clock in the morning. There was nobody there except themselves. When they had been at work for about an hour Kulikov and Aristov told Shilkin that they were going to the workshop, first to see somebody and secondly to take the opportunity of picking up some tool, which it seemed they were without. They had to go to work cunningly, that is, as naturally as possible, with Shilkin. He was an artisan from Moscow, a stove-setter by trade, and a shrewd, sly, intelligent, taciturn person. In appearance he was thin and puny. He would have been happy to go about all his days in a waistcoat and dressing-gown, Moscow fashion, but fate had decreed otherwise, and after long wanderings he had come at last to settle for ever in our prison in the Special Class, in the category, that is, of the most desperate military criminals. How he had deserved such a career I do not know, but he never showed any marked dissatisfaction; his conduct was equably peaceable; some-times, though, he got as drunk as a cobbler, but even then he did not behave badly. He was not, of course, in the secret, but he had sharp eyes. Kulikov, of course, tipped him the wink that they were going for the vodka which had been secreted in the workshop the day before. This had its effect on Shilkin; he parted from them without any suspicion and remained alone with the young recruit, while Kulikov, Aristov, and Koller set off for the edge of the town.

Half an hour went by; the absentees did not return and Shilkin began to put two and two together. He was a fellow who had seen much of the world. He began to remember that Kulikov had seemed in a peculiar mood and that Aristov had seemed to whisper to him once or twice, or at least that he had seen Kulikov wink at Aristov a couple of times; now he recalled all these things. There had been something odd about Koller, too: at least, when he left with them, he had read the recruit a lecture on how to behave in his absence, and there had been something a little unnatural, at least in Koller, about this. In short, the more Shilkin remembered, the more suspicious he became. Meanwhile, time was pass-ing, they did not return, and his uneasiness was becoming extreme. He very clearly understood how much danger there was to himself in this affair: it was on him that the suspicions of the authorities might fall. They might think that he had knowingly allowed his companions to get away, being secretly in concert with them, and if he delayed in reporting the disappearance of Kulikov and Aristov these suspicions would receive more credence. There was no time to lose. Now he remembered that Kulikov and Aristov had recently seemed very thick, frequently whispering together or walking behind the barracks, remote from all eyes. He remembered that even then he had wondered about them . . . He looked searchingly at his guard, who yawned, leaning on his rifle and most innocently picking his nose; and so Shilkin, without even condescending to communicate his thoughts to him, simply told him to follow him to the engineering workshop. Here they must inquire whether the missing men had arrived. But it seemed that nobody had seen them. All Shilkin's doubts were resolved. If they had simply gone off to the outskirts of the town for a drink and a good time, as Kulikov sometimes did, thought Shilkin . . . but even that was impossible here. They would have told him, because it was not worth while to conceal it from him. Shilkin abandoned his work and without going back to the barracks, went straight to the prison.

It was already almost nine o'clock when he presented himself to the sergeant-major and told him what was the matter. The sergeant-major was scared, and even refused at first to believe it. Shilkin, of course, put all this forward only in the guise of guesses and suspicions. The sergeant-major rushed directly to the major, and the major went immediately to the commandant. In a quarter of an hour all the essential measures had been taken. The Governor-General himself was informed. The criminals were important ones, and St. Petersburg might make a tremendous row about them. Rightly or wrongly, Aristov was counted a political criminal; Kulikov was in the Special Class, that is, he was an arch-malefactor, and a military one into the bargain. There had never before been an example of an escape from the Special Class. It was remembered, incidentally, that by the rules every prisoner in the Special Class was supposed to have two guards at work, or at least they must have one each. This rule had not been observed. Consequently this proved an unpleasant business. Special messengers were sent to every village and all the small towns round about to announce the escape and leave descriptions of the fugitives everywhere. Cossacks were dispatched to overtake and capture them; letters were sent also to the neighbouring districts and provinces . . . In short, there was complete panic.

Meanwhile, we began to feel a different kind of excitement in the prison. The prisoners, as they returned from work, learnt what the trouble was. The news was everywhere. Everybody received it with a sort of extraordinary hidden rejoicing. Every heart seemed to give a leap . . . Besides the fact that this event interrupted the monotony of prison life and stirred up the ant-heap, an escape, and an escape like this, evoked a feeling of kinship in all our spirits and touched long-forgotten chords; something like hope, daring, and the chance of changing our lot stirred in all our hearts. 'People *have* escaped; then why not . . . ?' And at the thought, everybody plucked up heart and looked at all the others with a challenge in his eyes. Everybody seemed, at least, to have grown proud, and they began to look patronizingly on the sergeants. The authorities, of course, at once swooped down on the prison. Our men were in good heart, and had a bold and even rather contemptuous look, with a kind of silent, staid severity, as if to say: 'We can make a good job of anything we set our hands to.' It goes without saying that our people had at once foreseen that there would be a general visitation of the prison by the authorities, and had everything securely hidden beforehand. They knew that in such cases the authorities are always wise after the event. And so it proved: there was much ado; they rummaged everywhere and searched everything and, of course, found—nothing. After dinner the escorts sent out with the convicts going to work were reinforced. In the evening the sentries visited the prison constantly; the roll was called once more than usual, and two or three more mistakes than usual were made in counting . . . This resulted in more trouble and fuss; everybody was sent out into the yard and counted all over again. Then we were counted once more, in the barracks . . . In a word, there was a great deal of commotion.

But the prisoners did not turn a hair. They all had an extraordinarily independent air and, as always happens in such cases, they conducted themselves that evening with unusual propriety. 'There must be nothing to find fault with.' The authorities, of course, wondered whether there were not some of the fugitives' accomplices still left in the prison, and ordered that the prisoners should be watched and their talk listened to. But the prisoners only laughed. 'It's likely, isn't it, they'd have left accomplices behind?' 'That sort of thing has to be kept in the dark, or it can't be done!' 'And is Kulikov, or Aristov either, the sort of man who wouldn't hide all his traces in a thing like this? They did it very cleverly and they haven't left a clue. They are fellows who know a thing or two; they can get through locked doors!' In short, Kulikov and Aristov had grown great in fame; everybody was proud of them. They felt that this exploit would go down to the furthest generations of convicts and outlive the prison.

'Ah, they're masters, they are!' said some.

'You see, they thought nobody could escape from here, but they *have* escaped, though!' added others.

'Escaped!' exclaimed another, looking round with some authority. 'Who's escaped, though? . . . Someone just like you, I suppose?'

At any other time the prisoner to whom these words referred would inevitably have replied to the challenge and defended his honour. But now he remained modestly silent. 'It's true enough: not everybody's like Kulikov and Aristov; you've got to show what you're made of first . . .'

'But why is it, brothers, that we go on living here?'

a fourth man, who had been modestly sitting by the kitchen window, leaning his cheek on his palm, broke the silence. He spoke in a rather singsong voice, with a sort of relaxed, but secretly complacent feeling. 'What are we doing here? We're alive, but we're not living; when we're dead, we shan't rest quiet. Oh, dear!'

'It's not a shoe you can kick off. What's the good of saying "oh, dear"?'

'But there's Kulikov . . .' one of the hotheaded ones tried to break in; he was a young lad and very green.

'Kulikov!' at once retorted another, squinting contemptuously at the young greenhorn; 'Kulikov! . . .'

That was as much as to say, 'Have we so many Kulikovs, then?'

'And Aristov, brothers, he's fly. Oh, he's fly!'

'Not half, he isn't! That one can turn even Kulikov round his little finger. Nobody's going to catch him!'

'I wish I knew if they've got far away yet, brothers . . .'
Immediately they began to discuss whether the fugitives had got far, and which way they had gone, and where it was best for them to go, and which group of villages was nearest. Men were found who knew the surrounding district, and they were listened to with eager interest. They spoke of the inhabitants of the neighbouring villages, and decided that they were not the right sort. They were too near the town and too clever; they would not give the prisoners aid but trap and betray them.

'The peasants here are a bad lot, mates. A bad lot, the peasants!'

'You can't rely on these peasants.'

'Siberians are a cruel lot. Don't let them catch you, they'll kill you.'

'Well, but our fellows . . .'

'Of course, now you can't tell which side will come out on top . . . And our men know what they're doing.'

'Well, we shall hear, if we don't die first.'

'And what do you think? That they'll be caught?'

'*I* think they'll never let themselves be caught!' chimed in another of the hotheaded ones, banging his fist on the table.

'H'm. Well, that's as may be.'

'I'll tell you what I think, mates,' Skuratov broke in. 'If I was a tramp, they'd not catch me, never in this world!'

'Oh, you!'

Some began to laugh, and others pretended that they did not want to hear. But Skuratov was losing his temper.

'Never in this world, they wouldn't catch me!' he repeated violently. 'I tell you, mates, I often think that to myself, and I'm surprised at myself. I think I'd squeeze through a crack in the floorboards so they shouldn't catch me.'

'I expect you'd get hungry and go and ask a peasant for a bit of bread.'

General laughter.

'Oh, would I? Liar!'

'What are you wagging your tongue for, anyway? Uncle Vasya and you killed the cow plague,[1] and that's what you're here for!'

The laughter grew louder. The serious ones looked on with still greater disgust.

'It's all lies!' shouted Skuratov. 'Mikitka made that up about me, and it wasn't even about me, but Vaska, and I only got dragged into it at the same time. I'm from Moscow, and ever since I was a nipper I've been used to being on the road. Even when the deacon was teaching me my letters and he used to pull me by the ear and say: "Repeat after me, Oh, God, lead us not into temptation, by Thy great mercy, and so on . . .", I used to say after him, "Lead me to the police-station by Thy mercy, and so on . . ." So that's the way I've been ever since I was a little nipper.'

Everybody again laughed loudly. But that was all Skuratov

---

[1] That is, they had killed some peasant because they suspected that he or she had put the evil eye on the cattle and caused them to die. There was one such murderer among us.

wanted. He could never resist playing the clown. They soon abandoned him and returned to their serious conversation. It was mainly the older men and the experts who expressed their opinions. The younger and meeker men only enjoyed watching them, and craned their necks to listen; a large crowd had collected in the kitchen; the sergeants, of course, were not there. If they had been, nobody would have talked at all. Among those who showed particular delight I noticed one Tartar, Mametka, a little man with high cheekbones, an extremely comical figure. He spoke hardly a word of Russian and understood almost nothing of what the others were saying, but he craned his head forward from among the crowd and listened as though delighted with what he heard.

'Well, Mametka, *yakshi*?'[1] Skuratov, spurned by all the others, accosted him for want of something to do.

'*Yakshi*! Oh, *yakshi*!' muttered Mametka, full of animation, nodding his comical head at Skuratov. '*Yakshi*!'

'They won't be caught, *iok*?'[2]

'*Iok, iok!*' Mametka babbled again, this time waving his arms about.

'You mean you're lying and I don't know what I'm talking about, is that it?'

'Yes, yes, *yakshi*!' Mametka took him up, nodding his head.

'*Yakshi* it is!'

And Skuratov, giving Mametka's hat a tap and knocking it over his eyes, left the kitchen in the highest spirits, leaving Mametka somewhat perplexed.

All that week there was an increase in strictness within the prison and zealous pursuit and search in the neighbourhood. I do not know how it was done, but the prisoners had immediate and exact information of all the manœuvres of the authorities outside the prison. In the first few days all the news was favourable to the fugitives: not a breath, not a whisper of them, they had simply vanished into thin air.

---

[1] 'Good' (Tartar word). [*Tr.*]   [2] 'No.' [*Tr.*]

Our prisoners only laughed. All anxiety about the runaways' fate had disappeared. 'They won't find anything, they won't catch anybody,' they said complacently.

'Not a trace; they were off like a bullet!'

'Good-bye, never sigh, I'll soon be back!'

We knew that all the peasants of the surrounding districts had been put on the alert, and all suspected places, all the woods and ravines, were watched.

'That's no use!' the prisoners laughed. 'They're sure to have someone they're living with by now.'

'Of course they have!' said others. 'They're not such fools; everything was arranged beforehand.'

Their guesses went even farther: it began to be said that perhaps the fugitives were still in the town, waiting somewhere in a cellar until the 'larum' had died down and their hair had grown. They would stay there for six months, or a year, and then they would go . . .

Everybody, in short, was in a somewhat romantic frame of mind. Then suddenly, about a week after the escape, there came the first rumour that the trail had been found. The absurd rumour was, of course, at once rejected with scorn. But that same evening it was confirmed. The prisoners began to be anxious. During the morning of the next day they had begun to say in the town that the fugitives had already been caught and were being brought back. After dinner we learnt more details: they had been captured in such-and-such a village seventy versts away. The sergeant-major, on his return from seeing the major, announced definitely that by evening they would have been brought in and taken straight to the prison guardroom. There was no longer any room for doubt. It is difficult to convey the impression produced on the prisoners by this news. At first they all seemed to fly into a temper, then gloom overwhelmed them. Later, an inclination to jeer showed itself. They began to laugh, no longer at the pursuers but at the recaptured men; at first it was only a few who laughed, but afterwards almost everybody except a few strong and serious characters, who thought for themselves and the course of whose reasoning was not to be deflected by jeers. They regarded the frivolous masses with scorn and kept silent.

In a word, Kulikov and Aristov were now just as much decried, and even decried with pleasure, as they had before been extolled. It was as if they had somehow done everybody an injury. The prisoners, with scornful looks, spread the story that they had been very hungry and that, unable to endure their hunger, they had gone to a village to ask the peasants for bread. This was the last degree of humiliation for a tramp. The stories, however, were not true. The fugitives had been tracked down; they were hidden in a wood and the wood had been surrounded on all sides. Then, seeing that there was no possibility of escaping, they gave themselves up. Nothing else remained for them to do.

But in the evening, when they really were brought in, bound hand and foot and guarded by gendarmes, the whole prison distributed itself along the stockade to see what was done with them. They could see, of course, nothing but the carriages of the major and the commandant standing by the guardroom. The fugitives were kept in solitary confinement, fettered, and brought to judgement the next day. The scorn and mockery of the prisoners soon died down of its own accord. They had learnt more details of what had happened and recognized that there had been nothing to do but surrender, and everybody began to follow with ardour the course of affairs in the court.

'They'll get a thousand,' said some.

'A thousand?' said others; 'they'll kill them! Aristov, perhaps, will get a thousand, but they'll kill the other, because, brother, he's in the Special Class.'

They had guessed wrong, however. Aristov was given only five hundred strokes, his former satisfactory behaviour and the fact that it was his first offence being taken into account. I think they gave Kulikov fifteen hundred. Both punishments were inflicted quite leniently. They, like sensible people, had not involved anybody else when they were before the court, had told a clear and precise story, and had said that they had run straight away from the fortress, without calling anywhere. I was most sorry for Koller: he lost everything, his very last hopes, underwent a heavier punishment than the others, two thousand, I think, and was sent somewhere, but not into our prison, as a convict. Aristov's punishment was administered lightly and compassionately; here the doctors were of assistance. But he swaggered and boasted loudly in the hospital that now he would tackle anything, he was prepared for everything, and would do something very different next time. Kulikov bore himself just as usual, that is stolidly and with decorum, and when after his punishment he returned to the prison, he looked as though he had never been absent from it. But the prisoners regarded him differently: in spite of the fact that Kulikov always and everywhere knew how to keep his end up, they seemed to have ceased to respect him in their hearts, and began to treat him in a more off-handed manner. In short, from the time of the escape, Kulikov's glory was sadly tarnished. Success means so much to people.

10. I Leave the Prison

WHEN all this happened I had already reached the last year of my penal servitude. This last year, and especially the very end of my time in the prison, is almost as clear in my memory as the first one. But why should I talk of the details? I recall only that during that year, in spite of all my impatience to come quickly to the end of my term, I found life easier than during all the preceding years of my exile. In the first place, among the prisoners I had by now many friends and well-wishers, who had finally decided that I was a good man.

Many of them were devoted to my interests and genuinely fond of me. The Pioneer was very near tears when he accompanied my companion and me out of the prison and when afterwards, although we had been released, we were kept a whole month in a government building in the town, he called on us nearly every day, simply in order to see us. There were, however, also some characters who were unfriendly to the end and who, God knows why, seemed to find it a burden to exchange a word with me. There seemed to be a kind of barrier between them and me.

Towards the end I had more privileges than during all my time in prison. Some acquaintances of mine, and even some friends of my far-away schooldays, turned up among the officers serving in the town. I renewed my acquaintance with them. Through them I was able to possess more money, to write home, and even to get books. For several years I had not read a single book, and it is difficult to convey the strange and disturbing effect produced on me by the first book I read in prison. I remember that I began reading in the evening when the barracks were locked, and read all through the night, until daybreak. It was a number of a magazine. It was as though news from that other world had come through to me; my former life rose before me in all its brightness, and I strove to guess from what I read whether I had lagged far behind that world, whether much had happened in my absence, what was exciting people there now, and what questions occupied their minds. I worried every word, tried to read between the lines, and strove to find hidden meanings and allusions to the past; I searched for traces of the things that had excited men before, in my time, and how sad it was for me to recognize to what extent I was now indeed a stranger to this new life, cut off and isolated. I should have to get used to new things and learn to know a new generation. I devoured particularly eagerly an article under which I found the name of a man I once knew intimately . . . But new names as well resounded now: new leaders had appeared, and I was greedily impatient to get to know them and fretted because I could see so few books in prospect and because it was so difficult to acquire them. Previously, indeed, under the old major, it had been dangerous to bring books into the prison. In the event of a search there would inevitably be questions: 'Where did the books come from?' 'When did you get them?' 'So you have connexions outside?' . . . And what could I have replied to such questions? So it was that, living without books, I had become wrapped up in myself, had set myself problems, tried to solve them, and sometimes tormented myself with them . . . But it is surely impossible to convey all this! . . .

I had entered the prison in winter, and therefore I was to emerge into freedom in winter, on the same day of the month as I had arrived. With what impatience I waited for the winter, with what joy, at the end of summer, I watched the leaves fade on the trees and the grass wither on the steppe. Now summer was already over, and the winds of autumn had begun to howl; now the first hesitant snowflakes began to drift down . . . At last the winter, so long awaited, had arrived. At times my heart would begin to beat thickly and heavily with the anticipation of freedom. But strange to say the more time went by and the nearer the end came, the more patient I became. During the very last few days I was even surprised, and reproached myself: it seemed to me that I had become callous and indifferent. Many of the prisoners, meeting me in the courtyard during our leisure time, talked to me and congratulated me.

'See now, Alexander Petrovich, sir, you'll be free soon, very soon. You are leaving us poor fellows all alone.'

'And will it be soon for you too, Martynov?' I would answer.

'Me? What a hope! I've got another seven years to drag through . . .'

And he would sigh and stand still, with an absent look, as though he were gazing into the future. It seemed to me that all of them had begun to be more friendly to me. I had visibly ceased to be one of themselves; they were already saying good-bye to me. One of the Polish gentlemen, a quiet and unassuming young man, was, like me, fond of walking in the yard in our leisure time. He thought the fresh air and exercise preserved his health and compensated for all the harm done by the stuffy nights in barracks. 'I am waiting impatiently for you to leave,' he said to me with a smile, meeting me once on his walk; 'when you leave, *I shall know* that I have exactly a year left before I get out.'

I will mention here in passing that, in consequence of our day-dreams and our long divorce from it, freedom somehow seemed to us freer than real freedom, the freedom, that is, that exists in fact, in real life. The prisoners exaggerated the idea of real freedom, and that is very natural and characteristic of all prisoners. Any ragamuffin of an officer's batman was for us all but a king, all but the ideal of the free man, compared with the prisoners, because he could go about unshaved and without fetters or guards.

On the eve of my release, at twilight, I walked *for the last time* round the prison stockade. How many thousand times I had walked round it during all those years! How, behind the barracks, I used to linger in my first year, solitary, friendless, and dejected! I remember calculating then how many thousand days still lay before me. Great God, how long ago it was! Here in this corner our eagle lived out his captivity; here Petrov and I often used to meet. Even now, he had not deserted me. He came running up and, as though guessing my thoughts, walked silently at my side, like a man wondering to himself about something. Mentally I took my leave of the blackened, rough-hewn timbers of the barracks. How unfriendly had been the impression they had made on me *then*, at first! Even they must have grown older since then, but I could see no sign of it. And how much youth had gone to waste within those walls, what great powers had perished uselessly there! For the whole truth must be told:

these indeed were no ordinary men. Perhaps, indeed, they were the most highly gifted and the strongest of all our people. But these powerful forces were condemned to perish uselessly, unnaturally, wrongfully, irrevocably. And whose is the blame?

That is the question, whose is the blame?

Next morning early, before the prisoners went to their work, when it was just beginning to grow light, I went round all the barracks to say good-bye to all the prisoners. Many strong, calloused hands stretched out to me in friendship. Some shook mine like comrades, but they were not many. Others understood very well that I was on the point of becoming an entirely different man from them. They knew I had friends in the town and that I should go straight from them to the *bosses* and would sit down beside those bosses as their equal. They knew this, and said good-bye to me, though in a pleasant and friendly enough way, not at all as they would to a comrade, but as if to a gentleman. Some turned away from me and surlily refused to answer my farewell. A few even eyed me with something like hatred.

The drum beat, and everybody went off to work, but I remained behind. Sushilov that morning had been almost the first to get up and had worked anxiously and earnestly to make tea for me in time. Poor Sushilov! He cried when I gave him my old prison clothes, my shirts, my under-fetters, and a little money.

'I don't want that, I don't want it!' he said, controlling his quivering lip with a great effort; 'how can I lose *you*, Alexander Petrovich? Who will be left for me here when you've gone?'

Last of all I said good-bye to Akim Akimovich.

'It will soon be your turn,' I said to him.

'I've got a long time, I've still got a very long time here,' he murmured, pressing my hand. I threw myself on his neck and we kissed.

Ten minutes after the prisoners, we too left the prison,

never to return to it, I and the companion with whom I had arrived. We had to go straight to the smithy to have our fetters struck off. But there was no longer an armed guard to escort us: we went with a sergeant. It was our own prisoners who struck off our fetters in the engineering shops. I waited while my companion's fetters were removed, and then went up to the anvil. The smiths turned me round with my back to them, lifted my foot from behind, and put it on the anvil . . .

'The rivet, the rivet, turn the rivet first of all!' commanded the foreman. 'Hold it there, like that, that's right . . . Now strike it with the hammer . . .'

The fetters fell away. I lifted them up . . . I wanted to hold them in my hand and look at them for the last time. It seemed amazing now that it was my legs they had been on a moment ago.

'Well, God be with you, God be with you!' said the prisoners, in gruff, abrupt, yet pleased tones.

Yes, God was with us! Freedom, a new life, resurrection from the dead . . . What a glorious moment!

THE END

EXPLANATORY NOTES

2 *a convict settler.* Persons sentenced to penal servitude in Siberia (*katorga*) were obliged to remain in Siberian exile for the rest of their lives after the expiry of their sentence. They were designated as 'settlers' (*poselentsy*), and were permitted to return to European Russia only in exceptional cases, as was Dostoevsky himself in 1859.

the little town of K——. K—— stands for Kuznetsk (later called Novokuznetsk, and Stalinsk), a western Siberian town about 600 miles east of Omsk.

6 *Our prison.* It is typical of Russian *belles-lettres* that Dostoevsky does not specify the location in which his action is set. But the description which follows is that of the prison at Omsk in which he himself served a four-year sentence in 1850–4. Omsk is situated on the River Irtysh in western Siberia. It was the administrative capital of that region and the seat of a Governor-General.

9 *about two hundred and fifty men.* This is one of the points at which Dostoevsky deviates into fiction. The actual complement of Omsk prison at the time of his own admission, in January 1850, was 148 inmates.

10 *It was a December evening.* Dostoevsky's own arrival in Omsk prison in 1854 occurred in the month of January. He again deviates into fiction here because he wished a description of Christmas celebrations to follow: in Part One, Chapter 10.

12 *different categories of prisoners.* Dostoevsky himself was assigned to the category of civilian prisoner, Grade Two. This meant that he wore a half-grey, half-black jacket with a yellow, diamond-shaped patch on the back.

14 *The staff-officer in immediate command.* This was a Major V. G. Krivtsov, who greeted Dostoevsky, on his first arrival at Omsk, by threatening to have him flogged for the slightest infringement of the rules. Krivtsov was dismissed, court-martialled

and cashiered for excess of zeal halfway through Dostoevsky's term of imprisonment.

15 *a commandant.* The Commandant of Omsk Fortress at the time of Dostoevsky's imprisonment was a Colonel A. F. de Grave.

16 *cell-system.* Reference is to solitary confinement, the introduction of which was contemplated by Nicholas I on the model of penal practices followed in London.

32 *gentlefolk.* Every citizen of the Russian Empire was specifically assigned to a social class or 'estate' (*sostoyanie* or *soslovie*). Dostoevsky himself belonged to the lower reaches of the Russian gentry (*dvoryanstvo*), the privileged caste which constituted only about 1 per cent of the Russian population. The peasantry (*krestyanstvo*) accounted for 80 per cent of the citizenry, and was the category to which the bulk of the convicts at Omsk belonged.

there were five Poles. See note to page 325.

33 *Akim Akimovich.* The real-life prototype of Akim Akimovich was an Ensign Yefim Belykh, who was serving a ten-year sentence for the murder of a Caucasian prince.

35 *an Old Believer.* The Old Belief dates from the schism which arose in the Russian Orthodox Church in the mid-seventeenth century. The Old Believers were those who refused to accept the reforms then introduced into the Orthodox liturgy by the Patriarch Nikon. They split into a variety of sects, some of which still follow their faith in the Soviet Union in the late twentieth century.

40 *Kursk . . . Tambov.* Towns in European Russia.

43 *Miretsky.* Reference is to the Pole A. Mirecki, born in 1820, who had been sentenced in 1846 for conspiracy against the Russian occupier of his native land. See also note to p. 325 below.

76 *a Russian translation of the New Testament.* According to an imperial order of 11 August 1850, convicts might not have any reading matter in their possession other than religious books.

78 *Gogol's little Jew, Yankel, in Taras Bulba.* Yankel appears in

Chapters 9 and 10 of the historical story *Taras Bulba* (1842) by Nikolay Gogol (1809–52).

90 *a moral Quasimodo.* Quasimodo is the hero of the novel *Notre-Dame de Paris* by Victor Hugo (1802–85).

91 *Brülow.* K. P. Brülow (1799–1852), the Russian portrait painter.

97 *Nastasya Ivanovna.* The real-life prototype was Natalya Stepanovna Kryzhanovskaya, who resided in Omsk and corresponded with Dostoevsky.

98 *the greatest egoism.* Reference is to the theory that rational selfishness is the key motive for human behaviour. Dostoevsky violently rejected this notion, of which the chief Russian exponent was his ideological enemy N. G. Chernyshevsky (1828–89).

121 *Napoleon.* Reference is to Napoleon III (1808–73) who became Emperor of France in 1852; he was a nephew of Napoleon I.

122 *Countess Lavallière . . . a book by Dumas.* The Duchess de Lavallière, a favourite of Louis XIV of France, is mentioned in the novel *Le Vicomte de Bragelonne* (1848–50) by Alexandre Dumas *père* (1803–70).

131 *K——.* Kiev, the capital of the Ukraine.

149 *R——.* Riga.

156 *there were only three such days in the year.* The prisoners were granted one day's holiday from work at Christmas and two at Easter.

159 *arranged for straw to be brought in.* This tradition commemorated Christ's birth in a manger.

177 *there was no theatre there.* Omsk indeed did lack a theatre, but amateur theatricals were not unknown in the town.

178 *The Rivals Philatka and Miroshka.* A popular Russian farce, subtitled 'Four Suitors and the Bride', by P. G. Grigoryev (1807–54).

179 *Kedril the Glutton.* A popular play dating from the seventeenth century, the text of which can no longer be traced.

194 *Glinka.* The Russian composer M. I. Glinka (1804–57).

199 *our military hospital.* A wooden building which still formed part of the city's hospital in the 1970s.

202 *T——.* Tobolsk, a western Siberian town about 350 miles north-west of Omsk.

236 *Marquis de Sade.* The French author and criminal (1740–1814).

Madame de Brinvilliers. The Marquise Marie de Brinvilliers (1651–75) attained notoriety as a poisoner who gloated over her victims' sufferings.

276 *Kirghiz tribesmen.* The left bank of the River Irtysh, which runs through Omsk, was inhabited by the Kazakhs: Turkic-speaking nomads who were erroneously called 'Kirghiz' in the nineteenth century.

286 *the Inspector came.* Reference is to a General Schlippenbach who inspected Omsk prison during the period of Dostoevsky's captivity.

325 *Boguslavsky, Miretsky . . . Zhokhovsky . . . Tokarzewsky.* These are the true names (given here in Russian spelling) of four of the 'five Poles' (mentioned on p. 32) who were imprisoned at Omsk at the same time as Dostoevsky. Tokarzewski's prison memoirs *Siedem lat Katorgi* (Warsaw, 1907) and *Katorznicy* (Warsaw, 1912) provide an independent, though somehwat prejudiced, picture of Dostoevsky the convict.

331 *the Governor-General.* P. D. Gorchakov was the Governor-General of western Siberia in 1851–3.

335 *there were men (one in particular) who were very sympathetic to us. . . . somebody had informed on us.* Reference is to an actual episode from Dostoevsky's prison life. The sympathizer was a Second Lieutenant K. I. Ivanov, the informer a Lieutenant-Colonel A. A. Martin.

THE WORLD'S CLASSICS

A Select List